Dream Laboratory

Dream Laboratory

CLARE BROWN

To Bill

Thanks and best wishes

Clare Brown

02/07/07

BLOOMSBURY

First published 2007
Copyright © 2007 by Clare Brown
The moral right of the author has been asserted
Bloomsbury Publishing Plc, 36 Soho Square,
London W1D 3QY

A CIP catalogue record for this book is available from the British Library

10 9 8 7 6 5 4 3 2 1

ISBN 9780747591535

Typeset by Hewer Text UK Ltd, Edinburgh
Printed in Great Britain by Clays Ltd, St Ives plc

To Dan

'I've dreamt in my life dreams that have stayed with me ever after, and changed my ideas; they've gone through and through me, like wine through water, and altered the colour of my mind.'

Emily Brontë, *Wuthering Heights*

Day three: Friday

Delphine left on Wednesday. My attempts to reach her have failed, so I've done little except stare out of the window, occasionally falling into bouts of quite pathetic sobbing, cursing her for giving me no warning, mentally pleading with her to return, as though my thoughts have their own wavelength which she can tune into, wherever she is, if she'd just make the effort. I can't believe she's gone; isn't that what one says in these situations? Belief in the obvious has never been my problem; indeed, right now I'd welcome a little disbelief, a little doubt. But it's clear as these tears that she hasn't just popped out to the shops and become distracted. Without her, these rooms are lifeless. And without her in my bed, I'm back to the night-time wakings I thought I'd escaped for ever. Back to the dry mouth, the aching muscles, the itching skin of insomnia.

All my usual distractions have lost their efficacy: I took my favourite book off the shelf, made a perfect cup of coffee, sat back in my armchair, then turned to the first page and waited for the magic to draw me in.

Aujourd'hui, maman est morte. Today, mother died. Mum died today. Today . . . whichever way you look at it, it's a fabulous way to start a novel. *L'Etranger* – often translated as *The Stranger* but *The Outsider* is more accurate – by Albert Camus, translation: Bert Snub. Loses something exotic and elegant in the English of course, but that only serves to humanise the man. Modernist thinker, literary stylist, a goal-keeper of note (though not, as is often stated, for the Algerian national team), French Resistance activist, trailblazer for some of the greatest artists of the later twentieth century; a man who was prepared to take on all comers until his untimely death in a car crash in 1960. A hero of mine. And linked, inextricably, to the day I met Delphine, because the very first thing I noticed about the woman sitting on a stool at the university bar was that she held a book whose cover was instantly familiar to me: the 1957 Hachette edition of Camus' greatest novel. I'd carried it with me across four continents and two decades and it saw me safely through what amounted to my youth and out on to the other side. That book was my primary sustenance and my ultimate stimulus for many years; it was already dog-eared and yellowing when I found it in a second-hand bookshop during my first year at Oxford, and when it finally fell apart, its pages flecked with sand and saltwater, foxed with specks of grease and splashes of cooking, I couldn't actually bring myself to throw it away.

And now it's a stranger to me. I can only read it with her voice in my head; that amused but also slightly scornful tone she used whenever we talked about it, and the words have lost their meaning. Or rather, they take on the meanings she would ascribe to them and begin to sound like accusations. For the first time, the *finesse* and poignancy of that book gives me no joy.

I'm in the study now; my brown study, with the chesterfield sofa and bookshelf-lined walls, typing at my computer whose hi-tech flat-screen monitor is perched incongruously upon the antique oak desk my father gave me when I came down from Oxford. Duruflé's *Requiem* is playing in the background.

Another French hero of mine, although he's hardly hero material in the way Camus most certainly is — in fact, there's something quite disappointing in his work, the eternal shadowing of the far more famous Fauré; what seems like the quiet and unambitious determination to do *as well as* his celebrated predecessor. But he's all about subtlety and subterfuge; knew more than the crowd-pleaser Fauré could dream of knowing, and the swell of his music makes my heart ache more than anything else ever did, except for Delphine.

My best bow is on display here too. It should be in a Great Hall; that grandeur is too overwhelming for my little study wall. I don't take it out anywhere near often enough. Delphine encouraged me to practise my archery more frequently; she was even considering taking it up herself. I was a little anxious that in her enthusiasm she would try to have me dress up in tights and chain mail to take part in some re-enactment of Agincourt. It's a very beautiful object, that bow; she often used to run her hand along the polished rosewood and tense her forefinger against the string.

And here are my souvenirs from Dream Laboratory: a colourful bundle of wires topped with neurological electrodes, their tiny metal cups not entirely free of the connective paste which glued them to my skull, and a framed printout of the most active period of my most impressive polysomnograph. Those zigzag lines mark the workings of my unconscious mind, the peaks and troughs of my brain's nocturnal mean-derings. If I stare at them for long enough I almost begin to read them as music. The modern stuff. No harmony.

My study looks on to the street. I'm up on the top floor of a Victorian mansion block at the Little Venice end of Maida Vale. Little Venice is a rather pretentious name, I've always thought, for the sake of a couple of canals, but I do like living near water. I can sit on the windowsill with a coffee and watch the passers-by below, then up and along towards Regent's Park and the Zoo. Nobody can see me up here unless I lean right out of the window; it's a perfect little hide-away, a dream-hole as we might say: an archer, or a shooter, a rifleman – any kind of sniper – requires a high vantage point like this which offers a wide view whilst keeping him invisible to onlookers. So here I am in my dream-hole, out of sight but seeing everything. Everything except the one sight I long for.

Delphine preferred to sit on the balcony at the back of the sitting room overlooking the large communal garden, and spot foxes or identify trees or just watch the local children play.

Although I had realised that there were elements of our life together which weren't entirely to her satisfaction, I thought she brought much of that *tristesse* with her. Admittedly she seemed more *distrait* than usual these past few weeks, and less inclined towards intimacy, but I thought it was just a phase that would pass and on the whole I believe – I believed – she was fairly happy. Certainly not unhappy enough to leave like this. Besides, nothing has gone; I've scoured the whole flat and everything is here – all the clothes and shoes I bought her remain in the wardrobe, all her lotions and potions are still piled in the bathroom cabinet, her perfumes and jewellery box remain on the dressing table. The clothes she was wearing when I met her seem to be missing, which is odd because I never saw her wear them again after that first occasion – I wasn't sure why she kept them at all. When I realised they were gone I thought it might have been some kind of sign. If someone had *coerced* her into leaving the flat I imagined her asking if she might get changed and choosing that outfit – a cheap black knee-length skirt and pale pink rollneck sweater, and those flat black pumps – to alert me to the fact that something was Not Right. Even her handbag was still on the kitchen table, containing her keys, her mobile phone and her make-up in the duck-egg blue soft leather purse I'd bought her for Christmas. What woman would deliberately, willingly, leave her handbag?

No, all that is missing is that outfit. That and her dream diary.

Day four: Saturday

Today, I have to face the facts. A woman has left a man. She has not contacted him since her disappearance, nor did she give him any word to suggest she might leave and all her possessions remain at the home she has shared with him for almost a year, but even so the circumstances are not what the police call suspicious, and my concerned telephone calls and visit to the local station have been met with a mixture of pity, incredulity, impatience and even amusement. So I realise, I have accepted, that no crime has been committed, and my initial conviction that my love had been the victim of a kidnapper or worse has been modified. The forty-eight nightmarish hours of fearing her dead have been replaced with a certainty that she lives. But for me that doesn't rule out foul play, and her absence is a mystery I must solve. Not easy, considering how little success I've had with solving the mystery of her presence. Coming home and finding her here never ceased to amaze me, so it's strange that being home and finding her gone leaves me just as surprised. Delphine was the woman of my dreams, or would have been if I'd had any. But dreaming is one thing she never managed to teach me.

I'd been going to Dream Lab for around six months when we met. I would have never expected to find myself in such a thing as a dream laboratory, even if I knew they existed, but my arrival there heralded an enjoyable period of unpredictability in my life, the zenith of which was Delphine's appearance. I dread it all falling back into the pointless routine of Before. And – more surprises – I find myself missing not just Delphine but Dream Lab itself and all its members – even Simon, even Sally – for our fortnightly meetings, our shared intimacies, our almost-friendships. Wishing myself back amongst that odd little group of restless sleepers and troubled dreamers to which I never truly belonged, it's not like me at all.

I suppose it's ironic that my job got me into the lab to begin with; the very act of undermining my professional capabilities opened a door into a life which gave me new confidence and vigour. The powers that be at the office introduced a mandatory medical for all staff members aged fifty and over. They didn't call it that of course – it was framed in newsspeak and packaged as though they were doing us a favour: 'a full health check, using the very latest technology, completely free of charge' whereas we could see they were just sifting the wheat from the chaff to help them produce their 'voluntary redundancy list'. They seemed genuinely to assume that none of us listened to the news, but we all knew what was coming, we were all watching our backs. It's hard to keep secrets in the civil service.

Health checks held no fears for me; I don't know any man of my age who is fitter, and I'm in better shape than most of the younger fellows too. The treadmill, peak-flow and blood tests served only to reiterate that fact and I remember thinking – aha, you'll have to find some other reason to get rid of me, chaps – but I was wrong-footed by the psychometric tests. All that business – sorting respondents into 'character types' and assessing their state of mind on the basis of a few multiple choice questions – is such patent guff that I had no intention of playing ball, and told them so in no uncertain terms. That's how I first got talking to Reeves, who was clearly ill at ease with my refusal to co-operate and hadn't a clue what to do with his recalcitrant patient.

Huw Reeves is a psychologist based at Central University – a decent establishment by all accounts, not one of those *arriviste* polytechnics and catering colleges and Lord knows what else which have all desperately started calling themselves universities – who'd been drafted in to carry out this part of the health check. He was ingratiating from the start, full of 'How goes it?' or 'How's it hanging?' to a group of people he'd never met before, and later, in the lab, he even came out with the odd 'boyo' or 'bach' just in case we'd forgotten his evident Welshness, or his even more evident pride at the accident of his birthplace.

I never could abide professional Celts. I once lost a delightful girlfriend to a squat, foul-mouthed, gingery Scot who neither deserved nor appreciated her. She lectured in sociolinguistics and should have known better, but told me she couldn't resist the way he called her 'darling'.

'But I call you darling!'

'Yes, but it sounds like – James, I don't want to be mean and it's not your fault, but when you say it, it sounds like something out of a 1950s radio play. Whereas Hamish–' (Hamish. I ask you.) '– says it so lightly; there's no hard "g", and that long open vowel sound, it's like a breath, he could be saying it to a baby. A posh English "darling" makes me sit up straight; a soft regional "darlin'" makes me melt.'

So that was that. Not only had I lost her, I'd lost the ability to say the word 'darling' with any unselfconsciousness or warmth and that's something I've never entirely regained.

Anyway, there was Reeves, his lilting accent utterly failing to beguile me, and there was I, questioning the wisdom of the job he was doing. At first he must have thought I was some silly old fool who had never heard of psychometric testing; he spoke to me in a kindly, patronising tone. 'Let me assure you,' he said, 'you've no need to be suspicious of these tests, they're a standard part of the medical and there's nothing in the least sinister about them.'

I corrected him at once. 'I'm not at all suspicious of them; I just believe them to be a waste of time. My employers will discover nothing about my state of health from these tests, and since that's what I'm here for I'd rather just leave it at that, thank you.'

He said, in a conciliatory manner, 'It's not only your physical health that we're taking a look at today you know, Mr . . .' he scanned the list of names on his clipboard, '. . . Mr Beauman. A lot of working environments put employees under a great deal of pressure, and issues like stress are very important . . .'

I interrupted him curtly, pretty sure of where that one was going. 'So they want to try and prove I'm a loony, do they?

Sadly for them, my mental acuity is tip-top so they'll have to do better than that.'

He smiled patiently. 'Suffering from stress is a long way from lunacy. Our mental health affects everything we do and most of the staff I've seen so far *love* this part of the health check; they find it fascinating. The colleagues you arrived with today have already finished and gone home, it only takes half an hour or so and the findings are confidential. If there were any – issues – we would discuss the results with you before agreeing any further action. Absolutely nothing at all to be worried about.'

I wouldn't budge so he began to pry. 'Are you not even vaguely interested in seeing what the results might be? Are you confident that there isn't just one element of your life, however tiny, where your mental or emotional state could be causing you some – disquiet?'

'Such as?'

'Well, let's see – occasional panic attacks. Mild bouts of depression. Problems with sleeping, troubling dreams . . .'

'Ah, on that score I can reassure you completely. I've never suffered from any kind of mental illness and, although my sleep is sometimes disturbed, I *never* dream.'

He corrected me sharply. 'You mean you never *remember* a dream.'

'No, I mean I don't have them.'

'I doubt that very much. It's extremely rare for someone to have no dreams; some people just remember them better than others.' His tone was rather arrogant.

'Allow me to know my own mind, Dr Reeves,' I said. 'I think I would know if I dreamt.'

'But you're asleep, how can you know?' he asked cockily,

and went on, 'Truly, it's perfectly possible for you to be dreaming regularly but not remember anything about them. It's rare to have no memory of dreams whatsoever, but it's not unheard of.'

He sounded very sure of himself and I couldn't be bothered to argue.

'If you say so,' I said in an unconvinced tone.

I can hardly bear to think about my interview with my Head of Section a few days later. Nica Jenson has never warmed to me; I've been aware of her speaking to me more critically and impolitely than she does to other senior staff, all of whom have a far less illustrious CV than mine. She took my refusal to fill out that damned form as a personal insult and the sharpness of her voice pricked my eyes and actually made them well up. That was the moment I should have walked out, told her to stick her bloody job and find some other mug who would jump through hoops for her. I was pretty well off, I didn't need to work; I didn't even enjoy it any more. That was probably the outcome she desired. But I found myself unable to speak at all.

'So James, we're agreed, you will see Dr Reeves next week and complete the full health test?'

I only just managed to nod my head in agreement before blundering out like a great overgrown schoolgirl.

Delphine knew a man who had something wrong with his eyes. He was massively myopic and his vision was impaired in some other way too which she didn't entirely understand, but he wore special contact lenses and had to insert eye drops several times a day. He was so used to the procedure that he had long stopped going off to the office washroom or finding a mirror, and would just pause mid-sentence, throw back his head and squeeze a couple of drops into each eye before resuming whatever he was doing. The first few times Delphine observed this she couldn't see the tiny bottle grasped in the depths of his large hand and was startled by what seemed to be an extravagant tic. Then she saw him pop the small white bottle back in his pocket and realised what he was doing. The first few blinks after each dose would send a clear blue tear down his cheek. It was exactly the same blue as his eyes and the first time she saw it, Delphine thought his eyes were *melting away*. Eventually she watched more closely – well, she stared, she admitted to me – and saw that the drops themselves were blue. She liked this man, who was wry and self-depre-cating and who looked after his terminally ill wife without complaint. One day she was chatting to him and he answered the phone on his desk. When he put it down he sat very quietly for a moment. Delphine saw that his face was wet, but it took her a good five seconds to realise he was crying.

'All that time he wasn't crying it looked as though he was. But when he truly cried, I didn't see it. Because they weren't blue, I didn't see his tears!'

I tend not to cry; no, that's not right, I *tended* not to cry and hadn't for years until that awful week before I went back for the damned test, when every imagined slight at work had me snivelling uncontrollably, and even alone at home I felt weepy. I felt less pain than I do now but wept far more copiously. That was worse, strangely. At least I know what my tears are for now; then, I was completely in the dark.

Day five: Sunday

To give him his due, Reeves didn't crow. His manner, when I reappeared for the tests, was utterly professional; in fact his very neutrality seemed like a kindness to me and I felt my eyes stinging once more, this time with gratitude.

When Reeves took the paper from me, unable to resist surreptitiously reading my responses, I tried to show him there were no hard feelings by referring to our previous conversation.

'I've been reading up about dreaming,' I said to him.

'Oh yes?'

'Yes, and I realise I was rather dismissive of your insistence that I do dream.'

'I didn't mean to be insistent, I'm sorry if that's how it seemed.'

'No need to apologise. It's your field, after all. Actually, I'm rather glad you mentioned it.'

'Oh?'

'Yes. It led to an evening of quite fascinating research for me. I've been interested in consciousness for many years now . . .' He seemed to suppress a smile as though I'd made a joke. '. . . although from a more philosophical than psycho-logical viewpoint, and I'd thought I was fairly well informed about it.'

At this he actually made a little snort and asked me, chirpily, 'So, do you think you've cracked it then?'

'What do you mean?'

'Consciousness. I've many colleagues who have spent their working lives trying to define it.'

I realised he was teasing me and was keen to show that I understood the complexity of the subject. 'I wasn't suggesting that I had "cracked" it. Just that the subject of how the human mind works has been my private study over the past few years. I wouldn't pretend to be an expert, but what I was going on to explain was how I'd almost forgotten Unconsciousness. What we can discover about the brain when the subject sleeps. So your comments about dreams led me to that area and I realise I have a lot more research to do.'

He looked mildly contrite. 'I'm sorry, I was being flippant. Unconsciousness – well, sleep – is my area of research, so it's a bit of a pet subject. You wouldn't believe the number of people I see who dismiss disturbed sleep as nothing to worry about but then discover it's the symptom of some quite grave underlying problem. That's why I asked you about your sleep patterns.'

'Do you think there is any possibility that my lack of dreams might be due to Charcot–Wilbrand syndrome?'

'You have been reading up!' he laughed, and then he looked at me with an expression I couldn't fathom and which gave me an odd trio of sensations: a discomfort at being scrutinised so closely, that tingling sensation which made me blink away tears, and a strong desire for the look to continue. I felt disappointed when his pale blue eyes broke the gaze.

'Look, Mr Beauman,' he said, hesitantly.

'James.'

'James. The Sleep Clinic at the university can do wonderful things. They have very good results. Why don't you come for an assessment and see if they can help you?'

'Help me with what? I don't have a sleep disorder.'

He waved his clipboard at me.

'I wouldn't be too sure of that. According to these responses, you've been an insomniac for all of your adult life.'

'Nonsense. I mean, I know I have trouble dropping off, but then . . .'

'. . . but then, according to this questionnaire, you wake three or four times a night, on average.'

'Yes, but that's never been a problem for me. It's only for a few minutes at a time, half an hour or an hour at the most. It's never affected my work or my health at all.'

'Perhaps not noticeably. But it's unlikely that the level of sleep disturbance you're talking about has no effect at all on your waking life. Highly unlikely. I would certainly recommend that you seek some help with your sleeping pattern. I can get you an appointment very quickly and we can take it from there. How about it?'

I'm not sure why I found him so persuasive, but I agreed all the same. I think I was intrigued and I suppose a little flattered, albeit wary. And, although I don't believe in Fate, I did feel strangely hopeful that something positive might come out of my fraught experiences at work and all the business over the health test.

The latter seemed symptomatic of what I can only describe as a campaign being waged against me by a little band of upstarts at work. Only a few years before I had been respected, not just by my staff but by the one or two people above me; they often deferred to my greater experience. More recently however, I'd suspected that the vindictive Ms Jenson was beginning to find like-minded allies. I had even begun to doubt the loyalty of some members of my own team.

So there had been enough unpleasantness and – *turgidity* – and perhaps now was the time to hitch a ride downriver, wherever it might take me. I wanted to know more about my unconscious life. Perhaps I'd sleep like a baby. Perhaps I'd even remember a dream. Reeves seemed to be offering his hand, and I was so eager to take it that I scarcely stopped to wonder why.

But my gratitude brought with it some resentment right from the start. He seemed too kind. That Chinese proverb: *Why do you hate me? I have never helped you.* It's a terrible thought, and I'm not quite sure why I think it, but it seems to make perfect sense.

Day six: Monday

I've extended my leave from work. Can't possibly contemplate going in like this. It's been a good nine months since I suffered from lack of sleep and I'm finding it hard to believe I put up with it for thirty-odd years without even acknowledging the effects. How did I keep going, feeling like this every hour of every day? Nothing to compare it to then, I suppose. The nearest experience to it might be the bundle of sensations one gets a couple of hours after a long-haul flight. You'll be on the train or in the car on the homeward leg of the journey thinking – well, this isn't too bad – and then it hits you. Even if you managed to snooze on the plane, a great wave of tiredness will engulf you; your eyes will sting and water, your skin will itch, your muscles

15

will twitch until you feel quite hysterical, you will be over-powered by a desperate desire to get home, make a cup of tea, have a shower and then lie in clean cotton sheets for an entire weekend. The reason you don't, if you're an insomniac, is that you know you won't sleep. Being tired isn't enough.

Insomnia marked me out from the common man. For all the time that sleep eluded me, I came to see that dependence on horizontal unconsciousness as shameful, as something only children or animals should need. I developed a theory that I avoided sleep almost by choice, because a man of my intelligence and ambition clearly had more important matters for his brain to deal with. Absolute nonsense: a few weeks of sharing a bed with Delphine cured me of all symptoms, including my self-deception, and I began to sleep soundly beside her. The relaxation this brought to me was blissful and I would fall asleep happily anticipating the wonderful experience of leaving the land of Nod naturally after the full seven hours, ready and able to cope with the wakeful pleasures of the day.

However, it appears that no cure ever occurred; it was simply that Delphine beside me was a lucky charm. And now my nights are filled with anxiety about her, which keeps me awake just as much as insomnia ever did.

At the Sleep Clinic, Reeves had arranged for me to talk to a neuropsychiatrist, complete yet another questionnaire and book myself in for a polysomnograph. I'm an old hand at PSGs now; it's amazing what you can get used to.

Nocturnal PSGs are a detailed log of brain activity, eye movement, sleep position, respiratory pressure, muscular movements and so on, and they're the central technical tool at the Sleep Clinic which uses them for diagnosis, to monitor treatment and for research purposes. I've seen mine – the equivalent of thousands of A4 pages all stored on computer and representing an entire night's sleep measured in seconds.

The first time was quite daunting – the 'prep' involved having some abrasive gel rubbed on my head before a couple of dozen electrodes were glued on to my skull, each attached by a long wire to a box by the bed. All rather *1984*. But Wayne, the chief technical chap at the Sleep Clinic, was wonderfully informative and answered all my questions about the procedure and what he hoped to achieve by it. I found his South Carolina drawl strangely calming. It could so easily have seemed like a scene from a ludicrous sci-fi movie, all that wire and bleeping machinery, but when I closed my eyes and heard his slow, long-vowelled explanations of the process it was more like listening to a story.

Delphine said, after her first PSG, that Wayne's voice and the hospital heat made her feel like Blanche Dubois. I wouldn't go quite that far, but I certainly relaxed enough to ignore the strangeness of going to sleep with little metal pads on my skull, near my eyes, at my jaw, and on my chin, plus a canula in my nose to measure my breathing and various bands around my torso and legs to note heart and lung events. 'We're interested in your ECG and EEG, obviously,' Wayne had explained languorously, attaching electrodes in conductive paste to my skin, 'and we'll wire up the ant. tibs on each leg for your EMG as well as the nasal thermocouple for heat measurements and three electrodes right and left for your EOGs, OK?' I could only nod. 'Right, give me fifteen to calibrate and we'll be off,' he said cheerily. I found it remarkable that I could get to sleep at all, but I did – that first time and every subsequent time – with no more difficulty than if I'd been at home in my own bed. My numerous wakings were a little disconcerting; it always took me a while to realise where I was, and possibly made it harder to get back to sleep again than if I'd been in familiar surroundings, but it pretty much mirrored a typical night at home. Wayne was happy to oblige my request for the printout of the night's most dramatic 'events' within my brain, which now adorns my desk.

On all the graphs, my heartbeat is reassuringly steady throughout.

All of my insomniac wakings were noted but despite the disturbances, and frustratingly for me, Wayne told me that my polysomnograph showed masses of REM sleep – the phase during which dreams most often happen – of which I could remember not one moment.

'You've a higher than average occurrence of Rapid Eye Movement periods, and greater REM density, according to the R and K score,' he told me, as though it were something I should be proud of.

'R and K?'

'Rechtschaffen and Kales invented this method of sleep scoring, splitting the sleep into phases.'

'So why can't I remember all those dreams I'm supposed to be having?'

'Well, really you should discuss this with a doctor, or with Huw . . .' he began, but was unable to resist suggesting his own theory, '. . . but one possibility could be that you come out of REM sleep stage very slowly – look here . . . and here . . .' He pointed out sleep phases on the screen in front of us. 'These delta waves increase from deep sleep very slowly so it takes a while before the Alpha phase kicks in, and so by the time you're fully awake there's far less chance you could remember anything. People who remember dreams regularly seem to leave the REM stage more quickly, whether or not they're insomniac, or they wake up suddenly – from a nightmare or very vivid dream or whatever – and so are able to recall what they've dreamt.'

I'd have been happier to discover that I lacked REM sleep, which would explain my dearth of dreams, than to realise I had a surfeit which my waking brain could not recall. Such a waste.

When I arrived for our follow-up meeting, Reeves was comparing the printouts of my PSGs with some other pieces of paper. He tidied up his desk quickly when I walked in, and smiled at me before saying, 'James. I run a little discussion group. Nothing formal: just a few people I've met via the Sleep Clinic at the university – as you know, my department works with them on a regular basis – who suffer from chronic sleep disorders. I've been charting their progress through a number of therapies for a few months now, and at the moment I'm particularly interested in how their disorders relate, if at all, to their dreaming patterns – whether different sleep problems tend to affect a patient's dreams in any predictable way, and if so what we can learn from that. We call it the Dream Laboratory. If you would like to come along – just on spec, to see if you'd like to join in – you would be very welcome.'

I felt inordinately moved at this invitation, but must have looked uncertain, because he started trying to persuade me. 'I have to be honest and say that it's not just patient care –

it's partly for my own benefit, because it's rare to have an ongoing relationship with a patient which isn't solely based on their treatment. This is a much more wide-reaching arena, dealing with issues which go beyond each group member's particular problems. I'm interested in gathering together some people who are keen to find alternatives to drug-based therapies and I'm also using the group as research material for another project I'm working on. It means that everyone must have a broader interest than resolving their own situation and at the moment the group doesn't have a straightforward insomniac, so . . .'

'But I don't dream – I don't remember any dreams. Surely I'd be of no use to your dream studies.'

'Not at all,' he insisted. 'I mean, think of yourself as, perhaps a sounding board. A *comparator*. Someone to whom we can turn and say – do non-dreamers feel x or y, do non-dreamers operate in this way or that? I don't mean that you've got to act as some blueprint for the non-dreamer – just that having someone who has no memory of dreams could be very useful for the group. Everyone else in this group has recurrent dreams or stress-induced dreams or vivid dreams or bad dreams. We need someone who has nothing.'

I raised my eyebrows.

'I mean, who has no dreams, who doesn't remember dreams . . . I'm sorry, I'm not explaining this well.' He looked rather flustered, which didn't suit his sandy colouring one bit; perhaps he thought my silence was an offended, rather than a thoughtful, one.

I reassured him. 'No, no, I do understand, I think. Perhaps I could be the *control*.'

Reeves beamed. 'The control. Just the job. So you'll give it a go?'

'I will.'

'Great stuff! And you might end up with a whole bunch of polysomnographs before too long! Every other Thursday at 7 p.m. in my office, starting next week.' He handed me his card and opened the door. 'Meet just before then in the bar and I'll come and fetch you when I'm ready. See you then.'

I glanced back through the window as the door swung shut, and saw him talking rapidly into a tiny hand-held voice recorder, one of those digital jobs I'd tried to use for dictation until it became obvious that my secretary's audio-typing skills weren't up to it.

He was pacing the room as he spoke and seemed terribly energised. I've always envied his enthusiasm.

3 October

James Beauman. Old school, public school, very old school tie. Safely cushioned by the Foreign Office. Probably thought of as 'eccentric' which usually means somewhere on the spectrum. Slight Asperger's maybe — his Myers Briggs score would support that. He must have been the kind of child people called 'intelligent' but never, never, 'bright'. And there's that intense smile which, I'm pretty sure, has no emotion behind it. Like he's trying to play a part but doesn't have the script. Probably wouldn't get through the FCO screening these days but you come across them sometimes, ones who've somehow slipped through the net. Certainly an odd fish.

So — about fifteen years older than me, a good few rungs further up the social ladder than me, a slow-talking formal type unlike me; scored low on empathy and high on systems absolutely unlike me; tall, dark and — and yes, you'd call him handsome I suppose, in that never-quite-grown-up-public-school sort of way, so . . . so . . . just about the very opposite of me.

But. And yet. A chronic insomniac, like me. Copious amounts of REM sleep, like me. No memory of dreams, like me. A PSG result that could have been the twin of mine. My older, posher, richer, weirder, better-educated doppelganger.

This might actually start making sense of the Thursday group which has yielded nothing of any value at all yet. Bringing in a 'control', ha ha, will give them even more opportunities to drone on about their latest nocturnal exploits. Plenty of time for me to continue testing

*out the Transmissions theory with the current group members, and
an outside chance that I can resolve — no, let's not be too ambitious
here — a tiny chance that I can examine my own problem . . . my
own lack . . . and maybe even work out how to remedy it — through
Beauman. Jesus. He's not the kind of body double I imagined. But
the match is too good to pass by. It's — work with me here, indulge
me — it's a dream come true.*

Day seven: Tuesday

I was depressed, of course, at that time. I had probably been
depressed for quite some years without noticing. It took me
a long time to use that word and I could never say it comfortably, even to Delphine. It was the most difficult admission
I've ever made, and it was only to myself. I never acknowledged
such a thing at work but the people in my team were clearly
more observant about my mental state than I was, because I
became aware of how some of them pussyfooted around me
and avoided anything approaching a confrontation with me.
The others – those I suspected of being in cahoots with Ms
Jenson – were off-hand and even dismissive. Everyone treated
me like a special case. I was determined to put a stop to it,
and after all that business about the medical I made special
efforts to behave as a fully-competent team leader should, and
matters did improve a little. Attending the lab seemed to give
me a certain confidence and ease which I'd never encountered
until then so that even before Delphine joined us I felt that
I was getting better, though I couldn't have defined from
what, exactly. The meetings were strangely therapeutic. I still
couldn't sleep, but that didn't bother me.

It is generally accepted that depression can reduce the
length of time a sleeper takes to fall into REM sleep, and
it is common for depressives to report troubling dreams.
Antidepressants suppress dreaming sleep. Chronic depressives
who are using certain antidepressant drugs often report an

improvement in their mental state which could be as much to do with a reduction in dreaming as in any directly chemical or physiological response. I haven't found any research on non-dreaming depressives. Perhaps I am an oxymoron in my own right.

The first Dream Lab meeting was an odd affair. I've never liked being in a small group of people. One to one I can cope with, and I quite like a crowd, but I used to dread tutorials at Oxford. My fellow students would assume a uniform expression of confidence and self-possession and I found it impossible to read their faces, which made me nervous. I overcame this with a trick which has proved invaluable ever since: any time I enter a room I look everybody in the eye and, whatever their facial expression, I smile politely. This always makes them smile back except in very rare circumstances, in which case the non-smiler just appears ill-mannered. The only way I can confront strangers in this way is to make sure that I don't really look them in the eye at all; I focus on middle-distance in the general direction of their eyes. This has three benefits: firstly, I seem confident; secondly, I don't have to try to work out what their faces are really saying; and thirdly, it reassures them about my innate friendliness and thus allows me to make discreet observations in my own time with impunity.

The first person I noticed when I walked, smiling, into the room the Thursday after I took Reeves' card was Simon. He was physically imposing and verbally forthcoming and, as the first couple of sessions were all about the current group members helping me catch up, he was able to dominate. They had been meeting for three months already but seemed unfazed by my arrival, and more than happy to tell me about their problems. As everyone defined themselves by their sleep disorders, it sounded like the stereotypical AA meeting in some American film.

'Hello, I'm Simon and I have a Circadian Rhythm disorder.'
    'Hello Simon.'
    'Right, what do you need to know?' he began but didn't wait for answer. 'OK, I've been aware of my problem – it's a fairly massive problem – ever since it started, in my mid-teens, but I've always avoided doing anything about it, you know, not admitting there was something "wrong" with me. You see, my normal timetable, right, is to fall asleep around 5 a.m. and wake up in the early afternoon – I'm practically nocturnal – and I just haven't been able to change that without being completely knackered. It's made me lose two jobs, it was the main problem in my marriage and last year I fell asleep at the wheel on the M25. So that made me wake up – ha ha – to the, erm, gravity of my problem and I became pretty keen to get it sorted out. I had an assessment at the Sleep Clinic six months ago, and they sent me off with an actimeter – looks like a wristwatch, notes your sleep patterns over the course of a week – and the psychiatrist told me I have a "Delayed Sleep Phase". I could have worked that one out for myself. And so far no treatments I've tried with the Sleep Clinic have worked so I've just about given up going to them.'
    Despite looking as though he was in his late thirties and clearly middle-class, Simon spoke in the kind of estuary drawl favoured by so many younger Londoners which always grated on my ear.

Reeves said, 'Remind me, Simon, what did they start you off on? Sleeping tablets? Waking tablets? Both?'

'No, at first they gave me a light box to use with my alarm clock and that worked for a couple of mornings but then I was somehow able to ignore it.'

Reeves saw my blank expression and explained, 'The message for the body to wake up can come from light as well as, or even better than, sound. For someone who finds waking hard and can sleep through all kinds of loud alarm-clock beeps, it's possible to position a light box near their face and even though they're asleep their eyes will become aware of the light and tell the brain it's dawn, it's time to wake up.'

'It's a great theory,' Simon went on, 'and I know it's solved the problem for some people, but not me. Anyway, they then tried it in combination with sleeping tablets, trying to aim for getting me to sleep at around 1 a.m. and the light box waking me at 8 a.m., but the number of tablets it took to put me out made me so groggy that the waking bit just didn't work. They wanted to try me with new combinations, including drugs to wake me as well as put me to sleep, but the whole thing made me feel really uncomfortable – ill, even – so I'm coming here partly to work out whether I *want* to change my sleeping patterns and if so whether I can do it some other way.'

Reeves seemed to approve of this approach. Simon was fortunate enough to have an understanding employer – he's a graphic designer so mostly operates alone in any case – who allowed him to set up an office at home and work during the night, so the pressing need to keep normal hours wasn't as great as it had been in his earlier life.

Simon had a careless, animal quality about him which

made me feel uncomfortable to be close to. It's not that he smelled bad, although I don't think he showered daily or laundered his clothes too regularly, and he certainly rarely shaved, but he had thick brown hair to his shoulders and too many teeth in his smile, and he was always making large, unnecessary physical gestures. In addition to his sleep disorder he suffered from a variety of nightmares which frequently caused him to wake in a confused, distressed state a couple of hours after he finally managed to sleep. The shaggy hair, the bristly muzzle and an image of him pacing his flat in the dark always brought to mind werewolves. I think I used to be a little scared of that big, restless body, all limbs and hair and *angst*. He seemed predatory and uncontrolled. He made me nervous.

'Hi, I'm Jagdev and I'm narcoleptic. Put simply, I fall asleep very quickly at inopportune moments. Stick with us and you're bound to see it happen.'

Jagdev was a postgraduate student, a protégé of Reeves in the Psychology Department as well as a Dream Lab member. He didn't say much more than that for the first few meetings, but subsequently took part in the sessions with great, garrulous enthusiasm. A handsome lad, gangly and long-limbed in the way I used to be, with thick, gelled rock-star hair and ripped jeans. All the makings of a ladies' man, but slightly too earnest to succeed in the role, even if he wanted to.

'Hello, my name's Sally and I suffer from Restless Leg Syndrome.'

She spoke as though I knew what that was and nobody picked her up on it so I didn't ask her to expand. Sally turned out to be an extremely talkative, and thankfully articulate, woman in her mid- to late-forties who would never let Reeves get away without explaining every answer to her satisfaction. I could tell he thought her a bit of a tartar but she was very commanding. Didn't give away much about herself though, unlike young Polly who said, giggling, 'Hi, I'm Polly and I'm a self-harming somnambulist.'

Polly usually giggled whenever she talked; thank heavens it was pretty entertaining stuff, and she didn't seem to mind our laughing at her comic tales of bizarre behaviour. She was a recent graduate in Drama, and had just taken a job as an 'animateur', whatever that might be, for an educational theatre company. She seemed rather head-girlish to me – a glossy brunette bob and a figure which was more athletic than womanly. I could see her on the lacrosse field, or toasting marshmallows in the dorm during midnight feasts.

'Evening. I'm Alfred and I have Obstructive Sleep Apnoea, for my sins.'

Alfred rarely spoke a great deal, but was nevertheless the most audible lab member; his dysfunctional respiratory system provided the percussive background to all our meetings. He was a pudgy, pale man whom I placed in his early sixties, and his condition made him permanently tired, since he spent every night holding his breath for up to a minute at a time and then waking with a shock and a disgusting rattle in his throat, sometimes more than a hundred times in one night. 'Our Jackie has to wear earplugs but they're not much use against a racket like I make,' he told us. His Jackie had courageously refused to leave the bed they'd shared for twenty years – 'our Jackie won't desert me' he would say with some satisfaction – and I was always rather touched by that.

At that initial meeting, looking nervous and sweating slightly, he had described the various methods he'd tried in order to resolve his sleep disorder.

'I know it's because I'm overweight,' he wheezed, in an accent which, added to his appearance, gave one the general impression of a Northern comedian who'd been playing the Working Men's Clubs circuit for forty years. I almost laughed aloud when I first heard him. '. . . and I have lost a few pounds, but let's face it, my neck's always going to be thick and I've never had much of a chin so even if I lost three stone I'd probably still have the problem. They gave me a See-Pap—'

Reeves cut in, for my benefit, 'That's CPAP, James. Continuous Positive Airway Pressure. Obstructive Sleep Apnoea is caused by closure of the upper airway which prevents natural breathing. The patient wears a special sort of mask to bed, usually covering the nose, and a gentle stream of air is introduced to the back of the throat which keeps the upper airway open and allows normal breathing. It's got a good track record.'

'Not for me,' said Alfred wistfully. 'I kept waking up and gagging. Couldn't get used to it at all. And sometimes I'd get Arousal Disorder — when you sort of wake up suddenly but not properly and your heart's thumping and the night terrors would start again.' His jowls wobbled at the memory. 'The only thing that works for a while is our Jackie pushing me over on to my side when I start; we're trying to train me to do it on my own. It's my heart we're worried about. You know . . .' he looked at Reeves almost pleadingly, '. . . the pressure on it.'

'Yes, apnoea does tend to put an extra strain on the heart. What about daytime sleepiness?'

'Oh aye, plenty of that. Once I was out of the pit I did an office job for the coal board as was, but I had to take early retirement because I kept falling asleep on the job. That's when we moved down south, spent my compensation money on getting away from all that. But the apnoea had already started by then. We should have probably stayed put and spent the money on holidays.'

Just looking at Alfred made me feel tired, even when I was sleeping well: his jowly, lugubrious face; a permanent sheen of sweat on his brow and the large purplish bags under his bloodshot eyes. Poor Alfred. Try as he might he never did lose much weight.

The final group member I met that first time, and the one who made the lightest impression on me, was Julie. She spoke so quietly I could hardly hear her introduce herself, 'Hello, I'm Julie and I have Chronic Fatigue Syndrome.'

She couldn't have been much more than thirty but her drawn, worn-out face made her look a decade older. Her parents hailed from Jamaica and despite having lived in Birmingham since she was a small child she had hung on – wilfully, surely – to a light West Indian accent which I always thought was an affectation. Mind you, if the alternative was your classic Brummie perhaps she was wise to do so. Chronic Fatigue Syndrome made her look permanently shattered, although right from the beginning it was obvious that her domestic situation – bringing up two small girls on her own in some grotty flat and working shifts at a hospital – made a significant contribution to her exhausted appearance. She developed CFS symptoms after recovering from some nasty infection, I believe.

'My work has made it ever so difficult to stick at any programme properly and I'm not sure I want to embark on

some of the drug treatments available. Not just yet. I'm interested in looking at the alternative first. And I'm really really
interested that we're going to be looking at dreams, so whatever
else happens, I'm going to make this session as often as I can.'

While I always found Julie to be a pleasant and friendly
member of the group, I wasn't terribly impressed by her
contributions to discussions and her shyness was occasionally
irritating. She was also interested to the point of obsession in
herbal remedies for sleep problems, a topic which I consider
total poppycock.

So we were what one could politely call 'a mixed bag'.
Nevertheless, the first few months were most successful; we
covered a multitude of subjects and enjoyed batting them back
and forth between us. Our discussions could hardly be called
intellectual – there wasn't really enough brain power in the
room to light a philosophical fire – but there were sparks,
and there was laughter and from time to time there was even
a sense of comfort and well-being, as though we were an odd
and rather dysfunctional family group whose members weren't
close enough for confidences but who nevertheless enjoyed
their limited time together. A couple of new members came
and went, but the 'core' remained solid and those fortnightly
Thursday evenings became a given that was also a pleasure.
The lab-less Thursday in between seemed dull by comparison
and I enjoyed the sense of mild anticipation I experienced at
work when the meeting day came around.

Nothing alerted me to the potential explosiveness of the
situation: the dangers of being the control in an environment
which resisted control, of losing my grip on what was
happening. Or of falling in love more deeply than I thought
I could, or ever wanted to.

Day eight: Wednesday

Today I slept through my alarm and was woken by the sound of the cleaning lady letting herself in to the flat. She has her own keys and has been 'doing for me' every Wednesday for five years but I've hardly seen her in all that time and had completely forgotten she would be coming. When Delphine first moved in I delayed going to work one morning so that I could introduce them.

'Delphine, this is Mrs Duda,' I said, trying to keep a straight face and wondering if she would find the name as amusing as I always did. But no, not Delphine.

'Oh, my mother lives next door to a couple called Doudah! You're not French are you?'

The woman smiled and shook Delphine's hand, saying, 'No, no, it's D-U-D-A, a Polish name. But you must call me Aniela,' which she had never said to me in all those years. After that they were friends, of course.

'Aniela is very beautiful, isn't she?' Delphine said one evening the following week.

'Aniela?'

She tutted. 'Your cleaning lady.'

'Oh. Well, looking good for her age I suppose. And she's got those cheekbones and all that. Yes, she's very attractive.'

'James, it's not like you not to notice a beautiful woman.'

'She's my cleaning lady! And a damned good one at that.

She does all my washing and ironing as well, you know, and most cleaners round here won't touch laundry.'

'Would she be less good at cleaning if you thought she was beautiful?'

'Of course not, but it's best not to complicate such a convenient arrangement.'

Delphine laughed. 'I asked if you thought she was beautiful, not if you had actually considered making advances towards her. They are two different questions, you know.'

This morning, Mrs Duda's pale blue eyes flashed at me in surprise as I appeared in the hall in my dressing gown and said, 'I'm sorry, Mrs Duda; it's not really convenient – I should have called you and asked you not to come this week . . .'

My voice trailed off pathetically but she nodded as though she understood my predicament and said decisively, 'OK, I will just tidy up a little and then leave it all until next week.'

She made me a pretty expert cup of coffee while I showered, and when she left the flat she turned to say goodbye and added, 'I hope she comes back here, Mr Beauman.'

'Yes. Me too,' I said, 'but don't hold your breath.'

Her expression was sympathetic as she closed the door.

Delphine was right, she is beautiful.

My past is littered with beautiful women from all over the world. I have sometimes wondered whether the pursuit of them sapped me, somehow, because my indisputable sexual success has never been matched in my professional life. I wasn't obsessive about these women; I never missed a morning in the office however hard it was to leave my shared bed, and I was sure to attend even the most inconsequential drinks parties at various embassies, whatever more appealing prospect awaited me elsewhere. I sacrificed nothing for the sake of pleasure. But every city I've ever worked in is filed in my head under the names of the women I bedded there, so perhaps my focus was distracted from my job despite every effort to show commitment and competence at work.

My excellent French, lack of family ties in Blighty and willingness to relocate at short notice should have made me top of the list for the best selection of jobs abroad. It started well. I did a few junior posts in the UK before moving on to positions in France and in French-speaking nations – worked my way up via Algeria and then Belgium, and was First Secretary in Hanoi before I was thirty, so ideally placed for greater things. I saw myself at fifty – suave, lean, debonair, a minister in Paris perhaps, angling quietly for the ambassador-ship to see out my final years in the service. The vision didn't materialise. Never Paris. Despite my indisputably fluent French – so close to bilingual the difference was academic – and having a couple of very promising interviews, I never landed the plum job I really wanted. What finally put paid to any hope I still nurtured was a realisation that my superiors were apparently unable to pinpoint precisely why I hadn't been successful. As though everything was fine on paper but they preferred a less qualified yet still, somehow, more suitable individual for the plum postings. I went to West Africa, I spent two years in Geneva working with the UN and then back to North Africa, Tunisia this time, for three years. I was well-paid, well-respected, worked on interesting projects. But I never got what I wanted, and it's only by looking back across almost thirty years of missed opportunities that I've been able to understand. There was something in my demeanour or my outlook which made them uncomfortable with having me represent them overseas at a senior level. I was alone in believing that my skills and my temperament were perfectly suited to the demands of a high-level overseas job. I may be exaggerating slightly, but by the time I was forty I seemed to be left in a pool which included all those who were habitually refused advancement: the bankrupts, alcoholics and homosexuals, but in my case it was for no reason I could see or was ever given.

After accepting that Paris was for ever beyond me, and tiring of waiting to see what second- or third-rate positions they could find for me instead, I requested a permanent transfer back to the UK — usually the prerogative of the family man, funnily enough — left the Foreign Office and have worked on Overseas Development ever since. It's fulfilling work — co-ordinating economic assistance to developing countries where I've been able to see some real improvements, and working with other agencies on all sorts of worthwhile projects. It used to be dams and power stations, but now we help set up television channels or internet access, fund medical research, and carry out community projects with other agencies. But it's all so far away, and there is always famine in Africa. It's one step up, two steps down, every time. I have no stomach for it these days.

The reason I'd slept in late on Mrs Duda's cleaning day was because I spent much of last night in my increasingly insomniac state: up and down for drinks of water or chamomile tea ('Smells of pee!' Delphine once said with disgust, and she was right, and it tastes of pee too, but I find it calming); listlessly turning the dial of the radio and finding neither soothing music nor stimulating speech; walking up and down the front room like an unhappily imprisoned bear. And thinking, obsessively, about making love to Delphine. It's been almost five weeks since the last time – which I didn't for one moment think might be The Last Time – and an enormous store of longing has built up in me, a ball–aching, gut-wrenching mass of desire which has nowhere to go. This looking back and gnashing of teeth is so much worse than the frustrations of adolescence where you have only your imagination to tell you what you're missing.

I'd been in passionate relationships before and, in my younger days, had clocked up the usual kinds of adventures, which always seem to boil down to a simple element of risk – and in these matters the risk is almost always of discovery, whether by the husband's Merc gliding silently into the garage while his wife's cries of pleasure ring out of the open bedroom window, or by a passing band of boy scouts on a ramble alongside the thrashing undergrowth in which illicit love-making is hidden from their view. But this went one step further. Delphine helped me to explore a new plane of sexual experience, which was a more than pleasant surprise to a man of my age. It wasn't that she was an exhibitionist – she never actually wanted to get caught – and nor was it some kind of cheap thrill; more an absolute insistence on when and how she wanted me to make love to her.

That makes me sound almost passive about sex; I wasn't, nor have I ever been. And many previous lovers have demonstrated enormous confidence in directing me sexually or in making spontaneous and unexpected demands. Delphine added another dimension.

Leaving an upmarket curry house (her most plebeian characteristic is a love of anglicised Indian cookery) and heading towards the local pub, she nodded towards the car park across the road and said, 'Let's go in there. Let's find a wall which you can take me against.'

I was aghast. It was barely 11 p.m., the car park was well-lit and although there was nobody about at the time, someone could easily walk by at any minute. But I allowed her to lead me by the hand and we casually sauntered, with beating hearts, along the perimeter in search of darkness. Turning the corner we came across the back of the police station, whose windows were all dark but which featured a line of bright halogen lights outside. There was a small courtyard at its centre and an appealingly shadowy doorway within.

'Here.'

'But someone might come past! And it's a bloody police station!'

'Nobody's going to be walking past here, and if they do we'll just be . . . kissing. OK?'

While she was talking, Delphine was reaching under her coat and skirt and pulling off her white cotton panties with one hand, while drawing my face to her mouth with the other. Aroused beyond belief, I clumsily undid my belt and trousers and was inside her in a moment. While I was thinking that the frequently uncomfortable vertical position for inter-course was in this instance delightfully easy, I saw that Delphine was entirely unaware of our surroundings. The rough brick scraped my knuckles as I clutched her buttocks and the cool wind on my backside ensured there was no possibility of my forgetting our environs, but her face looked just the way it did against a pillow. She was so relaxed, in such a reverie of pleasure. She pulled up and away from me briefly, only to turn around so that I could enter her from behind and I can still see her fist, clutching her panties, high above her head against the brick wall, and feel the smooth curve of her belly in my hands.

'I want you to see me when I come,' she said quietly, so we resumed our original position and I watched her lips part and her eyes close and heard her breath catch in her throat. Then she surprised me. 'Come inside me. Come inside me this time.'

Soon after we started seeing each other she went on the Pill, but this incident was before she had begun taking it so I knew we weren't supposed to be having unprotected sex. I had almost reached climax and had to make a supreme effort to disobey her, and was then surprised again as I pulled out of her and she dropped to the floor in a squat and took me in her mouth. When I had subsided she turned and spat neatly in the doorway. We repositioned our clothing in silence and walked arm in arm, both weak at the knees, away from the car park and to bed.

That spitting discomfited me. In the light of our intimate and adventurous sexual relationship it seemed to make her, briefly, rather distant from me. I'm not trying to suggest that a certain kind of behaviour is in some way *expected* from women. I've had lovers who are unwilling to open up to me in every way, and some for whom performing the act of fellatio was clearly tedious at best. It's just that the habit – of spitting – seemed so at odds with everything else we did to and with each other's bodies. I broached the subject later that night and she said, 'It's not made to *eat*. If it tasted nice there'd never be any babies.'

Delphine balked at nothing, even when I feared that I was asking too much of her small, light frame. Without meaning to boast, I have the good fortune to be well endowed; the shaft of my penis is thick and long while its head (circumcised as a family rather than religious tradition) swells to an even larger circumference. Long ago a girlfriend likened its effect to the barbs on a tomcat's genitals, which catch on the female on withdrawal and cause her to turn and bite him. The comparison titillated me at the time. When I withdrew from Delphine she often gasped.

'Just before you come out of me, it gets bigger,' she explained once, 'and I have to stretch around you a little. It hurts *nicely*.'

Oh dear. This was never supposed to be some frisky *exposé* of a love affair. It's just that whenever I think about Delphine I think about making love to her, and so much of what we mean to each other is contained within our sexual life. To gloss over all that would make this entire venture pointless; I have to be completely honest and honestly complete, and my intention is never to brag.

Delphine said I was the most honest man she knew when it came to sex.

'Have you *ever* had a sexual problem?' she asked me one night. 'I don't just mean a physical problem; I mean have you always been easy with the *idea* of it?'

I wasn't sure exactly what she meant. 'The *idea* of it?'

'Yes, you know. When you first learnt about it, or when you were young and wanted to approach a girl and weren't sure about what she would say. You know, that kind of thing.'

'No. No, never. I learned the facts of life – before they taught us at school, but not much before – and they made immense sense. It all tallied with those feelings I'd been having. And as for being nervous about girls, well, I'd make an approach and quite often it worked, and if it didn't – well, that's life.'

'You are very direct.'

That made me smile in the dark. 'Well, Mrs Pot.'

'Hmm?'

'You're Mrs Pot, you know, calling the kettle black . . .' She pinched me as I went on, 'Well, why not be direct? Two human beings over the age of consent shouldn't really beat about the bush, should they? I mean, one can do it nicely and all that, but it seems to me that directness is appreciated. By women. Don't you think?'

'Oh yes, for sure, it's an honest approach. And women want men to be honest more than they want anything.'

Delphine's last lover, in the first months of their affair, was the most physically uninhibited person she'd ever known. His natural state was to be naked; they spent whole days in her apartment without ever getting dressed and he revelled in his flesh and her flesh and all the things they could do together. He was forever grabbing her around the waist and touching her breasts and cupping her backside even when they were attempting discretion. She felt free and untethered when she was walking along with him or lying beside him and he helped her become much more liberated about her own body. Then as the relationship progressed he changed. He started wearing a vest and shorts to bed, he would come out of the shower wrapped in a towel, he never wandered around unclothed. When they made love, Delphine would have to gently pull his vest over his head so that she could feel his skin against her but sometimes he would wriggle out of her clutches and keep the garment on. Even when they were alone she would have to slip her hands beneath layers of sweaters, T-shirts, always that vest, and he was loath to take them off. They had been at the point when the only way of getting closer to each other's bodies would be to start paring skin off or climbing inside one another. But he had chosen to retreat instead, and to hide from her. She discovered his reasons a little later but at the time there was no explanation for the change and it confused her as much as it distressed her. Leaving him, she said, was the saddest thing she had ever done.

That night, the night of the car park, I should have asked her why she had asked me to come inside her. But there were so few possible answers and I couldn't think of one I wanted to hear.

Day nine: Thursday

Today I received a postcard from Delphine. It's now almost noon and for the past hour I have done nothing but stare at this little rectangle of text. I'm unable to say whether or not it was a shock: by the time I picked it up I had recognised her handwriting so it's difficult to assess how much of my response was relief, and how much hope, and how much dread. Even now, I can't quite place the cause of my shaking hand and this feeling of sickness that tightens the back of my throat. I know that I'm angry, but that seems an excessive response to something which amounts to almost nothing, a complete lack of information:

My dear James

I'm so sorry to do this, and in this way. I couldn't leave a note, didn't know what to say. Still don't know what to say, except again, sorry, sorry, sorry.

D

The card features a photograph of the Chagall window in Chartres, the postal frank matches. We were thinking of visiting the cathedral later in the summer, and going to Reims and Metz too, on a mini Chagall-and-church-architecture tour. Well, Delphine was trying to persuade me. We'd already seen his stuff at Chichester and at that little place in Kent and she was desperate to see more and, while I'm not that keen on him, I preferred the idea to her alternative suggestion which was a trek around some dreary north-western English cities to indulge her mawkish affection for the God-awful pre-Raphaelites. Anything but that!

Our tastes in art were poles apart, in fact she didn't really have any to speak of, but her Christmas present to me was an annual membership of the Tate Modern so I dragged her along with me every few weeks and she would dutifully walk around the in-house collections and allow me to point out works which intrigued or amused me, but she refused to buy tickets for any of the special exhibitions, saying very seriously, 'I resent paying for something that isn't moving.'

I was amazed. 'Not moving! Do you think that looking at art isn't an emotional business?'

'No, I mean something that doesn't *move*. Paintings and things. I mean, things happen at the cinema and on TV and even in theatre, if you can forget about the acting. You get swept along. But you can't possibly be swept along by staring at something which stays still . . .' She reconsidered, frowning mischievously, '. . . unless it's something like a dead person, which would be moving. Even though it wasn't moving. Actually, in that case it would be moving *because* it wasn't moving, and I suppose . . .'

I grabbed her and shut her up with a kiss when I realised she was teasing me.

That was a wonderful afternoon, and I don't remember anything about the art I saw that day; only the Tube journeys there and back, the weather, the arching, godless cathedral of the Tate's entrance hall, the custard in the blueberry muffins we bought in the café and that grand, fine feeling of walking out of the door and along the Thames with Delphine at my side, still making sweeping, ridiculous statements about matters she made no effort to understand, still making me feel full to the brim of love and life.

I was constantly surprised that our lack of common ground in the areas of musical and artistic appreciation never made me consider us incompatible as a couple; several of my previous relationships had foundered on this very basis and the notion that I would be happily, devotedly intimate with a woman who misunderstood Camus had never occurred to me. I also tried in vain to let her in on the great secret of Duruflé but she could only ever hear the familiar patterns of traditional church music and never understood how he subverted it. I can hear his superficially medieval chants assuming far more complex modern tones; in her mind's eye she just saw hooded monks going through their paces. Her preference was for dreadful, wordy popular music sung by gloomy men and whining women, the sort of thing my contemporaries would listen to in their rooms at Oxford and which I'd thought, happily, I'd left behind long ago. Delphine would indulge me by reading a book whilst 'my' music played in the background, but I could never bear to be in the same room as L. Cohen or J. Joplin droning or squawking their way through a series of one-dimensional tunes. But it didn't make me love her less, even when she wept at the most appalling schmaltz or hummed some trite melody whilst cooking.

This postcard gives me a sense of dread. Its lack of revelation only prolongs the agony.

Day ten: Friday

I have became bored of living on a student's diet so, in an attempt to clear my head of its anxious fretting about yesterday's postcard, I went to buy some more varied provisions. Provided I have a list, I've always quite enjoyed going to the local shops. Not supermarkets though. I can't bear supermarkets. All the shopkeepers round here have known me for years and usually I like to have a little banter with them, but my butcher opened with 'So, where is your lovely lady today, Mr Beauman?' and I wanted to flee. I managed to mutter something about her being on holiday but he didn't try to chat any more so my face must have given the game away. Though I'd ensured I was as well turned out as ever, I realised that on the inside I was still one of those unshaven men with stained shirts whose wives have left them. The butcher saw it at once, and so did the greengrocer and the girl at the deli, both of whom were more reticent than usual. Still, food has started to taste like food again, after a week of forcing down toast and cereal as though it were *fodder*, just to keep my strength up.

I bought calf's liver to cook with Marsala, a sirloin steak, some chicken to make escalopes, lots of tomatoes and chillies for sauces, vegetables to roast and steam, some fresh pasta, cream, prosciutto, a tub of porcini and good bread. I opened a bottle of wine this evening too, something I've been avoiding in case I take it too far. Just a couple of large glasses and no compulsion to have more, to my relief.

Delphine knew a woman who was often unfaithful to her husband. It was always a one-off; she'd pick someone up in a hotel bar each Saturday and spend the afternoon with him. Then she'd go home, stopping at the shops on the way, and prepare enormous quantities of wonderful food – the best cuts of meat, sauces swimming in cream, vegetables sweated in butter and wine, complicated puddings of sponge, nuts, meringue, more cream, and fine chocolates for afterwards. She would give her husband champagne and a bowl of olives then feed him all his favourite food with a good claret, and insist on his following the chocolates with a glass of port, or a brandy. By the time they reached the bedroom, hours later, she would no longer be feeling guilty about her anonymous tryst and he would be too sozzled and stuffed to attempt any physical expression of gratitude for his doting wife's weekly treat, except for a few loud belches and the rapid onset of snoring. But then the wife became too fond of one of her pick-ups – a personal trainer who worked at the hotel gym

– and made the mistake of starting to bring him to her home during the week. Inevitably, one day her husband left work early with the intention of surprising her with flowers and taking her out to a new restaurant. She and her paramour were upstairs making too much noise and expecting too much privacy so by the time she realised her husband was home, he was already at the bedroom door, a bunch of stiff, white lilies in his hand and a flash of shock on his face. After her lover had grabbed his clothes and departed, the wife walked sheepishly downstairs preparing herself for the confrontation. But the husband blamed himself entirely. He'd let himself go, he acknowledged, put on too much weight, eaten and drunk far too much, allowed her to spoil him. He'd let her down, taken her for granted, failed to live up to her expectations and needs. He apologised to her and asked if she would forgive him.

I miss having someone to cook for. I even toyed with the notion of asking someone to come and eat – Julie, perhaps, or Jag and Polly. But I don't have an *entrée* into their lives in that way. It would be uncomfortable for all of us.

Day eleven: Saturday

Another postcard arrived this morning. Chagall, again. From Metz, this time. The expulsion of Adam and Eve from the garden of Eden.

Perhaps she's doing the mini-tour on her own.

My dear James

Things are calmer now. Huw has gone – I expect you'll know all about that by now – and whatever was between us is over. It may not be much comfort to you but I'll tell you anyway, that what was between us didn't amount to much more than a research project for him and an escape route for me.

James, I'm going to try to explain myself, it only seems fair. I should have tried harder before but it became so difficult between us and a quick getaway was as much as I could manage. I'm sorry. And will try to stop saying that because it should just be taken as read, OK, under-lying all of this is my sorrow, and my apology to you.

D

So, she did leave with him. I can be proud of my prescience; I *knew* their relationship was becoming a threat to ours. But I didn't think it was a threat in the old-fashioned way. I thought he only wanted her dreams, and I thought that was all she would give him. I'm not quite sure what to do about this. Shelve it. I need to deal with Reeves, but not now, can't even think about doing anything about him now. I'm numb. I expected it, somehow, but it's still a shock.

I'm going to leave this for an hour. Do the crossword. Something.

I've been thinking about Delphine's history. Adoption has fascinated me for as long as I can remember. Like many children, I'd employed the notion of having been placed with a different (and, clearly, inappropriate) family as a baby, my own (exciting and perfect) parents having been killed in some tragic accident, and for Delphine the basic elements of this fantasy were a reality. I often asked her about it. She rarely offered any details off her own bat but generally seemed quite happy to oblige me.

My own relationship with my parents – indeed, with my family in general – has been somewhat strained for as long as I can remember. There were no traumas, I never ran away to join the circus or took drugs or even came home drunk. There is one memorable moment which seems to sum it up for me: I was down from Oxford for the Christmas break and had arranged to meet my one remaining school pal for a drink in the local pub. Coming downstairs, I'd met my mother on the way up and she had looked at me as though I were wearing a toga: 'James! You're not going out in public dressed like that.'

I was used to these comments. It was, after all, the early seventies when even the squarest young men wore the same kind of flared corduroy trousers, bright 'tank-tops' and loud, large-collared shirts upon which nestled long fronds of uncut hair. I responded reassuringly, 'Mummy, this is what *everyone* wears these days. It would look odd not to. It's OK, it's cool.'

She looked at me with such an expression of scorn it withered me. 'Cool? You sound as completely *ridiculous* as you look, James,' she hissed, before gliding past and leaving me to trudge down the road to meet my friend. At that age, of course, one rallies from such volleys but it must have hit home because it often returns to me when I'm heading towards the door, just before that final check in the mirror.

Delphine, remarkably, was never able to dredge up any such unpleasant memory. According to her, M and Mme Fournier – the couple who had taken care of her since the age of three, her mother having barely survived the perilous crossing from Vietnam and dying from pneumonia only weeks after their arrival in France – were loving, caring and completely honest with her from the beginning about her identity and her place in their family. The only dissatisfaction she could come up with was an occasional wish that she wasn't an only child. Other than that they were perfection itself. I found her rose-tinted opinion a little far-fetched and told her so.

'But they were French, white, in their forties with no other children. Surely there were too many differences for them to cope with – or for you to cope with. Surely you felt out of place sometimes!'

'Not really. I was curious, of course, about looking different from them. But there are a lot of Vietnamese people in France, and we lived just a little way outside Paris so it was quite cosmopolitan. You make it sound as though my parents were peasants; you know that Maman was a teacher and Papa was an engineer, they were intelligent people and they were careful to help me fit in. I made friends with a girl at school who came over a little while before us; she was a year older than me and lived with her mother a few streets away so her *maman* would tell me stories and some of the language and she even taught my mother some Vietnamese recipes.'

'Didn't your mother – your adoptive mother – resent that kind of interference?'

Delphine looked at me quizzically. 'James, there was no

interference. Just help and . . . support. A welcome. My parents were happy for me to know other people from my home country. They were good people. They would have been the same with any child, of any colour, because they knew that children needed love more than anything and if that was OK then everything else would be OK.'

'That sounds like one of Reeves's equations.'

'Well, it might be,' she sounded irritated, 'but so what? All psychologists would say the same thing. All parents and all children would say the same thing. Don't you see that?'

When Delphine becomes annoyed or otherwise impassioned her English is ever so slightly strained; it becomes less precise and an odd thing happens with her vowel sounds. I had listened hard to put my finger on it but couldn't work out why she began to speak differently, until I spoke to her adoptive mother (her adoptive father died three years ago) on the telephone. Her English was also good, not as varied and natural as Delphine's and with a stronger French accent, but with the surprising addition of vowels which were clearly northern in origin. Her time as a tutor in Leeds must have flattened them out, and since she was Delphine's main source of English conversation during her formative years they would have been passed on quite naturally. It was a comical intrusion, or at least I found it so, particularly when I realised that some of the dropped aitches and exaggerated 'u' sounds which characterised Delphine's speech at full tilt were in fact nearer 'ee bah gum' than the French vowel sounds my school chums and I used to parody as the bray of a donkey. My mouth would twitch involuntarily and I would have to hold back a little chuckle, although I was never so thoughtless as to mention it to her. The reason I remember that surge of suppressed laughter so clearly on this occasion was because I saw the irritation on her face and my smile dissolved at once as I tried to explain my concern for her. 'I just find it so hard, my love, to think of you as a little scrap of a girl, after that terrible journey from Vietnam, losing your mother so soon after losing your father and being placed with a family with whom you had nothing in common. It's almost *painful* for me to think about it.'

'James, you can't imagine this so you must believe me: it gave me no pain because it was never an *event*. It's just how I got where I was. I remember a few tiny little things about my time with my mother – precious things which I'll always remember, like how she tied her hair up with a clasp and a rag doll she made me which I lost on the way over – but I don't remember the journey from Vietnam at all, or anything about my father. So we *did* have something in common, the Fourniers and I – we needed each other. They were longing to be parents; I needed to be someone's daughter. It was easy, James, not painful. I'm sad not to know my mother; it's a sad story, but it doesn't give me constant pain. Why should it hurt you so much?'

'They didn't even let you keep your name!'

'That's not true! It's my middle name and I never wanted to use it. Would you like me to be called Nga? Would you? I like Delphine. And my parents asked my friend's *maman* to talk to me in Vietnamese and I learnt a little of it but then I didn't want to learn more. Don't forget, I've spoken English with my mother for most of my life; that was something she wanted to give me, what would you say – it was *in her gift*? And she gave it to me. Aren't you glad about that? And I was familiar with French already, it wasn't *alien* to me. James, you know more Vietnamese than I do!'

During my two years at the embassy in Hanoi in the late seventies I'd picked up a smattering of the language, but only enough for the barest formalities on the rare occasions there wasn't an interpreter around. I'd tried it out on Delphine in the early days at the lab and she had laughed in a slightly embarrassed fashion, unable to improve my pronunciation or teach me any more.

'Can't you see, James, that I don't feel *connected* to Vietnam. I left in 1978 and have not chosen to return. That's nothing to do with my French family; they've always encouraged me to go back, to try to track down my – my first family. But that's my decision, and it's not something I've wanted to do . . . It's not something I can do yet. And my history – my adoption – *does not* give me pain!'

I couldn't quite believe her, my brave girl. She was so warm and responsive, so keen on holding hands and cuddling; it was unthinkable that the loss of her mother had had no significant effect on her adult self. And I knew from my studies that her claims to remember her mother must have been fantasy; I knew that apoptosis – the programmed cell-death which wipes our brains clear of any infantile memories – would have made sure of that. She had obviously invented memories in an effort to soften the blow of loss. I didn't mention this fact to her, but after that conversation, whenever we spoke about her adoption, I could always detect the tiniest note of self-defence creeping into her words and feared that I had made her unnecessarily conscious of her place outside her adoptive family. I had introduced an awkwardness, and since she was usually the very opposite of awkward I wished I'd never asked about her family at all.

Delphine knew a man who, from early puberty, had found himself attracted only to older women with dark hair and eyes and olive skin, very much like his own. The attraction seemed to be reciprocal. At college, in his late teens and early twenties, his thirty- and forty-something female tutors were so notably enamoured of him that his peers used to tease him about it. The teasing became worse when the lads realised that their lucky pal was having none of it; however strongly these desirable women in the full bloom of their sexual vigour came on to him, he always resisted. He told Delphine what he'd never told his male friends: that he'd been adopted as a very young baby and could find no information about his father, although he had made a desultory attempt to trace his mother. He believed that his attraction to older women who looked like him was a dysfunctional and destructive means of searching for her and the consequences of finding her in that way were too terrifying to contemplate. It was a torture for him; one he would try to assuage by having casual flings with girls his own age. Blonde girls; he might have a sister. Eventually he got a reputation for being a 'user' of women and the few platonic female friends he had began to avoid him. Delphine helped him track down more details about his mother; they followed a complicated trail of names and addresses all over France which ended at a cemetery near Lyons, where his mother had died, of a cancer, two years earlier. His pale-skinned half-sisters showed him photographs of their fair-haired, blue-eyed mother. He cursed his swarthy, unknown father and returned to Paris, proposed to the Spanish tutor he'd resisted for a decade and now lives in Seville with the two children whose surprise arrivals had happily punctuated his wife's menopause.

Day twelve: Sunday

Today, I took my practice bow and gathered my kit ready to go to targets. I'm not accustomed to physical indolence; if even a few days go by during which I haven't been to the gym or for a swim or just for a good long walk, I begin to feel ill and, though this must be my imagination, it seems I also begin to look ill. My fingers were itching to get to work and I bounded downstairs purposefully, but I only got as far as the front door. Apart from my trip to the police station around the corner and that one visit to the shops, I haven't been outside since she left and without that desperate need I had to report her disappearance, or that desire to eat something decent, outside seems not exactly frightening, but certainly not welcoming. I stood on the front steps and the sky felt so oppressive; for a moment I could hardly bring myself to breathe. I could see the sunshine but I felt no warmth at all. A sort of panic attack I suppose, though I've not had such a thing before. So I'm back at my desk and my itching fingers will have to tap away at my keyboard instead of curve around my bow.

Archery, toxophily (Delphine hated that word – 'sounds like *poison*!'), is the best individual sport in the world. At my club, I've seen the youngsters join up hoping to mimic their heroes from the Tolkein films or their PlayStation games where contemporary Robin Hoods stalk the land wreaking violent justice, but very quickly realising that it's a more serious business than they'd imagined. You can see the thrill they get simply by standing with a bow. We all get that. If you concentrate, give yourself up to it, it's a purely sensual experience and like the very best sensual experiences it's all about anticipation; you are relishing all the things you have to do, all the mastery you must exert over your body, in order to arrive at something wonderful. That great surge of release. When it all works perfectly, when you are one with your bow, I've often thought of it as the most rare and joyful opportunity to combine male and female physicality. There's a strength and control which is thoroughly masculine, but the sensation of skin caressing polished wood, the taut string nestling against your shoulder and the openness of the stance – legs apart, torso stretched wide, pelvis tensed – are female, liquid, inviting. I would have liked Delphine to try it.

Perhaps I'll go tomorrow.

The most frustrating sessions at Dream Lab in the early, pre-Delphine, days were those in which we heard excerpts from the dream diaries. On the one hand I was fascinated to hear them; on the other I had absolutely nothing to contribute and was left in the position of voyeur, or its auditory equivalent.

Reeves got everyone to keep a dream diary – some of them already did – noting the date, time and subject of each dream with details of any drug or other therapies they were taking, and every few weeks they would report back on developments while I sat there, dumbly. But as time went by and I became familiar with the group members and their sleeping and dreaming patterns, my habitual note-taking and powers of recall became useful. Being outside the dreamers,

I was able to remember past sessions, to compare and contrast the dreams they were reporting, far better than they themselves could, and better even than Reeves, whose enthusiasm for the moment always took him into the middle of things, from where it's hard to see the whole picture. I'm not saying I was invaluable – had Reeves typed information from the dream diary records on to his spreadsheet after the meeting he would have been able to access the same information. But the ability to do so at the time of our meeting proved far more constructive and helped me overcome what I recognised as my *envy* of these dreamers. After I'd submitted to a couple of overnight experiences at the Sleep Clinic, I had evidence that I dreamed as much as, if not more than, any of the lab members, but try as I might I had no memory, not even a hint, of what I was dreaming. I started to long for it, for something that would wake me at the right moment for my dreams to become memorable, but it never came and still hasn't.

Not that dreaming seemed to give anyone much pleasure. Julie's dreams were the most mundane I'd ever heard – tiny scenes of domestic tedium in which she'd forgotten to turn off the tap or pack her daughter's lunch, or went into the garden and discovered that all the bulbs she'd planted had been eaten by squirrels. 'I think it's just because I'm anxious,' she said apologetically, as though we might censure her for her pedestrian unconscious. 'When I have nightmares, they're much more vivid and complicated.' She actually seemed to brighten at the prospect of sharing her bad dreams with us and thus providing us with some entertainment.

Polly's sleep disorder was the oddest for many reasons, one of which was the difficulty she had in separating her dreams from what had actually happened in the night. She regularly woke up with bruised ribs, lacerated hands or other disturbing injuries having no memory of their infliction, or having only 'dreamed' of doing something, such as building a wall. Sometimes she would find an actual 'wall' in the morning – a pile of books next to her bed arranged in the kind of tower a toddler would build.

'That's no problem,' she explained, 'in fact, I quite like those sort of things. But one morning last year I woke up with my fingers stuck to the sheets with blood. My fingertips were all slashed with tiny cuts. I followed tiny spots of blood across the bedroom carpet, on to the kitchen lino, and discovered that I'd tried to build my wall with utensils from the knife drawer.'

She was still laughing. And when not sleepwalking she dreamed prolifically and fantastically – looking at my notes I see that the most lurid phrases are all hers: 'The flashing lights became flowers and then it was like I was in a sea made of flowers but they had teeth and I knew that if I picked them I would be bitten' or 'I moved very fast towards the wall and I felt something sticking out the front of my head and just before I hit the bricks I realised, I was a *unicorn* and the impact could not harm me.'

Polly was convinced that if she discovered the 'meaning' of her dreams she would not only 'cure' her sleepwalking but would have also solved the mystery of life itself. For this reason she was never far from a little collection of tatty paperbacks which purported to analyse the 'true meaning of dreams' but which were really nothing more than the average output of a seaside Gypsy Rose Lee and caused us all great mirth from time to time.

I'd far rather listen to those crazy dreams than hear about Sally's, though. Without exception the subject of her dreams was sexual and we'd all shift uncomfortably on our plastic chairs as she related the most explicit scenes to us.

'I think it's highly significant that this dream was about anal sex,' she would say, unabashed. 'It was so graphic that it took me until after lunch the following day to open my bowels.'

Poor Reeves would have to ask her serious questions like, 'Can you remember anything about your leg movements that evening?' to which Simon was always quick to respond with some wisecrack like, 'Didn't you hear, Huw? Sally didn't have any movements until after lunchtime the next day,' to great guffaws all round, and even a wry smile from Sally.

So it wasn't as though I had any expectation that remembering my dreams would give me insights or understandings of myself or the world, though I hoped that mine wouldn't be as inconsequential as Julie's or as insane as Polly's. I suppose that my ignorance of them seemed to waste those unconscious moments. Still, even without dreaming there was a lot to learn, and although there were a few *longeurs*, most of the meetings in which we were discussing dreams were mentally stimulating and some were downright enlivening.

Reeves liked hearing about them, I could tell. Although his research wasn't actually too concerned with the details of dreams, you could see how entranced he was by them, and whereas normally he would encourage us – sometimes quite abruptly – to be brief and to the point in our discussions, he rarely cut short a retelling of a dream. Occasionally the meeting overran by ten minutes just so that somebody could finish. Simon could often remember the order of his dreams, which thrilled Reeves; the pair of them would sit there with his PSG printouts and try to match periods of REM sleep to specific dreams, Lord knows how. Personally, I couldn't see what good it did any of them, going over so much incomprehensible and unscientific ground, but Reeves actively encouraged and indulged them. I had nothing to add of course, as the Non-Dream Rememberer. There were sessions when I could hardly contribute two sentences.

Reeves used to scribble notes in a large lined hardback book during the sessions but he continued to speak notes into his Dictaphone directly after the meetings, and if any lab members returned to his office to retrieve forgotten coats or umbrellas, they'd often discover him hunched over his desk, or pacing the room, murmuring urgently into his hand. Simon used to joke about it, 'What do you think he's saying? I reckon he works for MI5; he'll be sending a message to some James Bond-alike: "Your mission, should you choose to accept it, is to submit to Wayne gluing electrodes on to your—" Oh, hi Jag. How you doing?'

Jag was quite protective of his mentor and even Simon was careful about taking his jokes too far. At the beginning, anyway.

As I soon realised, there was an issue in the lab about psychiatric treatments versus psychological approaches to their disorders and Reeves was at the centre of some heated debates. I remember something almost approaching a row between him and Sally, it must have been around our sixth or seventh meeting.

Restless Leg Syndrome is a condition I originally had some difficulty in crediting with any seriousness but I now understand can be most debilitating, not to mention painful. For Sally, the problem wasn't just the aching sensation of needing to move her legs violently as soon as she tried to go to sleep; when she finally did drop off she kicked energetically throughout the night and woke each morning feeling 'wrung out', as she described it, from acute muscular exhaustion. It was as though her body was both depriving her of sleep and forcing her unwillingly through a night–long aerobics session. She had finally presented herself to her GP who had told her she was depressed, which was causing insomnia, and prescribed some pills.

'What did your doctor give you?' Reeves asked her with a weary sigh.

'Antidepressants.'

He tutted. 'Bloody hell, what do they teach them? It's exactly what they shouldn't give insomniacs in any case, and antidepressants make RLS *worse*.'

Sally nodded. 'It was awful, and it was even spreading to my arms – that horrible pain, it's so difficult to make someone realise I'm not talking about tingling, or cramps, or convince them that I'm not exaggerating . . .' She looked distressed. 'I know that the Sleep Clinic treats RLS patients with other drugs, not antidepressants, and maybe I should give it a go.'

Reeves frowned. 'I thought you were very keen to avoid drug treatments,' he said.

'It's just the pain, if I could find something to ease that, I'd –'

'Do you know what drugs are used for RLS patients?' Reeves asked her. Sally shook her head. 'It's the same stuff they give to patients with Parkinson's.'

Sally looked shocked. 'Is there any link . . .?'

'No, no, no link between Parkinson's and RLS has ever been discovered. The drug treatments which are often the most useful for treating Parkinson's affect the dopamine receptors in the brain, and the same theory applies to RLS. But they're not to be taken lightly, put it that way.'

Sally didn't look entirely reassured as Reeves held up a finger and called for our attention. I'm pretty sure that Jag was absent from that session but all the rest of us listened intently. 'Listen up everyone. As you know, I think that mainstream medicine has problems with training non-specialists to recognise what underlies a lot of sleep-related symptoms. You'll find it hard to believe that sleep disorders take up a laughable *ten minutes* at most of a junior doctor's entire training. Now, the Sleep Clinic recommends a holistic approach; that's why I work with them. Working on your body and your mind simultaneously. But this group is *primarily* about taking a psychological approach –'

Julie interrupted. 'But Huw, if Sally's in pain she should try to sort that out, shouldn't she? I mean, the rest of us have been through all the options at the Sleep Clinic and have agreed to take a break from drug therapies. But she's not had any treatment there. Shouldn't she be given the chance to try it out first?'

Reeves seemed to be on the point of responding when Sally spoke. 'It's OK. I'll stick with this group for now. I really don't like doctors.' She blushed and added, 'present company excepted', which was foolish of her because of course 'Dr' Reeves has no medical qualification.

He was polite enough, or flattered enough, not to correct her. 'It's up to you. I can't tell you what to do. But if you decide to stay, then that's great! Now then, shall we start with your dreams from this week, Sally?'

He seemed ebullient and there was something else — I think it was relief.

Dopamine is a neurotransmitter substance, a chemical messenger. Certain drugs can manipulate it, to some degree, to change its message. They can tell someone — you're not sleepy, or — you are sleepy, or — you don't need to keep moving your legs around like that any more, or — for God's sake, move your legs, man! Clever stuff. But you have to get the levels right and Sally never seemed to be able to do that.

My legs are pretty restless but I can't leave the flat. Can't walk out of the door.

Even after we'd seen each other almost fortnightly for half a year I still didn't feel completely at ease in the lab, although I continued to enjoy it. Reeves' vagueness used to irritate me and I wasn't alone. Shortly after their little contretemps about the Clinic, Sally questioned him about the progress of his research and he was quite short with her. 'It's far too soon to have anything conclusive to say about it. I'm still collating information as it comes in; there's no possibility that I'm going to be able to present any conclusions for a long time.'

But Sally persisted. 'I'm not expecting a list of conclusions. But surely by now you will know if some pattern is emerging about *our* sleep and *our* dreams? Even if you can't extrapolate and make that general?'

Reeves shook his head. 'No, there are no patterns emerging.

Within this group I can't find a single factor which links a type of sleep disorder to a type of dream. Not one. And our wild card – that's you, James – ' a comment which raised more smirks than I cared to see ' – doesn't help much either. Your sleeping and waking patterns share many features with those of other group members but you can't remember dreaming whereas everyone else almost always does. It's not – well, it's not exactly all falling into place in terms of even testing a theory, let alone proving one. Nowhere near.'

'But you still think it's worth continuing?' asked Sally.

Reeves was keen to assure her and the rest of us that it certainly was. 'You never know, another few months of your questionnaires and my statistic juggling and we could come up with something. It's definitely worth sticking with. I do hope you feel it's worth it . . .?' He surveyed our faces and we all made encouraging and supportive noises.

I got the feeling that Sally was less than impressed but I knew that she wanted to continue coming to the lab and that her reasons were nothing to do with solving her sleeping problems. She and I had – well, I don't know quite what we had, a sort of affair I suppose, which had finished a couple of months before Delphine joined us. Sally was smartly dressed and quite trim, if not what you'd call a looker, and we tended to seek each other out at first, being the most well-educated pair in the group, and coming, apparently, from the same sort of class background. She was married to a doctor, some big-shot heart surgeon, who spent as little time at home as possible and her tales of his numerous infidelities were doubtless true, not that I thought about him a great deal. Things got to the stage where she and I were invariably the only ones left in the bar after the meeting and I finally realised that I was supposed to invite her back to my flat, which I duly did, and so the predictable occurred. Without wishing to sound ungallant, I did not find her at all captivating sexually. I never thought of myself as a *romantic* as such, certainly not before Delphine arrived, but I do need that spark, however tiny, to fly between my eyes and those of my lover. There was no such spark with Sally – enjoyable conversation, a few confidences made, a glass of wine, and then bang! To bed! And to a mechanical series of 'moves' which she seemed to enjoy but which made my heart sink. I felt obliged to go through these motions for several months, hoping that the novelty would wear off for her and we could mutually call a halt, but the longer it went on the keener she became until I realised I would have to end it myself, which I did, as kindly as possible. It was an awful conversation, in my car supposedly going to my flat but in fact heading in the direction of her house.

'James, where are we going? This isn't the way to Maida Vale.'

'No. Sally, I'm taking you home.'

Silence. Then, 'Just this week? You just can't take me to your flat this week?'

'No, I don't think we should go to my flat again. I am sorry, Sally, but it seems to me that there's no future in our continuing . . .'

'No future! Whoever talked about a future! There is a *present* isn't there? We can live for the moment.'

The sort of confrontation I have avoided all my life was upon me and I wanted to be anywhere but in that car with that woman at that time. As I struggled to find the right words to explain, kindly but firmly, that I wanted the quasi-affair to stop, I remember that the phrase 'ejector seat' popped, briefly but tantalisingly, into my mind. 'Sally, I don't − I don't have those sorts of feelings for you. I like and admire you enormously, and enjoy your company very much, but I don't feel . . .'

'You don't *fancy* me,' she said bitterly.

'It's not that. You're a very attractive woman, Sally, I feel privileged to have been − intimate − with you. But I don't feel that we are compatible as lovers.' I felt the urge for honesty. 'I mean come on. It wasn't magical, was it? You can't have thought the way we made love was the way it's supposed to be. Can you?'

'It was fine.'

I felt slightly insulted at such a lack of enthusiasm but relieved, too. 'Well, there you are. You deserve better than fine. We both do. You can't legislate for those things, it's chemistry. You do see that don't you?'

'It's been so damned long that just a warm body in the bed is enough for me; I wasn't looking for the romance of the fucking century.' Her coarseness made me flinch but I understood it was defensive.

'I'm sorry about your marriage. And that this didn't work out. I hope we can still be . . .'

'Friends? Oh yes, of course we'll still be *friends*. And nobody need know a thing about this little − business.'

I supposed that bitterness was inevitable but she then proceeded to bombard me with questions about why I didn't 'want' her, citing her weight, her looks, her sexual technique and finally her age as possible marks against her in some imaginary book I kept. They were all irrelevant but I felt obliged to protest at the latter. 'Your age? Sally, you're a good few years younger than I am and in any case I have never been the kind of man to choose a lover on the basis of her age. I promise you, that has nothing to do with it.'

She seemed slightly mollified by my reassurances, although we were both acutely aware that in denying every possible reason for my rejection of her we were whittling it all down to the fact that, as she had said to begin with, I just didn't *fancy* her.

We parked around the corner from her house, where her husband was on a rare visit home, while she dried her eyes and reapplied make-up.

'Where does he think you are?' I asked, conversationally.

'At Dream Lab. He doesn't know how long these things last. I really don't think he cares. Since the kids left home he hasn't noticed my comings and goings much at all.'

When she was ready to leave I dropped her at the end of the street. Before she got out of the car she turned to me and said, quietly, 'James, I have cared about you a lot more than you care about me. I know that's not your fault but I don't think you should have offered me the – the *encouragement* – of taking me to bed. Even though it obviously did nothing for you, you were making love to me. You did make me think you felt more for me – even simply more desire for me – than you did. That's going to be hard for me to forgive.'

There was little more I could do than offer further apologies for our misunderstanding before turning the car around and driving back to the safe solitude of my home. That night Duruflé played me to sleep in splendid isolation.

At the time Sally began questioning Reeves about his methods our affair was in full swing and I remember nurturing a faint hope that she would leave the lab, and thus save me the trouble of having to end it. I was disappointed that this wasn't to be the case, but Reeves was delighted.

Once we'd all assured him that we were still 100 per cent behind him he smiled and said, 'Good. Good, well thank you. And I realise that you aren't all finding these sessions as useful for your sleep problems as we'd hoped they would be, but please don't get too despondent. We'll persevere with that too, of course. And besides, there may be other research, other valuable information, which I just haven't worked out how to access yet . . .'

'Such as?' asked Jag, with the slightest hint of suspicion in his voice.

'Such as – I don't know. Not yet. You and I, Jagdev, will try to find that information, won't we?'

Jag looked relieved and nodded as his tutor continued, 'It's not wasted time, Jag, or wasted information. Everyone – believe me – not one minute of this will be wasted.'

We believed him.

I'm running ahead of myself. Before Delphine arrived, Reeves and I continued to get on reasonably well. My lack of dreams fascinated him without irritating him. And until she joined us, I only had the faintest interest in resolving my insomnia so I didn't share the desperation of the others; I didn't garland him with dramatic tales of sleepless nights and colourful dreams so I wasn't ever a burden about his neck. Having so many people put their hopes in you must be pretty stressful.

I had, from the beginning, eschewed all conventional treatments for my sleep deficit and only ever attended the Sleep Clinic for research purposes – the polysomnographs and so on. At first I'd had some vague interest in resolving my insomnia but when I joined the lab it sank into insignificance amongst so many more serious problems and, perhaps foolishly, I decided to ignore it. So I was the prize pupil, rather, until Delphine joined us: my refusal to seek medical help made me seem brave and bold and Reeves took me on as a personal challenge, offering all sorts of alternative treatments and therapies to help me sleep.

He was experimenting with what sounded like some pretty weird methods. There was the Transmissions Project of course. He and Jag were working, with Wayne at the sleep centre, on the supposition that the recording of a dreamer's brainwaves can be transmitted on to a visual display – and that one day that display could actually be a visual image of the dream itself. I had nothing to do with that crazy scheme and it didn't form the subject of many lab conversations, largely because it was at such an early stage of experimentation. But it didn't seem any more unusual than some of the non-drug treatments for insomnia Reeves used to try out on me. In one, the electroencephalogram – EEG – readouts of patients are converted into audible sounds – a sort of 'brain music', which is played to them through headphones as they go to sleep. In tests, a marked improvement in both the ability to fall asleep and to get back to sleep after wakings was noted by 80 per cent of those tested. Reeves couldn't understand my reluctance to try this method, and I couldn't think of how to explain that the idea of being lulled to sleep by the sound of my own brain terrified me.

'I don't know if I could cope with that,' I tried to explain, 'I mean, it doesn't sound at all restful, I don't like to have headphones on when I'm sleeping, and . . .'

'Just give it a go. Audible brain music – doesn't that

69

excite you? Doesn't that make you think – bloody hell, this I have to hear? Come on, James, let's have a bash, bach. Just once.'

And of course I agreed. And of course it was more than once, despite the fact that it seemed to make not the slightest bit of difference to me. It's an odd thing, but you end up treating it like white noise. The sound of my brain pattern was like an unecological fridge chundering along in the corner of a small kitchen. What an edifying thought.

So, we kept on trying things out and I kept on waking fitfully without any dreams to speak of, and I began to feel guilty about taking up so much of Reeves' time. I actually began to try to play ball: to concentrate on the hypnosis tapes, to put my mind through the relaxation techniques he gave me. I suppose I wanted to please him because he was making such a lot of effort on my behalf. But even when I tried it was no good: failure after failure, eternal disappointment.

But when I discovered my 'cure' in Delphine, I kept it quiet.

Now I'm wondering if I initially avoided trying to cure my insomnia because, without it, there would have been no place for a dreamless sleeper, for me, in the lab. Wondering, too, why in the final few months – when Delphine and I slept soundly every night – I never questioned my right to be in the group at all.

22 March

James is proving less useful than I thought he would. The hypnosis was a complete shambles. Playback of his own brain patterns didn't even result in better sleep, let alone stimulus of dreaming. I've never met a less responsive case. Still loads of REM though, even more than the first PSG suggested. I have to persevere with him; there's so little chance of finding a match that good. He's hard going though, fussy bugger. He's taken to correcting me when I 'get my facts wrong'. And of course, he's always right. He can quote back entire conversations and I'd swear they're near word-perfect; strange for his type to have such a good verbal memory. He remembers how *things are said too, like he's playing back the conversation just as it happened. He'd be worth a bit of study in his own right, even without Dream Lab. Yup, our James is a one-off, that's for sure.*

Difficult to convince the group that it's worth continuing when he's so clearly the odd one out though. Simon's already asked me if I think James is 'all there'. Sally is too curious about the research; next time she expresses doubts I think I'll send her off to the clinic and be done with it. I hope to God her dreams aren't going to provide the key to any of this; although their erotomaniacal tendencies would probably sell well . . . And Jag's suspicious. Obviously he's twigged that something's changed and is getting paranoid that he's not in on it.

The only thing you can count on: the self-obsession of any given person.

And I do include myself in that.

Can't string it out for much longer though; I have to test the new Transmission theory before the whole thing goes pear-shaped. It goes like this: brain patterns from a dreaming mind <must> act as a stimulus to another unconscious brain, I'm convinced of it. And amongst that group of frantic dreamers, James is the only one who would notice the difference. How I'm going to deal with Wayne isn't quite clear yet – a simple data swap of what's going through the headphones during Beauman's next PSG, but how to bring it about? And which transmission to select? Polly's are probably too vague; it's hard to see when she's dreaming. Simon's maybe, his dreaming periods are wonderfully defined and he can usually work out which dream's which. Amazing that the bloody hippy's the one with that kind of clarity. Jag's REM periods are too short. Same with Sally's, although using hers might give the old boy a treat. Can't see him getting much action, that's something we do have in common.

Alfred's might be the best bet for the time being – start with a flurry of light REM periods and see how we go. Poor old bugger; even if he finds a treatment that improves his apnoea his lungs are so shot from all those years underground that he's never going to sleep easy. He looks at me with too much hope and I've told him, I always tell him, that I'm not making any promises. Still, it's not like I'm making him any worse and he's certainly the best place to start.

Look you, James – you don't know what I'm letting you in for.

Day thirteen: Monday

Today I returned to work.

I've always loved the summer. Everybody does, I know, but it still strikes me as such a privilege to walk along an English street in my shirtsleeves and feel the sun on my neck, see people's gardens in full bloom − even blooming with weeds which shouldn't be there − and enjoy watching women in their summer clothes. We all do it, you know. Even if we don't admit it consciously, or feel we shouldn't, there's not a heterosexual man alive who doesn't feel a rush of blood to the head − and elsewhere − at the sight of light fabrics skimming smooth female skin. Pale shop girls with deep cleavages in strappy pastel tops; dark-haired foreign students showing flat brown bellies above white hipster jeans; young mothers in short silky skirts which flip from side to side as they push their buggies; tall black girls striding along, bright Lycra stretched over high buttocks; the odd pre-Raphaelite beauty with long hair and an empire-line print dress − I love them all. And what women see as their physical imperfections have always been the things which charm me most when I'm watching them on the Tube − some fetching facial asymmetry, a downy cheek, faint stubble under the strap-hanging arm, the line of a supposedly invisible bra-strap beneath a close-fitting T-shirt, a little dimpling on a long slim thigh. It takes so little to please us, Delphine was right about all that. She should be walking beside me, laughing at my helpless staring at all that female beauty, pointing out handsome men in tight T-shirts and giving the finger to the shirtless yobs on the building site who always whistle at her. This was the time of year we got together, the best summer of my life, and now here I am, walking alone.

I still saw the women on the way to work this morning and on the way home this evening, and I still noticed some lovely sights. I just didn't enjoy it as much as usual. I would never have thought that taking pleasure from female beauty was an activity which required a woman by my side, but Delphine's approbation, encouragement even, of my appreciation had made it something we shared. Other women I'd walked out with had been disapproving of my furtive stares, or pretended not to notice, but not her. 'It's a natural response,' she said with a shrug. 'You can't help it. But you can choose whether or not to act upon it, whether it becomes a "threat" is up to you. Do you think I don't find other men attractive any more? Of course I do – I just don't do anything about it because I'm happy with you.'

Perfect sense, of course, but refreshing words for me to hear from the mouth of my lover. Indeed, why shouldn't we look at beauty and admire it? If anything, loving Delphine made me see *more* beauty everywhere, and everything I looked at made me feel like making love to her. It seemed to be the same for her, as though we were revelling in our own gorgeous world of love and confidence without leaving that other, bigger world around us. We didn't need to hide ourselves away; our place in the bigger picture was secure, and wonderful. Now I'm worried that perhaps I should be careful where I look, and how.

There was a habit of mine – a not at all pleasant habit but one which always seemed to amuse Delphine in spite of her protestations at my unkindness – which was most prevalent in the summer months. As couples walked by I would assess their comparative attractiveness and whenever I saw two very ugly people together I would express my relief and pleasure at the rightness of their removing themselves from everyone else's gene pool. Although this was a piece of cruel fun, it springs from a genuine horror I have at seeing beauty with the beast. I realise it's not fair or rational, and even that it speaks of something deeply unpleasant within me, but the sight of some good-looking, well-dressed woman who clearly cares about her appearance walking hand in hand with a scruffy, spotty oik with a beer belly, gives me the creeps. It works the other way round too – only last week I saw a sweet-faced young chap, all dark eyelashes and cheekbones and a mop of black hair, with his arm around – or rather, *partially* around – the thick waist of a pale, puffy girl with the most gormless expression I've seen for a while. I *know* that personality counts for a lot, I *know* that you can't judge a book by its cover, I *know* that sexual attraction is a complicated matter. But we're not talking about leggy blondes marrying decrepit millionaires or gilded youths learning the erotic arts from wrinkled madams – couples where the pay-off is clear. These relationships of equals in which there is clearly such physical inequality confuse me. I'm not sure why Delphine indulged me in my nasty games; she was never unkind about ugly people herself. 'James, what a fascist you are!' she would say, but she could never resist turning and checking it out for herself and as she turned back I could tell that she knew exactly what I meant.

It was strange and uncomfortable to be back at the office and I couldn't concentrate at all; no chance of taking my mind off anything. My secretary – a pleasant but rather slow girl called Caroline who insists on calling herself my 'PA' but is actually my secretary, no more, no less – welcomed me smilingly and I received a few 'good mornings' from the staff as I walked through the main office but it was a relief to get into my own tiny room and spend the day dealing with correspondence – nearly all emails nowadays, which I respond to myself. I suppose that soon we won't need secretaries at all. Maybe when that day comes I shall call Caroline my PA. She hasn't forgotten how to use the cafetière, I'll give her that. And remembered to refill it swiftly, so that I could down three cups in quick succession. She brought a sandwich to my desk so I hardly needed to move all day except to go to the bathroom and stretch my legs. Nica Jensen wasn't around, thankfully; I don't think I could cope with her at the moment, and nobody else made any personal enquiries but waiting, nervously, for them to start was quite exhausting.

When I got back here after what seemed like far more than one day at work, I put Delphine's postcards, picture sides out, on the cork noticeboard she'd nailed to the kitchen wall very soon after she moved in. She liked to pin little bits and bobs to it – cards from friends, quotes and *bons mots* torn out of newspapers or copied out of poetry books, little messages and reminders to me and to herself, theatre tickets, appointment cards, all sorts of things. Initially, I had objected to this messy intrusion into my small, utilitarian, stylish kitchen. But long before she left I had become fond of this colourful rectangle on the white wall, overflowing with signs of friendship, culture, intellect, politics, and philosophy. Signs of life.

The kitchen was my domain; the one area which I used

to defend against all comers so when I handed it over to Delphine's not so tender care it was a key moment for me. For the bathroom and bedroom to become covered with clothes, brushes, shoes, stockings drying on radiators, bottles of gels and creams and moisturisers and all the rest of it seemed par for the course and I would happily wander around tidying up after her. But the kitchen was different. I know how easy it is for a man living alone to lose control over his diet, housework, laundry, even personal hygiene. That dependence so many men have on living with a woman and expecting her to feed and clean and clothe them is abhorrent to me and signs of that kind of self-pitying neglect which makes a grown man give up his personal grooming make me very angry indeed. 'For God's sake, sit up straight, man!' I want to shout. 'Have some self-respect. *She* won't be eating a Pot Noodle slouched in front of the telly wearing the same shirt she's worn for the past three days, will she? Is this your way of winning her back, to show her how much you *need* her? Need her to stick you in a shower every now and then, and comb your hair and put your bloody clothes in the washing machine? I'm sure she'll come *rushing back* to fulfil those needs, I mean there's clearly so much in it for her isn't there?'

But I never have shouted those things; I've always made the appropriate sympathetic sounds and exchanged those – poor sod – kind of glances with others in the office.

So the kitchen had become the symbol of my supreme ability to look after myself and was the scene of many an impressive three- or four-course meal served up to appreciative girlfriends over the years. I was always scrupulously clean in there; bought only the finest hardware for pursuing the science of cookery in a way as aesthetically pleasing as possible and nothing, absolutely nothing, was on display. All crockery and cutlery were assigned their places in the brushed steel drawers and cupboards and all white goods hid their ugly frontages behind matching steel doors. I would sometimes fill a soapstone bowl with fruit and put it on the table; otherwise all the food was stored invisibly too. Before going to bed each night I used to run a hand along my clean, uncluttered polished granite work surface. The only freestanding item in the room, apart from the solid beech block table and matching benches in its centre, was the bin, an Italian chrome number whose lid yawned open elegantly at the push of a discreet pedal on its base.

A week after moving in with me, Delphine broke the bin. She said she forgot about the pedal but I suspected – and still do – that the one-second wait for the lid to operate tested her patience. She came out of the bathroom with something rolled up in her hand, strode straight over to the bin and yanked up the lid. There was a small click and when she had discarded her rubbish the lid swung shut with a bang. She turned to me with her hand over her mouth. 'Oops,' she said with a tentative smile. 'I hope I haven't broken that, James.'

I tried not to look too concerned as I inspected the bin and discovered that she had indeed broken it. Lifting the lid manually, I feebly moved it back and forth in the hope that something might slip back into place and as I did so I saw what she had thrown away: a bloody sanitary pad, wrapped loosely in its polythene cover, which was now uncurling on top of my celeriac peelings. I flinched and said 'Oh!' perhaps too dramatically.

'What's the matter, James?'

I tried to be calm about it. 'I've just seen what you threw in here, Delphine. Would you mind using the bathroom bin?'

'It's full,' she replied.

Of course, it was full of her boxes and bottles and sticky leg-waxing strips and I had wondered if and when she would ever empty it but hadn't got around to doing it myself.

'Ah, right. Well, let's make sure we keep the bathroom bin emptied so that there's always room in there for – this sort of thing,' I suggested, trying to move away from the topic.

But she had a little smile playing on her lips and wasn't about to let it drop. 'What kind of thing, James?' she asked innocently.

'Your – your *feminine hygiene* things. I don't mind plastic and cardboard in here, but this is – well, this is *blood. Fresh* blood.'

'Are you afraid of attracting sharks?' she laughed. 'And James, you cooked lamb last night and the wrappings with the little lamb's *fresh blood* went in that bin, I saw you put them there.'

I gave up after that, and let her do whatever she liked, and I found that usually I liked whatever she liked too. I enjoyed the different styles of our cookery – her chaotic, instinctive and frighteningly speedy preparation of enormous pots filled with hearty French country meals, enough to feed a family, or dishes of Vietnamese delicacies and fragrant steamed rice wafting their aromas of lemongrass, ginger and chilli through the entire building, and then my more stately and time-consuming rituals of formal cookery, careful presentation, the production of intense reductions and sauces, precisely measured dressings, complex flavours. We made a pretty good team, I think, and both genuinely appreciated the very different skills of the other. She bought big old glazed china marmalade jars from the market and put my utensils in them. The fruit bowl was never empty and there were almost always flowers on the table. The work surface was full of little piles of ingredients and she never put the condiments away in their cupboard. There was rarely enough granite showing for me to run a hand over it and appreciate the gleam. I didn't mind in the slightest.

Staring at that corkboard covered in notes and cuttings pinned there by her — and those postcards, all those flying figures and odd faces, all that blue — dismays me. It looks as though all the life has come in from outside, as though I'd opened the door on a windy day and all manner of vegetation blew in and made itself at home. It's nothing to do with me.

Delphine knew a woman who worked in a café bar she used to help out at when she was a student in Paris. The woman's mother had been a fashion model and was very conscious about her weight and that of her daughter. At twelve the girl had been bulimic; at fourteen she was hospitalised with anorexia. Her treatment had been quite successful but this was no thanks to her mother, who encouraged her to err constantly on the side of under-eating and would say things like 'you shouldn't have eaten all of that bread, it's too much', which was an unacknowledged signal for her daughter to go to the bathroom and make herself vomit. She was still very slim as a young woman but felt as though she were enormously bloated all the time. She asked her friends to make sure that she sat down and ate a normal meal at lunch and dinner time but this had to be mainly smooth soups or very simple, unadorned vegetables or salad and could never include any fried food or more than a tiny bit of bread or rice or potatoes. Meat was impossible, cheese gave her cramps, pulses made her entire digestive system go crazy and the very thought of eggs made her gag. No food gave her any pleasure except chocolate and she would allow herself to eat one small bar a day, after her evening meal. She was convinced that this regime would be her lot for the rest of her life. She was a good waitress but Delphine noticed that whenever a customer ordered a glass of Diet Coke, she would always give them standard, full-sugar Coke, instead.

'I think it was just in case their mothers were starving them,' Delphine explained.

The night I met Delphine I arrived at the bar a little earlier than usual. As soon as I walked in I saw her, sitting on one of the high stools at the student bar wearing that pink sweater and black skirt. Her legs were bare; it was an unusually warm day in late April. As I approached to order one of their appalling coffees in a polystyrene cup, I realised she was reading what I considered to be my special book. I didn't hesitate.

'You're a fan of Camus?'

She looked up at me in surprise through warm brown dark-lashed eyes. 'I'm sorry?'

'Camus. That's my favourite book. I wondered if you were a fan.'

'Oh, I see. Well, it's OK. I haven't read it since I was about fourteen so I thought it was time to try again. This man – Meursault – he's a little annoying, I think. But the writing is good.' Her English bore just the tiniest trace of an accent and it was only the unusual cadences of her sentences which suggested she hadn't been brought up in this country. She was not exactly beautiful but nothing so common as pretty. Her face made you look again, and made you want to keep looking. Those eyes and that voice made me overlook the unsatisfactoriness of her answer, which must give some idea of how distracting I found her.

'You're reading him in the original.'

'Yes, I'm French. Well, I'm Vietnamese actually – originally – but when we . . . left we came to France and I was brought up there with my adoptive family.'

She said 'actually' like 'Ashley' and for a moment her mouth reminded me of Vivien Leigh's, which was disconcerting. I was curious about the biography and excited about the Vietnam connection. I told her, 'But your English is very good.'

She seemed pleased and smiled shyly. 'Oh, thank you. Well, my mother studied here – she was a language tutor in Leeds for a while, so she often spoke to me in English when I was tiny, and I've lived here for nearly ten years, ever since I graduated, and I've always worked here, and so – well, so it should be, I guess.'

Even the creeping Americanism couldn't put me off now. Assuming she'd graduated at twenty-one, I calculated, she must be at least thirty. For some reason, I was relieved to discover that she was comfortably more than half my age.

I wanted to question her further, but the others began to arrive and so our moment was gone. As they made their way towards the bar she asked me, 'Do you go to Dr Reeves' dream laboratory?'

'Yes, I've been coming for about seven months now.' I realised she might be joining us and asked, perhaps too eagerly, 'Is that what you're here for?'

'Well, he suggested I come along tonight and see if it feels right for me and right for the group, and then we can play it by ear.'

That sounded like Reeves all right. Play it by ear, my foot.

'Jolly good. Well, let me introduce myself and, if I may, ask your name and then I can introduce you to the other group members . . .' and I was just about to do so when Reeves appeared and took over the show, as ever, bounding into the middle of our gathering with the dignity of a puppy and heading straight for my new acquaintance, whose hand he grabbed and held in his own, practically pulling her off her stool, whilst turning to us with that lopsided grin of his and saying, 'Evening all. I'd like you all to meet a new group member. This is Delphine. She's going to come along to a session or two, see what we get up to, tell us a bit about herself and then we can all decide together whether she's going to fit into our happy band.'

Because I was still standing by Delphine's side I was facing the group and could see everyone's expression. Julie, as one would expect, looked pleased and welcoming in her open, foolish manner. Simon's mouth twitched lasciviously while his eyes traversed the not very considerable but highly shapely length of Delphine's legs. Sally just looked at her, tight-lipped, with a few sidelong glances in my direction, as though I were in some way responsible. Jagdev and Polly smiled and nodded hello. And Alfred just stared, with not a little suspicion. It must have been quite some welcome for poor Delphine, but she took it in her stride and radiated hellos and smiles all around before we decamped to Reeves' office, the man himself still ushering the newcomer along with many an unnecessary pat of the arm while the rest of us exchanged glances of surprise or pleasure or lust or mistrust or *chagrin*, each to his own.

Dr Reeves' assurances that Delphine had described a series of the worst dreams he had ever heard intrigued us all, as did his comment that she suffered from no sleep disorder.

'What's she doing here then, doc?' asked Simon slyly, '. . . and where did you get her from?'

Reeves frowned. 'I didn't "get her" from anywhere, Simon. Delphine has been temping in the Registrar's office and she took the minutes in a meeting I attended, after which we got chatting about the work of the lab and agreed it might be interesting for her to attend.'

'I'm sure it will be,' said Simon, smiling widely at Delphine, who looked a little anxious.

'Oh dear,' she said, 'I really don't want to impose, or to make anyone uncomfortable, it was just that Huw described what you were doing here and I told him about some of my dreams and we just – took it from there. But if you'd rather I didn't intrude I promise you that I won't be offended, I'll just . . .'

Simon interrupted apologetically, 'No, no of course not. I'm sorry, I was just taking the mick out of the doc.' Simon corrected himself and stopped drawling. 'I mean I was just teasing Dr Reeves. I didn't mean to make you feel unwelcome. You're very welcome, I swear. Isn't she, folks?'

There was a small hum of agreement and I heard Julie say in that vague way of hers, 'Oh yes, you must come back. It's nice for us to have someone new here, really it is.'

Delphine nodded politely and then sat back listening quietly for the rest of the session so I didn't get the chance to add my reassurance to Julie's and could only hope that she hadn't been put off by Simon's thoughtlessness. Once Reeves had done his summing up and made his farewells, she agreed, much to my relief, to accompany the rest of the group to the bar.

All of us tended to stay for at least one drink, largely because Dr Reeves rarely joined us and it gave us the opportunity to dissect a few of his — some would say more esoteric but I would suggest more *questionable* positings amongst ourselves. As soon as we'd made our way back into the almost derelict student bar, I manoeuvred myself next to Delphine and made sure that Simon wasn't the first to offer to buy her a drink.

'Do they do cocktails here?' she asked me, looking dubiously at our shabby surroundings. I didn't imagine they would, but insisted on making the request.

'What were you after?' I asked, once I had the attention of a barman.

'What I'd really like,' she said, turning her dark gaze upon him, 'is a French 75.'

My blank expression was matched by that of the young bartender — clearly a student earning some pocket money — and we must have made a comical pair because Delphine laughed and immediately waved the thought away with a gently dismissive gesture. 'Oh, I'm sorry, there's no reason why you should . . .' she began but the young man evidently felt that something important was at stake and asked for the ingredients. 'Well, it's a shot of gin — good gin — topped up with champagne and a squeeze of lemon juice. Served in a champagne glass.'

'The mixer is *champagne*?' I exclaimed.

She giggled at my incredulity. 'It's just something I tried recently and it's really lovely, but of course, a glass of wine would be fine, I'd be very happy with . . .'

She stopped to watch the barman disappear under the counter, then scurry off to the stockroom and return with a cold bottle of cheap cava, a saucer of lemon slices and cocktail sticks, a handful of plastic champagne flutes and a grin of triumph, saying, 'I'm afraid you'll have to stick with the gin that's in the optics, but we can have a go.'

By now everyone's attention was drawn to what was going on at the bar. Polly chipped in with, 'Ooh, that sounds *delicious*. Come on, Jag, that'd make a change from beer wouldn't it?' and Julie changed her order from a white-wine spritzer to 'what she's having' which gave Simon, who was getting the beers in for him and Alfred, a chance to curry favour with the new girl by joining in, so that the whole group except Sally, who refused to eschew her pineapple juice, ended up sipping the cold, dry, awfully sophisticated concoction. And although I drank it again – from crystal flutes, with the right kind of gin and vintage champagne, garnished with delicate curls of pared lemon peel – and always with Delphine – it never tasted as remarkable or was so intoxicating as that first evening. We stayed later than ever, long after the severely limited stock of cava had run out, until the bar was full of students and we were an unusual group amongst that crowd, too old and too smart, attracting stares from the surrounding clientèle. We stayed until tongues loosened and laughter sprang forth and the spaces between our respective thighs on the plastic-covered foam benches decreased little by little so that we became a homogenous mass of warm, drunken humanity, bound by our shared experiences, a sense of *bonhomie* and a strong curiosity about the woman who had made such an extraordinary evening happen.

Day fourteen: Tuesday

Another postcard. Reims, predictably enough. A rather tall and formal window, this one; I can't quite see the detail. I want to put a map on the wall and place pins in it. Understand where she's going, and why. See the pattern.

My dear James

All your funny sensitivities about France! I didn't mind it at all but I did mind how you could never admit them to me. You always wanted the upper hand, and you had it in nearly everything but you were still jealous of my little achievements — all of which were accidents, of birth mostly. Being French and dreaming — things I can't help doing, even if I wanted to stop — and they seemed to irritate you so much.

I wanted you to meet my mother and come to my country with me; you were more interested in dragging me off to Vietnam on the trail of something only you believed in.

D

I understand this one. She was often asking me to come to France and meet her mother, see her home town, visit the places where she went to school, hung around with her friends, rode her bicycle, had her hair cut, kissed boys. Normally I would have loved to go with her – I'm embarrassingly drawn to finding out my lovers' life stories and enjoy the tiniest details, and my desire to know every single little mundane thing about Delphine's early years was immense. But I didn't want to go to France with her. If I'm being honest, I think it was because I knew I wouldn't *impress* her. Previous girlfriends, even French speakers, had always been so full of admiration at my fluency with the language, my familiarity with the country and its people, its customs. That sounds a bit odd, as though I were talking about showing girls around some far-flung corner of the Congo or something, but I know many Brits whose impressions of France are that it's unwelcoming and mysterious, and of course there is that old rivalry which the French feel just as strongly, perhaps even more strongly, than we do. So to be taken out and about by someone who knows how to behave amongst the French, as well as how to speak to them, gave many of my former girl-friends a greater confidence in their ability to enjoy the country themselves in future. I even know one ex-lover who divorced her husband and bought a cottage in Normandy with the proceeds, so enamoured had she become of the place on a short break there with me. But I had never made love to a native French speaker and then taken her to her home country and I was strangely, stupidly, unwilling to do so.

The first real sign that something romantic could happen between us came one lovely late spring evening about two months after her acceptance into the lab. We had enjoyed a little conversational fencing during the meeting – by then it was obvious that her arrival had upped the ante for the rest of the group and discussions were becoming increasingly learned, with even Simon doing some background reading and proffering the odd half-intelligent comment now and then. And we continued to talk in the bar, sitting at the end of the group and sipping Australian wine – I had allowed Delphine to talk me into drinking one of those ostentatious New World young pretenders and been forced to admit that it was indeed superior to the university's cheap Merlot. As I listened to her speak and watched her fluid hand gestures I held on to each mouthful of wine for a few seconds and when I swallowed, my throat became infused with warm syrup, jam, pepper and a final tang of blood. It was one of the most concentratedly sensual hours of my life, so distinctive I can imagine tasting the wine now and my mouth fills with saliva in anticipation. Of course, it wasn't just the Syrah I was drooling over. My heightened senses were tuned in to the soft, low sound of Delphine's voice, I could see the tiny muscles beside her mouth move as she spoke and watch myself reflected in her dark eyes; our heads were close enough amongst all the surrounding racket for me to breathe in the subtle smell of her hair and my fingers itched to stroke the downy skin at the back of her neck.

She was questioning me in some depth about my apparently dreamless sleep. 'Have you ever dreamt?'

'Not that I can remember. My mother told me I had night terrors when I was very small, but from seven I spent most of my nights at boarding school,' I saw her expression soften at this but continued, 'and nothing untoward was reported there, or since. So I certainly don't remember dreaming.'

'Do you wish you did?' Straight in with the direct question, no pussyfooting around with pleasantries, that's my Delphine. On occasion, her questions were so direct that their force made me wince. I didn't mind it at all this time though.

'I'm not sure. I don't feel it as a *lack*. I see too many people who suffer in their sleep and I'm glad I'm not one of them. I mean, it must be terrible, it must make life very difficult for someone like Julie or Simon, for example – not only do they know they won't sleep properly, but they might have awful dreams as well.'

'Lots of dreamers sleep well; you just come across a lot of special cases here,' she pointed out, 'and your sleep is already disturbed. Are you sure you never, even occasionally, think that you'd like to read to us from your own dream diary?'

Her mentioning the diary alerted me to something, some significance about this conversation, which I wasn't yet sure about. My answer was supposed to sound sympathetic. 'Not if it was anything like yours!'

It sounded rude and abrupt but she laughed quite genuinely and brushed away my apologies. 'Don't worry, it's fine, I don't blame you for that!' But she still didn't release me from the questioning. 'But say if you had nice dreams, or surreal dreams, or just normal everyday dreams. Wouldn't you like to remember them when you woke and then bring them to tell the group?'

'I suppose so. Yes, I'm sure I would. But not if it came with a price. I'd like to remember my dreams but not if as a result my sleeping got worse.'

'I didn't say there would be a price. Do you *value* not dreaming?'

'I value sleeping well. That's my only aim now: to sleep well.'

'But you seem to connect them; you seemed to believe that in asking you if you'd like to remember your dreams I was suggesting you'd have to give something up, or pay, to do so.'

'I don't think I thought that. Although yes, perhaps there is a correlation in my mind between dreamlessness and sound sleep. And really, nothing that anyone in this group has ever said leads me to believe that it's a false correlation.'

'That's what I meant earlier,' she said earnestly, 'about this group not being a good place for someone who doesn't dream but wants to.'

'I never said I wanted to.'

'I think you do though, I think everyone does. But you probably won't be able to when the only time you ever talk about dreams it's with this group of people whose sleep is disturbed and troubled.'

She was looking into my eyes with a searching expression. I had noticed that Delphine always made eye contact, more than most people do, and I didn't want to miss this opportunity to connect with her, if that's what she wanted me to do. Her gaze didn't discomfit me except in a pleasurable way, and it was *curious*, not at all desperate, as though she was looking to see *if* something was there rather than looking *for* something. I was careful to look back at her while we talked and was surprised at the heady mixture of excitement and vulnerability I felt during our exchange. I knew it wasn't only the wine, and I knew, in one happy moment, that it wasn't only me. She patted my arm in a friendly manner and said, 'James, I wish I could help you dream.'

I replied gently, 'I'd like that. I'd like you to try,' and my voice sounded young, rather shy, more tentative than the words it was saying suggested. She nodded and took in a sharp breath before sighing it out with a little laugh, almost a nervous laugh. She left shortly afterwards, having written her number on a bus ticket which she handed to me as we said goodbye.

I didn't mean it. At the time, I wasn't actually thinking that I'd like Delphine to try to help me dream. Or at least, that seemed like a euphemism for what I'd really like her to help me achieve. Dreams feature too heavily as part of romantic iconography for me not to mentally translate her expressed wish into a number of bed- and sleep-related fantasies with which I had no doubt she could help me. Neither did I have any doubt that she had understood my response and acknowledged it, but I also think she meant exactly what she said at the time; she really did want to help me dream. Perhaps I should have wanted that more too, because a few months later I remember her delight at my recounting an explicit erotic daydream I'd had on the Tube home, and how the smile faded from her lips when I ended by saying, '. . . so you see, my darling girl, it worked, you have helped me dream!' and she shook her head in irritation and said, 'But no, James, that's not a dream. Daydreams aren't dreams, they're fantasies. You have always had those. Are you laughing at me for saying I wanted to help you really dream?'

Although I insisted I wasn't making fun of her I realised the extent to which she expected to take me at my word, just like I took her at hers. And it shocked me, that assumption of such precise mutuality. It sounds odd to say so, but I was counting on her intelligence, quickness and general savvy to help her read me; I hadn't realised that she expected me to match her directness, that she thought I would always tell her the truth.

It seems I'd got to a stage of my life where the truth had become an extremely relative state. For Delphine it was, however complex, fixed. Subjective and incomplete maybe; even she would admit that pinning down all the truth as though it were a moment in time is impossible, but when she 'told the truth' it was exactly what she thought was the truth. Not that it took any conscious effort for her to do so. I, however, found myself thinking carefully before answering her — is this right? Is this truly what I think or feel or did, or could it be some imaginary perfect answer? Some excuse or ducking of the issue? Some social smoothing away of rough edges? It became exhilarating to force my answers through this filter and I began to take pride in being scrupulous until Delphine said I sounded pompous. Now I fear I didn't do it enough, held back where I should have come forth, didn't entrust her with knowledge which might bring pain. The excuses I gave myself were all about protecting her but I should have put those very excuses through the truth filter, because I suspect they were very much about protecting myself.

The months after that night when Delphine had taken me on as a project were the happiest times in my life. Falling in love is always delightful but for the first time I had no notion of its habitual transitoriness. There was no worldly-wise voice in my head reminding me that this would pass so I should enjoy it while I could. Along with the thrill and adrenalin rush and the wonderful lovemaking was a calmness, a feeling that I had nothing to worry about any more. Where it came from I have no idea but it gave me such a sense of well-being, it actually made me feel healthy, relaxed, utterly fulfilled. My insomnia retreated week by week until it was normal for me to sleep through the night, and if I did wake in the early hours I found her there and was comforted back to sleep without an effort. There was no desperation in it, I think that was it. I'd never have described myself as desperate before Delphine, and still don't know if it's the best word, but the lover's motto of *carpe diem* had a new ring to it: I was telling myself yes, of course, seize the day, but seize every day, all the days, seize and consume and digest every single day with this woman and at the same time enjoy looking forward to seizing all the future weeks and months and years, together.

Delphine is only the second woman I've lived with. I've had relationships with women that have continued for five years or more during which time neither party has mentioned cohab-itation as an option. Often this is due to the surrounding circumstances − generally, that the relationship is clandestine − but even when I've officially been 'going out' with a woman I've always steered the conversation away from talk of moving in together. It has either suited them, or they have believed I will change my attitude in time and so persist optimistically, or it's the reason they cite for breaking with me. Most of them have probably gone through all three stages: women do seem to have this insatiable appetite for 'progress', and however 'alternative', independent or unconventional they may be, that always seems to involve setting up home with a man, even if it's with a view to changing the man every few years. I've had no such domestic daydreams and very much enjoyed living alone, although today it's hard to quite remember why. Admittedly, my experiences as a live-in lover before Delphine were fairly appalling, and I suppose that was mostly my fault since the tedium of fidelity for fidelity's sake is much more difficult to escape when someone is expecting your head on the pillow beside her night after night. At least both parties are allowed a certain leeway if they don't share a domicile, and provided no unpleasant questions are asked that has always seemed to be the most successful arrangement a civilised man and woman can reach.

I have always sought to live alone but actually I hate solitude. I don't mean making my own supper, watching a television documentary for half an hour then wandering into my study to listen to music whilst I read some taxing non-fiction or complete a crossword before pouring a nightcap and turning in for as relaxing a night's sleep as any insomniac could hope for. That's all fine. It's the prospect of never doing anything else which scares me; the fear that I could be trapped in my flat doing the same things night after night and never meet another human being at all. When Delphine moved in, every moment she was out made the place feel empty. At first I was scared of our living in each other's pockets; after a fortnight I wanted to put her in mine and keep her there for ever; every time she worked a little late or met a colleague for dinner or babysat for friends, I would resent my deprivation of her. I would plan evenings like the ones I used to have before she arrived, but when the time came they gave me no pleasure and I simply waited for her to return. Having spent much of my non-working life engaged in pursuing – and often catching – women, I had no network of chaps to invite round to watch the match and raise a glass or two, I didn't really have a bar to go to and in any case have always disliked the slightly grubby feeling of wandering into a public house alone and sipping beer in the corner while everyone around you smokes and laughs and talks. I've been pretty appalling at hanging on to the few people I know who might reasonably be called 'friends', and not just because of my years of living abroad.

I've collected some really excellent art from around the world. Unusual things, unique *objets*, all manner of mostly three-dimensional pieces and the odd contemporary painting here and there. I had found the perfect position for each one; woe betide Mrs Duda if she misplaced them by even a centimetre after dusting, she would get a sharp note from me the next week.

Delphine was forever changing them round. She would even take them into a different room or stand a large painting against a wall if no hook was available.

'It's so boring, keeping them all in the same place,' she said the first time I returned from work and was met in the hallway not by a set of abstract Shona stone carvings from Tanzania on the shelf opposite the door, but with a wonderful slipware vase I picked up at a potter's studio near Limoges.

'Where are the stone carvings?' I said as politely as I could.

'On the mantelpiece in the sitting room. They look so nice beside that soapstone dish, a little row of things to stroke.'

'The dish is kitchenware!'

'But it's lovely! And the colours of the vase look better against this wall, don't you think?'

I didn't know what to think.

'But Delphine, the slipware shelf will have a big gap in it . . .'

'What slipware shelf? I've mixed it up a bit. By colour, texture and scale. Come and see.'

She mixed it up every week according to no known aesthetic configuration, but to her *mood*. And it worked. I looked forward to opening the door to a new sight and finding, without any warning, a jug where there had been a carving; an oil canvas where there had been a plate. Nobody else would have dared – would have been able – to shake me up like that and make me enjoy it!

Sometimes, she even used the vases for flowers.

Delphine knew a woman with synaesthesia. She saw people's names as colours. The condition had fascinated me when I was reading up about it, that confusion of the senses, and I was curious enough to search out my old notes and ask Delphine if she could remember how it worked for this woman.

'Well, someone would introduce themselves to her and when she heard their name she would get a strong – vision, I suppose, like an apparition – of a colour. You might say, hello, my name's James, and she would think – though sometimes she might actually say out loud – ah, yellowy-brown.'

'Yellowy-brown!' I was affronted.

Delphine sighed. 'OK, reddy-green, is that better? Or irregular stripes of purple and grey? Or cerise with gold edging?'

'Hmm, it seems like rather a *womanly* form of synaesthesia,' I commented sceptically. 'I heard a man on the radio, who . . .'

'Or did you *see* him?' Delphine cut in playfully. 'Maybe you *smelled* him?'

'Ha, yes, very good. No, I *heard* him on the radio, and he was describing how he *saw* music as moving shapes and colours. It was remarkable. I wished so much that I could see Duruflé's *Requiem*, how grand and marvellous that would be.'

'James, I've never heard you wish for a dysfunction before!'

'It's not a dysfunction, exactly. It's more of a – a gift, I think.'

She looked excited.

'Exactly, a gift. That's what some of the Dream Lab people think. That's sometimes how I think about my dreams. To be different in some way – to see things differently or experience them differently – it might be scary and it's often tiresome but it's *special*.'

'Oh, I don't think there's a comparison,' I replied. 'The sleep disorders are more disabling than synaesthesia, which seems more enabling.'

'No, there's not that much difference. Just think, it might get really tedious to be introduced to lots of new people and be hearing all these names – hi, this is Jane and this is John and here is Fabrice, and Maurice and over there are Pascale and Patricia – and all the time you'd be getting these flashes of colours and patterns, it would be like being shouted at, it could get like a – like a . . .'

'A jukebox?'

'Yes, that's it, a jukebox. A floorshow. It could be really inconvenient; I think this woman used to get headaches. But it was worth it for her because it was so different and special.'

'Maybe.'

'It *is*! And anyway, don't you sometimes become almost synaesthetic about things? I mean, when I see purple liquid I think of blonde hair, because I had a flatmate who put peroxide on her roots every six weeks and the stuff she used was purple when she applied it but her hair came out ash blonde. And if I see a blue drink I can almost taste raspberry, because things like slush puppies and gummy sweets that are blue are usually raspberry. And when I saw a moonstone I was so disappointed because it sounds like something luminous and deep but looks like a cataract on someone's eye.'

'That's not the same thing at all.'

'It's not the same thing but it's partway there. It makes the real thing possible to understand. In the same way, you were tired all the time you were insomniac, so you do understand a little how it feels to be deprived of hours and hours of sleep like Julie or Alfred.'

'Ah, is that what you're getting at?'

'Not getting at anything, just showing you that you understand more than you think, that you've experienced more than you think.'

'How do you know how much I think I've experienced or understood?' I asked her good-humouredly.

'I think you think it's not much. And I think you think that's a good thing.' I shrugged it off and returned to my notes. Delphine turned to leave and I had a sudden thought. 'Delphine. What colour were you?'

'Hmm?'

'What colour did that woman say you were?'

'Oh.' She thought for a moment. 'She said my name looked greeny-blue. Or rather, bluey-green. Not jade, quite turquoisey, but deeper round the edges. With flecks of silver all around.'

'You're joking!'

'No. That's what she said.'

She turned to go again.

'Delphine.'

'What?'

'It's true. That's just like you.'

She looked pleased in spite of herself. And in spite of knowing, as I did, that I hadn't a clue why I'd said it.

I keep looking through her clothes in the wardrobe. I remember how it felt to hold her close and stroke her back when she wore the beautiful rose-coloured cashmere jumper I bought her, but without her shape to fill it, it caught on my dry hands and gave me a static shock. I even looked through the drawers to see if there might be a T-shirt she had worn briefly and put away without washing; something which might still bear her scent. What a deviant she's made me into, sniffing the seams of her clothes in desperate search of *something* to remind me. But everything smells of fresh laundry.

I haven't moved her bottles and jars away from their place in the bathroom and her white towelling bathrobe still hangs beside mine on the bedroom door, her waffle weave slippers are under the bed. Even though she's not here she seems more attached to everything in my life than I do myself. It's not just her things all over the flat, it's her *presence*. She is at the centre, wherever she goes, and I want to ask her how she does that. And can I ever hope to do that? I feel peripheral in my own home.

I haven't said much more about Alfred but he has been in my thoughts. It's hard to know what to say now. He was the quietest member of the group and the oldest, and everything about him made me feel as though we inhabited completely different worlds. I didn't get to know him well at all; less than any of the others and that's not saying much.

'Why do we dream?' he once asked Reeves, rather plaintively.

'Ah, I'm glad you asked me that. I was going to cover this in a couple of weeks, but shall we talk about it now?'

There was general agreement and Reeves asked each person in turn to explain why – or to hazard a guess about why – he or she dreamt.

'For spiritual enlightenment,' said Polly confidently, and Reeves made one of his 'well, you may or may not be right, who knows?' sort of faces, clearly coming down on the side of not but being too polite to actually say so.

'I see it as something more practical than that,' said Julie, 'a way of "practising" for events or problems and particular situations, making you feel like you've done something before and know what to do. Whenever I have a sense of déjà vu I think it might be because I've dreamt about the moment, or one like it, before it happens.'

'You believe you *foresee* the future, Julie?' I asked incredulously and she hastily said, 'No, no, not at all. I suppose that's how it sounded but no, I mean your mind just prepares you for very feasible situations that are likely to become real. Nothing supernatural or mystical about it at all.'

'I'm with you on the unmystical bit, but I think it's more like defragging a disk drive,' Jag joined in, matter of fact as ever. 'It clears your mind out and allows you to subconsciously file away information you need and jettison stuff you don't.'

When Reeves looked at Alfred to give us his view, I noticed the older man was looking impatient, and he said, with some bitterness, 'Clears out your mind I wish! I can't remember the last time I had a dream that was anything but a – a – an *imposition*. Even when they're not nightmares, I have these strange dreams I can't describe or explain and they just *agitate* me. They give me no peace.'

Simon agreed with Alfred, 'They all sound like really appealing explanations one way or another. But it just doesn't *feel* like that to me. I don't feel prepared or comfortable or enlightened and my mind feels *more* full and confused after I've had a very complicated and inexplicable dream; it's the very opposite of cleaning out and filing. Maybe my mental admin isn't as good as yours, Jag, but I never get the feeling that my dreams are any use at all.'

'So who's right then?' I asked Reeves, and he said that none of them and all of them were right; a typically frustrating answer.

We tried not to go over old ground too much after Delphine joined the group, but some of the questions we'd discussed in the early days came up regularly and I remember when this subject of the reason of, or use for, dreams was being talked about again. Reeves put the question to Delphine, 'Why do you dream?' and she looked puzzled and said, with a shrug, 'Because I can.'

Day fifteen: Wednesday

I took the day off. I remembered that Mrs Duda would be bustling in at around nine, so I was up and ready well before that. I did a little shopping but had no excuse, no desire, to stay out longer than I needed to, so I returned to the flat and spent several hours here in my study while all manner of vacuuming and cleaning and polishing went on in the other rooms. At one o'clock I came into the kitchen and made us some lunch – just fresh vegetable soup and bread with a couple of cheeses – and the poor woman's face was a picture as I told her to come through and eat with me. I think she brings some sandwiches or heats something up usually, but it seemed clumsy and unnecessary for us to each eat alone. We chatted a little, about her family in Poland and here, and she showed me photographs of her children, who have left home now, and her sisters in Krakow. They all have those cheekbones.

And then a walk in Regent's Park. Such a beautiful time of year; the beds are all in bloom, the grass littered with picnic cloths and daisies. Everywhere I looked brought a lump to my throat; I had to keep stopping and surveying the grey path, catching my breath back, so that all the vibrant pictures of other people's lives wouldn't hurt my eyes.

And I thought about all the things I want to ask Delphine. Back at home I took some sheets of paper and started to write a list, by hand, starting with the enormous, obvious questions about why she left, and why she had to leave with Him, but then I warmed to my subject and it went on for pages and became more and more embittered: did I no longer please you sexually? Were you ashamed to be seen with me? Why did you shout at me so harshly when I answered that call on your mobile two days before you left me? And then increasingly silly: were you just pretending to read Camus because it made you look good? Did you really lose the turquoise scarf I bought you in Florence or did you hate it and actually throw it away? Had my birthday book really not arrived at the shop or had you forgotten to order it? Reading it back made me feel ashamed until I realised that the great anger it expressed was mostly aimed at me, for not having asked her more, better, questions sooner. I am angry with her too; it comes and goes. She should have left me a note or told me that she was leaving, but I can hardly blame her for not doing so; it's precisely the way I've behaved all my life and I've always expected women to understand. I screwed up the paper and threw it in my wastepaper basket.

The basic facts: Delphine joined the Dream Laboratory in early spring last year; she moulded into the group seamlessly and became as well established as any of the rest of us very quickly; and she soon inspired great admiration and affection in all group members except perhaps Sally, although even she, in time, came round. It was impossible to resist the woman's charm which was as unconscious as it was appealing. Perhaps, had she been plain, we would have all said how *nice* she was, which sounds like an innocuous and even damningly faint word of praise, but is a genuine compliment. Being attractive as well as *nice* made her popular and so we all pursued her, whether for love or friendship or sex – or for *knowledge*, like Reeves did – or just so that some of it might rub off on us, like fairy dust. Every one of us was after her, one way or another. How shocked they must have been when she chose me.

I can't avoid Delphine's dreams any longer. We heard the first one around six weeks after she joined the group, when the session was focusing on nightmares. As usual, I couldn't voice an experience of a nightmare, or even summon up the emotional truth of it from anywhere in my being (a skill Reeves seemed to believe I should possess but which I never truly understood), and was both horrified by and envious of what other people were reporting.

Simon's dream diary was a messy, ragged reporter's notebook in which he had made a few notes in thick black pen. He flipped through it, seeking out nightmares, and then told us about his lurid night terrors which, being Simon's, occurred at around seven in the morning: 'So there's this creature, right, and it's got teeth like the alien in *Alien* – an inner set coming out of the mouth, they look like they're made of steel – and it's walking towards me but I'm standing on a river bank and when I turn around to jump I see that the river is full of boiling blood. The monster changes sometimes, even within the dream, but its teeth are always the same, and the dream usually ends either by its teeth reaching my throat or me jumping into the river and feeling the scalding blood touch my feet.' He looked genuinely scared as he recounted the horrific dream to us.

Polly's death-defying sleepwalking escapades in the clutch of awful visions were agonising, full of phrases which made me feel queasy despite their ludicrousness. I can remember her reading out bits of them, relishing the horror: '. . . and the wire in my spine pushes through the cartilage of each vertebrae slowly enough for me to *count* them!' she once said, wide-eyed and wincing.

Poor Alfred sometimes fell in and out of a nightmare in which he was falling from the top of a mountain and each time he woke – which could be dozens of times in one night – there was a moment when his heart was completely silent before thumping into dangerously rapid action.

Even Sally, who rarely had bad dreams, could tell us tales of waking with a sensation that someone was kneeling on her chest and finding herself in the period of muscular atonia, aware of everything around her but completely unable to move any part of her body for several fearful minutes.

On this occasion, Delphine was listening to each speaker intently, nodding occasionally, offering sympathetic tuts or little cries of shock at key moments. When they had all finally ceased trying to outdo one another the room fell silent and Reeves, assuming that unconvincingly wise expression he tended to don for our benefit, took a breath in preparation for summing up. It was at that point that Delphine spoke, quietly but firmly. 'Dr Reeves. Before we go on, may I talk a little about nightmares? About bad dreams?'

It wasn't Reeves' habit to ask questions of individual group members; there was always a free-for-all after he'd summed up each topic for the evening and he had explained that anybody who didn't want to contribute would be under no pressure to do so. While this suited me very well, I could see that Julie, for example, would spend five minutes building up the courage to talk and then just as she was ready he would bark a sharp 'Right! Let's move along then', and even the least sensitive man on earth could have seen her frustration. But when he realised that Delphine had been waiting for him to ask her to speak, he broke his own rules and apologised profusely for not having invited her comment. It was an important moment, and one which I'm sure the others would remember as clearly as I do.

In any case, she had our full attention by then but even if she hadn't the couple of dreams she described would have drawn us in to listen. I know they stuck in all our minds. We later discovered – via Reeves' questioning – that she kept notes of them all in her dream diary, had done for the past ten years, which is when she remembered their having started. We ended up studying a few of them – with the dreamer's tentative permission – in the group over the next few weeks, so Delphine dutifully typed them out and Reeves photocopied them for us. It seemed almost a violation of her, for the lot of us to be poring over those terrible manuscripts, rereading them with her voice in our heads; that matter-of-fact tone broken only by the odd moment when she actually laughed. These were the first dreams she read out:

A mother is tied up behind a pile of boulders on the top of an alpine mountain. She has a view through the rocks to the mountain's edge, where her child is playing near the precipice. If the child crosses a white line which is painted a foot away from the edge, then and only then is the mother allowed to cry out to encourage the little boy away from the edge. We then see that there are lots of mothers and lots of children – all crawling, toddling or rolling near the edge of the mountain. One woman sees her daughter's foot hover over the line and she screams. That's against the rules and the child is pulled, invisibly, over the edge. Another woman sees her son chasing a butterfly; by the time the boy crosses the white line it's too late for his mother's scream to stop the fall. Only occasionally does a child slowly cross the line, hear its mother and retreat, confused as to where the familiar voice is coming from. Most of the toddlers and babies are gradually falling over the precipice. The first mother keeps watching her child and scarcely dares to blink. We never find out what happens to her or her son.

A mother and her baby are on a high wire many hundreds of feet from the ground. It's foggy and she can't see anything in any direction. The child is a heavy toddler and the wire is very sharp; the woman has to keep changing her position on the wire as the skin on her palms, her arms, her thighs, is lacerated. There are other women, invisible to one another, along the wire. After a full day has passed some of them tie their babies to the wire and let themselves fall. Others drop their babies and tie themselves to the wire with coats, stockings, whatever they can remove from their bodies. Eventually only our mother and child remain. She is dangerously sleepy, and mother and child are coated in sweat and excrement.

After two days we see a young, nervous man in a white coat holding a clipboard reporting to his senior.

'Is that all of them?' the older man asks, looking upwards.

'I think so,' says the younger; then, seeing the irritation on his boss's face, changes it to, 'Yes, yes, that's all of them.'

We now see that there is a huge safety net underneath the wire and all the fallen mothers and babies are being taken away in vehicles.

'Good,' says the older man. 'Take this lot to get them cleaned up and then move the net. We'll take the wire down when the fog clears later in the week.'

We leave the woman, bleeding and exhausted, trying to tie herself and her child to the wire using the belt of her coat.

Of course, everyone except me had recounted dreams and nightmares or read excerpts from their own dream diaries, but the effect was quite different; the suspenseful detail and absolute awfulness of Delphine's stories was shocking and compelling, they were like the worst, or I suppose the best, kind of horror stories where what you imagine is happening is far worse than anything you can actually see happening.

After she'd read them there was a stunned silence before Polly started flicking nervously through one of her silly dreamers' dictionaries, looking up 'mountain' and 'butterfly' and 'tightrope' and suggesting that they were all auguries of a lottery win or meeting a tall dark stranger. Reeves was usually politely tolerant of Polly's mad theories, although he had made it clear early on that he wasn't a 'believer', but this time he shut her up quite sharply, saying something like, 'Polly, I think that the complexity and detail of Delphine's dreams calls for a little more analysis than your dictionary could cope with, don't you?' and poor Polly had meekly closed the book and, disgruntled, put her tongue out at Reeves when his back was turned.

Dimly at the time, I was aware of that session being the point at which Reeves' interest in Delphine was also sparked. There had previously been no sense of him as a sexual being in the way that you'd get from Simon, or even Jag. I was sure he had the hots for Delphine in the way that just about every man who met her had, and he'd mentioned his divorce so was single and eligible, but what really seemed to bewitch him was her dreams. I should have noticed the change in him; the way those sessions, however they began, all ended up focusing on the contents of her dream diary. I'm surprised nobody else did. It was in the back of my mind – his interest in her – when I first genuinely thought that she might want me but as soon as that thought was confirmed I was so over-joyed that I thought no more of the 'competition'. And yet the time they began to spend together, her increasing assistance in his research, would have made me feel insecure had it been any other man I can think of. I didn't think I needed to keep my eye on him as a man, rather than a scientist, at all. Now I can scarcely believe I missed the signs.

When Delphine saw our troubled faces, she gave a gentle laugh. 'Oh dear, I'm sorry, I've upset you all. Look, these aren't really nightmares. I don't wake up from them and I'm not bothered by them in the day. I'm *fascinated* by them but not *bothered*.'

'But they're absolutely *terrible*!' Sally said, sounding a little impatient. 'Dr Reeves, Huw – of course they're nightmares, aren't they?'

Reeves blinked and took his eyes off Delphine to answer. 'It's an interesting point, Sally. My research on this isn't finished yet, but it looks as though self-definition is the primary factor in categorising what's a dream and what's a nightmare. It's impossible to be objective, of course, because we can't make everyone dream the same dream and then tell us what they thought of it – not yet, anyway – but my department has been working on a nightmare distress questionnaire which gets people to "grade" the horribleness of their dreams or nightmares and then sets that information against details of their psychopathology. Unsurprisingly, those who tend towards stress or depression, or display schizoid characteristics, reported the most extreme negative response to their dreams and categorised more of them as "nightmares". But some people on the study reported a far higher number of "nightmares" which gave them no waking distress at all. Perhaps Delphine doesn't *suffer* from nightmares at all.'

'But surely,' interjected Jagdev, 'the type of the dream is important? I mean, I know that nobody bothers with dream analysis nowadays – we don't say aha, you dreamt that your teeth fell out which means you are anxious about impotence – well, nobody except Polly does' – at which Polly elbowed him sharply – 'but surely dreaming awful things is a sign of inner turmoil? With all due respect.'

He looked sheepishly at Delphine, who seemed unconcerned as Reeves answered, 'We don't know yet. Delphine's dreams aren't post-traumatic; they're not about things which have actually happened to her or people she knows. They *are* gruesome and frightening but she displays no sign of any emotional or mental disorder, so who's to say she's troubled in any way?'

Jagdev looked unconvinced, and embarrassed as he was at discussing this woman as though she weren't in the room, he ploughed on. 'But the dreams are about strangers, aren't they? And a tendency to dream about strangers correlates with a schizoid personality, unlike depressives who are more likely to dream about people they know, right?'

At this, Reeves tried to call a halt to the scientific discussion. 'Ah, Jagdev, you've a lot to learn. Delphine isn't even in her own dreams. She's not dreaming about herself in relation to people she knows or doesn't know. She seems to dream – and remember dreaming – entire scenarios, *as an onlooker*. As she says, they're filmic, she describes the view from which she sees the action happening and while sometimes it's more than close-up, and there's certainly some sort of empathy or even omniscience going on, she's never a protagonist and usually her view is as though from behind a camera.'

'Could be denial.'

'Of course it could be denial, in that her mind has decided to translate a dream in which she is the terrified protagonist into one in which she is the safe observer. But that doesn't alter the fact that she is not distressed by them. Maybe it's *why* she's not distressed by them but whatever way you look at it, she's not distressed. Are you?' he said, turning to Delphine.

'Well, I wasn't,' she said good-humouredly, 'until now, maybe. Look, these are just my dreams. They don't trouble me. I have other sorts of dreams – funny little surreal things like we all dream about – and which I remember bits of. And I know that occasionally I've had proper nightmares, classic things about being chased by monsters and unable to move, that kind of thing. But these ones I remember in full as though, like I say, they're films or scenes from films. The beginnings and endings are sometimes fuzzy but the action is all very clear. Maybe it's something to do with the period of sleep in which I dream them, I don't know. I'm going to the Sleep Clinic next week to have a polysomnograph and they'll look at all that then, won't they?' Reeves nodded. 'So perhaps that will shed some light on it. But truly,' and here she looked at all of us with some concern, 'truly, they don't trouble me. I'm not upset by them; in fact they're so over the top, so *camp*, that they're funny. But they're just my dreams.'

The image of Delphine lying sleeping in the clinic attached to the various bits of machinery and watched over by technicians and nurses aroused a strong protective instinct in me. By then I already knew that I was extremely attracted to her, and was almost certain that there was the tiniest shimmer of interest from her, though nothing to give me a clear signal on which to act. But at the moment I began to be familiar with her dreams, my fascination with her moved beyond sexual anticipation and on to a strong emotional pull towards her, a need which I felt quite physically to hold her in my arms, to place her in my safekeeping. This sounds paternalistic, as though I thought she were a little woman who needed a big strong man to take care of her. That's not what I mean. She was clearly strong enough to bear enormous amounts of pain, in a way I certainly was not. But I so much wanted to prevent her from further suffering; thought that if there was something I could do to keep her from harm then I would give anything for the chance to do it. It sounds quite chivalrous now, and I still believe it wasn't an entirely selfish impulse, although I would clearly benefit in various ways from holding her in my arms, and I know it was unlike anything I had ever felt before about a woman. I also identified – and it was hardly rocket science, given the nature of her dreams – that she had some 'issues', as they say, about babies, some deep-rooted anxieties in that area. It made me strangely hopeful that, because making a child was the last thing I wanted to do with her, it would count in my favour. That, despite my age, I might appear to be a safer prospect than a direct contemporary who would be more likely to require living proof of his virility. The excerpts she read from her dream diary kept all of us entranced and, in spite of their horror, made us wish for more.

No wonder they had Reeves, all of us, spellbound. I still believe that their provenance cannot possibly be a healthy or happy one, however much Delphine used to protest about the impressively even balance of her mind. And she clung to the fact that she was not their protagonist, absolutely refusing to accept that her memory of the dreams might be leaving her one cool remove away from the action.

If only I still had that diary, I've no doubt it would explain a lot. I can hold my hand up in all honesty and say that I never looked at it without Delphine's express permission to do so – even though she carried it with her at almost all times I could probably have rifled through her bag when she was in the bathroom, or got up on some pretext in the middle of the night and taken it with me to pore over in some quiet corner of the flat. Risky but not impossible. But, despite longing to read everything she ever dreamt I always resisted the temptation. Once a source of pride, now it's one of my deep regrets. But I have copies of a few, the ones she read to us in the lab. I almost dread to think of them, but they might hold the key to some understanding of her mind; I have to confront, to consider, the awful things my darling dreamt.

Day sixteen: Thursday

Today, another postcard. From France, but I can't read the bloody franking mark. Another Chagall window; the image of fire in the baptistry of Notre-Dame; it looks as though she's tearing these from one of those booklets of postcards you can buy in gift shops.

My dear James

You didn't fight for me. You knew I was sad but instead of trying to find out why, you just pretended I wasn't. Men are supposed to be brave; if keeping me was really important to you, surely you'd have made a bit more effort? Of course, the reason I'm still writing to you is because I'm not sure that's true. It's mad, but I can imagine you loving me as much as you say you loved me and still doing nothing. It must be unbearable, that passive acceptance of something you love slipping through your fingers; how do you live with it?

D

I was surprised to hear that's what she thought. The fact is, I did suspect she wasn't happy, but I thought she was unhappy because of me and therefore what could I do to help improve that situation? Keep my head down and try to be pleasant, I thought. How could I fight for her when the reason for her misery was *me*? It would be like fighting myself.

I can imagine her setting me some task to perform through these postcards, though I'm damned if I know what it is. That feeling of being her project continued to surface from time to time, especially when we talked about the lab. She was constantly surprised at how incurious I'd been about the other group members during all those meetings before her arrival and I suppose that, to someone as eternally curious as she was, it would seem odd and even frustrating. As for the lab members, I know absolutely that they were all taken aback at the speed with which Delphine and I had got together. She moved in with me later that summer, and that gave them all a shock too.

It must have seemed to Reeves and the others that my 'beeline' for Delphine had been the result of a carefully planned operation. As though Cupid fired that arrow right under the noses of all the oblivious onlookers? And I suppose I did 'pick her off' from the rest of the pack, make her my target, take aim and – fire. Delicate work, to send my arrow sailing towards her at just the right pitch and pace to strike her, tenderly and accurately, in the centre of her heart. There was my alter-ego – the sub-conscious James – tensing his bow arm and narrowing his eyes to slits, as tiny and dangerous as the fine arrow slit, the dream-hole, through which he was shooting. But surely, once the arrow was loosed, his cover was broken? However lofty his position, however well camou-flaged and well covered, he must have been knowingly risking himself to exposure? Perhaps it was so secure, up there in the tower, that he never even considered the consequences of the shot; didn't feel at all vulnerable at having given away his position.

An enjoyable extension of a metaphor but it's an uncom-fortable train of thought. The dream-hole allows the marksman to fire his bow unseen and remain impervious to whatever might fly back towards him. My view from up here has been so safe, the big picture so reassuring. And I know – can't believe anyone hasn't worked this out – that there was no premeditation, I had no plan. Sometimes, things just happen. Sometimes, you do something big and bold and it looks deliberate, conclusive. But usually you're just as surprised as anyone else. A combination of instinct and unawareness was what led me to Delphine: the former guided by desire and fascination, the latter fed by my huge disinterest in the people around me. Those two tendencies have resided in my being so comfortably for so long; this was the point at which they began to fight one another.

I remember giving her the low-down on everyone in the group a little while before she moved in, and it pains me now to remember the witty, acerbic *vignettes* I'd mentally prepared for her amusement.

'So what does Julie *do* at the hospital?' she asked me after I'd cruelly caricatured the whole group one by one.

'I'm not entirely sure – I thought at first that she was a cleaner but she talks about patients so she must be a nurse. Not sure what department or anything.'

Delphine was smiling at me, slightly dangerously. 'James, why did you think she was a cleaner? She's obviously well educated, and really bright!'

That wasn't an adjective I'd apply to Julie, whose singsong accent continued to irritate the hell out of me and she still rarely said anything particularly illuminating, but I let it pass. 'Anyway, she's on her own with two daughters in some block of flats and there's never been any mention of a man. I've seen photos of the girls, very pretty little things, mixed-race I'd say, so I assume their father – if they have the same father – is white but he's definitely not around. Apart from that I don't know much about her except that she visits her brother every two weeks, I believe he's in prison though I don't know what for, and it's a long round-trip so she gets even more exhausted than usual.'

'Poor lady. She does look tired, and she's very shy, but

she's always so sweet and nice to everyone. I think I'd be really bad-tempered if I had chronic fatigue.'

'Yes, I suppose she does cope with it pretty well. Anyway, it's good for the group to bring together people from different cultures and backgrounds so I'm very glad she's in it.'

'You make it sound as though she's just there to make up numbers, but every time I've been she's said one or two really interesting things.'

'Hmm, perhaps she has been on a bit of a roll recently. But before you arrived, I can honestly say I only remember her contributing half a dozen very minor points to the debate.'

'Maybe you weren't taking much notice,' suggested Delphine quietly and gave me no time to reply, instead asking, 'What about Simon?'

I viewed her closely while I answered. 'Simon is one to watch. I can guarantee that he'll be pursuing you avidly even though he knows we're together. I find him rather lecherous and unpleasant.'

She looked surprised. 'That's just an act isn't it? I don't get any real sense of being pursued; he's just one of those guys that like to flirt a little. And he's funny, like an overgrown boy. I think he's quite a kind person. I like him.'

'That's the act. He's not at all kind, I'm sure of it. He'll disarm you and then pounce.'

'James! You make him sound like a lion.'

I told her my werewolf theory and she laughed heartily before coming to sit on my lap and telling me that if Simon was like a wolf I was like a big grumpy bear with a sore head. I joined in with good grace but was always very jumpy about her relationship with Simon after that, and sometimes didn't succeed in hiding my hostility towards him.

During the three months before she left, we seemed to have quite a few heated exchanges. Delphine was definitely becoming more combative and fiery, and I assumed it was something to do with the psychology course she'd started on her days off work.

Money is supposed to be the subject which couples argue about above all others but thankfully that wasn't true of us. I explained to her when she moved in with me that my mortgage was paid off, my salary excellent, my pension very solid indeed, and therefore there was no need for her to make any financial contribution to the household. She did, of course, despite her part-time job being very badly paid – she was always paying for the shopping or buying me meals in restaurants, and insisted on taking out a loan to buy herself a second-hand car despite my offers to help her out. But she allowed me to buy clothes and treats for her, knowing what pleasure it gave me, and of course what woman wouldn't enjoy owning a few designer labels and good pieces of jewellery when she's never been able to afford such things on her own salary? So she had enough spare income to finance a part-time psychology course – not taught at the university, otherwise Reeves would have jumped in earlier, I suspect – and she was doing that for one day and one evening per week, which included a session of 'fieldwork' as she called it on Wednesday afternoons. I used to ask her how the course was going, but she never showed much willingness to discuss it with me, saying it was too soon to tell. I was a little resentful of her course because she would have to complete assignments when she should have been with me.

And she had to use my office. I offered to set her up with a desk and a laptop in the tiny second bedroom but she refused to even consider it: 'James, you don't have to spend any more money on me! There's hardly room for a desk in there and I don't need a laptop – I can just use your computer and save the files to a disk. And the light's much better in your room. Really, there's no need to go to any trouble.'

I wonder if she was teasing me a little even then. If she knew that ordinarily the idea of sharing my den with anyone was abhorrent, that I'd have paid a great deal of money to keep the space to myself. But in she waltzed, put her ring binder files on my shelves, her disk in my holder and it never bothered me in the slightest. I used to vacate the room for her and read the newspaper in the lounge until she'd finished, and I ended up enjoying the sound of her fingers tapping away at my keyboard. It turned out that with her, I quite enjoyed sharing.

29 June

It's fucking unbelievable. Beauman — that great over-educated, under-emotional arsehole — has taken up with Delphine, the girl with the fantastic dreams who sleeps like a baby and who gets everyone in that group to perk up just by the way she sits there. She can't be more than thirty, she's bright, beautiful, witty — I've no idea what she thinks she's playing at.

They came in holding hands. Like teenagers, only relaxed.

He just asked her. He just bloody asked her. They'd spoken in the lab and in the bar afterwards a few times, that was all, but he still thought that gave him the right to walk up and take her. I'd never be so — so sure of myself. That's what a private education buys you, that confidence. That's why there are so many twats walking around with their 'Oxbridge' (where's that then? Oh, middle England is it?) degrees who wouldn't last ten minutes — intellectually or any other way — in Cardiff or Glasgow or Liverpool. It's a kind of blindness. Or single-mindedness, that focus, that simplicity. Is that what women like? It's OK, he's on the spectrum but hey, he's got the superficial social skills required to use the right fucking fork at dinner. Jesus Christ. Jag and Polly have paired up, we all know that, but you'd expect it, they're young, they're full of hormones. This is — bizarre. It's unhealthy.

Transmitting to James when he's supposed to be having a PSG has failed completely. Even when the headphones are playing the most frenetic events from Alfred's REM sleep or the longest periods from

Simon's, they have no effect on him whatsoever. Maybe he's got neurological issues though nothing's come up on any of the tests . . . I'm not sure it's worth persevering with him, to be honest.

I can't lose Delphine though. I can't miss out on her dreams. The best PSG results I've ever seen. Great swathes of movement, and she watches them, she follows what's happening with her eyes. Never seen an ocular result this sharp; it's like lucid dreaming only she's entirely unconscious. If any dreams are going to transmit successfully, it's got to be these. I just wish she'd not chosen Beauman as her new paramour. Of all the people. I can't fathom it. I'm trying not to think about it.

Day seventeen: Friday

She is in Florence. Without me.

My dear James

I loved Italy, I loved our time here. I will never forget Florence. You believe me, don't you? There are things we have done and seen together which will stay with me always.

But the second time we went, later – did you not notice how much I was crying? You must have known. Why didn't you ask me why?

D

My reawakened interest in Italy was quite obviously something to do with my discomfort about taking Delphine to France; I can't deny it. *Bella Italia* was a delightful rediscovery of places I'd not visited for years and I took Delphine there twice – a whirlwind visit to the major cities in the summer and a week's holiday in Umbria early this spring. Her Italian was about as good as mine, if not slightly ropier, and she had only ever been to Rome before, so I was able to feel sufficiently propri-etorial about some of the places we saw. It sounds pathetic to say so, but that was a concern.

Now I think of it, I did notice her crying a lot earlier this year. We'd be looking at the view of a poppy field or resting from a walk in an olive grove and I'd turn to point something out to her and realise she was crying. It seemed like a perfectly reasonable thing to do in the face of such beauty; sometimes the sights of the *Bel Paese* brought tears to my eyes. I once put my arm around her shoulders and hugged her, saying something understanding and comforting like, 'It's so rich, isn't it, my love? Almost too much to take in,' and she wiped her eyes and squeezed my hand before we moved on.

Perhaps she wasn't crying at the view. Not the view in front of her at the time, anyway.

Florence was our place. I think that's what she's talking about in the postcard. We had one of our best days – one of the best and most memorable days of my entire life – in Florence. We had arranged the break only a few days earlier and Delphine had made the bookings on the internet, with her usual, unnecessary budgetary control. This involved an awful flight on a 'no frills' airline. For 'frills' read 'comfort', 'courtesy' and 'customer service'.

'Delphine,' I said in horror, 'what have you done? Look at the size of the staff! No wonder the baggage weight limit is so low; I'm amazed we got off the ground at all.'

She admonished me but giggled anyway, because I had a point. Or at least, the unflattering uniform of T-shirt, slacks and quilted body warmers made even the skinny ones look hefty.

'You are horrid, James. They're very friendly.'

'I don't want friendly. I want polite. I want subservient. I want free drinks! I want to see an over made-up woman of a certain age wearing a silly hat at a jaunty angle walking down the aisle and offering me a G&T!'

'Stop it! Next time you can book it, OK?'

'Agreed. And I hereby vow to pay whatever premium guarantees the presence of such hostesses in future.'

The hotel was not one I'd have chosen either – too central, overlooking a noisy street, with faulty air conditioning, and not as clean as it should have been. The room was dark even with the shutters open, and the heat wrapped itself around us without mercy. I was severely disappointed to find that the Uffizi, where I'd wanted to stand Delphine in front of the 'Birth of Venus' and watch her face, required pre-booked tickets so we'd had to buy them for the following day even though we were due to fly to Rome in the late afternoon. Instead of enjoying the cool beauty of Botticelli's masterpiece, we spent the morning at the Pitti Palace and Delphine laughed in disbelief as we progressed through room after ornate room hung with hundreds of paintings; the walls and ceilings covered, relentlessly, with mischievous cherubs, suffering saints, battling gods and reclining goddesses. She picked out a small painting of St Agnes and stared at it with her hand clasped to her mouth, whether from mirth or horror I couldn't tell at first.

'Look at what she's doing,' she pointed, 'look at what she's got on that plate!' The mutilated saint, serene and robed, proffered a golden platter heavenwards on which were arranged two perfect white hemispheres each adorned with a deep pink nipple. 'Her tits! She's giving God her tits on a plate!'

Delphine was so taken with the picture that she wasn't interested in seeing anything else and bought half a dozen postcards featuring the severed breasts to send to her friends who would be, she was convinced, just as impressed as she was. So we left the palace and walked all the way up to the top of the Boboli

Gardens and all the way down again, getting lost in the process and covering what seemed like miles in our attempt to find the path, before trudging back to the hotel for a siesta.

I was tired, hot and dusty, and flung myself on to the lumpy bed in relief. Delphine emerged from the bathroom looking annoyed. 'My bloody period has started. Damn, it's three days early and I haven't brought anything with me. I need to get some Tampax, James, there's a chemist across the street, I'll only be a minute.'

I grunted, half asleep, and was awoken five minutes later by her knocking at the door. As soon as I opened it and stood back to let her in, I noticed her expression and I immediately, and literally, sprang into action. We undressed rapidly, flung ourselves on to the bed and *gorged* ourselves on one another for the next two hours. She was bleeding heavily; it was every-where, all over my face and hands, sticking to my loins and belly, and at one point, as I pulled out of her from behind, I had to bring her hand downwards to make a cup between her thighs and catch a splash of the stuff while I rushed to get towels. We were wild: bruised, marked and swollen by each other's teeth and nails, dripping with sweat and semen and that glorious rusty stain streaking our skin, so that our bodies in the late afternoon light looked like they had come out of the earth. We exploded into orgasm at first, she came again and again until it made her laugh almost hysterically, and then we worked hard at them, dragged them from each other's aching bodies, the almost-pain of those tiny, frantically won climaxes making us moan as though we were engaged in mutual torture rather than the simplest, strongest expression of love and desire I had ever experienced. It wasn't just the triumphant atavism of a good fuck. We were often face to face and sharing a gaze which, in all its ecstatic fire, was grounded in openness, trust and certainty. I thought at the time – she's looking at my *soul*. And even in the heat and thrill of those hours I knew, was proud and joyful to know, my soul had looked right back at her, at hers. It was as terrifying as it was wonderful – the *energy* that came off us, the *power* – and we lay in each other's arms until late that night, kissing and dozing, every cell of our being throbbing slowly, silent save for our breathing.

At ten o'clock, our bodies cooled by the night air and the blood dry on our skin, we showered and cleaned up – Delphine washed the sheets and hung them by the window while I rinsed the towels as best I could – then we went to a restaurant around the corner to eat hearty bowls of *ribollita*, swimming with olive oil and torn basil, and great slabs of charred red steak with fried potatoes and salty zucchini, and huge glasses of Chianti. We devoured the food and threw back the wine with sparkling eyes and ridiculous grins and later, when we eased ourselves into what was left of our bed, just before I turned out the light I looked into her eyes.

'What do you feel now?' I asked her.

Sleepily, she looked back at me and whispered, 'Tired. Happy. Powerful.'

'As if nothing can hurt us,' I agreed with satisfaction.

She kissed me, turned around, and I just caught her whisper, 'I didn't say that.'

We slept for eleven hours and I didn't wake once.

'Delphine,' I used to say some nights after we'd made love and her head would be on my chest.

'Hmm?'

'Delphine, will you sleep with me?'

She'd give a drowsy laugh and say, 'James, you are a little forward! What a question!' And then she'd lean up to kiss me and say, 'But yes, yes of course I'll sleep with you. Now hush.'

I can't remember if I'd ever used that phrase before. Sleep with me. I didn't really use phrases, things usually happened wordlessly. But Delphine was the only woman I'd ever slept with – I mean, actually slept with – for a whole night and I liked to remind her of that. It was my battered, belated version of virginity.

Day eighteen: Saturday

My dear James

My dreams don't mean nothing but they don't necessarily mean *something*. Can you imagine how tiring it is to be in the presence of someone who believes that you require constant protection *from your own subconscious*? You thought them freakish. Huw could at least accept that they weren't, he was even able to help me laugh at them a little. But they fascinated him too, he still thought they were codes he could crack if he spent enough time trying to *understand* me. Understanding me is easy, I never shut up, remember? And I always say what I mean and I don't tell lies. You, with your no-lies-but-no-honesty-either, and him, with his private studies and preoccupations – you two are much more difficult to work out but you both acted as though you were normal and I was the deviant. I think that's the wrong way round.

D

Delphine thought I'd never told the truth 'properly', especially to women. However many times I assured her I had never strung anyone along, she always tried to disprove it. Having reached my half-century with the sexual aspect of my life in good order, the conversations I used to have with Delphine on the subject preyed on my mind even when she was here. Now, recalling them torments me. And the women torment me, or their memories do, all those warm, generous, sensuous souls who floated or trotted or zoomed through part of my life and took up all its time until I decided their time was up. And almost all of them took it so well. I preferred to let it fade away gradually until they realised that the phone had stopped ringing and the message hit home, gently. In the same way, I avoided loud confrontations, especially about 'the relationship', which I always associated with domesticity, the familiar contempt which grows between cohabitees. Women who showed signs of dwelling too much on The Relationship inevitably heard from me less and less. It seemed they wanted to own me, and as a young man and even into my early forties any lover who took too much of an interest in my life away from her seemed to be suffocating me. I'd calmed down by the time I met Delphine and had begun to enjoy the notion of a confidante: one woman in particular, Eleanor, reappeared in my life after a decade of absence and for several months we seemed to be combining a mature friendship with an uninhibited sexual relationship, an intelligent approach I thought, until she explained that she loved me. My surprised silence gave her every answer she wanted and I haven't seen her since.

But, as I told Delphine, Eleanor chose to finish the affair, not I. At no point did I lead her to believe that our relationship was anything but pleasurable to me. She just didn't get back in touch, went out of the door quietly and with a rather blank expression, while I sat there wondering when she'd call again and whether there would be new lingerie. Delphine disagreed with my analysis of the situation. 'You broke her heart,' she observed, talking in that quiet, neutral voice she always tried to use when commenting on my sexual past. 'You ended it, not her.'

'That's simply not true. Why would I pretend I'd been rejected if it was in fact vice versa?'

That put paid to the neutral tone; Delphine became very angry very quickly. 'It's not all about who dumped who, James! How *immature* of you to even think about it in those terms! You were behaving as though you loved her and taking all her love for you, and so what else could she believe except that it was reciprocated?'

I began to protest, 'But we never spoke in terms of *love*! We had great times together and were physically very compatible; we knew each other well.'

'Precisely! You'd known her for years; she would think that you had some kind of *respect* for her . . .'

'I did. I do respect her, enormously. In fact when I stopped seeing her the first time round I did consider trying to get back in touch because I – I missed her.'

'Did you tell her that this time?'

'Yes, at some point I think I did. It pleased her.'

'Well, don't you think that gives her the impression that you were rather more serious about it all this time? What kind of man would try to treat her the same way twice?'

'I gave her no false hopes. I made her no promises. I don't see why you're trying to demonise me in this way, Delphine, I . . .'

'You are like a demon!' She was becoming overly theatrical by now which always scared me. 'How could you treat her so badly if you liked her so much? Don't you think she might have believed you'd grown up in ten years? And that if you had the same stupid fear of commitment the last thing you'd do to a woman you respect is make her suffer because of it again?'

I was angry with Delphine for her downright refusal to understand the complexity of the matter. But I hated to see her upset and assumed – incorrectly, as it turned out – that her anger with me was down to simple jealousy. 'I'm sorry, my love, I shouldn't have mentioned Eleanor. It's not good for us to dwell on these things.'

Her face was flushed now and she practically screamed at me. 'My God, you think I'm *jealous* don't you? I'm desperately trying to understand you, to see how you can be like you are with me when you've been so horrible to women all your life, and all you can think is that I'm *jealous*! James, look at me, do you think it matters to me that you've had so many lovers? Do you think I sit around wishing you'd been celibate or that we'd met ten years ago? Of course not. What bothers me is . . .' she seemed to slump slightly, as the gale subsided, and she sat opposite me and held both my hands. '. . . what bothers me is this,' at which she leaned forward and kissed me. Our kisses were always beautiful: even when I bent down to kiss her goodbye before leaving for work I would feel the cool of her inner lip and I could never leave it at a peck, I was drawn inwards like the proverbial bee to honey and hated the moment of turning away from her mouth and going out into the world. That kiss – the kiss she gave me after being so angry – is something I will never forget. It was as though my heart were in my mouth, giving itself to her. When she had finished I had forgotten what she had begun saying, but she continued as though only a second had passed, 'and how you can do this with me but have acted like that with the others. Why have you changed the pattern? And what happens if it changes back again?'

I tried to reassure her, 'It's because nobody else has ever mattered to me this much. Nobody has affected me like you do. It's because I've never really loved a woman before.'

She looked shocked, and at first I thought she looked a little pleased too, but I was wrong.

'You have never loved a woman before me?' she asked incredulously.

'I don't think I have. I've been in love – I've done the infatuation bit and the fascination, even the romantic stuff, to some extent. But the feelings have never lasted. I don't just mean the sex; I mean the – the care, the concern, the enjoyment, the stimulation.'

The wonderful moment of our kiss was left hanging precariously in the air and I just couldn't understand how I had made that happen. 'Delphine, what's wrong? Don't you see what I'm saying? You're the first, the only woman I've truly loved.'

She looked anxious and a little impatient. 'I hope to God that's not true, James. I don't think it is true, that would be monstrous.'

'I'm not lying.' I sounded as distressed as I felt and her face softened. She stroked my hand.

'I know you're not lying. I know. But what you're saying still isn't true. I think that for a man who knows so many things about women you haven't learnt much about loving them . . . And I don't understand why that is.' She looked at me very seriously. 'Perhaps we can find out.'

From what she was saying it appeared that she thought there was something odd about the way I'd conducted my previous relationships with women. And I was disconcerted by her reaction to discovering I'd never loved anyone before her; a revelation which I thought would bring her great confidence in my true and unique feelings of love for her.

I do actually feel a bit sorry for myself, the self I was at that time, because it was all so unfamiliar and tricky that I really was out of my depth. It hadn't occurred to me that I might tell the truth − tell it how it was for me − and for that not to be true. And for someone listening to me to know both that I wasn't lying and that what I said wasn't true. Because she was right, of course. I see now that I can either own up to being a heartless automaton incapable of love or a foolish man who has closed his eyes and heart to love. Either way I have to own up to something unpalatable. It's the latter, of course. I could have loved other women. Not many, and not well, but I think there were three: a girl I went out with at Oxford but who ended the relationship after two years having caught me *in flagrante* with a friend; Cathy, the married colleague with whom I had a five-year affair, and Eleanor. So yes, I think I did love Eleanor, certainly the first time we were 'together' and possibly more recently too. To have acknowledged that Eleanor's departure left any sort of a gap in my life would have left me open to the most appalling level of distress and upset; easier to close the door and move along, with perhaps a philosophical sigh of regret.

Delphine even gave me the phrase which described how I'd treated love. 'You don't *honour* love,' she told me the morning after our argument. She often slept on a troubling issue and woke up with a fully formed idea or phrase to describe or deal with it. Sometimes it was quite annoying. 'You *have* loved women but instead of admitting that, to them and to yourself, which makes you vulnerable, you have found reasons to get them out of your life. But even then you don't want the responsibility for doing that; you have to try to make out that they're leaving of their own accord. You have done terrible things, not honouring love. I still don't see why you seem to be honouring this love, but I'm very glad you are.'

Her final words, arriving on the heels of such awful criticism, made me feel pathetically grateful. I suspected that the criticism was justified at the time though I couldn't quite comprehend it, and now I understand it very well but am a little more sympathetic to myself. She could be terribly judgemental.

I'd had a lousy childhood and an almost friendless adolescence and then when I was eighteen I'd discovered that I could make love to women. That I could approach them and woo them and they would respond more warmly than anyone had responded to anything I'd ever said or done.

Sex has been the most straightforward and satisfactory pursuit, the most downright honest act I've ever committed. It was quite shocking to think that the truth of it might be different. Or that Delphine thought I had acted like some misogynistic cad.

While she was talking I had been waiting for her to tell me that, as a result of my previous treatment of undeserving women, she was leaving. I wouldn't have let *that* happen without a word; I would have fallen to my knees and begged if it would make her stay.

She didn't force me to go to those lengths. In a way, such a gesture would have made me feel I was paying some penance for past behaviour, but why should I be allowed such an easy get-out? I didn't quite understand her insistence that honour was the greatest gift a man could possess, but I did my best. It always sounded so medieval when she spoke about it; as though a chap should carry the chivalric code in his back pocket, just in case.

I'm not unaware of the impression I give to those who don't know me. I realise that most people wouldn't think of me as the last of the red-hot lovers, for example, whereas that's actually an arena in which I'm extremely comfortable. No need for false modesty here; by anyone's standards I am an attractive man: six foot one, lean, good features, not completely grey yet. And I've taken excellent care of the gifts my genes have bestowed on me. Decades of bachelorhood and a lively curiosity have made me a devotee of the erotic arts; I am not one of the fusty, dandruffed, pinstriped half-centenarians you see on the Tube and whom you know in an instant haven't been near a naked woman for twenty years and even then they were probably paying. Whilst not being what one would call predatory, I am perfectly capable of exchanging glances with a woman, introducing myself, engaging in social intercourse and generally assessing our mutual compatibility before deciding whether or not to pursue the matter. And if I choose to proceed then yes, that is in a rather old-fashioned and courteous way, involving dinner out and visits to art galleries, followed by an invitation to my flat, a taste of my not inexpert home cooking and several glasses of very good wine – but then the manners are left with my shirt, hung over a chair or tossed on the floor, whatever seems appropriate in the circumstances.

The line between our social and sexual selves has always fascinated me and the ease with which I cross it – in both directions – has given me great pleasure. The women to whom I have made love sense that ease and, if that spark exists between us, happily surrender to the dark sexual world as easily as they accept the offer of a door opened for them by a gentleman. Women, I have learnt, can swoon deeply into the darkness and leap back into the daylight in a matter of seconds; I suspect that this knowledge is not common amongst men and that ignorance must lead to many a ruined love affair or marital dispute. And all that rubbish about male sensitivity and responding to a woman's needs has set the younger generation – both sexes – off on entirely the wrong track. What a woman needs is a man who knows what he's doing, and there comes a point at which a man must be 'outside', in control, of himself and what is happening, and when a woman's expression of pleasure must not be confused with a signal for a change of pressure or pace. Usually, they simply want more of the same and even if it takes a supreme effort of will and restraint not to go at it like hammer and tongs, patience will become its own reward. So much of what's touted as 'male sensitivity' comes down to the pure selfish anticipation of being awarded the scout badge for Best Lover. It's only natural.

I think that Delphine was surprised – and yes, perhaps even a little shocked to begin with – on our first night together, when I left the familiar character of James to inhabit the body of her lover. But I know that the transformation became a necessary secret between us and in no time at all she was leaving the Delphine we knew and loved, all modest and precise and only the faintest bit flirtatious, sipping cocktails at a smart bar, while in my bedroom she groaned and bared her teeth against my shoulder and her smooth pale limbs were writhing and unfurling around me.

Delphine knew a man who said that he always knew, infallibly, when it was time to end a relationship with a girlfriend. All the women he had gone out with or lived with, however different their characters, had the same habit of buying him little presents, leaving notes under his pillow, sending silly messages of love via text or email at odd moments, popping chocolate into his suitcase before he went away. He thought of this as a classic girl thing to do, a kind of multi-tasking whereby, despite carrying out all their daily duties at work and home, they were able to think about him continuously. He never reciprocated; it wasn't natural to him.

Anyway, in the first flush of love he would enjoy the girl's tender messages and surprise gifts. Then, in the calmer months following, the time of happy, easy getting to know each other, he would bear it cheerfully, if incredulously. Then one day he would hear his mobile beep while he was in the pub with friends, or the message window would pop up on his PC at work, or he'd put his hand in his pocket to get change for the newsagent and find a Love Heart sweetie saying Kiss Kiss or some such nonsense, and he would be *overcome* with a massive wave of intolerance. And then he would know, he would absolutely *know*, that he was going to have to end it all. But he told Delphine that he had developed a problem with this knowledge. He had begun to enjoy it perversely, to take great pleasure in those days or weeks before he delivered the *coup de grâce* when he knew what was on the cards but wasn't showing his hand. He would be giving the girl a kind of swansong to which she was completely oblivious and it gave him such a thrill, especially the sex, which was imbued, for him, with a strong tang of nostalgia and regret which made it exotic and delightful. Because of her ignorance of what was happening, it somehow felt as though he were making love to an entirely different woman. His behaviour towards the soon-to-be-ex would improve rapidly as the time for her departure approached, he would become as passionate and loving as he had been in the early days of their affair, and so it was the greatest shock for her to be given the heave-ho when everything seemed to be going so well. Nowadays, he told Delphine, he had started to long for that revelatory moment of irritation so that he could begin the exquisite countdown to breaking up.

That man wasn't one of her former lovers. In recent years she'd had a trio of affairs with married men: two were around my age and one, her last lover, about a decade her senior. They all ended badly. I found it hard to imagine her as the Other Woman; she seemed far too direct and honest – and demanding! – to want to share a man in that way, but when I expressed my surprise she just shrugged and said, 'I don't know exactly why it happened. I didn't go looking for married men. I know I've always been attracted to men who are a little older than I am but it seemed to me that the fact of their being married meant that they must really love me. To take the risk, you know.'

I'd never heard this take on marital infidelity. 'Do you think they saw it as a huge risk, really?' I asked her.

'No, of course not. That's what I finally realised. It was quite safe for them, because I would never exert pressure on them or try to make them leave their wives but I was always available to see them. A completely sane and single mistress is a useful accoutrement.' She sounded sad and a little bitter. 'And my other fault was to believe them. When they said they never slept with their wives. I believed they no longer loved their wives – I still believe that – so I just thought well, of course he doesn't sleep with her. I wouldn't sleep with a man I didn't love.'

'Even if the man was your husband?' I asked and she looked shocked at the question.

'James, if the man was my husband I would love him,' she insisted, a little primly.

'I think men see these things differently,' I suggested. 'They probably do love their wives *in a way* but they want the excitement of another, more passionate relationship.'

'I always thought they really loved me,' she said, and I remember feeling that it was a rather odd reassurance for me to have to give her as I said, 'I'm sure they really did love you. I'm sure they did, Delphine.'

But she didn't believe me. 'At the same time as they loved

their wives? You really think so? Then we mean different things when we talk about love, James, completely different things.'

But, whether or not we agreed on all such matters, it's certainly true that I, supposedly the sophisticated older man with so much experience behind him, found it hard and painful to confront the truth about my relationships with former lovers whereas my young, faithful, tender-hearted Delphine thought nothing of striding into my murky past and holding up to scrutiny whatever she found on the way. A shield-maid combing the field of battle for trinkets, or weapons, or severed heads. And it was never with reproach or vindictiveness; I see how she was trying to make me look back in honesty so that we could look forward, hopefully and trustingly, together. It saddens me to think that a year with me left her with neither hope nor trust.

Day nineteen: Sunday

Dream Lab was changing. After ten months – the latter three with Delphine as a group member – the signs of transformation, albeit a gradual one, were there. And it wasn't changing for the better; there seemed to be less of that feeling of camaraderie I'd experienced at the beginning and Reeves' sole interest seemed to be the nature of everyone's dreams. Indeed, he showed signs of impatience when anyone quietly mentioned their desire to get a good night's sleep. I assumed his research wasn't proving what he'd wanted it to prove.

He was once quite sharp with poor Jagdev. We had become used to the way in which the lad's narcolepsy would affect him – he would occasionally drop off mid-sentence or even mid-word at a speed I always found astonishing even after I'd seen it happen half a dozen times, but his recovery was usually within twenty minutes. The time I'm thinking of was just like all the others, apart from Reeves' response.

Jag was standing behind Julie, showing her some family photographs. His mother was widowed when he and his three younger sisters were all quite small, and it seemed that every other weekend he was escorting them all to some enormous family wedding in North London. The photographs were of the latest extravaganza and, looking over Julie's shoulder, I scarcely recognised Jag in a smart, if slightly sharp, suit, wearing a turban. Quite the family man.

'That's my middle sister,' he was saying, 'and that's my cousin Sukhdev, and that's . . .'

Julie said, 'Jag, are you OK?' and I saw that the hand which held the photograph was beginning to shake. Fortunately Simon was sitting beside Julie so the two of us were able to catch Jagdev with ease and were just placing a cushion under his head when Reeves entered the room.

He sighed. 'Oh for God's sake, not again! He did this in front of the Vice Chancellor at lunchtime.'

There was no mistaking the harsh tone, and I caught Julie's eye which mirrored my surprise. Delphine spoke to Reeves quietly in admonishment. 'Huw, you've been encouraging Jag to reduce his medication. It's not really fair to blame him for this happening, is it?'

He instantly apologised and made excuses about 'a bad day'

but it was so unlike him to be so rattled that I remember it very clearly. Even though Jag had been unconscious when it happened he must have picked up something in the atmosphere of the room when he came round ten minutes later. Perhaps it had already been in the air: he and Reeves had previously enjoyed a close working relationship but those days they certainly seemed less enamoured of one another. I wondered if Reeves was jealous that Jag was a part of this lab – or perhaps he felt that Jag's association with another group member was unprofessional.

I had realised, after a few months of our starting to meet, that Jag and Polly had become romantically involved, though they kept it quiet. It seemed a potentially calamitous match. In idle moments I imagined terrible incidents where she sleep-walked off into the night and he went looking for her, only for them to collide at the top of the stairs at which point he would fall into a deep slumber and one of them would drop to a messy death while the other awoke the next morning to discover a corpse in the hall.

Narcoleptics can be treated with the same kinds of drugs which are routinely given to children with Attention Deficit Disorder. Stimulants like Ritalin, which can help prevent narcoleptic attacks, often disturb the sleep patterns of children with ADD. A significant number of children with ADD already have a serious sleep deficit. So while the drug treatment initially improves their daytime behaviour, their sleep pattern becomes even more seriously disrupted, and any long-lasting behavioural improvements without further drugs are unlikely. I know people who like to joke that the contraindications on the forms which accompany their prescription medicines

142

always sound worse than the original ailment; even more worrying to me is the fact that they frequently sound identical to it.

Asleep, Delphine was impervious to everything. She seemed to be encased almost; an invisible force-field contained and embraced her. She would always fall asleep quickly, more so than I, and breathe fast and shallow like a cat or a child. Even if she fell asleep on my chest or in my arms, which was rare, she would instantly turn around and cocoon herself in her invisible coat and if I woke in the night, which happened occasionally, and wanted to hold her, my tentative arm around her or an attempt to snuggle up behind her were always met with a sharp rebuff, sometimes even a little kick. She was unconscious of it, of course, but I resented the way she kept herself from me in sleep, as though she inhabited a different world during those night-time hours, one of which I was no part. Once, I sulkily mentioned the way she 'treated' me whilst asleep and she thought it the greatest joke that I took it so seriously.

'How paranoid are you, James, if you begin to read significance into what I'm like when I'm *asleep*? Really, how can I even know what you're talking about, let alone try to change it? Or want to change it. I love my sleep, I don't snore, and you like me when I'm awake, why can't you be happy with that? You can't own me in my sleep!'

'I don't want to own you. But you push me away as though you want nothing to do with me.'

'Well, all I can say is that the sleeping me obviously doesn't want anything to do with you, or anyone or anything else. If I wake up and we talk in the night I like to cuddle up, you know I do. But you can't hold me responsible for being different when I'm *unconscious*.'

I wonder now if I seemed overly possessive. Or perhaps just petulant. Either way, I can see that her amusement might very easily turn to irritation at my unfair criticism. And now, of course, the idea of her beloved sleeping self lying next to me – whether or not she's inhabiting her own, exclusive world in which I can play no part – is what I long for. There have been times in my life when the sudden return of space to my double bed has had me rolling in it and spreading my arms out like a child in a bale of hay – freedom! All mine! – but these nights, ever since she left, I've occupied my side of the bed and I realise that it's become a fetish; I can't bear to cross the invisible line in the middle because that would signify an acceptance of her permanent absence and my future solitude.

She dreamt this dream the first night we spent together:

A mother is waiting for her husband and daughter to come home to celebrate the baby's birthday. It is a poor place, the little boy is small for his age and the clothes and furnishings are humble. There is trouble here; the village is occupied, there has been violence. Her husband is a village leader and known for his outspokenness; he has been beaten up once already and she can never relax until he and their daughter are both home for the day. There have been disappearances, mysterious deaths, whispers of dark deeds. This family birthday party is to be the first celebration they have held for months. She shopped at the market that afternoon and bought sugar to make cakes, such a treat! The girl should be back already; perhaps she has visited a friend after school. It is dark now. The woman is verging on hysterical. She is hugging the baby close to her, whimpering and peering through the curtains. Then she hears footsteps approaching the door – many people trying to tiptoe. There is whispering. Her first thought is to protect her child from a terrible fate. She cannot give up this baby to those men. A knock comes on the door she has bolted shut. A louder knock. A voice she doesn't recognise shouts, 'Open up, mother, it's a cold night!' She does not answer, and the people outside begin to put their weight against the door. The woman knows what she must do. She kisses the little boy then holds him to her body, forcing his face into the fabric of her shawl. He is strong for such a small one; the kicks and struggles go on for some minutes before he is still. At that moment the door breaks open. The woman's eyes are shut as she holds out the limp body of her son, saying, 'You shall never have him,' so she doesn't see the first, appalled look on the villagers' faces, on her husband's face, as they stand with lanterns and platters of sweetmeats and musicians, all dressed up for the baby's party. Her daughter vomits on the doorstep.

She told it to me in the morning over breakfast, and then retold it in the lab the following week. Nobody knew about us. I looked at everyone's faces and saw their reactions: Reeves' fascination, Simon's disbelief, Polly's disgust, Jag's confusion, Alfred's discomfort, Julie's concern. And it was hard not to smile because as Delphine was reading, I was remembering that scene – her rolling up the sleeves of my dressing gown which completely dwarfed her, and pouring tea for us – and her words only made me acutely aware of the lovely secret we shared. I sort of understood what Reeves meant about self-definition, and what Delphine meant when she said her bad dreams didn't upset her. Hearing that dream in those circumstances just made me proud.

'Just imagine what Delphine's dreams would look like if Huw's Transmissions project ever actually worked!' Simon said in the bar later. 'Move over, Stephen King!'

This received admonishing looks from Julie and from Jag, who said, 'Hey come on now. You're always taking the piss out of the project but don't forget, I'm working on it too.'

'Sorry. Sorry, mate. It just sounds so – twenty-first century. And Huw's standing there all earnest and excited, like some mad professor, going on about capturing our dream data and transmitting it to a visual medium, while we're being careful not to nod too vigorously in case we drop off.'

Alfred's wheeze cut through the ensuing laughter and turned it to silence. 'I think it's marvellous, what he's doing. Bloody marvellous. To be a part of something like this, to be able to help – even in some small way – with a science project that's so ambitious. Well. I think it's great.'

Simon looked abashed. 'Me too, mate. Really. I mean, I know I have a laugh and that, but honestly, I realise that we need people like Huw. It's just . . . it's just that I wish we could know about some results. Feel like there's some progress. If not with our own sleeping problems, at least with his – his and Jag's – research.'

Alfred nodded. 'I understand that. But I still feel – privileged. All the work Huw does with us, well, it might end up helping people like us, mightn't it? You know, in the future. And it might tell us all sorts of things that scientists don't know. Mightn't it?'

I don't know if anyone else heard Sally's *sotto voce*, 'And then again, it might not,' but I'm pretty sure Alfred didn't, because then he asked Jag, 'How's it going anyway, Jag? Did the last results from my PSG do the trick this time?'

And Jag answered quite dismissively, 'Don't think so, Alfred. Actually, I haven't talked to Huw yet about the latest round of research. Been working on my thesis, you know. I'm sure he'll let you know soon. Don't worry about it.'

He didn't usually sound so off-hand and I thought he looked slightly annoyed.

Day twenty: Monday

She can't be getting any sightseeing done at all.

My dear James

I wish you'd told me about Finn. That day he came to the flat is amongst my worst memories. Meeting your son should have been a sweet, good day for me but as soon as I discovered who he was all I could think of was how you had kept him secret from me. And me from him. Were you scared of what I'd say or do? Your fear made me afraid that you couldn't love me well enough. Love takes courage. Do you see that? Because it takes trust, and you have to be brave to trust and even more brave to welcome the chance to be trusted.

D

My son is a stranger to me, a fact that is entirely my own doing. I should have told Delphine about him much sooner than I did. And it's true that when our conversations skirted around the subject of offspring, I was as careful to conceal the truth from her as I was to avoid lying. My justification at the time, at every time, was that now was not the right time. It became a much greater issue than it needed to be. Perhaps I was too used to women entering and leaving my life without ever having learnt of his existence, let alone meeting him. It never occurred to me that he would just turn up out of the blue; it wasn't something he had done before and it was hardly as though we were on easy terms with one another.

His mother, Siobhan, was a recent divorcee when she flew into my arms on a powerful rebound after we got talking in a coffee shop. At that time I was in the midst of an increasingly ill-humoured cohabitation with my last university girlfriend, as well as a still-passionate affair with my married lover, Cathy. Siobhan, all flame-coloured hair and extravagant gestures – interspersed with some truly terrifying stony silences – thoroughly entranced me for three months, but all the feelings I had for her fled in the moment she told me she was pregnant. I wasn't kind, I'll admit that at once, but neither was I cruel. I was simply stunned by both the news and her attitude to it: 'James, my love, everything will be OK. I don't expect you to marry me or anything. But just think, a *baby*, how wonderful, how exciting. Darling, you're not *worried* are you? You do look pale!'

I felt cold as death, and slightly sick, and utterly unable to maintain any kind of social grace. Once Fright had done its paralysing work, Flight kicked me into action and, shaking my head in disbelief, I turned and left.

The next morning, after a troubled (but still dreamless) sleep, I shouldered the burden of my responsibility, consulted a lawyer and contacted Siobhan in order to make arrangements. She remained cheerily optimistic throughout our subsequent necessary meetings, always in the coffee shop where we had first met, and I genuinely thought that she was satisfied with the outcome of our affair (her husband had not wanted a child; that was one of the issues pertaining to the divorce, and it seemed that now she had carried out a successful plan to get one) and was greatly relieved by this. It was only on the day that I waved her train off on the first leg of her journey to Galway – her home town where her two brothers still lived – that I saw her break down in tears and ask me when she would see me again and it was only then that I realised she had been hoping for some change in my attitude as the pregnancy progressed.

'I'm sorry, Siobhan. We hardly know each other, and this happened so soon into our – relationship. It completely changed my feelings for you, which were in any case hardly developed beyond infatuation . . .'

'But we got on so well. We could try. I could move back up here with the baby and we can see how it goes. I swear, I shan't put pressure on you, but this baby needs a father. And I love you very much, I still love you.'

It was an awful conversation and I could see no way of avoiding the facts without storing up trouble for the future. When I say facts, I don't, of course, mean that I was about to tell her the true state of my complicated love life, although perhaps that would have been simpler in the end. I wasn't quite that courageous. 'No. I'm not in love with you, Siobhan. And the last thing in the world that I want is a child. I'm not saying you conceived deliberately – and I completely accept my culpability – but you want a child and I don't. I don't want to see it. I want you and the baby to be happy and I hope you'll meet someone who can be a father to it but I have to tell you now, it's not going to be me. I'm sorry, I thought that was understood, I had no idea you still believed we could resume our relationship.'

She was brave, I see that now, and always maintained a kind of honour about the business that I hardly deserved. After all, we were behaving as lovers behaved and she was under the impression – an impression I carefully did nothing to correct – that my girlfriend and I no longer made love, and of course she knew nothing about my other lover. But all's fair, as they say. And while I had assured her that I didn't hold her to account for the child's conception, privately I was convinced that she had engineered it in the belief that it would bring her a new and instant family. All that passion and intensity and the crazy belief that providing me with a child would somehow make my dreams come true as well as her own pointed to a mental instability whose signs I should have noticed before but, because I was its main beneficiary – such lovemaking! Even though it was sometimes followed by such awful black moods! – I closed my eyes to it. I was relieved that Siobhan would have her family around her to support her and ensure that her mood swings didn't affect the child too much. But that was the extent of my concern for the baby.

When Finn (a silly name, but it's not really a subject on which I was, or should have been, consulted) contacted me on his eighteenth birthday, his knowledge of me was sketchy but overwhelmingly positive. Siobhan had told him that he was the result of a doomed love affair and gave the impression that my absence from his life was as a result of an agreement she and I made to save him from complications and confusion. I told him the truth soon enough, because that's the only gift I had to offer him, and I remember his face when I described my cool dealings with his mother and my disinterest in all but his general welfare.

'I can see how you'd be upset at the time,' he said reasonably, 'but afterwards — even years afterwards — did you never sit down on my birthday and — and *wonder*? Did you never think about me at all?'

'I thought about you now and then. Your mother kept me informed of your achievements and your whereabouts. But I had no great curiosity. I didn't want to be a father, and I'm *not* a father. I fathered you, but I'm not your father. And I don't see how I can become that man even if I wanted it more than anything on earth.'

'You don't even want to try?'

'Don't take it personally. You're a fine young man and I think your mother has done a wonderful job. I truly hoped she would find someone — you know, get married again — and perhaps if she had you wouldn't feel the need to come here now.'

'I've dreamt about meeting you ever since I realised you weren't there. Even if I had a stepfather I'd want to know you. I'd hoped you might want to know me.'

'I'm happy to know you, Finn. But I don't think I'll be much use to you, I don't think I'll fill in any gaps, you know,' I looked at him wryly, 'I'm probably not the man of your dreams.'

'That's not why I'm here. I don't think that's why I'm here anyway. Look, I'm sorry if this is an unwelcome intrusion, but I'm coming to college in London and so – well, will you please allow me to visit from time to time?'

It should have been me addressing him in that faintly pleading tone; me taking an apologetic stance about my abandonment of him. Instead he had to cajole me into maintaining any sort of contact and I was always aware of his disappointment, his enormous disappointment, as we shook hands in farewell after yet another afternoon of stilted, unenlightening conversation which meandered everywhere except where he wanted it to go.

There had been a few moments when I almost told Delphine about Finn. On those occasions during which we were discussing children and my absolute intention not to have any, it would have made my life a great deal easier to give the obvious excuse for my lack of curiosity in this area – I've already got one. But I didn't want to explain the affair with Siobhan, and besides, I was plagued by daydreams – little panic attacks that descended upon me now and then – about her meeting Finn and falling in love with him. Silly of me, and so Freudian. He hardly even looks like me, favouring his mother's Celtic fair skin and auburn hair rather than my darker, Norman, features, although our eyes are the same brown and we are alike in height and build, and our voices can sound similar. He's a few years younger than Delphine, not her type, happy with his own girlfriend, too pleasant and straightforward to do anything as outrageous as steal his father's paramour. But still, I feared it.

And the more I heard about her dreams the more convinced I became that her terror of motherhood was as undeniable as it was inexplicable. There were plenty of terrifying scenarios in which mothers were responsible for choosing which of their children should die or how their children should die, but the mother's responsibility for the death was always central. I remember one in which the mother was given the choice of killing her child swiftly with a knife or watching it killed slowly by a torturer. Or another where her son and daughter were hidden beneath identical wicker baskets and their lives depended on her guessing which was which. She continued to grimace wryly after reading them but insisted they did not cause her any distress. Once, the usually stalwart Polly left Reeves' office before Delphine started reading from her dream diary, because she had an upset stomach and didn't want to make it worse.

Is it any wonder I couldn't bring myself to talk to Delphine about Finn? Any mention of offspring seemed unwise.

So when he arrived on the doorstep and they made their introductions, he was accustomed to knowing nothing about me and was therefore unsurprised to meet a new live-in lover, but she, who thought I had told her the truth, the whole truth and nothing but, was appalled. I'm convinced that she never quite recovered from that meeting.

I returned from work just after Finn had left the flat and Delphine confronted me at the door in an absolute rage of tears. When I tried to explain my anxieties about telling her the truth she looked completely disbelieving, and was as enraged as I'd ever seen her.

I suspected that she would berate me for abandoning the pregnant mother of my child, but in fact she was entirely unsympathetic with Siobhan's plight in a way which I thought may have been tinged with jealousy. 'It's the most awful thing, for a woman to get pregnant by a man she knows is someone else's. I'm not saying it's not your fault too – you should have been more careful, and it's right that you should contribute towards the costs of a child – but it's a kind of theft.'

I was amazed that she should be so disapproving of Siobhan. 'Some women are so desperate to have a child that they just get pregnant with the first man they meet,' I pointed out, 'and she must have realised that it was perfectly possible I wouldn't want to marry her and bring up the child.'

'Even worse!' Delphine insisted. 'To bring a child into the world just because *she* wants one. Without thinking that it needs a father and that she has no right to be so *selfish*!' She saw my look of surprise and explained, 'Because nobody has a *right* to it. If a woman hasn't got a man then she shouldn't have a baby. It doesn't mean there's anything wrong with her, and just having a man doesn't mean it's a good idea to have a baby, but these women who just feel they have a right to – I don't know – to fulfil their biological potential or something, make me *sick*!'

Such vehemence only served to confirm my already strong conviction that she had some terrible anxieties about babies and motherhood due to the trauma of her early years and growing up without her mother. Those terrible dreams and this outburst were, surely, all tributaries of the same fearful source. I started to speak comfortingly, 'Hush my love, it's OK. I didn't realise you felt so strongly about it, we don't need to talk about Siobhan again, all right?'

She was more relaxed now and able to dismiss my attempts at restoring calm: 'Oh, I'm sorry. It's not so much about Siobhan. Or even you. It's just – it just reminds me of somebody else. A postgrad at university, a woman who was *rabid* about her desire to have a baby. She had an image of herself as this lone, independent creature who would live in a remote place by the sea and become the Muse of artists – the kind of thing all fourteen-year-old girls who read a lot dream of – and she would bring up a child of nature who would be a creative genius. No thought about the child wanting a father, or her being scarcely able to take care of herself let alone a baby. She was the kind of person who would only give her cat vegetarian food.' Delphine had a problem with vegetarians although she respected vegans for their consistency. 'So she would hang around visiting writers and try to seduce them – which wasn't difficult; she was young and they were away from home – and try to conceive a child.'

'I don't think Siobhan was quite that bad . . .' I said, more defensively than I meant.

'I'm not saying she was. It just reminded me, that's all.'

I could tell that she wanted to end the conversation but I was curious to hear more, so asked, 'And did her plan work?'

There was a pause and Delphine took a deep breath as though she were about to tell me something of note. But then she breathed out sharply and shrugged, Gallic-fashion, and would only say, 'Oh yes. Oh yes, it worked. She conceived a baby with a man who was already someone else's man. A silly, gullible, arrogant man who acted as badly as she did.

They behaved – disgustingly. Awfully. Making a child *on purpose* that will never have a father is disgusting.'

She calmed down and looked at me with great sadness in her eyes. 'This is very hard. How can you stand there and tell me that you kept this enormous secret from me – kept your son hidden from me – just in case I'd fall in love with him? Why would I fall in love with him? Don't you see, he could have been like my brother? My little brother. Why are you so full of distrust? I can't believe you didn't tell me this!'

It was our first big row.

It wasn't just my avoidance of the truth which had riled her. Afterwards, I wished I'd asked her outright. I even wondered then if she, too, had a secret child. Where else did those dreams, those terrible dreams of motherly responsibility and fear, come from? Now, I regret not having asked her because I think we could have reached an understanding about all this. What she told me later seemed to back up my theory but I should have asked her then, carefully, when we were talking about *my* secret baby. I gave her the bare bones of the story and expected her to be satisfied, when I should have stripped myself naked, opened my heart to her, allowed her to flay me if that's what she wanted to do, but I locked it all in, and she knew it.

You know, I wouldn't have said any of that a year ago. Extended metaphors about locking in and keeping out and stripping bare and all that. Delphine had that effect on me, she changed the way I felt and thought, and how I chose to express myself. I found it so liberating to use language in a directly emotional way and it happened effortlessly, creeping up unexpectedly and filling my life with a new and delicious vocabulary which I delighted in using. Who knows if anybody around us notices these changes? Nobody mentioned it. But I'm sure I felt more warmth from people I spoke to, and enjoyed more smiles, more laughter.

That's gone now.

Day twenty-one: Tuesday

My dear James

You made such huge presumptions. All those things you said about people in the lab, you'd just made them up. Poor Julie! And Simon. None of what you said was justified.

Are you even a little bit ashamed of yourself?

D

This postcard confuses me; I'm not sure what I'm supposed to be ashamed about and even less sure how I can find out. It's the Psalm 150 window from Chichester Cathedral. Reds and salmons and rose-pinks, making a welcome change from that bloody blue. *Let everything that has breath praise the Lord.* Delphine wasn't sure whether she believed in God – probably not, she'd decided – but she used religion when it suited her. Entering any church, she'd scan around for the font to cross herself with holy water, and the stronger the scent of incense the better. She had that atheistic Catholicism which the French are so good at: enjoying the comfort of ritual without getting bogged down with belief. Anglican atheists are just atheists. But even Delphine wouldn't talk about praising the Lord. Is she tearing the damned cards out entirely at random?

I know I miss Dream Lab. I miss the others. It just didn't seem possible that they would ever find themselves *cured*. Or at least happy about, more accepting of, their disorders. Obviously, I knew that most of them were, from time to time, undergoing various forms of treatment – not all at the university and none under Reeves' supervision – but at times most members of the group embarked upon a course of therapy or drug treatment completely separately from their input into the lab. Occasionally, references to this other part of their lives were mentioned – if they were relevant to our discussions – but I never got the feeling that any *progress* was being made. Julie still looked tired, Simon continued to complain about his unsociable sleep cycle, Alfred's various attempts to breathe fluently through the night all singularly failed, Polly still arrived at the sessions sporting bruises and cuts from her nocturnal perambulations and Jagdev's tendency to fall asleep in a second continued to surface regularly. I suppose that they were all getting slightly less dramatic about their disorders and there were fewer signs of dysfunction, but I still sort of presumed that the lab would go on regardless, that we all needed that time and space in our lives.

Tensions about their treatment remained, I noticed, especially when one or other of the group members had been back to the clinic for another sleep study and had talked to one of the psychiatrists there. Invariably, they would advise drug treatments for any and all of the symptoms described, and when this was reported back to Reeves he began to get extremely twitchy. I remember one particular rant, when he said, 'There's no point at all in jumping in with a pile of drugs, just *throwing* them at the patient until, by some stroke of luck, you hit the right combination and hey presto! All sorts of side-effects can occur in the meantime, and you can just build up a dependency. You *have* to look at underlying psychological factors.'

He was talking to Jagdev that time, whose sympathies lay most naturally with his tutor, but who felt obliged nevertheless to modify what Reeves was saying. 'I don't think that's the line they take. The psychiatrist I was speaking to today was talking in terms of fixing the basic problem of brain malfunction and *then* looking at the psychology and trying that and all sorts of other therapies in order to get the patient off the drugs long-term, or at least on to as few as possible. She was adamant that you can't treat the psychological factors with any success until the patient is getting at least a reasonable amount of sleep.'

Julie joined in. 'That seems sensible. I mean, it's common sense that we all have one or other dysfunction which is giving us all sorts of symptoms which make it impossible for us to respond to a lot of treatments because we're too damned tired, or won't make the appointment at the right time,' here she nodded towards Simon, 'or we'll fall on the floor halfway through the session,' a sympathetic smile towards Jagdev, 'whereas if we can be made to feel just a little better and get just a bit more sleep, then maybe we would respond better to other treatments.'

Reeves was looking at Julie with undisguised dislike. 'I thought you were desperate to avoid drug therapies, Julie, I thought that was one of the reasons you were keen to take part in this group, to explore a more holistic approach.'

She didn't take kindly to this critical tone and was unusually feisty in her response. 'Huw, you know very well that's true; I wasn't making it up! But it's been so long now, and all the cognitive therapy and massage and acupuncture – the whole caboodle – it's expensive and it's not working. Surely you accept that for some people going down the drugs route is best?'

'I didn't mean bloody aromatherapy and basket-weaving! I meant proper analysis, a genuine attempt to get on top of the underlying stress and understand any depressive or schizoid tendencies. Look . . .' His voice softened as he realised that it was hardly fair to talk to Julie in that technical way, as though she were a colleague, almost. '. . . I'm sorry, Julie. You know my views on the subject. It seems to be a missed opportunity, to just grab some drugs and say – sorted. When the reasons you have a sleep disorder may still exist.'

Jagdev, who had been listening intently to the whole exchange, touched Julie's hand and smiled at her, and it was a gesture of such pure camaraderie that it almost brought a tear to my eye. He answered for both of them. 'We understand. We know what you're saying. Sometimes it's just – difficult.' Reeves didn't look sympathetic but Jag went on. 'And I think it's hard – harder – for someone who doesn't share this problem to really understand just how bad it gets.'

Reeves bristled. 'Meaning what exactly?'

'Just that it's maybe not that easy for you – someone who doesn't have a sleeping problem – to really see it from our point of view. To understand the kind of tiredness we're talking about.'

'How do you know I don't have a sleeping problem?' Reeves retorted. Jag clearly hadn't considered this possibility. 'You're making assumptions, Jag. But whether or not I "share your problem" is irrelevant to this laboratory, isn't it?'

Jag looked a little shamefaced and apologised. 'Yeah, I'm sorry, Huw. I suppose − I suppose I thought that if you had a sleep disorder you'd have − well, you'd have mentioned it. In all these conversations, something about it would have come out.'

'But it hasn't.'

'No. And of course you listen to us telling you about our dreams and you never say a word about yours, you never give anything away about your dreaming experiences . . .' Reeves didn't reply, although I was sure I saw his body tense. '. . . so − so, that's how it should be, that's the professional way of going about it. I'm sorry; of course it doesn't mean you shouldn't be running the lab.'

And after that uncomfortable exchange it was rare for anyone to mention their treatments at the clinic unless it was absolutely vital. It was almost as though any attempt by a group member to resolve his or her condition would be frowned upon, so after that session I had no way of knowing how successful or otherwise their treatments were proving. Having been worried about Reeves' lack of focus in the sessions I now began to lose respect for his methodology. His habitual air of *bonhomie* often seemed strained. I think I even began to resent him a little. Not just because I felt I owed him something − I was very aware that he'd held out a hand and pulled me up over some imagined precipice and that irked me as much as it gave me relief. But because he seemed to have stopped caring about the well-being of the other group members. The quality I'd grudgingly admired in him – that easy way he wore his humanity on his sleeve – was less in evidence in the months before the lab ended. He'd always seemed avuncular towards group members but as the jolly smile faded from his lips I began to feel paternal, protective of the others.

Reeves started to begin almost every session in the same way: 'Now then, let's have a look at your dream diaries.'

And out would come the PSG readouts and the bits of paper and his scrappy notebook and off we'd go. Well, off they'd go. Everyone except me.

Recurrent dreams were a fascinating topic discussed in the lab and we would revisit the subject every four or five meetings. Not everyone had them, but those who did described them vividly. After Delphine's arrival in the group everyone seemed more vivacious and expressive; I'm sure that was really the case and not just my imagination. During her first recurrent dreams session she reported that she had dreamt a few dreams twice, with minor amendments occurring halfway through, but Reeves felt it didn't amount to recurrence. This was one of those:

A mother is told that she must pay a forfeit in order to save her child's life. Her infant son is staring, wide-eyed and terrified, at the man with the big axe at his side. He is taken away from her and held fast in the middle of the village square. A box is brought out. There are scrabbling noises from within. A man puts his hand inside the box and brings out a mouse. The mother is relieved; she is not scared of mice, this will not be a torture. She takes it into her cupped hands when the man offers it. 'Now eat it,' he says. She is not allowed to kill it first. She can't do it. Every time she puts it near her mouth she is unable to put any part of it inside. She tries to imagine it as a sweetmeat, as something delicious, but cannot convince herself. She tries to quickly gnaw at it but its flinch makes her flinch. Eventually she shoves the whole mouse in her mouth and begins to chew wildly, feeling the crunch of bones and spurts of blood as the struggling creature bites back, bites the inside of her mouth, her tongue. She cannot get it into pieces, she cannot swallow it, she is too aware of claws and teeth, of tiny nails. Hysterical now, a huge retch comes from her belly and she vomits. The fatally wounded, still-squealing mouse writhes on the floor in front of her and before she can scoop it up for one last supreme effort, the axe is raised, and falls.

Afterwards she is not allowed to die. They follow her to ensure she cannot get hold of a knife, jump off a wall, take poison. She must walk in the town all day and everyone stares at her with disgust. She couldn't even eat a mouse to save her own son! they say. 'She couldn't even eat a mouse.'

'Well, thank goodness that one doesn't recur much!' said Polly, with her hand over her mouth. I don't think she was trying to control a smile, even though Delphine had said the last sentence through a genuinely amused laugh.

'Yes, it's a silly one, isn't it? I mean, I hate dreaming it but the fact it's so – so ludicrous, so *daft* – that makes me hate it less. Do you see?'

'Whatever you say.' Polly looked unconvinced and then Reeves said, 'OK, let's move along shall we. Polly?'

He wasn't exactly disapproving of Delphine on that occasion, but he tended to discourage her commenting on her dreams with even a modicum of humour. You could see he didn't like her describing it as 'daft'. He liked to take them very seriously indeed; even more seriously than I did sometimes.

He had plenty of recurring dreams to concentrate on after that: at least once a month Polly dreamed that she was trying to open the fridge and would wake the next day with a hand injury, anything from a scrape through to serious cuts. She would sleepwalk to where she thought the fridge was and then try to open it and its 'handle' could be, in reality, anything from the rough brick chimney breast to the knife rack.

Simon had a regular series of anxiety dreams in which he lived an entire day in great detail – from waking to returning to bed and falling asleep – only to wake and realise that the day he thought was over had only just begun. As he described the minute detail of mundane, domestic activities his dreaming self experienced he was leaning back in his chair in his usual casual pose, but I felt that what he was recounting was far less tolerable than he was making out. He pushed his unruly brown hair away from his forehead and sighed, saying, 'So I get through the most boring and tedious day of my life. I go through each tiny motion the average – and I mean really average – day holds and it's a relief to get to bed and think that's the end of that. But then I wake up and discover that no, that's not the end; it's the beginning, again. Sometimes it feels as though I risk dreaming that I'm living the same day over and over and never actually get to the bit where I wake up in real life.'

Reeves was leaning forward, interested. 'You mean you think you'll die before you wake?' he asked.

Simon's laugh displayed long teeth and a lot of dark pink gum. 'Nothing so dramatic, doc. Nah, I mean that I'll spend the day dreaming and re-dreaming the same dream hundreds of times in a row so when I do wake up I'll feel weeks or months, even years older, like all that time is gone, wasted.'

'Do you ever wonder whether this is a dream, what's happening now?' Reeves asked him, which was the question I would have asked him at that point too.

'No, this is different. When I had to start work at 9 a.m. I used to spend the first half of the day in a dreamlike state which was really because I was dozing on the job. But in the recurring dreams I'm talking about here, there's hardly any interaction with other human beings, only the most basic stuff like buying food in a shop or paying for a Tube ticket. Even if people I know are in the dream, we're just making arrangements on the phone or something factual, not having conversations of any depth. These dreams are a nightmare – I mean that, they are like nightmares to me – because I guess they play on all my fears about days and timing and stuff. When I wake up on a normal day it's usually early afternoon and for the first few seconds when I see the clock, even now, I panic because I think I've overslept and am going to get fired or dumped or generally shat on. Even though my nocturnal schedule seems more natural to me now, I can't shake off the old chronologies.' His face looked pained for a moment, then he shook his head, shrugged and grinned toothily again. 'So. Bummer, eh?' he said to the group in general.

Our sympathies were with him but all attention swiftly moved to Sally who reported that all of her recurring dreams – rather like her non-recurring dreams, come to think of it – were of a sexual nature. She dreamt of a huge Heath Robinson-type contraption in the middle of a room the size of an aeroplane hangar, all light metal poles and bars, levers and hinges, in which were built a large number of specially constructed seats. Sally was strapped, legs akimbo, into one of these seats, and a man she didn't know occupied another. The two seats were brought together in such a way as to make sexual penetration unavoidable. Then the machine parted and reunited Sally and her helpless lover, slowly at first but building to a pneumatic climax with a great pumping of pistons and hissing of valves, 'like a steam train!' Sally said. These dreams were a little frightening to her but quite pleasurable – she didn't feel that rape or violation was taking place – and she was able to see that some wish for an abnegation of sexual responsibility was at the root of the fantasy.

Sally's dreams of mechanically operated sexual antics were already familiar to us, and caused great hilarity (and a little smirking behind her back) amongst the group as a whole, but only I knew that she was omitting some 'material' from her re-telling: their effect upon her waking life. She was the kind of woman who made unwelcome confidences as soon as a man made love to her, as though that act were a signal for all sorts of floodgates to open. Our conversation had, naturally, frequently fallen to the subject of sleep and dreaming, and while during our 'courtship' this remained very much in a 'swapping notes' sort of spirit, the very evening of our first tryst she entrusted me with the most intimate details of her private life, completely uninvited. At the time I considered her fortunate: my trustworthiness in these matters was without blemish; I am not one of those men who love to kiss and tell.

Reeves' pat analysis of the dream – the creation of an arena in which promiscuous sexual activity could take place with no blame attached – convinced everybody. But there were certainly darker forces at play too, as Sally's *conscious* mind had become convinced that 'they' – presumably the operators of the machine – were prone to become nasty and the form this nastiness took was to demand that some feat be performed at their bidding or else innocent people would die. In Sally's case, 'they' were going to insist that she achieve orgasm within thirty seconds, at any given time of the day or night. And although she knew, rationally, that this wasn't going to happen, she still felt obliged to be prepared for it, and so set herself the task of masturbating, successfully and at speed, in appalling circumstances. When the ten o'clock news featured newsreel of fly-infested starving African children, Sally would be there on the sofa frantically wiggling through her tears. And whilst listening to a tragic drama on the radio she would jettison her sympathetic attention in favour of desperate frottage with whatever kitchen implement came to hand. She was very nearly within the thirty seconds every time, she had told me cheerfully. After I had broken with her I obviously couldn't ask for an update on her progress.

Delphine knew all about that. I had wondered how she would respond to my breaking Sally's confidence but I realised within a month or two of our being together that Delphine was happy for me to spill the beans on former lovers in spite of her generally fair code of honour. She explained this incon- sistency with wry knowingness. 'You have to tell me everything about everyone,' she had insisted, 'even if you promised them you wouldn't. You know that I won't tell anybody any of the things you tell me. About other women. I'll guard their secrets too. The important thing is that you haven't kept it secret from me.'

'OK, OK,' I put up my hands in surrender, 'whatever you say.'

But she carried on in earnest, 'But if you ever leave me you must *never* tell a soul *anything* about me. Not even my name. Do you see?'

'I don't need to see. I will never leave you.'

'Promise me that, if you did, you would keep all my secrets. You would keep me a secret from your future lovers.'

This conversation made me uncomfortable. There wasn't the slightest chance I would leave Delphine. It sounded as though she were considering it as a real possibility. 'I promise. But there's no need.'

'Yes, there is. There must be something to make me different from anyone else . . .' I was about to enumerate the multitude of ways in which she was different but she stopped me. 'If we're not together, I don't want anyone to know we were. I don't want to be just a name on the list. Better that I'm not on it at all, that I — we — never existed.'

This seemed to be such a dramatic and fearsome moment for Delphine, and so bewildering for me, that I wouldn't have breathed a word even if one had sprung to mind. I squeezed her hand and kissed her.

Perhaps she didn't trust me. She always said that my past didn't bother her and I was so clearly besotted with her that it seems impossible that she didn't feel completely confident about my attachment to her. But we seemed to have quite a few conversations in which she was imagining herself as being the current last name on the bottom of a list which hadn't yet stopped growing. There were times when my disagreements with her about sex and love – and especially honour – seemed to make her almost jumpy. I used to think it was just her irritation at my refusal to accept all of her theories wholesale but I suppose it might worry her in other, deeper ways. My track record is not impressive.

In bed that night I tried to show her how truly and well I loved her, and only her. During our lovemaking she looked lost and happy. After she had climaxed for the third time I turned her head towards me and slowed down my movements until her feet came to rest lightly on my back. 'Look at me,' I told her. She opened her eyes and our gaze didn't falter as I resumed the long final strokes up to and beyond my orgasm. The moment we usually missed, my private completion, was offered up to her and she took it. She must have seen what that meant, she can't have doubted me. She took it.

Day twenty-two: Wednesday

Today I visited my father.

I had no appointments at the office and felt such an urge to 'do something' so I called John first and insisted – so forcibly that it struck him dumb and he mutely agreed to my demands – that he fetch me at noon and drive the pair of us to the home in Hampshire where we put Father a decade ago, shortly after Mother died. She had been caring for him, with the help of a daily nurse, for five years, ever since the massive stroke which flattened him, completely *flattened* him, had done its shameless work. John and I were both surprised at the new tenderness and care which Mother showed him — their relationship when he was fit and well was always strained, with her mood swings and his occasional affairs spilling out nastily every few years and making life hell for us all. Our ungenerous conclusion had been that she was glad to have him where she wanted him and could afford to be Lady Bountiful now that nobody else could get their claws on him. I suspect there was an element of that — and now, I think who could blame her? — but there was no need to be quite so assiduous in the way she looked after him and she was probably, I think, making up for lost years in the only way she knew how.

It was too late, of course. Some of his vision and most of his speech had gone for ever — at first he would try to talk but the blorting, dribbling sounds which emerged from his loose lips disgusted him as much as us and so he soon gave up trying. He had limited use of his limbs and tried physiotherapy for a while but showed no interest in going anywhere in the house apart from his bedroom, even if he could have moved there unaided. Mother tried to play his favourite music — those awful afternoons of Wagner booming around the house to nobody's enjoyment, I'm sure of it — and read to him, but there were so few signs that he was taking any of it in that everyone else just stopped talking directly to him. A year later he had a series of smaller strokes and after that the assumption was that there wasn't much point in talking to him at all. Occasionally, if Mother was present, we might say 'Hello, Father, how are you today?' never knowing whether to leave a polite silence for the answer which would never come, or just to prattle on, but otherwise we talked over him or, preferably, in another room. As we told each other – he's just not *there* any more.

That didn't go down at all well with Delphine.

'Not there! Not there! What are you talking about?'

'I mean it's not really him any more. He doesn't hear or see well, he has no interest in anything outside, nothing can make him happy or interested . . .'

'But he's your father!'

'Yes, that body is the body of my father but *he* isn't *there*!' I shouted a little, unusually, and she became quieter.

'James, do you *know* for sure that he doesn't know what's going on around him?'

'The medics have never been sure. They say that there's lots of brain function and some days he will respond to requests to move his arm or blink or whatever but more often than not he won't. He's just limp. So while there's no solid evidence, I can only use my own eyes and knowledge of him – of what he was like – to judge that no, he isn't there any more. He's distant, uncommunicative, cold. And there's nothing I or John or anyone else can do which might bring him back.'

'What was he like? Before he was ill.'

I considered for a moment, and said, 'Distant. Uncommunicative. Cold.'

Delphine sighed impatiently. 'Is that all?'

'Yes, mostly. When I was younger I remember him being a little more involved – I vaguely remember things like having horse rides on his back and playing cricket in the garden, that kind of thing. But after we'd both left for school we seemed terribly unconnected. That was the time that he started taking mistresses as well, I believe, so he cut off from Mother as well in some ways, although that was always pretty understandable.'

'You really didn't like your mother at all, did you?'

'We were never close. She was very critical. She was quite a troubled woman and there was nothing I could do to make her better, that's for sure.'

Delphine's face softened and she hugged me. 'My poor brave boy. It's so sad that you didn't have a lovely mother to take care of you. But it's not all your father's fault. How often do you see him?'

I resented having to interrupt the delightful experience of being rocked against her firm little breasts, especially when I knew she wouldn't like my response. 'Once a year since he's been in the home. At Christmas time. John does his birthday, which is in July, and I do Christmas.' Sure enough, the rocking stopped. 'And at no point does he respond to either of us. We blether on and take gifts and he might sip some whisky on a good day, but he just stares into space and doesn't react to anything.'

She squeezed my hand and looked into my eyes with great urgency. 'James, I think it's really important that you sort this out. This is a *chance* for you to make peace with him. It doesn't matter whether he's there or not; it's just up to you to act as though he is. That's your *duty*, don't you see?'

'No, I don't see. I've said already, we weren't close and now I'm convinced he neither knows nor cares whether I'm there or not.'

She tutted impatiently. 'James, you're not *listening*! It is terribly sad if he isn't there any more, but *even sadder* if he is. You have a chance to let him know all the things about you which you never told him before, and perhaps even a chance to have some sort of reconciliation. At least to let him know that you have *forgiven* him for not being the best of fathers.'

'I'm not sure I have.'

'Well, do it, James. Forgive him *now*, quickly. You can't carry that nasty feeling around in your heart for your *father*! I will help you. Let me come with you, let's visit him, James! I'd like to, truly.'

Begrudgingly, I agreed to sort out a visit in the next month or so. But I never did. A few weeks after our conversation Delphine asked me if I'd called the home yet and I muttered something about being on the case but I couldn't bring myself to do it. A little while later she stopped mentioning it and I never talked to her about my father again.

But today there we were, emerging after an almost silent, but comfortably so, journey, from John's Bentley. I'm not sure why I wanted him to drive, it just seemed more appropriate somehow. I've a weakness for stylish cars and it's one of the few areas in which France has failed to satisfy me, though I notice that a couple of the new Renaults are looking pretty good. But just because I'm a Francophile it doesn't mean I have to overdo it. I love a French farmhouse kitchen, but only in the French countryside. And I'm not about to start covering my ceilings with blowsy floral wallpaper. So it was fine to pootle about trendily in a little red 2CV when I was a student but these days I drive – and thoroughly enjoy driving – a metallic-blue Alfa Spider. Cars and coffee; the Italians beat the French on both counts, I'm afraid.

Delphine's last lover didn't drive. She said she knew a lot of academic types who didn't. He explained it by saying that he was too neurotic to attempt to take control of a vehicle, and that even the thought of learning made him anxious. At first she found his lack of interest in cars appealing – too many past boyfriends had turned their heads at passing MGs with a longing she couldn't comprehend. But as the reality of his lack of mobility hit home and she was invariably called upon to ferry him to and from their assignations, drinking water while he enjoyed a bottle of wine with his meal or a few beers in a bar, she began to think of it as an affectation and it became an increasingly irritating feature of their relationship. Eventually she concluded that it signified a pathological retreat from taking responsibility for his own fate.

John's elegant, gas-guzzling motor – one of his ill-gotten gains from flogging mediocre wine to ignorant restaurateurs – felt like it was made to crunch up the gravel outside the terribly exclusive Rectory; a tastefully converted vicarage and stable block with two dozen well-appointed ensuite rooms decorated in varying degrees of chintz. Father's room was the most masculine available, with inoffensive leafy William Morris wallpaper, a dark brown leather armchair and a cinnamon-coloured carpet. For some reason, being able to bag him that room had given me tremendous satisfaction, despite being sure that it wouldn't make any difference to him if he ended up in one of the sickly pinky peachy alternatives. The Matron, whom I had always liked, largely because her expression never even hinted at criticism on my annual visit, came out to meet us. 'My goodness! Mr Beauman *is* honoured, seeing both of his sons at once!' she beamed, apparently without any sarcasm at all. 'He's in the lounge; would you like me to take you through?'

John and I exchanged surprised glances. Father never usually left his room. Matron noticed our looks. 'Ah yes, he's really perked up in the past few months. Still not talking, but much more responsive and the physio is very pleased with him. Follow me.'

I'd never seen the lounge properly before, just glimpsed it through the doorway, and it had always seemed to be a rather deathly place in which a few old dears sat gawping at the loud television set on the wall. Today, the TV was indeed on loud – some nature programme – and a few people were watching, but elsewhere one woman was knitting, another was doing *The Times* crossword, a couple of the men were playing cards and outside the window I saw a few smokers, their expressions identical to those you glimpse huddled under fire escapes outside office blocks – that world-weary give us a bleedin' break nonchalance combined with something like glee at being, effortlessly, the naughty ones in the class. Father seemed to be asleep in an armchair near the window, but then we saw that he was wearing headphones. Matron gently touched his hand to let him know she was there and his eyes opened. I'm sure he looked surprised to see us; certainly he seemed more expressive than last time I'd visited. His hand gestured clumsily towards the Walkman on the arm of his chair and Matron gently removed his headphones and switched it off but not before I'd recognised the honeyed voice singing 'Every Time You Say Goodbye'. Ella Fitzgerald! Whatever happened to Wagner?

'Your boys are here to see you, Mr Beauman,' she said cheerfully. 'I'll leave the three of you to it.'

Having demanded John's presence at this moment, I now felt entirely incapable of demonstrating why, and the only thought that drove me on was Delphine. I sat beside my father

175

and clasped both of his hands in mine. 'Hello, Father. John and I are here to see you. We'll be coming to see you more often from now on; I hope that's all right with you.'

There was no response from him, but John's raised eyebrows and tight lips told me his views on the matter straight away. I spoke to both of them. 'We were never sure whether you knew we were here. We convinced ourselves that you didn't, that our visits were of no benefit to you. But I think that doesn't matter. *We* are here, with you, and if there is anything we can do to help, or amuse, or entertain you, then we'd like to try. I'm sorry, Father, for being so remiss, and hope you'll let me make it up to you.'

I stopped talking when I noticed that Father's eyes were watering. It looked as though he was crying. John knelt down by the other arm of his chair. His eyes were glistening too and his face looked just the way it did when he was a boy and would feign nonchalance about a beating; that subtle clenching of his features as he battled to control them, to show it hadn't hurt. He managed to speak in a low, slightly strangled voice. 'Yes. Sorry, Father. We'll – we'll come more often.'

Matron appeared with a tea tray which she set on a nearby side table. She had assessed the situation accurately and discreetly placed a few tissues near Father's hand. I wiped his eyes and John, still looking like himself aged nine, wiped his own with the heel of his hand.

It was the first time I'd touched Father in that way. I had to place one hand against the side of his face so that I could gently dab his eyes. I steeled myself to meet his stare. All that stuff about the eyes being windows to the soul seems misguided to me. Close up, an eye is a big white ball with a coloured circle on its visible curve and a deep black hole at the centre of that. Without the surrounding muscles to shape it into a smile or a frown it's the least expressive feature of the human face. The skin around Father's eyes droops and his lids are heavy; he usually looks either sleepy or glum, but today, when I tilted his head to wipe away the tears, they fell open and the gaze which met me didn't falter. I don't know whether it was a searing glimpse into my very soul, or a look of compassion or irritation, or even of utter disinterest. He may have been gazing somewhere else and not seeing me at all. I didn't consider how I looked to him; now I hope my eyes didn't betray the uncertainty I felt during that encounter. I hope I looked like a caring son.

I've never held a child's head still and told it to blow its nose. Until today, I've never wiped away anybody's tears except my own, and never with any tenderness.

Still, Matron seemed to find it all most satisfactory. 'There, I knew he'd be pleased to see you. He's come on so much in the past few months, haven't you, Mr Beauman? Realised this isn't such a bad place after all, haven't you? Mind you, a certain lady visitor has helped, I think.' She winked at Father, who didn't respond, and told us, 'We've had ever such a good volunteer coming once a week for the past few months. I mean, quite a lot of people come and help us out with this and that, but they've never been as useful to us. She's a lovely young woman – doing a psychology course and wants to work in geriatrics. She just chats to everyone really, they all love her, but she's made a special friend of your father and she was the one who persuaded him to leave his room and join in with things a bit more.'

I knew at once. 'What day of the week does she visit?'

'Wednesdays, though we haven't seen her for a little while. She wrote to me and said she was travelling. We've all missed Delphine, haven't we, Mr Beauman?'

Father didn't respond, again, and although John and I stayed to chat a little longer – doing our best to come up with subjects which might interest him and realising in shared shame that all John could talk about were the kids and the house and the state of the French grape harvest while my conversational topics were a recent office redecoration and the cricket scores – there was no sign that our presence was appreciated. But it didn't matter, certainly not to me and I think not to John either. Despite our limited ability to communicate with Father and the extreme unlikelihood of any sort of reciprocation, I did feel as though we were doing some good. As much for me as for Father, but good nevertheless. I didn't talk to Father about Delphine; I wonder if she told him who she was.

John and I hardly spoke on the journey home, but he insisted on driving me to my door rather than dropping me near a Tube line as I suggested and we agreed a schedule of further visits, alone and together. He's going to take the kids to see their grandfather, or at least try to persuade them. They haven't seen him for years; Stacey thought that visiting the home would upset them and John didn't push it. I wonder what Father made of us today. And whether he's any more proud of us than he used to be. John was always more of a mother's boy and she was delighted when he decided to use his university contacts to help set up his own business; it seemed exciting and go-getting to her but our father was less impressed by the notion of trade. His hopes were set on me to follow him into banking and even though my choice of career was hardly radical, I knew that he was disappointed that I'd rejected his own steady, lucrative calling. He saw my desire to travel as a foolish affectation and one which would cost me any stability in my life. Thinking about my days at the desk in the office and my painfully unglamorous working life, I may as well have been a banker. At least bankers don't have great ambitions to be thwarted.

Father was a very handsome man; I look much the same as he did at this age and I do all that sort of stuff, catching a terrifying glimpse in the mirror and thinking for one second that I've turned into him, same as anyone else. All my own hair, and while it's peppered with silver there's still plenty of black there too. Hazel eyes with lots of green flecks. Strong features, dark brows, visible cheekbones. The same height and leanness and smooth skin which tans gently in early June and is never pale. While poor old John tends towards fat and is almost bald, Father passed on some useful genes to me for which I am now, finally, thankful. Even today, the state he's in, you could see what a good-looking fellow he'd been in his younger days. I wonder if he'd ever thought about doing something other than following his father into the bank, if he ever dreamt of a different life. My only consolation, knowing that if I asked him now he couldn't answer, is that he probably wouldn't have answered me fifteen, twenty, twenty-five years ago. Perhaps he *was* thwarted.

This was here when I got home:

James, whenever I smile into a camera, I'm always smiling at you. I saw a photograph of me taken two weeks ago. I remember being very miserable. But I'm smiling out, even my eyes are smiling, and I look happy. When I

looked at it and wondered how I'd hidden being sad,
I realised about those smiles.

D

Still Chagall – water, this time, from Notre-Dame Baptistry.
The card was from Hanoi. She went to Vietnam then. Without
me.

And yet – am I being too optimistic to see this as the
most positive thing she's said to me for weeks? Months,
even. Surely by telling me about her smiles, all her smiles
being for me, it suggests that she still has feelings for me,
perhaps feelings of which she hasn't truly been aware until
now? I'm putting aside the paranoia about who was taking
the photograph, and where she was when it was taken, and
trying to think about what she wants me to *do* with this
knowledge. That's always confused me; it's obvious that she
doesn't want me to reply and last week I got back another
unopened envelope from her mother's address so any
attempts to do so have been fruitless. Yet there must be
some *point* in it, something more than catharsis for herself.
She could get that by just writing the cards and throwing
them away or putting them in a scrapbook. I feel sure –
and I do realise that I *want* to feel sure so am testing the
sensation carefully and daily – that I am supposed to do
something, that these messages are supposed to have a
particular effect on me. It feels like a test. Perhaps I will be
examined on their contents at some point, in some way.
The thought excites me; I feel exuberant about the possibility
of a test. It would be something to aim for, at least. I'd like
Delphine to send me a treasure map and a list of clues which

180

shoot me off around the world in search of her. I expect it won't be quite that glamorous, this thing I'm supposed to do. Perhaps she doesn't even know what it is. All I know is that it's my quest and that in pursuing it I shall wear her colours and seek her favour.

Day twenty-three: Thursday

I can't quite remember when Reeves started to take Delphine off for sessions on her own but it must have been about six months after she'd joined. Not just for PSGs but for all sorts of other tests. 'Mostly just questionnaire sort of things,' she told me nonchalantly. I do remember how odd the lab felt afterwards. It was something to do with Reeves' cutting-edge project which he called 'Transmissions', and although it was supposed to involve Jag it really seemed to rely on the technical expertise of whizz-kid Wayne from the Sleep Clinic. The notion of 'harnessing' a subject's dream and 'transmitting' it on to a screen sounded like such a mad fantasy that I didn't give it much thought, but Simon and a couple of the others continued to be intrigued.

'Do you really think, Huw, that some day we'll be able to *see* people's dreams?'

Reeves nodded with great certainty. 'Oh yes. I don't doubt it. The fact that the machinery which measures brain activity is becoming so much more sophisticated – and so quickly – means that it's going to be a wholly natural progression.'

I thought this was preposterous. 'What, you really think

that at some point in our lifetime we're going to be able to *project* our dreams on to a screen for everyone else to see?'

There was an uncomfortable pause as Reeves thought how to respond but he evidently decided not to pull his punches, as he said, 'In *my* lifetime. Yes, I think that will happen.' I blushed, a rare response from me, but more from anger than humiliation. He went on, 'But obviously we're right at the start of it all. Wayne and I are experimenting with the technology but it's way beyond both our level of expertise and what's possible in terms of science at the moment. Top people are already working on it in the US and elsewhere but there's not much information available just yet. We think that what we *can* do is start trying to identify which areas of brain activity are most likely to undergo successful transmission . . .'

'You mean the strongest signals?' I asked. 'The greatest REM density?'

'Probably. But it may be the most prolonged activities of REM sleep that transmit better. Or those which take place in a particular part of a REM sleep phase. We're not sure yet.'

I remember Julie asking a question then, and I was surprised by the sharpness in her voice. 'Huw, you haven't spoken about this element of your research to us very much. I know you've worked on it a bit with Alfred and Simon, and now with Delphine. But do you think you could fill us in a bit more?'

Reeves shuffled a little. I sensed he was wishing he'd never brought the subject up. 'Well, it's been a topic I've *wondered* about for years. But I've only really got together with Wayne to work on it in the last couple of years and it's been – well, it's been a sideline. You know I've been looking at your REM phases with this in mind, don't you? And we hadn't got much further than that, but now I think I'm actually making some progress.'

In his enthusiasm, he had completely forgotten his discomfort; so Julie's annoyed tone seemed to give him a jolt. 'So when you got this group together – the Dream Lab – you had this research in mind?'

'Not exactly, no. Well, partially, perhaps. Wayne and I collaborated on who might be the best people to have in the group . . .' his voice faltered.

'Best on what basis?' asked Julie. 'You told us that we were representative of different sleep disorders and that your research was all about the effect of those disorders on dreaming. This business about transmitting dreams was scarcely mentioned. What were the real criteria for being "the best"?'

He seemed even more nervous now. 'It *was* for that reason, exactly as I said. But in addition, we ensured that all of you – everyone I invited to join this lab – had produced polysomnographs which showed long periods and high densities of REM sleep. In the hope that this was the area which might possibly lend itself to transmission.'

I joined in at this point. 'So I'm not here as the control?' I asked, irritated at having been kept in the dark about all this.

'You are, of course you are. All our discussions have been about dreams, haven't they? And about your not remembering them, whatever the level of your insomnia. I had no ulterior motive when I asked you to join us; it just so happens that your PSGs showed a similar level of REM intensity and a higher than average percentage of REM sleep, just like everyone else's in the group, so . . .'

'So even though *I* have no idea of what I dream about, you quite fancy trying to make it into a home movie?' I asked indignantly.

Julie spoke before Reeves could reply. 'Huw, this is a bit of a surprise. Why didn't you mention any of this before?'

'It was only a secondary interest,' he tried to reassure her, 'and to be honest, in technical terms it's such pie in the sky that it wasn't really worth mentioning. But I haven't found any useful correlation between your disorders and the kind of dreams you have so it's moved into – sharper focus in my mind, I suppose. In any case, we're working on it more intensively with Delphine now so it doesn't involve anybody else at all and needn't detain us . . .'

'Why Delphine? Because of her dreams?' asked Julie.

'Yes. We don't know, of course, whether it will work out, or even if we'll be able to make any useful kind of assessment, but the fact that her dreams are already so filmic does perhaps make them the most appropriate to begin looking at. At this stage.' Reeves looked at our questioning expressions and sighed. 'OK, I'll try to explain. There's been some research on lucid dreaming – you remember we've talked about that a few times – the state in which someone goes into a dreamlike trance while remaining fully conscious. I know that the whole area is a little suspect and Delphine doesn't claim to be a lucid dreamer but the research might be relevant: it suggests that recordings of eye movements during dreaming demonstrate that the eye is *fixating* on an object and sometimes *scanning* a scene. As though the brain isn't just *thinking*; it might actually be *seeing* a dream. Delphine's ocular movements are similar to those described and this happens during periods when her heart rate increases too, which is another factor to consider. It just makes it more likely that she's experiencing something *visual* which may one day be transmittable.'

Delphine seemed uncomfortable, though she smiled as all eyes turned to her. I think she looked a little apologetic to all of us, but mostly to me. 'We've only just started to talk about it,' she said, 'and I had no idea that it was something that Huw was thinking about earlier with the lab.'

Polly looked cross. 'Jag, why haven't you said anything about this lucid dreaming business?' she asked.

Jagdev had been quiet throughout and when he spoke it was tersely. He looked at Reeves as he replied, 'Because I didn't know anything about it.'

Nobody stayed for a drink that night.

As Reeves' interest became so clearly focused on Delphine and his special experiments, Simon threatened to withdraw from the group. This had happened once before and it was hard to gauge his seriousness, since that time he'd announced his possible departure by leaning back luxuriously in his chair, arms folded above his head, an ankle crossed over his knee and actually yawning widely as he said something like, 'Doc, this isn't working for me at the moment. Fact is, I need *more* sleep in the day now than I ever did and that just wasn't the idea. I'm thinking of quitting.'

Of course, the idiot Reeves instantly began his emollient persuasion, joined by the women and their 'Oh Simon, don't go now, please just hang on and see how it goes for a bit longer, we really want you in the group.' Alfred and I exchanged a heavenward glance and young Jagdev arranged his face into something approaching concern but we knew damn well Simon was only bluffing. He was like a schoolboy trying to get attention from Teacher and the girls, which he got, in buckets.

But this time he spoke quietly and looked uncomfortable and Reeves' attempts to dissuade him seemed half-hearted.

'I'm sorry to hear that, Simon,' he said, sounding anything but sorry.

And then Sally said, as though she had just thought of it, 'Actually, Huw, I've decided that I really am going to leave too. I really am this time.' There was a surprised silence as she continued. 'I did enjoy the lab in the very early days and when we changed the focus on to dreaming it seemed to make sense. It was fascinating. But lately there hasn't been much direction, your extra-curricular interests have been taking over, and I haven't been happy about the way in which you've discouraged me from curing my RLS.'

Reeves looked annoyed. 'I don't think it's fair to say I've actually *discouraged* you . . .'

'Well I do. You know of my antipathy to doctors and I think you've played upon it. I don't quite know why. At first you really did seem to want us to find inventive, healthy ways of improving our sleep. But in the past few months you've been saying things which go against that completely. Almost as though you want to keep us in this unhealthy state.'

If any other lab member had made this speech Reeves would, I'm sure, have been floored. But because Sally was always the one who took him to task over matters great and small, he was able to behave almost graciously. 'Sally, I'm so sorry that's the way you feel, and sorry too if my manner has seemed to suggest anything of the sort. It was entirely unintentional. I do wish you'd reconsider.'

Even I understood that his final sentence meant the very opposite of what he had said, and Sally was always good on nuance. She must have been feeling bloody-minded that night.

'Well, perhaps I will, Huw. If you're sure.'

Reeves couldn't muster the grace to look relieved or grateful and for a moment nobody could think of what to say, and it was Jag who broke the silence with a question. 'This is such a small group, Huw. A couple of people think about leaving and suddenly it looks like the whole thing could go down. It's shaky. Is it really sustainable as a research group?'

That did surprise Reeves. He sat on the edge of his desk and tried to look relaxed and thoughtful but his eyes were flicking around the room and his voice, when he spoke, was strained. 'How about a break? Perhaps people are thinking about leaving because we've been doing this for over a year now and as far as you're concerned not a lot has happened. But really, it would be such a shame if the whole thing fell apart now. I feel like I'm getting somewhere, I'm on the brink of discovering an important correlation. But we're all a bit tired of it at the moment. So look – let's take August and September off. A whole two months. I can do some work on what I've already got and you can all have a break. Start afresh next term. What do you think?'

I was certainly game and the others, all except Jag, agreed to this suggestion quite happily. Jag agreed grudgingly, but I got the feeling he couldn't see the point.

Although it was a silly time of year to visit such a tourist trap, that was the first time I took Delphine to Italy. A quick tour to Verona, Siena and Padova, our wonderful three days in Florence and a night and a day in Venice, which she found utterly entrancing.

I wanted to remember our time in Venice and have just looked in the photo album I've kept only since knowing Delphine. There are lots of pictures of her — sitting at the edge of a fountain; at a café table in Piazza San Marco; next to the Doge's Palace with the boats arranged behind her, straight out of a Canaletto painting. She rarely took photographs, though there are one or two of me, and a slightly lopsided one of the pair of us which we asked a passer-by to take. And there are several pictures of gondolas — the black and gold ones with red plush lining and gondoliers in full gilt and velvet costume with feathered hats — every one of them full of Japanese tourists. Delphine found it hilarious that everyone else refused to pay the exorbitant rate for a showy gondolier when they could get a riverboat for a few euros, and had taken several photographs showing timid-looking Japanese couples or family groups hunched in front of snooty gondoliers punting their passengers along with bored expressions as they played crackly tapes of 'O Sole Mio'. So she photographed them with great enthusiasm whenever she got the chance. They make me smile now.

She always viewed the world from an angle I'd never have considered. I used to think that a careful overview was the best way — assess the situation before you commit and then stride in masterfully, that kind of thing — but now I wish she had taught me her trick of looking again, taking a squint *behind* what's actually happening and waiting for the true moment to reveal itself.

I still dread going to work. I do really appreciate the beautiful weather we're having and I start the day with a healthy breakfast and leave the house with a spring in my step, but when I remember where I'm going I slow down and feel gloomy. Before Delphine, I'd go to work fairly happily except for that little dip I had around the time I met Reeves – the time of my depression – and while she was here I positively enjoyed working, knowing that she and I would share the end of each day. Every day I've been in the office since she left, I've found everything tedious except the small bursts of chat with colleagues. Even that's odd, because the constant interruptions to my concentration caused by members of staff jabbering on about their private lives used to irritate the hell out of me, whereas now I always listen and sometimes even join in with the conversation. I don't know what's more enjoyable, that joining in or seeing the looks of surprise on people's faces when I do so. But the work itself, it's unbearable. I can scarcely concentrate on it and am less motivated than I ever have been. Of course, at first I put it down to my sadness and the strangeness of going to work without having kissed Delphine goodbye, but now I'm used to feeling this quotidian pain of loss so I think it's actually to do with the work itself. I can hardly be bothered to complete the more challenging tasks I'd have dealt with swiftly and cheerfully only a month ago.

What's worse, my Head of Section has returned from her break and continues to treat me with less respect than she should. After I'd kowtowed to her over the medical things got slightly better. There was nothing she could pin on me; more's the pity for her. So there was a brief period after that – lasting a few months, when I was at my most depressed – when her manner seemed to be gentler, kinder, towards me, which I found highly disturbing. But then I got back to normal and so did she and these days we only speak when necessary which, given my autonomy within the section, isn't very often outside the normal meetings structure. She met Delphine at the office a couple of times and I remember her surprise when I introduced them. She couldn't prevent herself from saying, 'James, I didn't realise you had a – erm – hello, hello, I'm very pleased to meet you!' while staring at Delphine and shaking her hand with great vigour.

Didn't realise I had a private life, I suppose was what she was going to say.

She offered me redundancy today. A very generous package. I turned it down.

So I'm clearly not the only one who's finding my presence at work close to pointless at the moment. My deputy, a very able chap who's not yet forty, has been covering for me. Partly for his own ambitious purposes, for which I don't blame him at all, not for a second, but also partly out of kindness. I can see that. Caroline found out about Delphine's departure via a few subtle questions and it looks like she spread the news. I don't mind really; people have been terribly kind, even those whom I hardly speak to have made the effort to say hello and let me know about the numerous little drinks dos and birthday celebrations which happen, in-house and at the pub after work. There's one in a couple of weeks' time, a retirement drinks party being held for a man who graduated with an Oxford PPE degree at the same time as I did but who transferred for domestic service after only ten years or so in the FCO. I always liked him; I should go to raise a glass.

14 August

Dream Laboratory's days are numbered. They're becoming far too jumpy about the Transmission project. Shame about Jagdev; perhaps I should have tried to involve the lad more. Conflict of interests though. I suppose he has a right to be pissed off with me, he's been kept in the dark as much as the others. And Wayne can see that I've lost interest in his clever machine. I mean how much time can you spend staring at moving dots on a screen when you've no way of knowing what those dots mean and no idea how to find out? Transmission has to be to someone not to something. Screens and projectors are all very well but the information must transmit more accurately, more directly, to another brain. Another sleeping mind that doesn't need the translation of media like his daft machine. Unfortunately, the only suitable sleeping mind at my disposal – the only empty sleeping mind around apart from my own – is bloody James Beauman's and he's not responded to a damned thing I've thrown at him. Brain music. Pah. It has no more effect on his REM sleep than playing random sounds at exactly the same volume. Useless.

It's got to be more than that. More direct. Forget the headphones. I'll transmit directly via electrodes. Surely to God that'll do <something>.

The bloody Sleep Clinic isn't going to play ball for much longer either. That prissy Ms Andrews has started to look a little too closely at the PSG bookings records and keeps talking about 'limiting my Wayne hours'. Fuck sake.

This is my window of opportunity. It's small, and closing, and I have to jump through it, and I have to take Beauman with me. And Delphine, of course.

She's started to confide in me. Not a lot – she's too loyal – but enough to see that he's bugging her. Leave a fool for long enough and he'll bugger up all by himself.

Day twenty-four: Friday

When we returned from our break Reeves made a great show of being attentive to all of us, not just to Delphine. He dutifully listened to everybody's dream diaries, discussed the results of masses of questionnaires and checked his facts with me before making notes. He also became quite excited about yet another PSG he wanted me to undergo.

'But I've already tried this brainwaves theory several times, and absolutely nothing has happened!' I protested. I didn't like to spend a night away from Delphine and had been quite happy that Reeves' interest in my sleep, or lack of it, had waned.

But he was adamant. 'This is different. We've got a better method of transmission. Much clearer. It's much more likely to have a real effect this time.'

At that point I realised that Reeves was going to find me out and had to come clean. 'Um. I think you should know . . . my insomnia seems to be – umm – in abeyance, one might say.'

'What?'

'That is to say, I am sleeping quite well, these days. Very well.'

'How many wakings?'

'Um . . .'

'Round about how many? You don't need to be precise.'

'None.'

'What?'

'Yes, I haven't mentioned it before because I wasn't sure whether it was a trend or just an anomaly, but . . .'

One of the reasons I generally tell the truth is because I am such an unconvincing liar. But Reeves looked only the slightest bit anxious. 'And I suppose you're going to tell me, somewhat belatedly, that you spend all night having amazing dreams?' he asked.

I shook my head. 'Sadly, no. Lots of sleep but still no dreams.'

He looked relieved again. 'That's not a problem at all. In fact, it might even be better.'

I was confused. 'Well, why would I need to listen to my brain sounds to help me sleep when I can in fact sleep very well without them?'

He had an answer ready. 'This is a bit different. We're not using headphones – we're going to try transmitting your previous PSG results directly through the electrodes. It will still be useful to see if the transmission disturbs your sleep in any way whatsoever. And completely safe, of course.'

I was still feeling slightly abashed at my 'fraud' being discovered and so could hardly refuse the request.

The summer break had brought about several changes in the laboratory. Both Simon and Sally were still uncertain about remaining and nearly everybody had returned to the Sleep Clinic to embark upon drug therapies or other mainstream treatments for their problems. I only know that because Delphine told me, but I hope I would have noticed the changes in them over the next few months even if she hadn't. The bags under Julie's eyes shrank. Simon cut his hair and shaved more so that, in certain lights, he looked almost boyish. Sally's face looked less lined and Polly rarely sported sleepwalking injuries, while Jag's narcoleptic incidents became very rare indeed. Only Alfred continued to wheeze through the sessions looking pale and sweaty but when anyone suggested he might return to the clinic he refused outright. 'They can't do anything else for me. I tried everything before I came here.'

Polly tried to convince him to give it another go. 'They're discovering and refining techniques all the time, you know. Something might work. Isn't it worth going just to find out?'

'They've nothing to help me. I do keep up with developments in treatment, you know,' he sounded defensive and Polly blushed, 'but drugs have never worked for my apnoea and all the gadgets make it worse, so I'm just going to carry on coming here.'

I think we all had the same thought at this, and it was Jag who took it as his professional duty to speak. 'Alfred,' he began tentatively, 'you do know, don't you, that Huw isn't trying to find *cures* for us? The research he's doing, it's not going to help any of us to sleep. The stuff he's finding out about dreaming might one day help someone with your kind of disorder, but just coming here and talking isn't going to *cure* any of us.'

Alfred sighed impatiently. 'Look, lad. I know you're trying to help, but you've not credited me with much intelligence. I know exactly what this group's for and I know that it's not going to solve my problems. But Huw's been good to me and I've no wish to spoil his research by leaving just because there's nothing directly in it for me. So thank you, and you Polly, but I don't need that kind of advice. All right?' They nodded, shamefaced. 'Now cheer up the bloody pair of you and stop fretting, d'ye hear me? I'll be fine.'

That was more words in one go than Alfred usually uttered those days, and it was an effort – a real physical effort – for him to get them all out.

Delphine's last lover had swept her off her feet. He lectured in post–1950s British and American poetry, a challenging postgraduate course which she began on her twenty-sixth birthday because she missed learning. She found the length and breadth of his knowledge hugely impressive and more than compensatory for his average looks and the very beginnings of middle-aged spread. For the first two years he had pursued her avidly and charmingly but never overtly, and had flatteringly confided in her about his unfortunate home life, entire sexual history and iconoclastic personal philosophy, swearing to her that she was the first woman to whom he had told the truth about himself for at least twenty years. She did her best to disbelieve him but ended up being convinced that his wife couldn't possibly understand him and so they began a passionate relationship. Very soon after becoming lovers, they began to talk about children. He already had a two-year-old son and a baby daughter – both conceptions apparently engineered by the scheming wife – but told Delphine that, while he knew it was impossible, he longed to have a child with her. She was tempted; her biology played tricks on her and while she didn't quite become careless she realised that the start of her period was a monthly disappointment. But she controlled the urge to manipulate the situation and found herself waiting for him to give the word. It never came. A year later he began to plead guilt.

He swore he loved her and no other but the fear of discovery and of destroying his family was too great. They continued to meet, he continued to kiss her like a lover and eventually she had to put an end to their affair because the discrepancies between what he said he wanted and what he actually did were making her a nervous wreck. A few months after that she discovered that at around the time he had begun to mention guilt, he had started an affair with someone else and impregnated her almost immediately. Delphine was heartbroken.

A few months ago I recall her returning from one of her psychology lectures all sparkling and excited. She told me that she had finally understood what had happened. 'It's all about Alpha males!' she cried.

I was confused. 'Aren't they supposed to be great intellectual and physical specimens whose genes are so much in demand that they have to fight the women off them?'

'Yes, yes, but he was trying to get round the evolutionary trap of his being short and average-looking by going out there and *offering* his sperm! And because he was so eloquent and intelligent, women overlooked the less than perfect physical bit – which they can always do if they're just looking for a shag, but which they usually think about a bit more carefully if they're Alpha females wanting to make Alpha babies – and *accepted* it.'

'You didn't.'

'No, because I was always waiting for him to say it. But he so much wanted to be the Alpha male that he could never say it – to me or his wife or the new woman or anyone – he just set us up and waited for us to behave *as though he were* the Alpha male. If he'd overtly asked us to make a baby it would be no good; he wanted to believe it had happened because his genes were so much in demand. Whereas of course no woman would have actually set her cap at him to get a baby until he started all that sweet-talking about how it was fate and how he longed to make a child with her above all others and then their ovaries went crazy. I'm sure we're more suggestible than we think, especially about reproduction. Women, I mean.'

Women have been the source of pleasure and confusion, in equal measure, and my time with Delphine has done nothing to upset that balance.

Take her mother, for example. Now, my image of Mme Fournier was of a loving, sensible woman, with plenty of liberal French pragmatism in her outlook, but there was one very unsound piece of advice which she gave her adoptive charge at the tender age of sixteen or so, and Delphine remembered it word for word. I'll translate, of course: 'Only have sex with a man with whom, if the worst came to the worst, you would be prepared to have a baby.'

'That's preposterous!' I said, when Delphine repeated it. 'That's a classic piece of motherly interference dressed up as wisdom! It's something that a mother might have told her daughter fifty years ago but what about the Pill? What about legal abortion? Women aren't tied to their biology in that way any more.'

Delphine bristled at the insult to her mother. 'She wasn't dressing it up as anything. It's what she thought. And I think it was good advice; she wasn't saying save yourself until marriage, and she wasn't suggesting that if I did get pregnant I should therefore have the baby. But she wanted me to have a happy sexual life, she wanted my lovers to be good, honest men who loved me back and would accept the consequences of their actions. *If the worst came to the worst*, James.'

'I'm sorry for being unkind about your mother. I'm sure her intentions were good. But my darling, this is the twenty-first century and there is no need for anyone to have a baby if they don't want one, so the advice seems pretty outdated now, don't you think?'

'You still don't get it. It's nothing to do with babies. It's all about *love*. I was sixteen years old, I was still a virgin but I had a steady boyfriend, and she saw me about to embark upon my sexual life and wanted to tell me, to remind me gently, that however sophisticated we are about birth control, sex is still a reproductive act, whatever else it might be, and that's worth bearing in mind. Because even if you don't intend to reproduce, there is some sense, to me, in making love with a person with whom you *could imagine* having a child. Even if you don't want one. Don't you see that?'

'And have you kept with the programme?' I asked, feigning amusement but really being concerned about this bizarre take on sex.

'Mostly. And the times I haven't – when I was a student and did silly things with men I didn't really know – I have always regretted it. I don't beat myself up about it but I feel I didn't treat myself well sometimes. I haven't had many lovers, James. Since I grew up, it's never been just for fun. And for the last ten years, yes, I have kept with the programme.'

She was waiting, I could tell, for me to join up the dots she'd drawn for me but I was too agitated. I didn't dare ask her about what would happen to us if *the worst came to the worst*. The subject was so fraught, and I was so scared, that I chose to misunderstand her and feigned hurt feelings. 'You used to say you didn't mind the fact I'd had a lot of lovers. But now it sounds as though you're saying you've behaved well and I've behaved badly. Whereas you've had affairs with married men, just as I have had affairs with married women . . .'

'I'm not saying I'm morally perfect!' she shouted. 'I've sometimes behaved badly, I know that. It's just that I behaved badly with men I loved.'

I tried to reassure her. 'My love, you know that if I could turn back the clock I'd act differently, I hate the thought of my past upsetting you . . .'

But I think she knew that it was all so much flannel on my part, because usually she was quick to reassure me that my history didn't detain her for a moment, but this time her response wasn't sympathetic. 'It's nothing to do with that. Nothing at all. It wasn't a comparison. But it has shown how very different our views are on the subject.'

'Not on love. Our views on love are the same, Delphine, whatever route we've taken to get here.'

'Maybe. But I don't think so. It's like colours – you see blue, I see blue, but how can we possibly know whether in fact your blue looks like my red? There's no way of knowing.'

'We have to trust in it. We have to have faith in it.'

She looked into my eyes, her expression unfathomable, and I turned away first.

Yet another negative instance of babies appearing – or not – in Delphine's life. I was so sure that it was my duty to ensure that the subject would never rear its ugly head and upset her again. Now I'm sure of very little, except that I got it wrong. That I misinterpreted her and, especially, her dreams. It seems I'm not alone in that but I, of all people, should have tried harder.

One day I walked into the bedroom to find Delphine dressed only in her panties, viewing her figure from side on. Her hands were cupped around her breasts and she smiled as she saw me. 'They're very small, aren't they?' she said, matter-of-fact.

I wasn't sure how to respond. 'But perfectly formed.'

'Still small. I wonder what I'd look like with larger breasts.'

'I hope you're not considering plastic surgery, my love? Your breasts are perfect and they match the rest of you.'

'Of course not. But I saw Mia today and she's been breastfeeding her baby for three months now and her tits are *enormous*. I was trying to imagine what mine would look like.'

'Enormous and perfect, I expect,' I said hopefully, still not at all confident of where this was going. To my relief, she just kissed me and shimmied out of my grasp to put her clothes back on and make supper.

Delphine knew a woman whose husband only made love to her once a month and insisted he never wanted children. She selected her lovers on the basis of their physical similarity to her husband. 'Just in case I get pregnant,' she explained.

22 October

It's such a beautiful, simple idea. To make the dreamless man dream. To transmit data from the REM sleep of a vivid dreamer while he sleeps and stimulate his own dreams. Brainwaves introduced directly through electrodes on his skull.

They won't be the same dreams, of course. These are early days. Besides, I wouldn't wish Delphine's dreams on anyone, even James, however much of a prick he is. Although, one day, that will be possible, I know it will.

There must be something there; some frequency, some pattern, of her transmission which, if I time it right, will occur slap in the middle of a major REM phase.

He is the perfect control. Not a shred of evidence that he's remembered a dream all his adult life. Imagine the moment when we unhook him and start removing the electrodes. I'll casually ask, 'So, anything to report?'

And he'll think a bit, look confused, then concentrate and remember, and then smile and say, 'Yes! Yes! I had a dream! I can remember a dream!'

These moments contain everything; all the hopes and fears that potential — potential anything — throws up. Benign manipulation of brain activity during sleep, something you can really control, could go a lot further than helping the dreamless dream or the insomniac sleep. It could offer a treatment for depression and anxiety without the use of drugs. Never mind giving a visual display of someone's dreams; that's schoolboy stuff and the Americans are going to get there first, if the Japs haven't already done it. Well, let them play. This is the real deal.

And not benign, of course. Other kinds of brain manipulation. Transmitting through the telly to make everyone buy washing powder. Well, that's all been tried before and it'll be tried again. It's not going to be my problem. This is going to be my solution.

Day twenty-five: Saturday

My dear James

I could tell you weren't a liar. But I began to wonder why the truth is so important to you and I began to suspect that it was nothing to do with honesty; it was about fact. Telling the truth for you is saying what is factually correct. That doesn't always leave room for honesty. I have loved too many liars; now I think there are other kinds of deceivers.

D

That honesty/truth business sometimes really got my goat. She was always throwing scenarios at me and I did my best, I wanted to support her coursework, but I didn't always like her tone.

'OK, imagine you're at the deathbed of an old lady.'

'Oh please God, no!' I'd groan but she wouldn't let me escape.

'Hush, listen carefully. The old lady is about to die. She has always been very careful about her appearance but this illness has made it impossible for her to even hold a hairbrush. She is very fretful about how she must look, and keeps asking for a mirror. She grasps your hand,' here Delphine grasped my hand, 'and says, "How does my hair look?"'

I considered. 'Well, obviously you can't tell her that her hair looks marvellous . . .'

'Why not?'

'Because it doesn't. And because she'd know you were lying.'

'How would she know?'

'Well, common sense would tell her that hair which hasn't been brushed for weeks wouldn't look good.'

'In that case, why does she ask the question?'

'I have no idea. Really, Delphine, why do they give you these silly examples? It's completely unrealistic – as if a dying woman would care about the state of her bloody hair!'

'I think it's very realistic. I think that's exactly the kind of thing she might think about. And you wouldn't bend the truth for her sake!'

'All right then, I'd get her a mirror like she asked.'

Delphine's expression of shock was entirely genuine; she seemed to flinch when I said that. 'What? You'd do something so brutal? You'd . . . you'd . . .'

I cut in while I had a chance. 'I'd do as she asked. Without telling a lie or bending the truth or having to pretend. What's wrong with that?'

'If you don't know then I can't explain,' was her answer.

There was one awful time when I asked Delphine to play along with a story I'd invented. Well, John invented it really and I allowed him to believe it because it was so typical and so annoying of him to misinterpret everything I did. John and I rarely spoke on the phone and we were having one of those conversations in which both parties were trying to be gracious and brief simultaneously.

'How are Stacey and the kids?' I enquired.

'Fine, fine. Matthew's come back from his gap-year adventures and will be going to Durham in October and Jayne's waiting for her GCSE results but thinks she's done OK. How about you?'

'Yes, thanks, absolutely fine.'

'Are you – erm – will we be meeting anyone new at Christmas?' This was his way of asking if I had a new girlfriend and was as tactful as he could manage.

Unusually, I told him he would be meeting Delphine, because without even thinking about it I'd written her in to our tedious family Christmas and indeed to any aspect of my future life I'd considered. And she had only just moved in! This realisation struck me as I was talking to John so that I wasn't paying much attention as I responded to his unsubtle questions about the new woman's name, age and provenance. I was unprepared for the approving way in which he exclaimed, 'Vietnamese eh! And twenty years younger than you. Well well well, have you got one of those mail-order brides then, James? Not a bad idea, seeing as you're getting on a bit and don't seem to meet the right kind of lady, but I must admit I'm surprised. So, does she do *everything* you ask, eh?'

I was irritated. The fantasy of introducing Delphine to what was left of my family disintegrated in an instant and I responded angrily, 'Yes of course, John, unable as I am to attract female company I've been forced to resort to paying for it. And clearly subservience is up there at the top of the list along with timidity and a lack of ambition.'

'All right, all right, keep your hair on. Look, I've got no problems with it, and I shan't breathe a word to Stace, OK?'

He had clearly read my rage as defensiveness and I didn't have the energy or the will to explain. We said goodbye stiffly and I heard no more from him until he telephoned a few weeks later. His car had broken down and the trains to Hampshire weren't running and could he stay at my flat for the night?

'Give me a chance to meet your new lady friend, eh?' he added, with the vocal equivalent of a wink. I had no choice but to invite him over. But then I had a brainwave about how Delphine and I could have the last laugh at his prejudices. I rushed to find her.

She was not at all keen on my idea. 'Surely he won't really believe that you've ordered a mail-order bride, James! Why can't I just meet him as – as me?'

But I was insistent. 'He's always trying to score points over me and pour scorn over my life. Just because I have a steady job at the civil service instead of what he sees as the thrilling life of a wine merchant, and I didn't get a Stacey and a Matthew and a Jayne and a big pile in Hampshire. Darling, please, it would be a huge favour to me, and we can have some fun with it. He's such a bigot; this is exactly what he deserves.'

Eventually she agreed, so I picked her out some clothes and we worked out a plan of action.

It would pain me too much to go into every detail here, but to summarise: Delphine spent the evening dressed in a very low-cut black bodice which she usually wore under a sheer blouse, and a long, green and gold Chinese silk skirt which we'd found at Portobello market. She couldn't help looking sexy and delightful in this outfit but the revealing top made her feel uncomfortable and so she was slightly round shouldered whilst wearing it, which helped give just the right impression of shyness and subservience I was after. I wanted her to look like the kind of oriental woman one might find in an upmarket catalogue of brides hoping to appeal to fat western men who lacked the social capacity to interact with women as equals. John couldn't take his eyes off her. She served us food and drinks, said not a word unless she was spoken to, and even then responded in a tiny, slightly accented voice, and sat listening to me making the most absurd claims about how she carried out all of my housework and cooking, devoted herself utterly to my physical and sexual well-being and only left the house in order to undergo various beauty treatments designed to keep her as decorative as possible. At first Delphine was fantastically convincing and seemed to be actually enjoying herself, but as my brother became more and more loathsome in his lewd appraisal of her the whole act became too uncomfortable to sustain so she made her excuses – apologetically – and went to bed early. I had to stay another hour drinking whisky with John while he made comments like, 'She's a bloody cracker. You lucky devil, Jim. I tell you, this is the best thing you could've done, m'boy.' Despite his being my junior by two years, John has assumed an increasingly patronising tone towards me, which I've traced back to the day he married. 'Wait till I tell Stacey. Her and her bloody whingeing about who does all the "child-care" and her washing-up rotas and her "you iron your own shirts". She won't believe it.'

When I managed to get him off to bed in the spare room and join Delphine in bed she was still awake. She looked sad. 'What was that for, James?'

'I told you, he's such a bigot. He really believes women

should behave like that. And he's got that whole thing about oriental women.'

'What thing?'

'You know, that they're delicate little flowers who want a man to tell them what to do, and know their place and so on.'

'Do you think that?'

This was so plainly silly that I laughed but she remained silent. 'Delphine, darling, you know such a thought has never crossed my mind. I don't see you like that. I've never seen any woman like that. And I'd never *oppress* you, or make you do things for me, or treat you like a servant. I'd *hate* that.'

'That's what you did this evening.'

'But that was just play-acting. That was for John's benefit.'

'I know.'

And that was all she would say, although she allowed me to curl in behind her and kiss her neck before falling asleep.

Every morning that I woke to find her beside me I felt insanely grateful – to whom or what I can't say – and the pleasure of watching her lovely face in repose always fought with my urge to wake her. When John had his first child, Matthew, I was struck by the depth of his obsession with the small, red bundle which I found utterly charmless. John and Stacey spent the first few weeks just staring at the baby and for many months after that I would ask my brother a question or make a comment only to be met by silence as he looked, oblivious to anything else, in anxious awe at his firstborn. My impatient tuts would bring forth attempts to explain himself and I remember him telling me, with an embarrassed laugh, how often he and his wife found themselves gazing in that way.

'You can't understand until it happens to you, James,' he assured me, 'but it's such an amazing thing, you can't control it. We even watch him when he's asleep. Stacey's always making excuses about needing to check he's breathing and that his sheets are still on and that the room temperature is OK, but I don't even bother pretending: all I want to do is watch him. And if I go to see him in the morning before work, I hate to leave him like that so a few times I've actually woken him up so that I can say goodbye to him properly. Which isn't fair to him or Stacey because he sleeps so little as it is, but I just kind of want him to see me seeing him, to see how much I love him, the little bugger.'

I must have thought about Finn when he talked like that, but I have no memory of doing so. John didn't know that I'd already had a son a full seven years before. That's something he still doesn't know. I suppose I shall have to tell him soon.

Anyway, what he said about the desire to watch Matthew and the longing to wake him, that's just what it was like when I woke before Delphine. And when she did finally open her eyes – whether as a result of my tossing and turning and unnecessarily loud coughing or of her own accord – I loved to see her focus on me, brush her hair away from her face and look at me with an expression I could never quite fathom. 'You look pretty,' I would say, which was always an under-statement, and her response could be any number of things – a contrived flutter of the eyelashes, a sweet 'So do you', a ludicrous cross-eyed grimace, or just a tiny smile. When I was a younger man, if I woke next to a woman I was instantly aroused, but in the past ten years or so that ardour has slowly cooled and I've had less energy for sex in the morning. With Delphine the mere sight of her eyes looking into mine would make me hard and we often made love before I got up for work. I loved to roll lazily, almost reluctantly, on to her and she would yawn and wrap her legs around me as I began with luxurious sloth, knowing that in due course we would build to a sweating urgency which would leave us prone and panting side by side, sated and ready to sleep again.

I hope she knows how much I appreciated her, how much her presence meant to me. Women are always complaining about being taken for granted; I'm sure that's one sin of which I was never guilty when it came to paying attention to Delphine.

I'm not avoiding the issue about Reeves. That is, I'm not avoiding thinking about it. It's hard to know what to say about it though. I'm still surprised that the tiny gleam of sexual interest he displayed had ever been made overt. Or that it had been welcomed by Delphine. I knew that he visited her for chats during work – her part-time temping job at the university became a permanent post and so she occasionally had to work with him – but he definitely sought her out more often than he needed to. She always mentioned their encounters and recounted their conversations until a couple of months ago, when she stopped mentioning him much at all. If I'm to be sensible about this, I should guess that's when their relationship took an unexpected turn towards something more intense.

Around that time, I'd arranged to meet Delphine in the bar a little earlier than usual before the Dream Lab meeting, but she wasn't there so I knocked on Reeves' door to ask if he'd seen her. She was in his office, sitting on a chair holding her dream diary, crying. I'd felt annoyed at him, for allowing her to become so upset, and said, with some irritation, 'I don't think you should be making Delphine go through that diary again, Dr Reeves, it's clearly not something she enjoys doing and surely your research doesn't demand it?'

Reeves looked angry and began to say something but Delphine interrupted him and said, 'He's not making me do anything, James. I wanted to talk to Huw about this. It doesn't upset me at all, he's not upsetting me.'

'Then why are you crying?' I didn't mean to sound so accusatory.

'*I'm* not upsetting her,' began Reeves but Delphine shook her head at him and he said no more. We left his room and went to the bar but she was quiet all that evening and I was privately cursing Reeves for having been so thoughtless as to make her go through those painful stories any more than she had to.

Yes, yes, I now realise it was me that was upsetting her, somehow or other. I'm not entirely stupid. I know these obvious, glaring mistakes should have occurred to me some time ago but I am, slowly, understanding them. Oddly, I don't feel terribly jealous of Reeves. I'm angry, and I refuse to think of the two of them together, but I believe what Delphine says about him – about his not mattering to her – and I also feel that I'm to blame, in a way. For not seeing the danger or guarding her vulnerable side more carefully.

One advantage of having slept with so many women is that I am able to see how much or how little sex can mean. How it is so often the thing that two people do with each other because they don't have the vocabulary, or the imagination, or the sheer energy, for anything else. It's a default position for a man and a woman who find themselves alone and communicating. And if they're not on guard; if one of them doesn't jump up to make a cup of tea or pour a drink or suggest a long walk, there's a sad inevitability to it. So often I've found that even the sweetest sexual encounters, those wonderful erotic surprises which life can put in one's path from time to time if one's on the look-out for them, can leave a bitter aftertaste. Something lost. A book closed. Even, rarely, shame. I've still welcomed the chances though, what man wouldn't? A couple of times since getting together with Delphine I've been in a position which, had I pursued it, could have led to my making love to another woman. But each time, I was able to pull away, quite consciously, and with only the faintest tang of biological regret, soon to be superseded by relief. I was overwhelmed by a conviction that I was being honourable. I was acting as an honourable man. There are few things in my life of which I'm more proud.

I suppose I shall have to see Reeves at some point. Not yet though.

Day twenty-six: Sunday

'When did you last read this damned book?' Delphine asked me one day. She was waving my ragged copy of *L'Etranger* at me, the one whose twin I had seen her reading at that first meeting.

'I can't remember. Five years ago? I almost know it off by heart. Why do you ask?'

'Read it again. Just read the first few chapters and the last few chapters and then tell me what it reminds you of.'

'What for?'

'Please, James, just do it. Then we'll talk.' Her face was glowing with excitement as though she had made a remarkable discovery. I took the book from her and leafed through it, half-expecting some little note or tickets to drop out of it but no, it was just the book.

'Must I do it now?'

'Yes,' she insisted, removing my newspaper.

So I did. And when she returned with coffee twenty minutes later she found me looking extremely contemplative. She poured the drinks and handed me my cup before asking gently, 'So?'

I knew what she was getting at. 'Look, I think I can imagine what it reminds you of . . .' I began but she wasn't taking that.

'Uh-uh. What it reminds *you* of. What that voice reminds you of.'

'Well, I suppose that it is a bit–' I could hardly bear to say the word. She was right, of course. The short, factual sentences. The lack of emotional or social engagement and of any religious or spiritual beliefs or interest. Experiencing and failing to control some basic human instincts and lacking others entirely. The refusal to bend the truth even for his own survival. The steadfast naivety. 'OK, autistic. He sounds what we might describe nowadays as a bit autistic.'

Delphine punched the air triumphantly, such an unusual pose for her, and it reminded me of a schoolboy celebrating a goal, imitating the aggressive antics of his footballer heroes. She was too small and graceful for such extreme gestures.

'Yes! *He sounds a bit autistic.* That's exactly it.'

'Look, I'm sure Camus wasn't intending to write about autism. I bet it hadn't even been defined when he was writing. He's talking about society and man's place within it, about the power of the individual, about the pressure to conform, about the absurd . . .'

Delphine made a dismissive *pouffe* sound.

'The whole thing about the absurd — it's a very *male* idea isn't it? Are there any women who write about the absurd? No, because it's all about dislocation and alienation whereas women want to make connections. We want to join things up.'

'And your point is . . . ?'

She shrugged. 'No point. I'm just glad you agree. Since we met, I know that you've been really pissed off that I don't think this is the best book ever written. And you've believed that I just don't "get" it, you thought I was a bit too slow to realise that Meursault is an anti-hero without convictions who nevertheless and so very ironically dies for Truth. But I've always known that. I've also always thought he's a bit *stupid*. Too stupid to merit having grand convictions about the truth; I mean, he's hardly Galileo, is he? And very, maddeningly *irritating*. He doesn't care about anything enough to lie. Not even his own life. He's so outside it all that there's nothing to keep him in. And so his death is no kind of tragedy; it's not even a miscarriage of justice because he *did* shoot the Arab, and he feels no remorse and he could easily kill someone else next time he gets a bit hot.'

I was taken aback by her eloquent literary dissection. 'Well, I'm not entirely in agreement about that reading, I've heard similar things said about Meursault's lack of moral empathy and so on, and I do see what you mean about his voice; it's an interesting theory. Personally, I think that's too simplistic, it ignores the great sensual drives which animate him. But Delphine, why are you so excited about it? Why are you trying to convince me so – rabidly?'

She looked at me in astonishment and banged her hand against her forehead, yelping out a very French 'Ai–ai–ai, this man, this stupid man!' before grabbing the book, returning it to its shelf and throwing herself into the armchair opposite me. She looked tired. I tried to talk to her about it again but she made a little sign – a no go – with her hand raised palmwards towards me.

'Delphine, it looks like you're directing traffic!' I joked and she smiled but kept her hand up.

She reached for her coffee and said, 'End of conversation.'

And that was that.

A person whose emotional cortex in the brain becomes separated – which can happen as the result of head injury or brain surgery – but whose other faculties remain intact should, in theory, be able to make perfect decisions. Without the complications of subjective emotions, he should be able to look at a situation in a genuinely rational manner, weigh up the pros and cons of each potential course of action and plump for the one which is most likely to be successful. But that's not how it works. What he actually lacks is *instinct*. The emotional cortex – I shan't go into the technical terms because it's extremely complex, but that phrase will do – is a vital part of decision-making because it informs the brain about all those subjective and erratic factors, it makes judgements about likely outcomes based on its knowledge of other people, on its *empathy* with other people. Lacking those instincts, a person can't even trust himself to make decisions; his brain is a bit like a computer, which we would never leave to decide anything, however powerful its processor. The messy emotional bit is what makes us different, what will always make us different, from computers.

When I discovered that fact in a book a few years ago, I felt that all the time I'd spent in pursuit of consideration and control had been wasted. It was a great shock to me, to learn that the complicating factors, the soupy mess of anger and fear and love in which we flail about, and which I'd sought to escape, are the vital ingredients for making decisions. And that all my standing back, observing, calculating before making my well-aimed move could never be enough. It makes sense of course – the successful businessman of whatever class always has the whiff of something feral about him. There's a palpable excitement at a deal being struck which is more than simple greed, and the calculations he's making aren't only about profit; they're a fearsome mixture of emotional knowledge, experienced second-guessing and nerve-holding *panache*. He can *smell* victory and his skill isn't due to his behaving like an animal; it's about his enjoyment of life as a human being.

Delphine must have thought I was being very stupid, to fail to make the rather obvious Meursault connection. Shortly after we spoke, it did occur to me that she was trying to draw a link between me and my 'hero' in a less than flattering manner. Not that she can honestly think I'm autistic; otherwise why would she have had anything to do with me in the first place? Could she really think that I'm the Outsider at fifty? That if Meursault had slipped out of the noose and run away to become middle-aged, he'd be like me?

The day after that silly argument, I remember her saying, 'James, do you know the difference between being honest and not telling lies?'

'Aha, a riddle!' I said with enthusiasm, but her serious face showed me it was no riddle. 'Can you – explain a bit further, Delphine?'

'OK. Let's see. A simple one: a child throws a toy at his younger brother, and it hits him on the head. Their mother rushes in and finds her baby holding his head and sobbing, the toy at his side. "Did you drop that on his head?" she asks the older child, and he answers, wide-eyed, "No!" His mother is sure he is not lying. But is he being honest?'

'Ah. Well, I suppose that strictly speaking he is telling the truth, because he threw the book rather than dropped it.'

'And not strictly speaking?'

'His mother meant did you make the baby cry? But she phrased it badly.'

'And so, the child is *right* to answer in that way?'

'Well, he's not lying.'

'But he's not being honest either.'

'Well . . .'

Delphine dismissed my attempt to speak and said, 'The fact it's a child makes that one more complicated. Let's have an adult example . . . you never told Eleanor that you loved her, because that would have been a lie. And yet you continued to act in such a way that she thought you loved her, and that behaviour was dishonest.'

'Oh, I can hardly be held responsible for someone else's reading of my behaviour!'

She carried on as though I hadn't spoken. 'We talked about babies many, many times and not once did you tell me that you had a child—' She stopped my interruption with her hand. 'And don't you dare tell me it's because I never asked. You weren't honest with me. You don't tell lies but you aren't interested in honesty. "Telling the truth" or "not telling lies" is a childish concept based on asking the right questions. Honesty is a state we aspire to, especially when we love.'

I couldn't think of anything to say to that.

But whatever she was getting at, I know that I *can* have moral empathy, I do have a sense of society and collectivity, I am at ease with the sensual world. And I'd lie, tell the truth, stand on my head, eat my hat, do whatever is asked of me in order to get Delphine back. I have *passions*. I am a passionate man.

I visited Father again and told him about Delphine. He still doesn't respond, although sometimes he seems to squeeze my hand. Occasionally I'm almost convinced that it's in answer to something I'm saying but other times it's probably just a spasm. Now that I talk to him as though he gives a damn about what I'm saying, I find it quite easy to gabble on to him. Talking about Delphine was a breeze. She had sent him a postcard; I saw it on his bedside table where Matron had placed it. I didn't read it because he didn't invite me to. I mean, he couldn't obviously, but I felt as though to take a peek would be prying. I'm quite proud of not having looked, although now I'm mad to know what it said. Perhaps next time I go I shall ask him if I may read it and see if there's any response.

Day twenty-seven: Monday

Delphine wouldn't let it lie. She noticed that I never read any other novels. I explained that I'd read all the classics in my youth and now wanted to focus on philosophical and scientific texts rather than try to keep afloat in the ever-rising sea of new fiction.

'But it's a bit strange, to only ever read the same novel over and over again,' she argued. 'I mean, you don't even read any more Camus. Have you read *Sisyphus*? That's much better, much more universal. And actually,' something else dawned on her, 'you *only* listen to Duruflé's *Requiem*.'

'Nonsense, look at how many CDs I have.'

'You have them, and they're all in beautiful alphabetical order, and you sometimes put them on when we're having dinner, but the only thing you ever play in your study is that requiem, and the only novel you ever read is *L'Etranger*!' Her voice was getting louder and her manner disturbed me. I don't know why I felt so defensive about it, but all I could do was shrug uncomfortably. I don't have the time to read everything. I have striven for many years to learn about new subjects, to keep an active mind and a focused intellect. You don't get that from reading novels.

I've just looked at *Le Mythe de Sisyphe* in my *Collected* Camus. It's confusing because the writer describes this man – sentenced by the gods to pushing a rock up a hill and releasing it, then repeating the act *ad infinitum* – as the perfect absurd hero. He says, 'His scorn of the gods, his hatred of death, and his passion for life won him that unspeakable penalty in which the whole being is exerted toward accomplishing nothing. This is the price that must be paid for the passions of this earth.' But that doesn't sound like Meursault at all, quite the opposite in fact, and *he's* supposed to be the perfect absurd hero. I don't know why I never noticed that inconsistency before. Rather disappointing of Camus to change his mind like that.

'Hmmm, I can't quite work out your brain,' Delphine said one evening after she had been at her course. She was always trying out little tests on me and chatting away about the psychology lectures she had attended. Odd, now, to think of all she kept from me. It must have been hard for her to be so inhibited.

'That's because it's a highly sophisticated piece of machinery, my dear,' I joked, but she looked quite serious.

'Yes, yes,' she said impatiently, 'but is it male or female or balanced?'

I'd come across such terms but they smacked of the silly stuff that Reeves occasionally peddled, and had never looked at them in any depth.

'Explain, please.'

'In a nutshell – no, *to the layman*,' she enunciated solemnly, 'the male brain tends to excel at *systematising* and the female brain at *empathising*. Do you want me to explain the terms?'

'No, I can imagine,' I replied dryly. 'So why am I difficult to work out? Am I not extremely manly?'

'It's nothing to do with that. Well, not much. It's not as simple as having a man's brain or a woman's brain. But I've done these tests on your behalf – as if I were you – and I've decided they haven't been designed with someone like you in mind.'

'What do you mean "someone like me"? Did this test by any chance tell you exactly what you wanted to hear about yourself?'

'I have a very well-balanced brain, thank you,' she said quite proudly, 'only very slightly more female than male. I can read maps *and* cry at films. But you're a real fusspot about grammar and brush technique in paintings and the structure of buildings. And you're not interested when people tell you about themselves. So you should come out more conclusively on the male brain side. But you're really good at shopping – you always pick out lovely things for me, things my girlfriends would choose. And you care about food and objects looking beautiful – not just clean and tidy, but *beautiful*.'

'So can't I be balanced too?'

'I'm not sure. I need to think about this; it's very strange.'

I didn't want to delve into the strangeness of my mind, particularly not via some ludicrous multiple choice test, so I flattered her instead. 'I could tell you're perfectly balanced. Up on that tightrope, never needing to look down.'

But she didn't take the compliment; she looked concerned and said, 'James, it's not a tightrope. It's a really wide path; most people walk on it easily, they just tend to stay towards one side or the other. But you seem to . . .' she searched for the word and found it triumphantly, '*veer*. You *veer* from side to side.'

'Like a drunk.'

'Or a lunatic,' she said, crossing her eyes and making a mad face.

'Or a fascinating maverick?' I suggested hopefully, and she fixed me with a disapproving glance. 'Delphine, I'm trying, I really am trying,' I told her and she avoided the obvious pun and came over to kiss me so I moved the psychology book from her hands to the floor and led her to the bedroom.

Afterwards she held me tight and said she loved me. 'You make me *mad*,' she added, 'but I love you very very much.'

I couldn't get that idea of precariousness out of my head.

I have a claustrophobic feeling. Admittedly, I've spent too long cooped up in this room, but even now I'm back at work I feel as though I'm always in too small a space with no hope of escape. I'm tempted to turn my back on consciousness or unconsciousness, and perhaps apply myself to improving Italian or South-East Asian cookery. The type of thing I *can* do up the road in the community college. Dreams, nightmares, daydreaming about dreaming, daydreaming about Delphine's dreams – it's trapping me in a web of fascination which risks becoming obsession. I don't want to think of nothing else all my life. I want to jolt my mind back to consciousness and stay sharp, leave these nocturnal studies of phantasie behind me and move back into the real, stable, steady world of waking.

Day twenty-eight: Tuesday

Sally stuck it out for another few months but left the laboratory at the beginning of this year. She only stayed to rile Reeves, I'm certain of it. And his great attentiveness to us all began to wane. Once I'd done that final overnighter at the Sleep Clinic he barely spoke to me.

It was an odd experience. Not the actual PSG, that was just the same as ever: Wayne hooked me up to the machinery and left me to it, and I only woke once, very briefly. But when I woke properly in the morning, I heard an unexpected voice saying, 'Good morning, James. Sleep well?' Reeves. He wasn't usually there after a night of monitoring – it was always Wayne who removed the electrodes and brought me a coffee; Reeves just wanted to see the technical results. But that time he was the one hurriedly removing electrodes with a smile. It reminded me of what he'd been like the first few times we'd met. That energy and positivity all bouncing off him. More recently his mouth had been tensed or downturned and there was rarely a sparkle in his eyes, but that morning he seemed puppyish again.

'Not bad at all, thanks. I think I just woke up once –'

I looked around for Wayne to confirm this but Reeves said, 'I took over last night; Wayne will be in in a moment or two.'

'Oh.'

'Yes, I was particularly keen to be here. The duty nurse was there too, of course. But I looked after the equipment, made sure the transmission was working and so on.'

'Right.'

'And so yes, there was just one waking period I noticed, at around 3 a.m., and it only lasted for a few minutes. You certainly look like you've had a good night's sleep. Now then, apart from the waking, is there anything else you can remember?'

'Not really.'

'Nothing at all? I tell you what, why don't you go to the shower block and have a think about it while we go through the results?'

I returned twenty minutes later, showered and dressed, and saw that Wayne had appeared. I was shocked by the expectant look on Reeves' face when he turned to me. 'Aha, there you are. Right, so anything to report?'

'I'm afraid not. What were you expecting?'

'I wasn't *expecting* anything. Just thought that you might have experienced something – different. Are you absolutely sure now?'

'Completely. But different in what way? What did you think this transmission would do to me that it hadn't done before, with no noticeable results?'

At that point Wayne called him over to look at something on the printout and the two of them pored over several pages with great interest. 'What is it?' I asked. 'Can you see something different on there?'

Reeves shook his head dismissively and covered the paper with his hand but Wayne, who was still examining the printout, said, 'Sure can! Come and have a look at this.'

Reeves said something to the young man which I didn't catch but he stopped talking as soon as I'd reached the desk. Wayne looked uncomfortable as he pointed to my printout. 'See here? These are your eye movements. You always have a lot of REM, as you know, but at key points last night your ocular movements changed quite radically. See here . . .'

The top two lines of the histograph, which had been hooked up to the sensors by my left and right eye respectively, showed a period of REM sleep in which the activity was so dramatic that the zigzag lines of the graph crossed over one another on many occasions. 'If my eyes had been open I'd have looked like Marty Feldman!' I joked to Wayne, but he was too young to know what I was talking about.

'So what does that mean?' I asked.

Wayne looked at Reeves and then shrugged his shoulders. Reeves said, 'Something or nothing. Not sure yet.'

'You seemed quite excited by it a moment ago.'

'It's been a long night. It's . . . it's just a change. It's interesting.'

I looked more closely at the printout.

'Those movements – they look like Delphine's REM. They look like the periods in which you said she was lucid dreaming.'

'I didn't say she was lucid dreaming.'

'I mean, that her eye movements were like those of a lucid dreamer.' I felt impatient now, I couldn't see why Reeves was being so uncooperative. 'That's right, isn't it?'

'We'll need to study it more closely. Without anything notably different for you – without your remembering anything about your night's sleep – it's probably not very useful material.'

'Well, Huw, we don't know that yet . . .' Wayne began, but he subsided weakly and shrugged. The look between us was sympathetic and yet I didn't understand what sympathy I felt for him or him for me.

If Reeves knew I'd been asleep almost all of the night, this great thing he expected me to have noticed must have been something that took place when I was unconscious. It must have been a dream. Why he thought I might begin dreaming as a result of having my brainwaves transmitted back to me – me, the man whose dreams are invisible or non-existent – is a mystery to me even now.

I had let him down. He never said so, but that's how he made me feel.

And then Alfred died. It shouldn't have been such a great surprise; as successive attempts at curing his apnoea came and went without any improvement he was looking increasingly grey and sounding wheezy and exhausted. It was his heart which went, failing during a minute-long attack. Jackie, lying next to him, mistook the rattle of death for the familiar rasp and gurgle during his resumption of breathing so dropped back to sleep and then woke an hour later in a cold panic at the unfamiliar silence. Dying whilst holding one's breath must be a strange thing, like a death within a death. Which brings to mind dreams within dreams and Simon's fears of continuous dreaming with no real life in between. I suppose that for Alfred every night was a bit like that, with a multitude of little deaths and tiny dream-memories winding their roots around him, around his heart, as though each night he lived a hundred lives and died a hundred deaths. None of us could cope with that. I got the cold shiver you might expect from hearing about the death of someone I'd been seeing every two weeks for a year and a half, with the added frisson of discovering that he was only five years older than me. I'd originally placed him at a good decade my senior.

The others went to his funeral but it was on one of my working days and I had a large backlog of paperwork to get through so I didn't go. I couldn't tell whether Delphine was annoyed with me and now I worry that she was, although at the time she seemed to understand how it was unavoidable. Truly, I'd have liked to go, partly to pay my respects but also to meet the long-suffering Jackie, and pay my respects personally. In nineteenth-century France, a man called Hervey de Saint-Denys carried out a series of experiments into lucid dreaming from which he concluded that it was possible for the average person to exercise considerable control over what, and how vividly, he could dream. Saint-Denys harnessed his own sense of smell by associating a particular perfume with a woman he admired. Once he was sufficiently familiar with the scent, he was able to sniff some of that perfume on a handkerchief before going to sleep and then have some very satisfactory lucid dreams about the relevant woman. Actually, I think he did it with at least two women and two perfumes, which makes the whole thing somehow questionable. I bought Delphine Arpège, whose old-fashioned muskiness delighted her. Last night I sprinkled a little on to my pillow in the faint hope I might conjure my love, but the first time I woke, at about 3 a.m., all it did was make me cry.

Day twenty-nine: Wednesday

Today I met Delphine's mother.

The urge to *do* something became too great and it's not as though I'm indispensable at work at the moment. I couldn't get a decent flight so broke my vow and ended up on one of those godforsaken budget flights again, but this time I suffered gladly and almost enjoyed myself. I laughed warmly at the antics of the plump trolley dollies of both sexes and had two beers before reaching Paris and realising I hadn't even booked my accommodation. One of those kiosk places at the airport sorted me out with a perfectly good hotel in the Cinquième.

She was expecting me to show up at some point. When I knocked on the door I could hardly believe that it would be answered, that it would be that easy. I'd brought a pen and paper and had already begun to draft the note I would leave through the door giving my contact numbers and requesting a meeting. All unnecessary, in the event. A small, slightly greying and very chic woman in her late sixties answered the door and looked up at me calmly.

'Mme Fournier?'

'James,' she said, and it was not a question. 'Come in.'

The house was unremarkable. Contemporary, not cutting-edge but not continental rustic either. There were a few nice prints, and a little collection of Chagall postcards in clip frames which I imagined had something to do with Delphine. Her mother showed me into the kitchen and asked if I would like a cool drink then brought in a bottle of *sirop* made of plums picked from her garden, with a carafe of iced water.

I began to explain why I was there and to assure her that I wasn't going to try to apply any pressure to her or be difficult in any way, but she stopped me politely and asked, 'Please, could we speak in English? Your French is perfect, but I could do with the practice.' The way she speaks English is so much like Delphine; far more so than during our brief telephone conversations, I could hear all those unusual little inflections, the tiny, subtle details which previously had been unique to Delphine. It was disconcerting, hearing them from the lips of a stranger. 'She isn't here, you know,' she told me.

'But you know where she is?'

'I know vaguely. But I don't have an address. She has been travelling — Europe and then Vietnam. That's where she is now. She came to see me in between her travels.'

'To pick up post?' I asked ruefully and she looked uncomfortable for the first time.

'I had strict instructions to return anything.'

'Did she tell you why she was returning it?'

'No. Except to say what had happened and that she didn't know what to do next.'

'I was worried that you might not allow me in, that you might think I'd mistreated her in some way,' I explained. 'I mean, I think I have mistreated her but not deliberately and not obviously.'

She was shaking her head. 'No, no, she was clear that it wasn't anything like that. That would have been easy to deal with. To be honest with you, James, she hasn't really talked to me about it much at all.'

I was disappointed that I wouldn't be hearing any explanations from Mme Fournier. I'd had some vague hope that she would have some specific knowledge, that Delphine would have confided some secret in her which would shed light on these past few weeks. But it looked at that stage as though she was as much in the dark as the rest of us.

'How is she? Her health I mean? Does she seem to be OK?'

Mme Fournier looked at me shrewdly. 'She's not pregnant, if that's what you mean.'

I was flustered. 'That's not what I mean at all!' Then, 'Well, it's something I wondered about but that wasn't why I was asking.'

Her mother sighed. 'She seems fine. I know she's been swimming a lot, and reading. I don't quite know how she's paying for it all; I suppose she's got a job or something.'

'You know, I would happily help out with money if she needed it. With no conditions. I just want her to be – happy.'

'You think she'd take your money? She won't accept any help from me, so I'm perfectly sure she wouldn't from you.

As for being happy – who can say? Maybe she doesn't want to be happy just now. She seems quite happy being unhappy.'

I must have looked bemused because she laughed quite kindly and leaned over the table to pat my hand. 'You love her, don't you?'

'More than I've ever loved anyone!' I sounded so fervent, and felt quite adolescent but didn't care. 'I hope she knows that. That's why I've been sending her letters and trying to contact her. At first I just wanted her to come back but now I want her to find what she wants to do. And be happy. And so all she needs to know, while she's thinking about what to do, all I can tell her is that I love her. More than ever. Can you let her know that?'

If it were a film, that would have been the moment when the back door opened to let in a stream of light, and Mme Fournier would have looked up and smiled in delight, saying, 'You can tell her yourself right now!' and Delphine would have come in from the garden wearing a light print dress, holding a basket of apples, flowers arranged with artful carelessness in her hair.

Instead, her mother nodded and said, 'Of course. I couldn't make her open your letters, you know. I suggested we save them until she felt like looking at them but she insisted I return everything.'

'I understand. But if I send something to you by email, can you forward it to her? You do have an email address for her don't you?'

She looked uncomfortable again. 'I don't know if I should. She insisted she didn't want anything to be forwarded.'

But I persisted. 'I want her to know about a service, a memorial service, for somebody we both know who has died.'

'Alfred, the poor man who couldn't breathe in his sleep?'

'Yes.'

'You wrote about that on an envelope and I told her the details in an email.'

'Thank you for doing that. Do you think she might come?'

'I have no idea. Vietnam is a long way to come for a church service,' she commented wryly. 'As for anything else – truly, I don't know. But look, if you email something to me I will send it on, I promise.'

'Thank you so much. I do appreciate it.'

'James, I feel very sorry for you. But Delphine has always been so independent and so single-minded and I was very surprised when she told me that she had started to live with you. It's been a long time since she lived with a man. Those affairs – they kept her from making that kind of relationship. Perhaps she just can't do it, or is afraid of it.'

'I think it must be my fault,' I said, 'even if what you're saying is part of it, I don't think I helped exactly. I was silly about her dreams . . .'

Mme Fournier looked puzzled. 'What do you mean?'

'You know, those awful dreams. I never accepted that they were just bad dreams; I always thought they meant something. That they were about her fear of motherhood or something.'

'But Delphine always wanted to have children! And she doesn't have nightmares. She did when she was tiny, but she told me that in your little dream group you and she were the only two who could get to sleep at all! Except for that young man who couldn't stop himself sometimes.'

'Jagdev. So she told you about us all, then.' That pleased me. 'But OK no, not nightmares, just those awful dreams she has. Had. You know, terrible things about mothers having to choose between two children or kill their babies and all that?'

Mme Fournier put her hand to her mouth. I saw that she knew nothing of this. 'Tell me,' she said.

So I told her.

She listened intently and then said, 'Oh dear. Oh Delphine. I think those dreams must be about her brother.'

For several seconds I could see Mme Fournier mouthing words at me but I could hear nothing except a sound like the sea inside my head.

Mme Fournier told me the story which Delphine had not felt able to tell. The Fourniers had received very little information about their adoptive daughter but they were given some notes which had been scribbled down by the French nurse who had cared for Delphine's dying mother. Desperate to leave her daughter with the only gift she had left – information – the sick woman had gasped out her child's date and place of birth, the name of her father, and the fact that after his disappearance she tried to leave with both of her children but was only allowed to take one with her on the boat. Delphine's younger brother, not quite a year old, was left at the dockside with an uncle, their mother's youngest brother.

'Naturally, we tried to trace him,' Mme Fournier told me. 'My husband went over there – it was very dangerous but we had to do it for Delphine, and we got help from a church group which had been quite successful in tracking people down. But although he found out some possible leads it didn't work out that time – her father had disappeared completely, we didn't know her mother's family name and there was no proper record keeping, so it would have been hard even if it hadn't been chaos over there. If Delphine had been younger we might not have told her about it, but she was three when she came to us, and she often used to ask for her brother. We had a Vietnamese neighbour who used to translate in the early days – at first Delphine didn't speak French at all even though she knew some of the language – and this neighbour told us that Delphine seemed to understand that her mother had gone but couldn't accept that her brother wasn't there either.'

My eyes filled with tears and it was hard to ask the right questions, so eager was I to hear more. 'Do you still speak about it – I mean, did you talk about it later, when she was older?'

'Yes, from time to time. When she was a teenager we planned a trip to Vietnam and made all sorts of arrangements to start the tracing process again, we had made some quite good progress in fact, had a few trails to follow, but Delphine became almost hysterical at the idea of going; she couldn't be persuaded, so it all had to be cancelled. Once my husband became ill it was never a possibility and although I've mentioned it since he died, she's been just as firmly against it.'

'Why? Why do you think she didn't want to go?'

Mme Fournier was becoming visibly upset. 'She never said. And after that, every time we raised the subject of going there – even just for a holiday, just to get a feel for the place – she would walk out of the room. It became our taboo. We had always been so careful to keep her culture, her past, in focus, but she didn't want it. We really felt we had failed on that score.'

'I'm sure that's not what Delphine thinks. She's always spoken very admiringly of how you brought her up. But she just kept telling me she was French and not at all interested in Vietnam.'

Her mother looked me straight in the eye. 'Do you know what I think? I think she was scared. Not scared of feeling out of place in the country of her birth, or of meeting members of her family who were strangers; she could have coped with all of that. I think she was scared of discovering that her brother was dead. That her mother's choice had spared her life. That she was saved and her brother was dead.'

So now I've cried with a complete stranger. It seemed to do us both good. When I finally left I held Mme Fournier's hand with both of mine.

'Thank you. I hope we'll meet again.'

'You're welcome, James. And I hope so too. Au revoir.'

Au revoir. The door is left open. I think she liked me.

I don't know what to think about all the rest of it. All the awful, tragic rest of it. My poor Delphine. Why didn't you tell me?

20 November

I was angry when James told me he'd remembered nothing. So angry. But now I'm relieved. At the same time as wanting, wanting so much, to hear about a night full of memorable dreams, I hated the idea that I'd put her inside him in that way. I was disgusted with myself for being so — clinical — about it. But I needed my dreamless subject and he was the perfect choice.

Something happened that night. Something happened in his head whether he remembers it or not, and it happened just at the points I fed in Delphine's transmissions. This really is something massive. Hugely important.

Wayne is causing me problems. He was suspicious when I sent him off the other night, put up quite a fight to hold on to his precious machinery. I pulled rank and he'll not be pleased. He's too straight to be trusted on this one, though. Too full of best practice and patient care from all those courses he goes on.

He says he's 'lost' the data from Delphine's PSG readouts. He says he's sure it's just a missing file and he'll track it down but in the meantime they're just not there. Christ, I nearly hit him. Just managed to look a bit irritated and mutter something about him letting me know when he finds it.

So I need one more PSG from Delphine. And then I'll have another bash at it. And this time, forget my body double; I'll be the subject. I'll be the dreamless man whose head is filled with her. I'll be the man who sleeps with her voice in his mind.

Day thirty: Thursday

That little trip to France exhausted me, but I still paid a visit to the Unlucky Gym before going to work. This kind of exhaustion benefits from putting my body through its paces in order to give my mind a rest, and I've been neglecting my exercise.

The Unlucky Gym was so christened, of course, by Delphine. Part of the little collection of moving-in presents I'd bought for her was a membership of my health club and she was delighted with it, absolutely taken with the idea of keeping fit, going for a swim, having the odd sauna. She'd done a bit of aerobics in the past, a little yoga and plenty of swimming, but was bowled over by the vast array of machinery in the cardiovascular suite and the gleaming equipment which filled the floor of the immense weights room. The huge blue pool, adorned with a hot tub at one end and a sauna and steam room at the other, made her clap her hands with glee on the first occasion I took her there to show her the ropes.

But she never took to the habit of exercise. It's been part of my life for as long as I can remember, and not just the archery. I didn't enjoy the rugger and cricket element of my school sports, but took up membership of the running club and particularly liked cross country. I had a good build for middle-distance too, and enjoyed the odd game of squash. I bailed out of the competitive stuff before my knees went, swapping the muddy fields and sweaty courts followed by the team bath, for the more gentlemanly pleasures of the gymnasium and the luxury of hot showers and soft towels afterwards. I am in excellent shape and it's certainly kept me healthy as well as fit; I've rarely had a day's illness in my life. Of course, there's an element of vanity to all this as well. What man doesn't feel that powerful combination of bursting pride, pure sensual pleasure and overtly sexual anticipation when he gently tenses his arm and feels the bulges of different, carefully developed muscle groups filling out and then stretching the short sleeves of his T-shirt? There is no woman alive, I swear it, who is not pleasantly surprised to remove the clothes of her new lover and find that underneath his skin is an impressive set of well-toned muscles. He needn't ever use them overtly; the simple fact of their being there gives her, and thereby him, immense pleasure.

It's not the same vice versa. Although a well-toned female body is delightful, it's easy for a woman to overdo it and when I've been in a few rare situations where a lover's musculature is almost as impressive as my own, I've not enjoyed it. There's no 'give'. I realise that this sounds appallingly sexist but heigh ho. For me the joys of the female body are legion and I've never subscribed to any notion of having a 'type', of limiting my enjoyment to women of a particular size or shape or hair colour – preposterous! – but the common pleasure in them all is their *softness*. Even the slimmest woman (I've never gone for skinny or bony types – Siobhan was the thinnest woman I've slept with and she was by no means skeletal) has a little flesh about her waist, the gentle curves of her breasts and the slopes of her thighs. I don't like to meet with too much resistance; a woman's body needs to yield. Which again sounds like the male aggressor, but I'm afraid it's the truth.

Delphine had almost no spare flesh on her at all, but when I held her close to me I experienced only her softness and a certain compactness. Her hips and ribs were just about visible but when I lay against her they didn't intrude into the embrace. Her elbows were incredibly bony and she used to force rings over her prominent knuckles, where they would slide around her much slimmer finger, but the general impression, to the look and to the touch, was of an intensely feminine body.

All that, Delphine would agree with. And she never planned to become a body-builder, just to look after her heart and keep in the wonderful shape she already was without having to think too much about what she ate. But every time she went to exercise, some minor disaster struck – the class for which she had booked was cancelled, the steam room was out of order, the fire alarm went off, the showers were too cold, she lost one of her favourite pairs of earrings – so before too long it became the Unlucky Gym and nothing could have convinced her that going there could be in any way enjoyable.

'The only thing I like about the Unlucky Gym is the changing rooms,' she announced after another fraught attempt to take an hour's uninterrupted exercise.

'What do you mean?'

'I like seeing all the women getting changed.'

'I'd like that too.' She swiped me with her towel as she put it into the washing machine. 'But *how* do you like that? I don't like watching the men. In fact, I could get into serious trouble if I did.'

'I don't stare at them. I just like seeing these women with no clothes on looking like they belong to different species. There are huge fat ones and tiny anorexic ones, of course. But even in the middle, you get someone who's one metre eighty . . .' (I could never persuade Delphine to use the imperial system for my sake) '. . . and built like an Amazon – powerful, with big hips and a small waist and full breasts and strong thighs – and someone next to her who's probably the same height but has a flat chest and goes straight down without a dip for the waist, to a great big bottom and very well-developed calves. They're so different, it's as though the scale is wrong. I love to see it.'

I was picturing the scene myself and becoming discomfited, but Delphine went on, 'And I love seeing who uses the private changing rooms. There are only four of them, in the corners of the room, and they're almost always empty but sometimes I see someone's feet poking out from underneath and I actually wait – I don't go into the gym till I see who it is, or I take ages getting dried and dressed for the same reason. You'd think they'd be used by really old wrinkly women, or very fat ones, or someone with one leg or a massive birthmark or whatever. But no, usually those people just get on with it in the communal room with the rest of us, and the person that comes out of the cubicle is almost always a very young, very beautiful girl. She'll have a swimming costume on, or her gym kit, and it will be high cut and tiny so you can see that she's gorgeous.'

'Why does she hide away then?' I asked, unable to stop licking my lips.

Delphine continued, with a disapproving look. 'I think it's just shyness. They don't know how lovely they are. Or maybe some of them are disgusted by all the rest of us – their older sisters or mothers, with marbled flesh or droopy bosoms or fat bottoms–' She saw my longing expression and remonstrated, 'James, stop it, I'm not even talking about the beautiful sixteen-year-olds any more.'

'Sorry. It all works for me. You just keep talking about all these naked women.'

She pretended to ignore me. 'And I want to say to them – stop! You don't have many years of being like this. Let us all be able to look at you and enjoy how lovely you are and remember our young selves. Because when you're thirty you'll be out here with the rest of us wishing you'd flaunted it a bit more earlier on.'

'It's hardly as though you're one of the mottled-thigh types, my love.'

'That's not the point. I don't have youthful beauty any more. I don't mind; I'm a woman and not a girl. But it's such a shame that we don't make our daughters proud of their bodies. There isn't enough communal nakedness.'

'I absolutely agree. But I liked it better when you were telling me about the thighs and bosoms and bottoms. Can't we go back to that?' I pleaded.

'No.' She was mock-haughty now. 'And if I ever have a daughter I'll say to her every day – just look how *beautiful* you are, my lovely girl, look at your soft skin and your strong legs and your peachy bottom and your round little tummy with its sweet belly button, look at your open face and gazing eyes and shining hair; you are a work of art, be proud and happy.'

A sudden thought occurred to me and I asked, 'Are boys allowed in the women's changing rooms?'

'Over eight they have to go to the men's room even if their daddies aren't with them, but eight and under come to the women's changing rooms with their *mamans*.'

'The lucky little bastards!' I couldn't help exclaim.

Delphine protested at once. 'Oh James, they're little boys, don't sexualise them like that!'

But on this point I was positive. 'Delphine, believe me, at well before eight years old I'd have killed to enter a ladies' changing room.'

'I don't believe you. Most of them are completely unaware and of course some of them stare a bit, but I think that's good, and hopefully they'll remember . . .'

'Oh, I can guarantee they'll remember every minute of it,' I smirked.

'Oh shut up. I mean when they get to adolescence they'll know that women come in all shapes and sizes and that the female body isn't just a standardised thing they see in adverts or pornography,' she insisted reasonably.

In an instant, I was fiercely jealous of all those bloody boys allowed to gaze unhindered at Delphine's navel or her perfect little breasts or her dark strip of pubic hair. Perhaps they'd see her week after week and note the changes in her body; her slightly rounded premenstrual tummy, the soft short hairs which appeared on her thighs and legs and underarms between waxing appointments, her fading tan marks. I was becoming frantically envious until Delphine pointed out, 'And it's the same for girls. If their daddies take them swimming they go into the men's changing room until they're eight years old.'

My growing bubble of jealousy was effectively pricked as I had a vision of small sweet girls staring, appalled, at the mass of hairy-arsed men dangling their fearsome bits and pieces at eye level.

'Poor little darlings!' I said.

Delphine knew a woman who was an old-fashioned Methodist, very conventional and quite shy. They had struck up a friendship over the coffee machine at her last job before coming to the university and discovered they both enjoyed swimming. They arranged to meet at the municipal pool the following Saturday and went to the changing rooms. Delphine wouldn't have been surprised if the woman had opted for a private changing room, but had no intention of using one herself, so went up to one of the communal benches, put her money in the locker and began to undress and place her clothes inside. When she turned around to put on her costume she found that her colleague was getting changed next to her. And the shy Methodist woman had the most daringly minimal bikini wax Delphine had ever seen apart from in the uninvited images she sometimes found in her email inbox, plus a pierced navel, a nipple ring and a gold-and-green dragon tattooed on one buttock. She had said nothing; the woman had not referred to her adornment either. 'But it goes to show,' said Delphine, 'you never can tell.'

Delphine knows so many people. I mean really *knows* them. Her ceaseless anecdotes about people, all those funny, sad, awful, grim stories she told me, aren't the fruits of observation. She talks to people, all the time, and they talk to her. She has friends you wouldn't believe; people who she's no reason to give the time of day to, and who will be able to do nothing for her, but with whom she nevertheless gets along splendidly.

'You're a collector of lame ducks!' I accused her one evening, when she was late home because one of her 'acquaintances' had accosted her coming up the steps from the Tube and she had walked him back to his sheltered accommodation. I had put champagne on ice in order to make her a French 75 to sip on the balcony while I prepared supper, and was put out that she had chosen instead to spend her time with a man whose favourite tipple was most likely methylated spirit.

'Sean was depressed. I could see it. He needed someone to talk to, not a stranger, and by the time I left him he was much more settled. I'm sorry that you're put out, James, but I'm glad I spent the time with Sean because he needed me.'

'I need you!' I realised how silly this plaintive cry sounded and modified it before Delphine's expression of disbelief had fully set on her face. 'Sorry, that was pathetic. Of course you did what you had to do. And of course I'm glad too, that you were able to help. I'm sorry, my love, I was being selfish.'

She was mollified, and we had a lovely evening on the balcony exactly as planned. After that I was careful not to be so jealous of her time.

I once asked her why she picked up so many strange companions on her travels, and she said that it was because she was foreign. '. . . and I'm small. I have a friendly face . . .' here she grinned an enormous cartoon smile '. . . and so some people choose me to talk to because I don't look threatening, and others because they identify with being "different" in some way – don't laugh, James, I'm serious. You don't know how it feels, to walk along a street and be the only person who looks like you, unless you're on holiday somewhere exotic and that's different entirely. I'm not complaining about it, it's not a bad thing, it's just something which I can sympathise with, empathise with, even.'

It was a good point well made, but I didn't just mean the care in the community types who gravitated towards her. It was the giggly girls at her office with whom she'd go for drinks in awful bars, or the boring postman who brought the mail to her desk for sorting each morning and grumbled incessantly while she made him a cup of tea, or the chubby office junior who was finding it difficult to come to terms with the dual, and apparently conflicting, facts of his obvious homosexuality and even more visible breasts. The gall of these people in even approaching someone as wonderful – as clearly, obviously, strikingly wonderful – as Delphine amazed me. I was outraged on her behalf, because I suspected that they did indeed see a small oriental woman who spoke with a slightly foreign accent and that they therefore felt she was fair game, or even that almost, she should be grateful for their taking the trouble to 'include' her in their conversations. I feared that stupid people might think that they were actually being *kind* to her.

I do have a heart. I may not attract the lame and the halt like Delphine does, but I do my bit, I have several direct debits to reputable charities and make large donations at Christmas time. I won't give money to beggars, although if I didn't live in London I probably would. But I will go and have a chat with *Big Issue* sellers – buy a copy of the magazine, share a jovial comment or two; I've even bought a sandwich for them from time to time. Cheese. I thought that was pretty thoughtful; everyone likes cheese sandwiches and they're OK for vegetarians. Vegans be damned; that's taking it too far. But those chaps are always so polite and pleased with their sandwiches, I know they appreciate it and I can be sure it's not being spent on drink or drugs or a flutter on the horses which would do them no good at all.

Julie telephoned me this evening. She's cooking dinner for Simon on Saturday night and wondered whether I would like to join them, if I had no other plans . . . She must have sensed my surprise, and my hesitation was tangible, but while I mentally stumbled through the confusing messages my brain was receiving she waited patiently and even interrupted my clearly insincere ummings and ahings about where I'd left my diary with a little encouragement: 'Oh, I do hope you've not got anything else on, I know it's short notice. But, well, I miss the lab and the people I knew there . . .'

'You do?' I'd suspected that I was the only one who missed those meetings.

'Of course. I mean, I'm glad things are moving on for me, but I miss those sessions, and the people. Simon and I were just saying how we'd like to catch up with you.'

I sensed her sensitivity and said, 'You do know that Delphine is – no longer here with me?'

She answered quietly. 'Yes. Yes, we were sorry to hear that, James. She's in touch with you though, isn't she?' which meant that she was also certainly in touch with Julie, and I hoped, briefly, that she might be able to tell me how I could contact her.

'Well, she's written to me. But I don't know where to send my replies; her email address bounces anything back to me and the things I've sent to her mother's house have come back unopened. I don't suppose you know . . .'

Julie sounded genuinely sorry. 'No, James. She sent me a postcard from France but there was no reply address. I'm sorry I can't help.'

I was acutely aware of my vulnerability at this point. I had made an open plea for help, and a clear admission that I didn't know where Delphine was. But I didn't feel ashamed, or not much ashamed at any rate, and suddenly I surprised myself by saying, 'Never mind, it's not your fault. And I don't have anything arranged for Saturday night so it would be very good to see you and Simon. Thank you, I'd love to come.'

I took her address and we said our farewells.

At the session after Alfred's funeral, the group was inevitably in sombre mood. There was much discussion about what a good service it had been, how well-attended it was, how many friends Alfred had gathered around him throughout his life. I felt very regretful that I hadn't been there, and wanted to make this clear.

'I'm so sorry that I wasn't able to come,' I began. 'I would have liked to be there at Alfred's send-off and give my condolences to Jackie in person.' Several heads nodded sympathetically and I went on, conversationally, 'How do you think she's coping?'

Reeves, who had also been absent from the funeral owing to work commitments, snorted, and Jagdev began to chuckle helplessly. Polly stepped in with some soothing response, 'Jackie's coping very well. They've expected it for a while so Alfred had "put his affairs in order", and they had lots of friends who are being really supportive.'

I nodded and said, 'Well, they'd been married for a long time, hadn't they?' at which Polly, smirking, caught Jagdev's eye and he erupted into full-blown laughter. I was at a loss, unable to understand why such a perfectly reasonable question had elicited this response, and from someone who only a moment ago had seemed to be in deep and genuine mourning. Something must have triggered a little green light in Jagdev's brain, allowing some of the stress and tension of grief to escape. Unfortunately, his hearty laughter also led to one of his rare attacks of cataplexy and he slid to the floor. Polly got her hand beneath his head before it hit the ground, and the other men present helped to lift him onto the couch where he fell into a deep slumber – as usual he had dropped straight into REM sleep with no preamble – for almost twenty minutes.

By that time all the attention was on Jag and so my question seemed to be forgotten, but Delphine was annoyed with me and I couldn't tell why.

Inspired by Julie's invitation, I called Finn and invited him for dinner tomorrow. He sounded surprised, and then suspicious, but agreed to come in spite of the very short notice. I haven't a clue what I'm going to say to him. And then Eleanor called to invite me out to lunch on Sunday, so I'm on a bit of a roll, socially speaking.

Eleanor's call has been troubling me. If she had got in touch when Delphine was here I would have been pleased. Perhaps I could have tried to make amends for how I treated her, tried to explain all the things I had realised about what happened between us and how I had spoiled it. But the fact of her contacting me now has made me uncomfortable; I don't want to see her or talk to her when I don't have – the protection, it feels like – of Delphine. There is no way on earth I want to make love to another woman now, but if I did, I suppose that woman would be Eleanor. And whether or not she knows it, and I doubt she does, it feels dangerous to me. I don't quite know what to do about it, wish I'd called her months ago in an attempt to salvage a friendship or at least apologise for yet again treating her badly. I agreed to the meeting. There wasn't any hope detectable in her voice, in fact she just seemed friendly, but still I feel some disquiet. Earlier today I was annoyed with myself, and fearful that the intensity of my feelings for Delphine were beginning to wane in the face of her continued absence from my life. But it's inevitable that this level of – of what, I don't know – of longing and loss and anxiety and hope – has to fall off a little. I don't mean that my feelings for her will be reduced, but their expression is bound to. I'm on day thirty already, how will I feel if I get to day forty, day fifty; if I begin to count this journal in weeks, or even months? When she first left I would have signed up to completing year five without a moment's hesitation, but now there are new ways in which I can think about my love; things which seem so much more connected to her and our life together. And if she does come back – and I imagine it daily but I can't quite believe it's going to happen – then what do I want her to find? A sad man hunched over his keyboard in some act of pointless commemoration? Or just this flat, clean and tidy, decorated with her postcards? And me answering the door and making her a coffee and talking in the kitchen about all the places we've been and the people we've talked to. Surely she would want me to get out of here sometimes, to avoid it becoming some kind of mausoleum?

I'm still crying a lot. I did go through a phase lasting a few days, when every time I started to well up I couldn't allow myself to sob; I felt so stupid I had to stop. The sounds were inhuman. Delphine used to say that the only thing which scared her about getting older was the possibility she might cry more than she already did.

'Not a chance!' I assured her. 'I don't know anyone who weeps like you do at the craziest things.'

It didn't have to be some emotionally manipulative film in which you knew damn well that the scene with the dying wife and distraught husband was designed to force tears from the hardest heart; she could cry at something on the news, or in a book, or on the trashiest TV soap. She cried about love, death, friendship, joy, courage; she cried about powerlessness and coincidence and faith. One morning I popped out to buy croissants for breakfast and returned to find tears streaming down her face as she listened to a reporter's strained voice speaking about a disaster on the radio. I recognised the report at once, and rushed to explain, 'Delphine, don't cry, it's not happening now. It's about a place called Aberfan, in Wales, and there was this terrible landslide on to a primary school. I remember it happening, it was in '66 and it felt like 9/11, everyone was distraught. This must be the anniversary. But it's not happening now.'

She was not to be comforted. 'One hundred and fourteen children died, and lots of adults. I've just heard a man who said . . .' She could barely repeat it. '". . . it's a terrible thing, for three of you to walk to school in the morning and only one of you come back."'

'I know, I know. It was terrible. But it was a long time ago, love, don't cry about it now.'

'What difference does that make?' she said, dismayed. 'They're still dead, aren't they? Am I only allowed to cry at sad things which are happening *now*? I bet lots of people will be crying at this however many times they've heard it. They'll be crying *because of* how many times they've heard it.'

'My darling girl, you're so sensitive, you mustn't let things get to you like this.'

She looked puzzled again and, through her nose blowing and eye-wiping, just asked me, 'Why not?'

So she feared an old age in which all she could do was cry, at everything sad happening in the world, and everything sad which had ever happened, and at finding things sad which before she wouldn't have found sad at all. 'And if I had children I'd be even worse,' she said, 'because mothers cry at silly things, they start when they're pregnant and then they can't stop, all my friends with babies tell me that's true. So just think, I'd be *inconsolable*.'

'It won't come to that, my love,' I said soothingly. 'I'll make sure you don't cry more as you get older. I'll make sure you cry less now!'

But she didn't seem to believe me and I think perhaps she quite liked crying after all. I'm certainly finding it comforting, now that I've got over the shame of it.

I'm so tired. The insomnia remains, and bothers me far more than it used to, when I thought it was a normal part of my life. I tried to explain what that tiredness felt like to Delphine and she asked me, 'What are you tired *of*?'

It was a good question. Before I met her I'd been rather tired of life but she made life seem far more compelling. I stopped being tired of things when I started sleeping with her.

This is desperate. I've even started to look at the little herbal remedies pamphlet that Julie handed out to everyone in the early days of Dream Lab. I went to the wholefood shop near the Tube on the way to work, and realised it was the first time I had ever been in one of those places since I was a student. That fusty, lentilly smell was just the same, although the array of products was rather more impressive. You could spend a fortune on taking evening primrose oil for your joints and garlic capsules for your blood and fennel for your indigestion and echinacea to prevent colds and all manner of vitamin and mineral supplements for everything else you can think of. Surely a healthy diet and a scarf in winter would do the trick for most of us? I bought some valerian, which Julie recommended, and lemon balm because I liked the name.

They even sell hops which apparently gives you 'a natural night's sleep with no headache'. Sounded ominous to me. I'd rather drink it in the form of beer. I also bought some 'natural' liquorice and organic peanut butter. I shall be wearing sandals next.

I'd told Delphine that as a young man in the seventies I'd been very scornful of those from my circle who became vegetarians, and strongly resented having to sit in smelly cafés to indulge their affectation. 'They were all so pleased to be *homogeneous*,' I explained. 'As though it was acceptable for one's eating habits to define one's political viewpoint, cultural interests, even one's clothing. Why should someone who chooses not to eat meat automatically want to eat wholegrain rice and lentil broth on bench seating in some basement?'

Delphine thought my irritation highly amusing. 'Most vegetarians do it for political reasons. Ethical reasons, you know. So of course they share some other ideals about fair trade and organic produce and so on.'

'But lots of people stop eating meat purely for health reasons. And even if they don't believe they should eat meat it doesn't always follow that they give a damn about where their bananas come from, or give up drinking proper coffee. For a while I seriously thought of opening a vegetarian café where they would serve decent French food on mahogany tables, accompanied by choral music. Copies of the *FT* and *The Economist* would be available and the wine cellar would be amazing. Delphine, what's so funny?'

'A right-wing vegetarian café!' she hooted. 'Oh James, that's *wonderful*!' and she kissed me hard.

Delphine would want to go to Alfred's service. I sent an email to her mother, giving the full details. I also wrote that if she wanted to get a message through to one of the group to say she was coming, I would be prepared not to attend. I don't want to make her feel uncomfortable.

Even during wartime, Winston Churchill liked to stay in bed until midday, seeing any visitors and holding meetings with cabinet members whilst still in his pyjamas. Everyone knows his reputation as a power-napper too, able to grab ten minutes of shut-eye and be bright and alert for the next four hours. That doesn't seem like such a waste of time; in fact it seems like the perfect way to while away a dull moment. He must have been so relaxed, to be able to drop off like that. I'm not running a country or overseeing a war; why is it so difficult for me?

I've been re-reading some of my early notes about sleep-lessness. It's odd, the way that not sleeping hastens the big sleep from which we never wake – like Alfred with his constant wakings, his restless nights, just managing to grab half an hour of decent kip here and there, and usually not even that. Whereas if you sleep well you will, all things being equal, be more successful at postponing death. Is it Buddhist, that notion of having a fixed number of heartbeats in your life, hence the need to impose calm and relaxation in order to breathe more slowly, reduce your heart rate and make life last longer? It's a bit like that, or like a kind of fealty – we lesser mortals, we serfs, have undertaken to spend a certain number of hours of our lives in a state of unconsciousness and if we fail to do so our feudal lord – whoever He is – can take what's owed to him and make up the underpayment by imposing upon us the ultimate unconsciousness earlier than expected. So whether you're a stressed businessman who's at his desk by seven in the morning and goes to bed late after taking all his paperwork home, or a long-suffering insomniac who does all he can to sleep but fails, you're punished either way for not putting in the hours of shut-eye. We must each have our own individual tariff because some people can survive on remarkably little sleep. Margaret Thatcher, I seem to recall, could rest for four hours and then be up and ready for battle in the morning.

Sleep deprivation is harmful to all species. I read about a nineteenth-century Russian scientist called Marie de Manacéïne who used puppies as her guinea pigs. They were forced to remain awake and they all died horribly after around four or five days. One's metabolism goes to pot and however much food one eats it's never enough to stave off exhaustion, or skin lesions, eye infections, breathing difficulties – a long list of debilitating symptoms, until the heart gives out. When I read about those experiments I was extremely disturbed. I'm no great anti-vivisectionist; I have all the standard ethical objections to shampoo being squirted in rabbits' eyes, but would allow millions of mice to die if the knowledge gained would save a human child. But I had two spontaneous reactions to this experiment: firstly, what kind of woman was she? And secondly, did it have to be *puppies*?

Adult dogs last a little longer without sleep – up to seventeen days – and rats can hold on to life for three weeks.

A man will die from lack of sleep far sooner than he will die of starvation.

There's a terrible summer storm outside. The sky is quite yellow and the air is prickling with electricity. The hairs on my arms are upright. I fear for Delphine in this weather. I see her bedraggled and shelterless. I know she can take care of herself, but that's not the point; I want to do it.

Day thirty-one: Friday

Finn brought his girlfriend to dinner. He called this morning to ask if that was OK and I could hardly say no, although my first reaction was to feel hostile towards the idea. Despite having no plans about what to say to him, I did assume that we'd be having what one might call a heart to heart, which would be hardly possible with someone else there. Then again, my playing the part of his father cooking a meal for him was already so laden with peculiarity that the presence of somebody else was probably a mercy.

They've just gone. I've learnt at least two big important things about my son this evening. I discovered the first as I brought out the roast with a flourish and was about to start carving. I thought that the silence from the two of them was awe, but then caught the look on Finn's face.

'You don't like lamb?' I asked.

'Erm – actually, I'm really sorry, I should have told you, I forgot you didn't know, but actually, I'm vegetarian. And so's Charlotte.'

It could have been a terrible moment. I was angry at first; that beautiful leg of lamb had been marinated and roasted to perfection and my son was now rejecting it. In that instant I remembered my mother's face when we didn't express the right level of appreciation for the food she served us or, worse, left something on our plates. She rarely cooked for us except on what amounted to showcase occasions, and we always felt the pressure. I remembered the fear at having angered her, the pain at having upset her, the irritation with myself that I simply *couldn't* swallow the mouthful, and the resentment that all this was happening without my being able to stop it. And I controlled my anger. I wouldn't make Finn feel that way. Harder to control was the urge to cry; here was this young man, my son, and we had never eaten together before. Never broken bread together. I felt so ashamed, it was hard not to show it but what I actually did was neither shout nor cry; I laughed.

'I'm so sorry! I should have checked. Don't worry at all, give me a moment and I'll sort something else out,' I said, and the look of relief on their faces was a joy to behold.

I set the lamb and its gravy to one side and covered it up. The potatoes, having been cooked beneath the lamb to catch the drips of fat, wouldn't do either. I had a dish of buttered baby vegetables, which I put in the oven to keep warm, and then casually looked through the cupboards in as unconcerned a manner as possible.

'Do you both like porcini?' I asked hopefully.

'My favourite,' said Charlotte, perhaps out of politeness, and so I put them to soak and rustled up a risotto, splashed around a bit of Marsala (having checked that they weren't teetotal as well!) and went heavy on the cream and parmesan, and we ate that with the vegetables and some bread, and I could see that they were impressed by the speed with which I assembled it as well as the finished result. I put the claret I'd picked out for the lamb back in the wine rack and opened the bottle of Bardolino they'd brought with them, which was rough and ready and much better suited to the meal.

As we talked I learnt the second big thing about Finn: he is getting married. He has been going out with Charlotte for three years now, has a steady job in the research department of one of those ecological charities working on 'renewable energy', not a job I'd have envisaged for any son of mine but it seems to suit him, and they are going to tie the knot next spring. They are in the process of buying a flat, in Kilburn of all places. Not far from me in terms of mere geography, although in other respects a world away.

I did know that Finn had a girlfriend and might have dredged her name up from my memory, given time. But it never occurred to me to suggest that I might meet her, or that she might like to meet me. And now here she was, my prospective daughter-in-law. How much catching up I have to do! They looked so pleased with each other, so happy, and I wanted to offer help but realised that all I had which might prove useful was money, and it seemed indelicate to mention it at that point. But Finn brought the subject up. 'Mum set aside the money you sent for me,' he explained, 'she managed to save nearly all of it, with a bit of help from my uncles and by doing bits of work here and there. So it's grown into a really good deposit we can put down on a flat. I've not touched it until now.'

'I had no idea your mother wasn't using that money while you were growing up,' I began, amazed that Siobhan had been so resourceful. 'There were no conditions attached to it . . .'

'Oh, I know, it's OK; Mum said it was entirely her decision. We didn't go short or anything, not really. I mean, she refused to send me to public school didn't she? Well, that saved a bob or two. And I did use the allowance you gave me for when I went to university, so as not to get into debt. It was just that she knew that otherwise she wouldn't be able to save – she's usually terrible with money – so she saw it as her only chance.'

'I wish I'd known. I could have sent more . . . Finn, I'm terribly sorry if you feel that . . .'

'No, Dad, really, I didn't tell you that to make you feel guilty. It was just to explain how we can afford to buy a flat. You know, the London conversations about property prices and all that, I just assume everyone's going to ask us what we're paying and how much we're putting down and what the mortgage will be and so on. Sorry, it wasn't meant to come out as a criticism or anything of the sort – it's great for us, it's made buying the flat possible . . .'

I wasn't listening very closely, and he knew it, because he'd noticed – a little after me but he'd noticed – that he'd said 'Dad' for the first time, and he saw my eyes fill with tears which made him slightly flustered so it was remarkable he got to the end of his sentence at all. Charlotte, sensitively, began to clear up the plates and pile them by the sink and I patted Finn's arm rather nervously and said, 'Well done. And congratulations – about Charlotte and the flat. I truly hope that you'll be very happy in both of them.'

And this time it was Charlotte who burst out laughing first, closely joined by Finn, while I took a little while to cotton on and then felt mortified at my unusual verbal clumsiness. But soon enough I joined in the laughter too.

We spoke about my family and his. He's going to meet John and Stacey and the kids and introduce them to Charlotte. He seemed so pleased when I suggested it. 'I don't have any cousins anywhere near my age because Mum's brothers are both so much older than she is and their kids are in their forties,' he said, 'and I always wanted more kids in the family. I used to nag Mum for a brother or sister and when I realised she'd need to find a bloke first I was always trying to set her up. Mind you, my uncles were just as bad; they'd always be bringing these single friends of theirs home to meet her on ridiculous pretexts – she had to place a ban on it in the end.'

'Why do you think she didn't marry again?' I asked.

He looked thoughtful and a little uncomfortable. 'I suppose you don't really know Mum that well – I mean, you didn't know her for very long. She had a few problems you see – she was a bit up and down emotionally, mentally. It was fine – once I was born she was really careful about using the medication properly and it's pretty much under control. But I think it made her very wary of being with someone who might not – well, might not understand it. So in some ways I think she held herself apart, didn't get involved with men. And of course there wasn't much choice around. She said that there were obvious reasons why her brothers' single friends were single. She did see a couple of men, one when I was very young who I don't remember at all, but he was already married and it wasn't that serious anyway, and another when I was in my teens. That lasted about three years, but it never seemed to develop and she ended it.'

'Did you like him?'

'He was OK. He was always pretty nice to me. Maybe he was just a bit of a commitment-phobe, I don't know. I've never really spoken to Mum about it in any detail and she didn't seem heartbroken. She's always said – no regrets.'

'And do you believe her?'

'I believe that she wants me to believe her. You know, she doesn't want me to feel as though I'd ruined her life or anything.'

'I'm sure she feels quite the opposite, Finn. She very much wanted a child. If anything, I ruined her life, or at least I didn't help make it any easier for her.' He looked uncomfortable again but didn't reply. 'What do you think she would say if I asked to see her?' I went on. 'Do you think she would object?'

'No. I'm sure she wouldn't. I mean, we'd like you – Charlotte and I would like you – to come to the wedding and it would be good if you could have met before . . .'

'I'll call her soon,' I promised, sounding braver about the prospect than I felt.

Delphine's last lover often had black moods. He would be sullen and morose, and although he would always assure her that it wasn't her fault, it was equally clear that she had no beneficial effect on him at those times.

'Whatever I said or did couldn't cheer him up,' she told me. 'I think he enjoyed it somehow, feeling so down. He talked about "the black dog" and used to hint that he was thinking about suicide.'

'The black dog. That's depression. Do you think he was depressed?'

'No. I think he wanted to be. Maybe he was once – he'd been treated for depression when he was at university, or at least he said he had, but whenever I saw him in one of his "depressed" moods it just looked like grumpy to me. And I noticed that it was usually something to do with guilt, something he'd forgotten to do which he'd promised he would or, towards the end, something I'd say which would make him angry.'

'What kind of thing?'

'You know, asking where he'd been or who he'd been with. I tried not to seem suspicious but he used to get mad with me, and then he'd slump and say sorry, his head was in a bad place, it wasn't my fault but there was nothing I could do, this just happened to him from time to time.'

'You don't sound very sympathetic.' In fact, her ferocity startled me.

'I've met enough people who are really depressive to know that he was just making excuses to make me feel sorry for him. He *always* felt sorry for himself, he was always talking about how he didn't get the recognition he deserved and how hard his life was, which wasn't true at all, and he used to say that he didn't like himself, that he wasn't worthy of my love, that kind of thing.'

'And you didn't believe that either?'

'I did, for a long time. Even after I'd finished it I still hung on to that idea, that he'd been unfaithful out of weakness and hopelessness, almost as a *justification* for feeling unworthy of me. It was the baby that made me realise.'

'Realise what?'

'That he was lying about feeling worthless. It was just another element of his egotism, to talk in that way. In fact, he thought he was such a wonderful human being that he should attempt to reproduce himself at every opportunity. I'd thought he wanted *us* to make a child, but really any woman would have done. A man who was truly depressed wouldn't have chased another woman while still swearing that he loved me and a man who hated himself that much wouldn't be so

260

keen to have more children.' It sounded feasible, if a little simplistic, and I nodded in faint agreement but that didn't satisfy Delphine. 'You think I'm just trying to make sense of it, don't you?' she said sadly.

'No, I mean yes, in one respect that's true of course, but what's wrong with that? I do see what you're saying, and it's probably true, especially the stuff about babies . . .'

As a man who had never considered having children it seemed extraordinary to me that her ex had been so obsessed by the subject; I'd always assumed that men had children because their women wanted to, so it was difficult for me to imagine myself into his shoes, in which I felt uncomfortable in any case. After Finn's conception I frequently considered having the snip but never quite got round to it. Cowardice, I suppose, at the prospect of a medical operation which never seemed vital: the Pill had always taken care of everything for me. I was *trying* to imagine her lover's point of view though. 'But love is such a complicated thing, it's not just a set of emotions you transfer from one person to the next. Perhaps you don't want to admit that he may have still loved you in spite of being unfaithful to you.'

'But he said he loved her too!'

'Perhaps that was true as well,' I suggested tentatively.

We had covered this ground before but clearly not to Delphine's satisfaction and she looked at me in disbelief. 'James, do you really think a man can love two women – sexually and passionately – and tell them both that he wants to have a child with them – and *actually mean it*?'

'I do think that. I can certainly imagine it. Perhaps he did mean it.' She shook her head impatiently.

'OK, so let's say that somehow or other he's convinced

himself of that, that he's found that way of excusing himself and allowing it all to happen as though it's not in his control. Let's say that he really does mean it. But do you think it could be *true*?'

'Yes, I think so,' I answered honestly. She was adamant in her disagreement.

'But no! If you love a woman – and you are in love with her – you can't possibly fall in love with another woman at the same time. I don't mean that a man can't love his wife after twenty years of marriage but still "fall for" someone new and exciting, I'm not naïve, James. But I'm talking about a situation in which we were still passionately in love, he was still declaring himself to me all the time, and that didn't stop him going crazy about someone else, someone who'd fit his baby-making plan better than I was doing. I couldn't do that kind of being in love with two people at the same time. I would always have to love just one person. Could you do it?'

I thought about meeting Siobhan and responding to her flirtatious approach. My girlfriend of the time didn't merit a second thought, but Cathy, my lover, did. And I know what I did; I put her from my mind. I remembered her husband and her child and how difficult it was for us to meet. I remembered how miserable she used to look when we parted. I remembered how I hated the long weeks between our meetings. I avoided thinking about her eyes and her body and the way she said she loved me. I knew that I loved her dearly, but I put her from my mind. How could I admit to such a thing? I simply couldn't.

'No,' I said, looking earnestly at Delphine. 'No, I couldn't.'

She didn't look convinced. I thought she looked anxious. But I think now that she was scared.

Now, I would tell her that I had done just that. I would tell her that I had dishonoured love out of pure selfishness and justified it to myself by claiming temporary insanity. I would tell her about the weariness I felt about Cathy, about a love which was making no progress, which seemed to be thwarted at every turn and which I should have taken with both hands and held on to, whatever the world would have said. I would tell her that the worst thing I did to Cathy, who so desperately wanted our child, was to recklessly rush off to make a child with a stranger. And the worst thing I did to Siobhan was to allow her to believe that my love was true and deep, so true that she believed I would never leave her. The truth is that my version of love was a poor scrap of a thing, too bound up in me to ever reach out far enough and firmly enough to link itself to another human being, to a woman. I saw Siobhan's deep red hair and slim, nervous body and I wanted her. And all the love I had for Cathy was squashed into a box at the bottom of my heart where I couldn't hear it calling. I was just like Delphine's last lover, flailing about in a mire of desire and denial without the faith to hold on to love. Everything she told me about him used to make me feel secure about the vast differences that existed between the two of us. Not far apart in age and class perhaps, but worlds apart in terms of what we expected of life and what bits of it we respectively wanted Delphine to provide. I know that early on those differences comforted her. But I'm afraid that she discovered them to be superficial; she found out that he and I shared some inherent traits.

And I want to tell her that now I have changed. I could never fall in love with someone else when I am so in love with her. My love has become a strong, living thing; it won't bend to the breeze or snap under pressure. I know what she means by love, at last. When she was in front of me I didn't think about it, but now that she's gone my love is a weight upon my heart. This time, I will bear it. I will be an honourable man.

Delphine's last lover never once, even at the end, admitted he didn't love her. He insisted that he had been in love with her from the beginning and that his love for her had continued to burn bright as ever, if a little bruised, throughout his affair. I know how it's possible to do that. Possible for men, some men, to do that. Or convince themselves that they do indeed love two women, without examining what that means, whether that's true. Does it diminish the love, for either beloved? Certainly, if they find out about it. And I suppose that a love which is so non-exclusive is *worth less* than a monogamous devotion. It never felt that way to me; I made sure I wasn't caught out. But Delphine said that if she was with a man like that it meant there had to be more than 'I Love You'. If 'I Love You' could be sincerely said to two people then it couldn't possibly be enough for one. Not for her. She had a disclaimer too, one she told him: when she said 'I Love You' to a man who was saying it back to her, the truth of the entire dialogue was conditional on their telling the truth to one another. Her love was for the man she saw reciprocating it, the man who was faithful. If he was deceiving her, taking her love under false pretences, 'Then it is not love,' she said. 'It's not love at all, because everything it's based on is untrue. So how can it be?' And she said, to that faithless lover when she left him, 'How funny this is. You have deceived me, yet in spite of your behaviour, and your claiming to love another woman, you will not admit that you don't love me. Whereas I have thought I loved you all this time, have acted as though I love you and been true to you, but only now discover that I loved someone else; the man you pretended to be. Which means that as soon as you deceived me all my love meant nothing. Do you understand? It was an illusion, one which took us both in. And now it's gone. I don't love you.'

When she said that to him, he cried. And she felt nothing but scorn for him, because she had no belief left, even in his tears.

I suppose I am feeling my age at this moment. Fifty-one isn't supposed to be that old nowadays, it's hardly even middle-aged, and I've always relied on looking younger than I am to buoy up the way I feel about myself. But having a grown-up child, and one who is about to become even more grown-up, due to be mortgaged and married within the next twelve months, has made me sit back and take a deep breath. In not so many years' time I could be a grandfather. How will I manage to do that, when I've been such a failure as a father? And as a son. I think I'm scared, for Finn and Charlotte. I'm fearful of how strongly I fear for them. As though all the years I should have spent fretting and worrying about Finn's happiness and friendships and exam results – or the company he was keeping and whether or not he should have a motor-bike, all those classic parental anxieties – have been saving it all up to throw at me now. It's floored me, this duty of *care*. I care so much for him, despite hardly knowing him, because of hardly knowing him. I hope he wants to know me.

Sometimes I wanted to reassure Delphine that my love

for her was nothing to do with the age gap between us; that the fact she was twenty years younger than me didn't give me some frisson or make me feel as though I'd won a trophy, that I would have loved her as much and in the same way even if she'd been older than me. I expressed myself badly though. 'Delphine, I wish you were the same age as me!' I once said, sincerely, and for a moment she looked shocked as she translated that wish into its potential consequences: wiping out decades of her life, bringing her nearer to death.

But then she saw what I meant and she laughed and understood. 'I know, you're not the child-catcher,' she said, and kissed me.

I called Sally after Finn had gone. She seemed surprised to hear from me, but not displeased. She said she was sorry to hear about Delphine going, and it sounded like she meant it. I asked her if she'd like to have a coffee some time and she said yes, that would be nice, but she was just about to go to Barcelona for a week with a friend so she'd call me when she got back. Her voice was lighter than usual, and I said, 'You sound very cheerful.'

'Yes, it's been hard but I'm having a good time now. Feeling more settled. Well, settled into not being settled, I suppose. I should have done this years ago, you know, but I was always too scared.'

'How is your health?' I enquired.

'Very good. The RLS is much better now and in a little while I'll only need to attend the Sleep Clinic for check-ups every few months. All I needed to do was to get some sleep. It was that simple. As soon as I was able to get a couple of weeks of normal sleeping my mind cleared as if by magic and I finally felt able to make lots of decisions.'

'I've become something of an insomniac again,' I confessed, with a little feeling of something like pride, not that Sally was likely to be impressed by it.

'Oh James, I am sorry. Of course you'll have been having a bad time of it, I'm so sorry to be prattling on about how wonderful things are for me.'

'Not at all, I'm very pleased for you, I really am. It just feels as though everybody else is getting their sleep problems sorted out while mine are just starting up again, so I'm playing catch-up. As usual.'

'Do you think she'll come back?'

The question floored me. Nobody had asked it before, and that fact had made me fear that it was so evidently not a possibility that mentioning it would have been in bad taste. I asked, 'Do you think she might?'

Sally must have recognised my hopeful tone and probably regretted having asked in the first place. 'Oh James, I really don't know. She wrote to me a few weeks ago and didn't say anything which suggested she would or wouldn't come back. I just wondered what you thought about it.'

'I don't know either. She left everything in the flat, you know. Why might she do that, do you think?' Then, in the silence which followed, I checked myself. 'Forget I said that, I'm sorry, it's the last thing I should be asking you, Sally.'

She dismissed my apology in a friendly manner and assured me, 'You can ask me anything, James, I don't bear you any grudges, all right?' and I bathed in forgiveness as she went on, thoughtfully, 'Hmm, I think that if I did that it would be for two very different possible reasons.'

'What are they?' I desperately wanted to hear them.

'Remember, this is just my take on it, OK? Well, if I wanted to leave someone for ever and leave all my life with him behind, I would do just that. I might actually clear it all up and throw it out actually, but if I wanted him to suffer I'd leave it all where it was.' I felt crestfallen, but she went on. 'On the other hand, if I wanted to leave everything so that I could walk back into it then I'd do the same thing.'

I perked up. 'I'd narrowed it down to those two possibilities, I'm glad to hear you still think there's a possible positive outcome,' I told her, and she immediately backtracked. 'James, I did say it's what I would do, but I'm not Delphine. You asked me a question and I answered it but please don't read anything into it, I don't think these sorts of things obey such — such neat rules.'

'I understand, really I do. But the latter scenario — her just coming back and living with me again — it's what I want to happen, but how can I do anything about it when I have no way of contacting her?'

Sally paused. 'There isn't anything you can *do*. But that's not the same as thinking or hoping. Is it?'

'Thinking and hoping are all very well but what do they achieve?' My voice sounded pathetic even to me.

'They are their own achievements. Thinking and hoping that Delphine will come back to you won't make anything happen, or at least it won't make her come back or not come back. But whilst you're allowing yourself to think and to hope you never know what else might happen; things which you *are* in control of or can affect somehow.'

'What do you mean?'

'It sounds more mysterious than it is, James. All I know is

that as soon as I began to take the time to really consider my life and try to work out what bits of it I could salvage and what I'd have to change, I realised that I'd actually never reach a conclusion. Moving away from home was obviously a big thing to do but I didn't confront my husband and demand a divorce, and nor did I say I "needed my own space" or anything like that. I just told him that I didn't want to live there any more and I didn't know how long I would feel like that – and that was that.'

'How did that help?'

'It helped because it wasn't me trying to go through the motions you're supposed to go through when you leave. I don't know if I want to leave my husband; I thought that's what I wanted but now I'm not sure. All I did know was that I wanted to go away for a while, so that's what I told him. And our conversations since then have been the most productive and respectful for years.'

'Sally, I'm glad for you, but I still don't see how that has anything to do with me or Delphine . . .'

'Me neither. I was just trying to explain this *process*. I'm not trying to make massive decisions or cut things out of my life or make a new start or anything like that. When I come back from Spain I may even go back home, at least for a while. Gerard and I have been married for nearly twenty-five years; I want to make sure that whatever happens I'm not destroying things or upsetting people I care about. Even if I'm not sure how I care about them. Nothing is definite, and I thought that would be terrifying but it's the most relaxing, comforting state I've ever been in. Do you understand?'

'I'm not sure. I mean, of course I'd hate to *know* that she was never coming back, but then again that kind of certainty would allow me to – move on, as they say.'

'But you don't want to move on, do you? You can't tell yourself lots of *reasons* about why you should move on and then expect it to happen. In any case, that's not moving on, it's turning away. Running away maybe. You have to go *through* it, one way or another.'

'You're talking like a psychologist!'

'I know, those phrases are so naff aren't they? But they do make sense.' She paused. 'James, this is something I talked about with Delphine. We spoke on my last night at the lab and then we met up a couple of times after that. She was a great help to me.'

'She seems to have helped everyone,' I commented, 'or nearly everyone.'

Sally ignored my sarcasm and said thoughtfully, 'You know, the odd thing is, sleeping more – spending far more time completely unconscious – has made me much more *conscious*. All those disturbed nights and mad dreams – which have stopped now, you'll be relieved to know – were making me walk through my life as though I were dreaming. Sleeping more has made me wake up to what's really happening, what's really at stake. Isn't that strange?'

Delphine's last lover never knew that she had miscarried his child. She told me how she found out she was pregnant just after she'd discovered that his new lover was also expecting his baby.

'Why didn't you tell him?' I asked her, surprised that she had taken so many months to mention this, after we had had so many conversations about him.

270

'There was no time. I miscarried when I was about nine weeks pregnant and I hadn't told anybody. And there was no point in telling him after that.' Her voice was flat and quiet. The air was prickling with danger; I didn't know what she felt and therefore couldn't think what to say.

I remembered her tirade against Siobhan and women who have babies 'selfishly' and asked her, 'Was it – she – the student you spoke about? The woman who was desperate to have a baby with any man she met?'

She nodded and at that moment she looked so sad but I couldn't tell whether that was about the miscarriage or the relationship or the infidelity or anything else. Instead of asking her what she felt – such an obvious thing to do and yet I was fearful of doing so – I said, sympathetically, 'That's an awfully difficult way for you to prove your mother wrong.'

She looked up sharply and my heart sank.

'What do you mean?'

'You know . . . about only having a relationship with a man you would have a child with and all that . . .' I stammered.

She looked into the middle distance and said, almost dreamily, 'If the worst came to the worst. Well it did. He chose to have a child with someone else while swearing he loved me. I can't think of much worse. But, James, my mother was right.'

'You wanted to have his baby?'

'Of course I didn't want to have his baby!' she snapped. 'I would not have chosen to have his baby, not in those circumstances. I had been very careful not to have his baby, I'm not like *her*, I wouldn't make a baby who couldn't have a father.' She gave a bitter little laugh. 'You know, it sounds ridiculous, but I still don't know how it happened. Biologically. It was the wrong time of the month to conceive. But women can ovulate twice in a month, I discovered. Nobody ever taught me that at school. Did you know that?' I didn't. 'So no, I didn't want to have his baby. But I wanted *my* baby. I didn't want to lose my baby.'

She cried and cried and I held her close until she stopped but I don't think I was any help at all.

'Like wine through water' is how Emily Brontë's Cathy described the effect that dreams had on her mind. She meant to convey how her dream life was rich, vivid, and suffused her waking life, but when I asked Delphine what she thought about the phrase she shivered and said, 'All that makes me see is a swirl of blood in a test tube.'

Day thirty-two: Saturday

Sunday morning actually. I was too tired to write yesterday night. Julie is a very good cook. She has mastered seafood, my one great culinary shortcoming: despite having worked my way steadily through all thirty-one lobster recipes in *Larousse*, any successes were hard-won, and I never had the *feel* for it. But Julie's *bouillabaisse* was as good as any I've tasted in Marseilles, and probably more hygienically prepared. There was a moment, sitting with Simon in the tiny dining room of Julie's beautiful flat (yes, not the dilapidated council block I'd imagined, and some really wonderful abstract pieces of art on the walls), both of us using slabs of Turkish flatbread to mop up the last of the soup and *rouille*, when I felt utterly contented. Neither Simon nor I felt obliged to talk as we cleaned our bowls until the porcelain gleamed, and when Julie walked in with a big, wobbly sponge cake sandwiched with strawberry jam and whipped cream I felt quite excited! And I'm smiling now, as I recall the moment at which I had just complimented Julie on the superb quality of her baking, and taken another greedy mouthful, only to be told that Simon had made the cake, and subsequently almost choked in surprise.

'Is it that much of a shock?' he asked in amusement. 'I've lived alone for a few years now, how's a man supposed to spend his time? And anyway, Delphine told us that you were a great cook, the pressure was on!'

It wasn't the first time she had been mentioned, but it was the first moment at which I felt the pain of her absence sharply instead of the usual ache. 'Did she?' was all I could say.

'Oh yeah, after one of the lab sessions she was going through a list of your specialities and it sounded amazing.'

'Well, I've had lots of practice. You'll have to come round and try some. And anyway, Delphine's not such a bad cook herself. You know, I never saw a person make so much food out of so little. That was the main difference in the way we cooked, that and the *speed* she did it at. I'd heave bags and bags of choice ingredients onto the work surface and, after hours of close work, serve up these minuscule, exquisite little platefuls. Whereas she'd breeze in through the door with a carrier bag containing a few items and emerge half an hour later with masses of food.'

'You make it sound as though Delphine worked miracles,'

Julie said, at which Simon laughed, 'The Feeding of the Two! From only one loaf, two fishes, and a sprig of coriander, Delphine transformed the meagre fare into a feast.'

I could see Julie watching me in some concern, as though she were afraid that I'd take offence, but I didn't, couldn't, not when I was laughing along and talking about Delphine.

If Simon had known the way I used to speak about him I wonder if he'd have been so pleasant to me. During the course of our conversation he referred to his 'bad time' as though I knew what he was talking about and when I looked at him questioningly he seemed surprised.

'I told Delphine about all this a few months ago,' he said. 'I thought she'd have passed it on . . .'

'No, she didn't mention it.' I was embarrassed but he didn't seem to be.

'Oh, well it's just that after my wife divorced me four years ago I went through a really bad patch. Lost my job, wouldn't speak to anyone and couldn't cope with the sleeplessness and so on. Got very depressed. I ended up sitting with a bottle of pills and a bottle of whisky but instead of downing them, I phoned the Samaritans.'

'I'm so sorry, I didn't realise . . .' I began.

'No worries, it's not something I talk about a lot but I've not got a problem with talking about it either. I told Delphine because I knew she wouldn't look at me differently – you know, as someone who'd had such a serious emotional problem, mental health issue, whatever you want to call it.'

'And Simon does two sessions a week with the Samaritans now,' said Julie. She sounded proud of him, and I noticed that he was about to admonish her for giving away his secrets but then stopped and gave her a little smile.

'That's very – commendable,' I said, a little stiffly because I was feeling so awful at the assumptions I'd made about Simon, about his predatory wolfishness. I didn't know what to say. 'I suppose I didn't ever ask you much about your life before the lab . . .'

'No, we didn't talk much socially did we? Still, Delphine's so good at getting information out of you – I've never known anyone be so charmingly nosey.'

That was certainly true, but Julie took him to task. 'That's not the right word at all! She's just very – connected, very interested, in everything and everyone around her.'

As she spoke, Simon cupped his hand to his face and mischievously mouthed 'Nosey!' just in Julie's eye-line.

She frowned tolerantly at him and went on. 'When I mentioned that I was a widow she was so sympathetic without being embarrassed. People don't like young widows; they resent you using the word. But she makes you want to talk about stuff you don't necessarily talk about with other people that much.' She noticed me looking blank again and explained, gently. 'My husband died from a brain tumour three years ago, when my youngest wasn't quite three, and I hadn't completed my training. He'd been ill for quite a while; that's why I was so late graduating and why I'm only just specialising now that both kids are at school.'

My brain, fortunately, caught up so I was able to digest all this information quietly and realise that Julie is not a cleaner, or a nurse, but a doctor. I even managed to ask, 'Ah yes, what is your specialism?'

'Geriatrics. I love it. I was so pleased when Delphine showed an interest; she's been to my ward a couple of times and asked for a lot of advice. I do hope she's going to keep it up; she'd be great, I'd love to have a psychologist like that at the unit . . .'

I felt like telling Julie about my father, but decided now wasn't the time. Besides, there were more coals to be heaped upon my head, as Simon said, 'Of course, Julie thought about haematology because of her brother.'

More blankness from me.

'You know, her younger brother who lives in Birmingham and has sickle cell anaemia? He's not bad at the moment but the attacks come and go so she's had to do a lot of hospital visiting and liaising with his GP and so on because he can't really look after himself but he doesn't want to move down here to be nearer her. She's become quite an expert on the subject, haven't you, love?'

'Only because I had to. And really it's not the sickle cell that's the main problem; it's his inability to manage the condition – my mum had him when she was in her late forties and he's got quite severe learning difficulties so that makes it really tricky because he doesn't fully understand what to do to look after his health, but he's independent enough to live in sheltered care and he has friends there and everything . . .'

I felt ashamed, but more than that, humbled. The criminal brother was nothing of the sort. I couldn't remember why I'd thought he was.

'I didn't realise you had quite so much to cope with, Julie,' I admitted. 'I knew you had the girls to look after and your job and so on, but I didn't know what your visits to your brother entailed, or that you'd lost your husband.'

Julie looked at me seriously. 'James, you never asked.'

She didn't sound disapproving. I considered more apologies but felt that would be self-indulgent so decided to talk about the paintings. They were stunning: lots of blues and russets, blocks of colour and of translucence; the kind of thing I can sit in front of for hours without worrying that I can't see what it means. At one point, when Simon was taking plates out to the kitchen, I had lapsed into quite a reverie gazing at the piece which faced me.

'And I didn't realise you had such an interest in art. These are wonderful! Who's the artist?'

'My husband painted those. He was just beginning to sell stuff when he became ill. Do you really like them?'

'I noticed them as soon as I came in. I really like them enormously, he was very talented.'

She seemed genuinely pleased. 'You know a lot about art, don't you? Delphine told me about your visits to the Tate.'

It seemed that they knew all about me and Delphine knew all about them and I knew all about nothing.

We spoke about Dream Lab a lot as well, naturally. I think I've been rather slow on the uptake. They both felt that Reeves had been misguided in setting it up in the first place.

'Ethically speaking, it was rather sharp practice,' Julie said, 'because he was helping out with the research at the Sleep Clinic ostensibly to further his own studies into dreaming and sleep disorders, but what he actually did, with Wayne's help, was filch several patients and volunteers and sort of hive us off into a separate group. And although he never explicitly "banned" us from remaining in touch with the clinic, you must have noticed his attitude to any mention of it.'

I nodded. 'Yes, I remember him getting much more extreme about it too. And he used to get into all sorts of arguments, even with Jagdev who used to be on his "side" if you know what I mean.'

'The split with Jagdev was what really signalled the end of the group, at least that's what we reckon,' said Simon, 'because until that point Jag had been his protégé, and then he started getting drug treatment and having fewer and fewer narcoleptic attacks and Reeves didn't like it one little bit. And Reeves' relationship with Wayne and the projects they were working on began to take precedence. Jag felt pretty much left out of it and very unsupported.'

'Why do you think that was, though?' I asked. 'I mean, Jagdev couldn't possibly get much practice with clients without controlling the narcolepsy, I'd have thought Reeves would be pleased he was getting it sorted out.'

Julie's expression was troubled. 'You'd think so, but actually – and look, James, we're not sure about this and it's not something we're taking as read but it's just a possibility we've considered – we think that as time went on Huw might have been getting a bit obsessive about it all. The things he was doing with Delphine – all those weird transmission experiments he was working on with Wayne – I think those began to take over everything else he was doing and so our dreaming, rather than the effects of our disorders, became the most important factor in it all. I certainly began to feel as though he didn't want me to get better, that it suited him to keep me – all of us – in our disordered states just so he could finish his research. I noticed that as I was getting a bit more sleep I was dreaming less, and Simon had the same experience. Maybe Reeves was worried that this group of people with remarkable amounts of REM sleep was going to disintegrate and leave him with fewer subjects for his research. He was really throwing the dream questionnaires at us in the last few weeks; I kept feeling as though I didn't have enough material to fill them in properly, which is hardly what you're supposed to think about a scientific study. Didn't you notice?'

'Now you mention it, I do recall there were a lot of them. But because I never filled in any of the dream stuff it didn't really make a difference.' I remembered something. 'And actually, Delphine didn't fill them in either. She began to hand them in blank. I thought that she hadn't had time, or even that she was making some sort of protest. I knew that something was going on with Reeves . . .' Here both Julie and Simon began to look uncomfortable so I did my best to reassure them of my ability to continue with this line of thought. '. . . nothing like that, I don't mean I realised that anything *untoward* was happening between them. But I felt that there was some tension, and so when I saw the blank questionnaires I assumed it was part of their − argument, or whatever.'

'Why didn't you ask Delphine?' said Julie, puzzled.

'I didn't want her thinking I was interfering, and I was, stupidly, never jealous of the attention Reeves paid her. You probably find that hard to believe, but it never occurred to me before, even though it all makes sense in hindsight.'

'If it's any consolation, I don't think anything was "going on" for long,' Julie said. 'I think that what happened happened very rapidly and finished just as quickly. I don't think you were being deceived for a long time or anything.'

'You're kind to say so, and I think you're right. But, oddly, that's not my concern now. I'm very interested in this notion that Reeves wanted to keep all you lot frozen into your sleep disorders for his own benefit. That seems extraordinary to me. You see, I think that he was obsessed with Delphine's dreams . . .'

'I think we all were,' Simon pointed out. 'I mean, they were pretty unforgettable.'

'Yes, but I mean more than just intrigued in that – tell me more sort of way. I got a postcard from Delphine – she's sent me a few postcards – which mentioned Reeves' fascination with her dreams. And said that although he kept telling her that of course they weren't proof of some kind of inner dysfunction, or even disquiet, she felt that he considered them proof of *something* and he wanted to find out what. Even though he only claimed to be interested in them for his research.'

'She stopped dreaming,' Julie said abruptly. 'That's what she told me. She started sleeping badly and she stopped dreaming. She didn't have any dreams to write about.'

There was a pause. I'd known about Delphine's problems with sleep, of course – I'd sometimes wake up in the early hours, reaching out to touch her and finding nothing beside me, and discover her making hot chocolate or reading a book or just wandering around listlessly in an effort to get sleep again. It was as though we'd changed places. Now that I've reverted to my old sleepless ways, I'd wanted to mention my new-found knowledge of insomnia to Julie and Simon, and was feeling quite proud of having tales of a sleep disorder to share with them after being embarrassingly 'cured' without any effort on my part, but this news was taking time for me to digest.

I asked, 'When did she tell you that?'

'In a postcard I got a few days after she left. She's only sent two – that one and the one which asked me to . . .' She stopped with a small gasp and I surmised that the second one asked her to ask me to dinner, but I pretended not to notice as Julie stumbled through, '. . . asked me to do her a favour, nothing important. But in the first one that's what she said.'

I turned to Simon and asked him wryly, 'Do you get postcards too?'

'Sadly, no. Delphine puts her best regards to me on Julie's.'

Only then did I remember that 'love' Simon had casually placed at the end of a question to Julie and see their easy familiarity and realise that they were a couple. I wondered how long that had been going on. 'But she sent one to Sally, and Polly and Jag have had one,' Simon continued. 'Not saying much, except not to worry about her and sending love, and . . .' he tailed off so I finished for him, '. . . and asking you all to make sure I'm not starving.'

He looked sheepish as Julie explained. 'James, Delphine did ask me to see how you were. But Simon and I wanted to ask you for dinner, that was our idea. And all Delphine did really was to give us – permission, I suppose.'

'Permission?'

'Yes, to contact you. We weren't sure if you'd want us to. We all wanted to say something and we were all concerned but you're not – well, you're quite – I mean, you're not really . . .'

I stopped her, mercifully. 'I know what you mean. I'm not the most approachable of men, and I've not been good at getting to know you or the other group members. I didn't take the time to ask you anything about your lives and so I'd made all sorts of assumptions which she got very annoyed about. Rightly annoyed about, it was stupid of me. But I really do appreciate your inviting me here tonight and I know you're not doing it just because you felt obliged. Truly. It's wonderful to see you both.' Julie looked relieved and I felt confident enough to say, 'And I obviously missed out on quite a lot, because I didn't realise you two had got together. I had no idea! You sly pair.'

They both looked embarrassed and pleased. 'We didn't want to make a song and dance about it,' Simon explained, 'because Polly and Jag had already started seeing each other and so we thought that if we made it overt the whole thing would turn into some sort of couples therapy or something. When we realised that Delphine and you were serious about each other, we thought it was amazing, the lab had worked like a dating agency without the slightest effort. It was just a shame that Alfred and Sally were unlikely to get together really!'

I was relieved to note that neither of them seemed to know a thing about me and Sally, and steered the conversation back to Reeves.

'Do you think he was annoyed that some of us had paired off?' I asked Julie.

'Maybe. I can't imagine him liking any kind of complication to the lab, and that's what it would represent to him. And I'm sure he was jealous of you because it was fairly obvious he fancied Delphine from the start.' I was glad that my suspicions had been more than paranoia and that Julie shared them. 'But he never said anything. As long as we remained sleep-deprived and resistant to drug therapies – and as long as we kept dreaming – he was happy enough.'

Something occurred to me. 'Do you think he knew that Delphine had stopped dreaming?'

'I've no idea. He would only know if she told him and we can't know that.'

'But she would have hated that! That would have really upset her! Don't you think?' I asked Julie.

'James, I couldn't say. She didn't say. There are all sorts of reasons for stopping dreaming, or stopping remembering dreams. I think it works a bit like the dreams themselves in terms of being self-defined – if she thought it was a problem then it could easily become one, whereas if it didn't bother her she'd be fine.'

Now that I know Julie is a doctor it seems so obvious. How could I have missed the quiet authority with which she discussed medical matters? I think Delphine would be proud of just how ashamed of myself I am to have jumped to such unfounded conclusions about people. The shame and the knowledge of the extent to which I was completely wrong have made me feel unsteady. Who knows how many other assumptions I've made over the years which have deprived me of friendships and of knowledge?

We continued talking and drinking until Simon looked at his watch and announced that it was 'Oh Christ hundred hours' and I ordered a cab. When I fell into bed I was too full of good food and wine and too genuinely, luxuriously sleepy to worry about Delphine and her lack of dreams. I fell asleep quickly and woke eight hours later, spread-eagled across all six foot of the bed's width. It didn't feel like treachery at all.

I have begun to think of Delphine as an angel. Moving in mysterious ways, mending broken walls and laying discreet trails back and forth between people who have lost their way with one another. But she wasn't, isn't, an angel. I don't want her mystery and her supernatural thoughtfulness. I want her, the real Delphine, the warm body and the smiling mouth, the silky skin and the fingers flying, flying over whatever they touch; cutting vegetables with the sharpest blade at heart-stopping speed, typing emails to friends around the world like an express train, opening the milk carton, with which I always struggled, in two seconds flat and pouring it over her cereal at the same time; twirling a pen between them whilst considering a crossword clue. I want her back, on this earth, in my arms. I want her back now.

Day thirty-three: Sunday

Eleanor is getting married. It's a man she met just before taking up with me again two years ago but whom she had stopped seeing because of me. When she told me that, I felt mortified – she certainly had been taking the relationship more seriously than I had ever imagined she might – and hugely relieved that this chap got back in touch with her after we parted and has been wooing her ever since.

'Do you love him?' I asked her and she couldn't control her start of surprise at my uncharacteristic forthrightness. But she smiled happily and said, 'Yes. It's taken a while, I was so cautious. But now it's all perfect and I love him very much.'

'I'm so pleased for you, Eleanor. I truly am. And I'm sorry that I've been so remiss in contacting you, I should have been in touch earlier, I've been meaning to . . .'

She put her hand up gently. 'Hush, James. It's OK, there's nothing for you to apologise for.'

Her new happiness had afforded her a gracious forgiveness

which it was tempting to accept mutely and say no more, but I took a deep breath and told her all the things I did, in fact, need to apologise for. Stammering and ineloquent, I must have seemed like a real idiot, especially when we should have been celebrating her impending nuptials rather than going over the past, but it was something I had to do and in the end I think she appreciated my having made the effort.

She was quiet for a minute before taking my hand and saying, 'I loved you for ten years, James. I allowed myself to believe that you loved me but that time, all that time, seems like a dream to me now. When I "declared" myself and you said nothing I was sure that I'd been deluded. And now you say you did love me after all – well, you had a very funny way of showing it.' I braced myself for a litany of complaints but none came. 'I'm not berating you now. But that night I spoke about love, I looked at you and found – nothing. Absolutely nothing. As though you weren't even there. I hope you don't think me unkind to feel very glad, very relieved, that you're not saying that you love me and that even if you did I wouldn't jump! I'm settled, content. Excited too, but mostly settled. I'm happy to be over you.'

'Me too!' I said with a fervour which made us both laugh, and then we spoke about the film she'd just been to see and promised some book swaps and made a vague arrangement for me to meet her fiancé.

I managed very well. I did the things you're supposed to do when an ex-lover announces her marriage. But I didn't feel as gracious as my behaviour implied. Eleanor still looked lovely to me and I can't believe that she doesn't remember some of the wonderful times we had together. Had I been honest to myself about my feelings for her almost a decade ago – or even two years ago – she and I may have been married by now. In which case, I wouldn't have joined the Dream Lab, or met Delphine, or fallen in love with her.

There is a little resentment creeping up here, resentment of Delphine and my love for her; I can feel it. I wonder what would have happened this afternoon – what I'd have made happen – if Eleanor wasn't so clearly happily attached to another man. I'm not entirely sure, but I suspect I may have tried to make love to her. Taken her somewhere – back here I suppose – after lunch. I'm not simple enough to believe that if I'd said – Eleanor, I love you too! – when she made her feelings known two years ago everything would have been perfect; in fact I'd probably have continued to blunder about in ignorance and ruin everything and she'd have divorced me by now. But even the fact of my *knowing* irritates the hell out of me. Delphine has given me all this understanding and created the new honourable James and then buggered off and left me to it. That feeling I had when Delphine was here and I successfully avoided the advances of other women – that gentle pride – isn't what I'm feeling now. I feel frustrated and cheated of a delightful afternoon in bed with Eleanor. Even though it wasn't my call, even though Eleanor gave me not the slightest sign that such an afternoon would be possible, I can't help blaming Delphine for my deprivation. She had no right to leave me, not after she'd made me see that what I thought was love – what I thought love was – is a sickly cousin next to the real thing.

The Real Thing. Listen to me. What tosh, what dross, what garbage. Words are failing me. Words fail me.

Day thirty-four: Monday

Today is the tenth anniversary of my mother's death.

It was sudden and unexpected. I was on a six-month place-ment at the High Commission in the Gambia when the news came. I called John, who had got to the house already, made the necessary travel arrangements for the following day and then sat in my apartment wondering what to do next. I began to think about Mother, and about Mother not being there. I felt uncomfortable and went to fix myself a cool drink. I caught a glimpse of my face in the hallway mirror; I looked *sullen*. I looked how I used to look when Mother told me off or criticised me. I rearranged my features in an attempt to look more suitable – sad would be a start, if not grief-stricken. But the sulky teenage expression wouldn't budge. I didn't want to stay in the flat, blissfully cool as it was, so I decided to do what I did every afternoon at about that time: go into Banjul town for a swim.

The hotel up the road gave FCO staff passes to use their facilities so the girl on the desk knew me and waved me through with a smile. After swimming a swift mile in the almost deserted outdoor pool I showered and dressed and then saw the same girl in the hotel foyer on my way out. It was the end of her shift. We got chatting, I asked her if she'd like a drink, which she did, and she came back to my place. She was twentyish and quite pretty, with that deep black skin which looks like velvet and long, lean, athletic legs. Unlike many of the local girls, she was also what we called 'game' and made no pretence of shyness or inexperience when I kissed her and started to remove her clothes.

Afterwards, we dozed for a while but when I awoke and saw that it was almost midnight I shook her gently and told her she would have to go because I needed to get an early flight back to London the following day.

'You are leaving?' she asked, feeling obliged to look politely upset at the possibility.

'I'll be back in a week,' I explained, 'I have to go home for my mother's funeral. Then I'll come back.'

The girl just stared at me and I realised that my words must have sounded odd to her but there was no retracting them now. She dressed quickly without showering while I called her a taxi. As she left the flat she nodded at me in farewell and I smiled at her. 'So I expect I'll see you at the hotel some time next week?' She ran for the cab which was hooting outside.

That encounter used to be one of my best memories. I have – *had* – a series of unforgettable sexual experiences which seemed to mark out the milestones of my life. Getting my A level results, graduating with a First in PPE, hearing about the death of a school friend in a car crash, attending the wedding of a girl I thought I was in love with, going to my grandfather's funeral, getting the call from Siobhan's brother to say that Finn was born, seeing my father after his stroke – after all traumas or thunderbolts or celebrations my priority has always been to make love to a woman. Sometimes it was a woman I knew, often it wasn't. There was something immensely cathartic in that stringless, meaningless tangling of limbs and exchange of fluids. I used to think that it was my way of commemoration. Losing yourself always does seem to be a wonderful thing to do, especially if yourself is in the midst of pain or confusion or loss, and using sex to celebrate is surely a basic instinct. I always felt immensely powerful afterwards. But now I think that it wasn't strength which took me from every significant moment of my life and plunged me into the body of a woman who could be any woman; it was weakness. Cowardice. What I saw as my lovely set of erotic souvenirs were more like cheap pornographic playing cards from a seaside shop: the precise opposite of romance. Whether I have felt euphoria or grief my first instinct has been not to share my pleasure or pain with loved ones but to mark it with a pointless hedonism that gave nobody anything of value. I have tried to substitute anything painful in my life with the experience of sexual release and having avoided the pain I have also missed the joy which is its flipside. This dream-hole I've clung to, peering out and calling the shots all my adult life; what protection it has afforded me! What safety! What empty solitude.

I told Delphine about my mother's death and the nameless girl. She did tell me her name at the time but it wasn't important and I can't remember it.

'Grief makes people behave oddly,' was her first, charitable reaction. 'You were in a strange place with no friends, you wanted to be comforted, I can see how . . .'

I didn't let her finish. 'No. I felt no grief. I was bored and uncomfortable and didn't know what I felt. So I did something I could understand very well, something I could do very easily. Are you shocked?' How cold I must have sounded.

'Not shocked in the way you mean. Not about your fucking

a girl, a stranger, like that. You think that's a surprise? Hardly. But I don't believe you could be so careless about your mother's death.'

'Sorry, Delphine, I was. Am. You can't understand how distant she always felt.'

'Always?'

'As long as I can remember. Her death was shocking because it was sudden, a heart attack, and John and I had to deal with Father and so on. But I didn't cry about it and I never have and I couldn't if I tried.'

She didn't answer.

She must have been aware of the Camus connection. Meursault goes swimming and meets a girl he knows and makes love to her the day he hears of his mother's death. He can't cry about it either. It's hard to believe, but it wasn't in my mind at all at the time; it was only when I was at my mother's funeral that the link came to me. I avoided mentioning it to Delphine but she must have known and thought my failure to mention it at least odd, if not sinister. Perhaps she thought it was some kind of copycat incident.

If we'd had that conversation more recently, I'd have broached it differently and had a better understanding of why I behaved in the way I did. The facts can't be changed but my feelings about them have changed immeasurably. I was almost *boasting* to Delphine about how little my mother had meant to me. I wasn't lying, not exactly, but nor was I allowing even the slightest possibility of doubt to enter the proceedings. How silly I must have sounded to her.

Aujourd'hui Maman est morte. It's a fine way to begin a novel but a terrible sentence to read a hundred times without ever feeling a sense of loss.

I need to deal with Huw Reeves. This is what I emailed to
him:

> I feel it would be a good idea for us to meet. Do you
> agree? If so, perhaps you'd like to suggest a time and
> place which would suit your schedule. Preferably not at
> the university. I look forward to hearing from you.

It took an age to come up with such a bland few lines. I'm
not exactly sure why I feel this is something I should do. But
seeing Julie and Simon made me acutely aware of – I don't
know what of, exactly – the *possibility* I suppose. Just that.
The possibility of tackling things and making them resolved,
or better, or just *open*. I've been imprisoning myself in this
flat and there's been nothing open here for weeks, just layer
upon suffocating layer of memory, regret and pain. In truth,
I've been wallowing in it, the stultifying, paralysing, *stasis* of
memory. This journal, this long-winded stab at probing has
been nothing more than me digging a deep hole in the sand
and carefully placing my head in it. I intended to shine the
fierce light of truth, and of accuracy, at the dark path behind
me and so discover its secrets but almost all of my little discoveries have come about when I've stopped standing still and
looking back, when I've gone into the world. It takes more
than consciousness, memory and study to get to the heart of
the matter. I should have known that. I should have thought
about what Delphine would have done, and what she would
have wanted me to do.

There is so much I want to tell her now, so many realisations
and apologies and even bits of news, things I've read in the
paper which I want us to talk about, a TV documentary I

saw last week about the Uffizi which I just know she would love as much as I did. You're 'supposed' to miss the mundane things about the departed one first, finding it hard to get used to the empty chair, the space in the bed, the table set for one. But they're not mundane, they're about the ground we shared and how I allowed it to crumble and how it has almost swallowed me up. Not quite though. I'm going to pull myself up and confront some of my demons. Bloody silly psychological phrases she used to use, but they're only silly because they're bandied about at every turn by politicians and pundits and lyricists. Demons is what this feels like. I don't care if it sounds silly.

Delphine's last lover had a highly developed sense of pride. If he sensed any slight from his lover – any doubt being cast upon his whereabouts, for example, or who he was supposed to be meeting – he would fly into a rage and make all sorts of counter-accusations. Then he would insist upon an apology, he would *lay claim* to it as though it were owed him. Without the word 'sorry' being uttered there would be no rapprochement. Delphine (and, she imagined, countless others before her) would bite her tongue and remind herself that she loved this man and that what he asked cost her nothing, really, and she would quietly utter the word. Then he would hug and kiss her, say he was sorry too, sometimes even weep with the surfeit of triumph, of vindication that he was feeling. But Delphine (and those others, she was sure) *knew* that sometimes he was lying. Whether or not there was a reason for the lie, and whether or not her suspicions were of his plotting some deception against her, she knew for a fact that sometimes he lied. And these times were no different from the others; there was no lessening of his sense of hurt and disappointment in his heart, that his love had doubted him, even if that doubt was entirely justified.

Delphine had a friend whose husband had beaten her quite severely, but carefully enough for nobody else to notice, for several years. Whenever the friends in whom she confided urged her to leave him she would always say the same thing, 'But he's so sorry afterwards. I know it's not right, but he does love me, and afterwards, he's so loving to me; it's just like when we were first together. I know I can help him with it.' The words had chilled Delphine when she heard them; it echoed the excuses she made to herself each time she let lie a lie from her last lover.

Eventually Delphine presented the man with proof of his lying: she found (wasn't looking, but just found) a receipt from a local restaurant in his jacket pocket bearing a date on which he was supposedly at the other side of the country. He was livid that she had sneaked around behind his back; outraged that she should think anything was amiss or that there wasn't a simple explanation, and insistent that she apologise immediately. That was when she left him.

'When I hear Elvis sing "Suspicious Minds" I always think about him,' she told me, 'because that song is so heartfelt, he's begging the woman to stop being suspicious. But she's probably got every right to be. He focuses on her suspicion as though everything's her fault. He probably uses her suspicion as an excuse for why he's forced to be unfaithful, just to get away from her every now and then. That's what my last lover would do.'

I remember thinking, poor old Elvis, and was about to point out the foolishness of this attitude to Delphine, but instead I said, 'Delphine, I'll never be unfaithful to you. I'll never give you any cause to be suspicious.'

And she just said, 'We'll see.'

Day thirty-five: Tuesday

The last Dream Lab happened in March, one month after the session in which Jag had passed out so dramatically. In a way, Alfred's death and his funeral had prevented anyone from talking about the business we were supposed to be there for, so I think it prolonged the meetings unnaturally. Julie in particular was getting irritated by Reeves' failure to answer her questions about his 'secondary' research project and Jagdev was clearly resentful that he hadn't been involved or even informed. An air of suspicion surrounded our mentor, so the previously easy-going atmosphere was spiked with discomfort. Delphine was contributing far less to the conversations in those last weeks and didn't seem to like it when Reeves referred any comments about the other project they were working on back to her. When asked for an update, he would say something like, 'Well, let's ask Delphine how it's going. She's seen the gizmo which Wayne is developing, basically feeding her brain-wave readings during different phases of sleep into a computer which will then "translate" them into images.'

And as expectant eyes turned towards her she would be tight-lipped, almost frowning, and say dismissively, 'Oh, it's far too complicated for me to talk about. I only understand the very basic theories really.'

Then Reeves would use her unwillingness to talk about it as a means of avoiding the subject altogether and it was hard for anyone else to bring it up without appearing to be unkind to Delphine.

All this seems pretty obvious to me now, but at the time I wasn't aware of all the little tensions in the room, or the issues behind them. I suppose I was put out that Reeves had this subtext, but because my dreams were still something I knew nothing about I didn't have the – protectiveness, I suppose – of some of the others.

At that last meeting we'd all been a bit jumpy and unsettled, which I'd put down to the absence of both Sally and Alfred. I thought we just needed to 'find a new group dynamic', as Reeves himself might have said. Probably did say. But then Simon had clearly decided that he wasn't about to be put off any longer and tried to have a proper conversation about the Transmission project. Sally had tried, and failed, a couple of times previously and I think the rest of us should have given her more support but she was always so tetchy with Reeves, and questioned everything so thoroughly, that I don't think we realised the importance of her persistence. Simon must have wanted to take up the baton for all sorts of reasons. 'You know the images you talked about,' he began, casually, 'what form do they take at the moment?'

It wasn't a query Reeves could pass over to Delphine so he answered, reluctantly, 'It's just lights at the moment. A bit like the way most computer software that plays music has onscreen visuals which move in response to the frequency. Very simple.'

'But that's hardly new technology, is it? I mean, that sounds like reinventing the wheel,' said Simon provocatively.

Reeves was beginning to warm up in spite of himself, and obviously couldn't let this slight pass. 'No, not at all. We're not suggesting *that's* something we've invented. That's just sound waves output to a visual display; nothing so complicated as a brainwave which contains visual, audio, all sorts of data we can't even understand just yet. That kind of transmission is just a means to an end, a step along the way. We're more interested in the form in which we *capture* the data and then *input* it. We're seeing if that's an area that we can play with. Wayne believes that it may be.'

'What, so if you find the right way to input a dream from Delphine's mind it will suddenly appear onscreen?' asked Simon disingenuously.

Reeves looked impatient. 'Of course not. Not your standard PC screen. And there's no question of transmitting entire dreams here; if we can work on the notion of one, unclear, fuzzy sort of image we'll be very lucky. We're talking about work which will need technology we're only just dreaming of – pardon the pun – right now, but which *will be* developed. But just because it may be decades away, that doesn't mean we can't be as ready for it as we can, when the time comes.'

Simon looked thoughtful. 'OK, so just say that all happens. Just say that in ten or twenty years' time you'll be able to hook Delphine up to some contraption for the night and capture her dreams on some magic tape and then feed that into a machine which projects it for everyone to see. Just say that happens, OK?'

'OK,' Reeves said, tentatively.

'Why?' Simon's tone carried a mixture of disbelief and disapproval which Reeves just couldn't understand.

'What do you mean, why? Can't you see what a break-through that would be?'

'No. What good would it do? To anyone at all? Don't know about anyone else here but if there's one thing I wouldn't like to see it's Delphine's dreams. Bad enough hearing her read them; I don't think I could cope with them on the silver screen.'

Jag joined in. 'Simon's got a point, Huw. I don't just mean about Delphine, but generally. You take the piss out of Polly's dream dictionary, but why is this business any more useful or significant than that? What therapeutic or positive health outcome is the aim of these experiments?'

Reeves responded angrily. 'Don't you start trying to put me through my paces, Jagdev,' he almost shouted. 'Since when have you been in a position to question my clinical methods?'

Jag had his answer ready. 'Since you stopped telling me anything about them.'

Reeves tried to draw a line under the conversation by suggesting they talk about this later and couldn't we all get on with the discussion, but everyone was clamouring to join in by now and he finally said, angrily, 'You seem to have got hold of the wrong end of the stick, folks, almost as though you think there's something weird or sinister about what we're doing. That's the trouble with dreams, always has been – and it's not just Polly who can get a bit carried away with inter-pretation and premonitions and all the rest of it; it's all of you. We're talking about the absolute cutting edge of psycho-logical scientific research and you lot are going on as though it's witchcraft!' There was silence and Reeves spoke more appeasingly. 'Right, I tell you what. We'll fix a time – one of these meetings – for Wayne to come over and show you what we've been doing. And that will be the moment to ask all the questions you're asking now, OK? Now please, can we talk about your dream questionnaires, as planned?'

That seemed to satisfy most of us – certainly I was happy to stop talking about the subject – but at that point Delphine raised her hand and said, 'Huw, would you excuse me, but I don't have anything to discuss about the questionnaire. I think I'll go now if that's OK?'

He looked concerned but could only agree. I got up to join her but she told me not to. 'No, James, you stay, I'll meet you in the bar afterwards, OK?'

She looked pale and I realised how tired her eyes were. I hadn't realised her insomnia was having such a great effect on her and it made me angry, so while she stood there ready to go I turned to Reeves and said, 'Look at her! All this business is wearing Delphine out. Can't you see what you're doing to her, making her go over and over those bloody dreams as though they're nothing but strings of words and pictures for you to – play with, to *amplify*! Can't you *see* how upsetting she finds them?'

Delphine looked embarrassed at my outburst, an embarrassment I thought was due to her needing me to defend her, but I'd obviously needled Reeves so he retorted, 'Please, James. She isn't upset by her dreams, how many times has she told us all that?'

'Oh, come off it. She doesn't want anyone to worry. But it's obvious, isn't it . . .' I appealed to the whole group. 'It's obvious that all those dreams about mothers and babies in danger, or mothers failing to save babies, or mothers *killing* their babies, for God's sake! – it's obvious, isn't it, that Delphine has serious anxieties about motherhood which she plays out subconsciously, and the last thing she needs is for you to be – *using* her for your ridiculous experiments . . .'

I'd heard Delphine's sharp intake of breath and as I looked at her I saw her face reddening. I thought she was about to cry.

'That's enough, James!' bellowed Reeves. 'You're talking about Delphine as though she's not even there, and just listen to what you're saying! Delphine,' his voice was soft, 'are you OK?'

She had regained her composure. 'Yes. I'm fine. I'll sit in the bar.'

She didn't look at me as she left. I sat back down again.

When she had gone Reeves had also calmed down. He appeared to be more relaxed, as though a weight had been lifted from his shoulders. He sighed and looked admonishingly at me and at Simon. 'You know, far from my work with Delphine being the problem, it's more than a bit thoughtless of you, James, to suggest that her dreams are the outward signs of some deeply unhealthy impulses. And Simon, do you think it's a good idea to suggest they could *damage* people?'

'I never suggested anything of the sort!' Simon replied indignantly. 'I just think it's an odd choice of dreams to want to *project*. And yeah, yeah,' he added, as Reeves was about to interrupt, 'I know it's not going to actually happen until we're all a hundred and three, but even so, it's an odd choice.'

'As I've already explained, Delphine's dreams seem to be the most appropriate for the research, not because of their content but because of their clarity and the very strong visual sense she describes.' Reeves was openly impatient. 'We may find that it simply doesn't translate into an image in the way we hope – who knows, maybe James' dreams which never even enter his conscious mind as memories might "transmit" more successfully?' He didn't sound convinced. 'But we have to try a variety of approaches and it's going to take a long time. Meanwhile, it would help if you'd at least *modify* your obsession with Delphine's dreams.'

Simon was open-mouthed now. '*My* obsession! That's a bit rich. We all know who has the obsession with Delphine's dreams, don't we?' At this point Julie placed a restraining hand on his knee, and he continued more quietly, 'To be honest, Huw, I think the lab has run its course. We're all in a much better state sleep-wise than we were when we started and your interests at the moment seem more to do with this transmission research business than the stuff we all signed up for. What do other people think?'

There were nods of agreement from everyone except me. I never thought that such a dramatic ending was in sight. I was astonished, especially when Reeves said, in a tone I could only read as surrender, 'Perhaps you're right, Simon. I'm sorry if you think I've been wasting your time recently; that wasn't my intention, it's just that − well, that it was always a bit of an *organic* process, this group and these meetings, so I suppose things − my studies − have just . . . developed away from it.'

And so it was agreed. That was the last meeting. Reeves, sitting on his desk as usual as we gathered up our bags and coats, and looking rather less upset about the end of the lab than I imagined he would be; Simon, still bristling slightly from their run-in; Julie looking sad; Polly watching Jag with some concern as he waited to have a word with his disappointing tutor; and me, probably looking confused at best but most likely blank. No Sally. No Alfred. And now no Delphine.

We had our last little drink together in the bar. For a

change, Reeves joined us, which made the occasion even more sombre. He and Delphine hardly spoke to one another and while she did chat to the others and swap telephone numbers and email addresses and so on, she seemed subdued. We all left at the same time and as Reeves said goodbye to Delphine I heard her say, 'So, that time's OK, yes?' and he nodded. I wanted to ask her what time? What did she mean? but didn't want to be accused of prying and in any case I assumed it was something to do with his mad experiment. That was probably the moment they planned their 'elopement'. Right in front of me.

In the car on the way home we didn't talk much, though I was racking my brains to think of things to say. And that was the last night I made love to her, gently and in the dark. I thought she was crying but wasn't sure. A month later she was gone.

Drinks with Polly and Jagdev tonight. Polly called me this morning. I'm enjoying something of a social whirl.

Drinks is what it was. Hardly anything to eat save for a few peanuts, so I'm far more pissed than I should be. Polly and Jag are going through an amicable break-up and I seemed to be an unwitting part of some ceremony to mark this fact. I sat between them on the sofa in Polly's shared house, with assorted theatre folk drifting in and out throughout the evening, and we laughed cruelly about her recent injuries through somnambulistic forays to the fridge, Jagdev's unfortunate episode of narcolepsy whilst holding a crystal vase in John Lewis at the weekend, and even my initial panic on finding that Delphine had disappeared.

'You went to the police!' shouted Jagdev. 'They must have thought you were barking!'

It was all most cathartic, if raucous, and as I hugged them both goodbye, Jagdev's insistence that I come to see him for a drink after work one day soon sounded utterly genuine. Polly is off to India to work on an educational project with her theatre company and will be away for at least six months, hence their rather practical decision to split up. They asked me if I was going to Alfred's memorial service which is taking place at the weekend. I said I wasn't sure.

'You do know about Alfred and Jacky now, don't you?' asked Polly drunkenly. Jagdev was smirking.

'Know what about them?'

'That Jacky's a man. That Alfred was gay.'

I could almost hear lots of little pieces of information shuffling themselves around in my mind until they finally slotted into their rightful places with a pleasing click. Jackie was, in fact, Jacky with a 'y'.

'Ah. That explains a lot. Like your last attack of cataplexy, Jag.'

'I was already in such a state, and you going on about them having been married and all that, it just made me hysterical – and so down I went!'

'But how did you know?' I pleaded. 'How did everyone else know this? I mean, Alfred was a big burly bloke from Yorkshire!'

Polly looked at me disapprovingly. 'They don't all wear cravats and wave musical theatre programmes around,' she said, 'and Alfred never made a secret of it. You probably weren't listening properly.'

'It just didn't occur to me,' I protested. 'It was always "our

Jackie does this", or "our Jackie looks after me", it just sounded as though he was talking about his wife.'

'Well, he wasn't. Although they were certainly like a married couple in a lot of ways. But it's amazing that you never twigged.'

I was humbled yet again. But they didn't let me feel down for too long and we had a marvellous chat about all sorts of things before the night was out.

I may be an old romantic fool but I have a little suspicion that they won't find it that easy to impose their separation. Perhaps it's a hope, that distance and absence needn't always be the enemies of love. Whatever, they are sweet young people and I was touched by their friendliness.

Somnambulism often runs – or rather walks – in the family. Polly's mother has been a sleepwalker since she was a child. She doesn't harm herself like her daughter does, but she used to have terrible weight problems as a result of sleep-eating. Without any knowledge of doing so, she would go to the fridge in the early hours of the morning and eat whatever she found there – cheese, yoghurt, ham – and then go through the cupboards to demolish chocolate biscuits, peanut butter, bread, nuts, dried fruit and so on. When her children were at home there was little she could do about this – locks on the doors were no match for her sleepwalking self, who always remembered where the key was, sometimes better than her tired waking self – but when Polly and her sister left home she took action. So nowadays there is very little food in the house which does not require cooking – and thus far she has never cooked in her sleep – and there are no easily demolished

303

snacks apart from fresh fruit. So Polly's poor father has lost almost as much weight as her mother, and when he visits his daughter he roams around her kitchen searching for nibbles.

This was here when I returned. She's gone all the way down to Ho Chi Minh. I want to know how she's been travelling, and if she's OK. There's no date on this, I can't even tell when she posted it. I have her safety to worry about now too.

James — did you know, I stopped dreaming? I was becoming more and more unhappy and I no longer dreamt anything at all, not the awful ones, not even little ones, each morning I woke and remembered nothing. That's never happened to me before. When I've been sad or down in the past I've still dreamt, I've sometimes dreamt more sad things but I've still dreamt. But this — void. I've never had anything like that. I hated it. I like to know when I've been asleep. Everything began to merge into one when I couldn't even remember a dream.

I'm ridiculously pleased that she told me.

There was a response from Reeves too. We're meeting on Thursday.

8 February

I can't take any more of this crap. It's been going well, really well. Delphine comes to see me, or I drop by her office, every other day and we've stopped pretending we need a pretext. We talk. She talks to me. So I knew she'd help me out if I asked her, she wouldn't question why I need another PSG from her. Hell, I told her the truth – that Wayne's 'lost' her previous data and my research will be useless without it. And that's the moment she chooses to tell me she doesn't dream any more. And that she's insomniac. Nearly a year in my Dream Lab and the world's best dreamer stops dreaming and then stops bloody sleeping as well. I'm doing really well here.

Completely stymied. Wayne has been sneaking about in my data files – he's precisely the reason I don't leave any of this stuff on the computer; there's not a firewall or password that boy couldn't crack. So he won't find anything of interest but that's precisely the point. If he bothers to look closely he'll find very little at all from the past six months. And he's the kind of guy who'll look closely, I don't doubt it.

I need to get away. I need to relax for a bit, think this through. Not give up – never give up – but try a little patience. I've played the long game for so long, what difference does a few months make?

I'm going to take her with me. Not as a hostage or a captive; she wants it, I know she does. She's miserable as hell and cries every time we talk. Last week, when we went for a drink after work, we spoke with our faces almost touching.

It's been so long. So long since I felt I could go for it and it would work. Delphine and I will go – somewhere – Paris maybe, I've always wanted to take a girl to Paris – and we'll have a marvellous time and then when I come back I'll play all the right games and calm Wayne down. I could claim stress, get some time off maybe, that'd explain my lack of data. Anyway, I'll bide my time and we can try it out together. I'll talk to Delphine about it. She must want to help; I know she'll want to help me to dream.

So fantastic to think of sharing this with someone. With her. To get it out in the open. I'll find the right moment — I won't lay this on her all at once, I'll wait till it's all ready. I want to ask her to marry me. Do it properly this time. Kids, even. I've not had these thoughts for years. But for now, I'm going to ask her just to come away with me. I'm just going to walk up and ask her.

Day thirty-six: Wednesday

Last night, I had a dream. I actually remember a dream! I've still been taking an age to get to sleep but once I manage – usually in the early hours of the morning – I've been tending to stay just about asleep until a rude awakening by my radio alarm. But I must have managed to drop off at around 1 a.m. and then woke with a start around two hours later and as my heartbeat slowed down and my mind grappled with what had happened to break my sleep, I remembered it!

There was a woman standing in the sea. I couldn't really see what she looked like, it was a vague figure wearing blue clothes and I knew it was Delphine. I knew that in the dream; it's not something I'm adding now. I wrote it all down very quickly for fear of going back to sleep and forgetting it so I'm not just relying on my memory here. I couldn't quite see what she was doing but I knew that she was crying and counting and I realised that she was trying to cry seven tears. It's from the story of the selkie-wife: my nanny used to read to me at bedtime, before I started boarding school, from a book of Scottish folk tales. One night – the only time I can remember but perhaps there were more – Mother read my bedtime story instead. Perhaps my nanny was ill. And this was the one she chose. The selkie – or seal – can leave her pelt hidden on the beach and take human form temporarily, but this selkie-maiden loses her pelt and so is forced to remain on land and marry a human she doesn't love. Come to think of it, I think the husband is the one who hides her pelt, in order to trap her. She goes to the sea and searches every day but never finds her skin. I can't remember exactly what happens then in the version of the story my mother read to me – I think perhaps a human child takes pity on the woman and helps her because she is powerless on the land and there's something to do with having to shed seven mortal tears into the salt water to contact the selkie folk and secure their help. I remember, once Mother had left the room after reading me the story, trying to think of the saddest things in the world so that I could squeeze out the requisite seven tears but I could scarcely manage a couple and concluded that it would have to be a girl who helped her because girls cry all the time. Anyway, whether by human intervention or not, she finds her pelt and returns joyously to the sea. I believe Mother sang to me that night as well, although I don't know what she would have sung, and I can't be sure that she did.

Of course, I didn't dream all that. My dream (how odd that phrase looks written down. Even odder to say it aloud) was simply Delphine in the sea trying to cry seven tears and it's not difficult to find all sorts of metaphors working their way through my knowledge of the selkie-wife's tale and helping to draw uncomfortable conclusions, but I'm trying not to do that. I'm trying to think that my dream is just a dream. But it's more than that, even if it doesn't signify anything particular, even though it's not some kind of divination, it does feel like the most enormous *achievement*. As though this is the real deal. I could go to the lab and recount this dream and it would start a great discussion about folklore and symbolism in dreams, like the time we talked about Sally and lions (you can imagine!) or Simon and flocks of crows or

Polly and the dark tower or Jagdev and the jester figure with bells on his hat. I loved all that! I thought everyone was mad to dream those dreams and madder to confess to dreaming them but now I wish I could tell them all about my dream. I wish I could phone Delphine now and tell her!

Some species are uni-hemispheric; they can split their brain function in two. It turns out that this is especially useful in sleep, because one half of the brain can be 'switched off' while the other keeps watch for predators, and then the two sides can swap. Many small birds can do this, as well as dolphins. Dolphins need to breathe air every few hours so complete underwater sleep would be extremely perilous. I wonder if there's a slight uni-hemispheric tendency in men's brains. Men's, not Man's, I mean.

This morning I dusted down my Rolling Stones CDs and played them. Fauré's too serious for me just now and in the old Stones versus Beatles war I was always on the side of the wild bunch. We caught a bit of the Stones live on a late-night TV show a few months ago and as we watched Jagger prancing about like a leathery, overly energetic frog, I told Delphine how my admiration for him had waned in recent decades and she smiled at me approvingly and said, 'Yes, it's that Alpha Male thing again. Success, money, celebrity – added to confidence and an evident intelligence – make it obvious that Mick Jagger will wander about impregnating women willy-nilly.' She'd taken to using some of my more arcane phrases and they always sounded so pretty when she said them. 'But it's tragic because in the end none of them want *him*, nobody wants to know *him*, they're just programmed to want his sperm and his babies because of what he *represents*. People like that, they seem to be an object of envy for men but really there's nothing at all to envy.'

'I don't envy him at all,' I assured her truthfully. 'He could never attract a woman like you, so what's to envy?'

'There,' she said with some satisfaction, 'just as I was giving up all hope you say something like that and redeem yourself.'

Day thirty-seven: Thursday

I met Reeves in a pub at Piccadilly Circus; one of those smoky, vinegary-smelling places where the safest drink is Guinness. He looked absolutely awful and my first thought at seeing him was – poor man! My second, third and fourth thoughts were all less charitable but I still think it's significant, and pleasing, that I was able to pity him. Not that it helped us much in the end. I approached his table and he half stood up but neither of us proffered a hand, so we both nodded and took a seat. There was an uncomfortable pause. I had already decided not to speak until he did, and evidently he was similarly determined but eventually he seemed to realise that, even though this meeting was at my request, it was his responsibility to break the silence. He said, gruffly, 'James, I shouldn't think this will matter to you much at all, but I do want to say that I'm sorry.' I just looked at him. 'She's a grown woman and I didn't force her to do anything but I acted badly. I am sorry.' At this point his face reminded me of John trying not to cry at our father's side. I still couldn't think of anything to say. 'I always . . . I always felt an attraction for Delphine. I mean, it wasn't something trifling, or . . . I was really very shocked when I realised you and she had got together, I found it hard to believe.'

'Thanks very much.'

'I mean, it was amazing how *easily* it all seemed to happen. Come on, you can't really be offended by my surprise. I mean, you kept yourself to yourself — didn't have much to do with anyone in the lab — but then she arrived and suddenly you lit up. And you decided what you wanted and just went for it. And it worked! I kept wondering why.'

'I wondered too. Am still wondering.'

'I asked her. Just before she left me in Paris. It was so obvious to her that she'd made a big mistake; I didn't try to argue with the decision. But I did make some bitter comments, some — comparisons.'

'Between you and me?'

He nodded. 'And she got so angry. She said I'd never understood what you were really like and how much in love the two of you had been.'

'She said that?'

'Oh yes. And that she hadn't stopped loving you but found there was too much of you that she couldn't understand. Too much you wouldn't help her understand.' Reeves looked at me closely. 'But, there you are. She loves you. You're the lucky man. She sees something in you that the rest of us don't. Do you know, when I realised you were an item, I thought — my God, there's hope for us all yet.'

I pretended not to notice his rudeness and said something which had just occurred to me. 'I don't think she saw anything in me. I think she just saw me.' It was true, but it was an odd thing for me to say. So I went on quickly, 'I thought it was her dreams you were after.'

He looked uncomfortable.

'My big mistake was similar,' I confessed. 'I thought I knew what the dreams meant.'

'Fear of motherhood, right?'

'Ah yes, I did air my theory rather publicly, didn't I?'

He nodded. 'The night of the last lab meeting. When you stood up and said it in front of everyone, it was the final straw for her. She'd always felt very manipulated by your interpretation of those dreams, but thought it was something to do with your own fears of having children . . .'

'She's probably right.'

'. . . so decided to just let things develop and see if you changed. But then she found out you have a son, don't you?'

'She told you that?'

'I'm sorry if you didn't want me to know . . .'

'No, you're right, she's right. It shouldn't have been a secret.'

'Well, after that she thought the subject might appear a little differently to you but apparently there was no change. And she was worried about how you treated your father and your brother and didn't like your mother, and . . .'

'You know my life story, don't you?' I said, annoyed.

Reeves became more animated. 'This is what we talked about! It was like seeing a client, do you understand? She was telling me why she was unhappy and hoping I could help. The trouble was, we let the fifty minutes run over, time and again, and we thought that there was something between us that wasn't there at all. She just wanted to talk to someone and I – well, that's me. Someone people talk to. I had the right kind of couch. I really think that was all there was to it.'

He exhaled deeply and looked down at his drink. I asked him, 'Why are you telling me this?'

'Why not? You wanted to meet, I don't know what for exactly but it must have been for information one way or another. To hear my story. That and my apology. So I'm telling you. Isn't that what you wanted?'

'I wanted to make peace.'

He looked surprised. 'You did? Do you still?'

I didn't exactly feel like the winner but I was beginning to get the distinct impression that he was losing. So I said, 'Yes. I still do.'

There was a pause which I broke by saying, 'And by the way – you might be interested to know that I've been dreaming. I've had a dream. Not sleeping brilliantly, although not as bad as I used to. But I had a dream. What do you think about that?'

I'm not sure why I told Reeves this and, when he remained silent, I regretted having done so. I said, 'Anyway, that's all by the by. All of it. So yes, I still want to make peace.'

For a moment I thought he was going to shake my hand. But then his expression changed and the control he'd managed to exert thus far was gone in an instant. He didn't raise his voice – the bar was too small for that – but his red, angry, screwed-up face was so close that I could hardly focus and his fists were tight as he spat out the words and his teeth were so clenched, he was so livid and so *Welsh* that it was hard to understand what he was saying.

'Peace? You sit there in your handmade fucking suit and your public schoolboy's haircut, talking all la-di-dah and so fucking *civilised*, and you expect me to shake your hand and make peace? What, so you can give me your forgiveness, your blessing? So you can say no hard feelings, old chap, let's forget all about it? How do you expect me to believe you give a *shit* about Delphine? If you felt like I feel about her you wouldn't be *able* to sit there like that. If you felt like I feel about her you'd have walked in here and smashed my fucking face in. I can't *believe* she'd ever go with you. And I can't believe that you, you of all people, are claiming to be a dreamer. That's a club you'll never join, don't you understand? You don't have the – the *capacity*. The depth. It's not possible because there's nothing to you. Nothing at all.'

He downed the rest of his glass and pushed the table away from the wall, and into me, as he barged out.

Delphine knew a woman who wanted to be a prostitute. Not on the streets, more in a kind of *Belle de Jour* sort of a way. She saw herself in white four-poster bedrooms with handsome men whose hectic lifestyles made relationships impossible; with young guns eager to learn how to pleasure a woman; with decent family men whose disabled wives could no longer fulfil their needs. 'And if I were a whore, I'd always kiss them,' she insisted. 'They all say, don't they, that it doesn't count because there were no kisses, there was no love. Well, what's the point of sex without kissing? Kissing's the best bit. I'd kiss them better than they'd been kissed in their whole lives. And they'd fall in love with me and make love to me ardently, as though we were lovers. Then they'd pay up and go home and I could do as I pleased.'

'Why don't you just kiss lots of men?' asked Delphine. 'Take lots of lovers. Why must you be a whore to do that?'

Her friend had been shocked. 'I'm not a complete slapper,

Delphine! They'd be paying me – it would be my job. I don't just want to shag lots of men. This is completely different.'

Delphine said that she would rather die.

Delphine believed that most people invent a romance in their lives. She thought that very few people genuinely find love but the urge to do so – no, the urge *to have done so* – is so strong that it can overshadow any amount of truth.

'It's like when you see a television programme interviewing war widows,' she explained. 'They probably got married to someone they hardly knew, got a handful of censored letters about the awful food and needing more socks, and if the man came back they had forty years of being bored and having children. But as soon as they're interviewed, it turns into the greatest love of the century; they talk about receiving love letters which were practically poetry and enjoying a life of perfect bliss and joy. Why can't they just admit that they got on fine, that they loved their children, that they had no big complaints? It's so *fake*.'

I thought she was harsh. 'War is hardly a normal background for getting together. Everyone is feeling more mortal and more desperate, so of course they're going to have a heightened notion of what they're feeling and how important it is.'

'I was just using that as an example because I remembered that documentary we saw last week. And it's almost impossible to talk to old ladies nowadays who *didn't* marry during the war so it overshadows everything. But I guarantee, in forty years' time when my friends are being interviewed about their married lives, they'll come out with exactly the same sort of rewriting, exactly the same delusions.'

'What do you want them to say?' I asked, bemused. 'They're

not going to say – well, it was OK, we got on just fine. Are they?'

'Why not? Why not if that's the truth, which it almost always is? A long marriage is an achievement to be proud of, so why pretend it can ever be an effortless journey? It's like a job only you sign up indefinitely. You can do it well or you can do it badly. Why talk about it as though it's supernatural?'

'Delphine, I promise I shan't try to recruit you to that job!'

'I wasn't talking about us.'

'I know, but just in case you ever worry, I've no intention of trying to sign you up. All right?'

To me, marriage has always seemed to be a very silly contract. I suppose it may be a good idea if you want to bring up children, but otherwise what possible benefits can it bestow on a man and a woman in our century, in our millennium? I've never made promises I can't keep and all that loving and honouring till death us do part, forsaking all others, is too much to ask of any man. Of anyone. But every now and then, after Delphine had been living with me for a few months, I did used to have little fantasies about marriage. They were almost girlish – I thought about what we'd wear and concocted menus for the wedding breakfast – and they always took me by surprise. I wonder what she'd have said if I'd asked her to marry me.

I don't quite know what I feel about my meeting with Huw Reeves. It was unpleasant, shocking even, but then how I thought it might be amicable I have no idea. I was going there to find out what I could about Delphine and didn't know whether he'd be angry or resentful or calm or apologetic. I feel I've let myself and Delphine down by being so – passive. Sitting there listening to the things she had told him about me was the oddest experience and not one I'd like to repeat. But all the stirrings of indignation and humiliation I was beginning to feel were swept away pretty quickly by a tide of curiosity. In some weirdly inverted form of egotism, hearing what she had told her lover about me seemed to bring me closer to her. I couldn't get enough of it, wanted all the details of what he knew, not to feel aggrieved or abused in any way, but just to imagine her saying it. To picture her mouth saying my name and to think that she told him she loved me! It was the sweetest, happiest news I'd had for ages, and when he said – there's hope for us all yet – my heart leapt in agreement. It's a shame he spoiled it with insults. And yet by insulting me he was doing *something*. He was kicking out. When he was hissing in my face I felt exactly as he described me. Perhaps I should have punched him. He's a little fleshy, a little out of shape. I did a bit of boxing at school; I could have taken him on despite the age difference. Behaved like a man. That's what he thinks, that I'm not a man. And he is clearly in love with her and isn't ashamed to let that flood over him, overcome his better judgement, make him behave badly. In a way, I feel as though I should be grateful that he thinks it's worth shouting at me at all.

When he stormed out, he left his jacket hanging on the back of the chair. I didn't fancy his chances of getting it back from that place so I brought it home, thinking that I could always drop it into the Sleep Clinic reception some time. His Dictaphone was in the jacket pocket. It's tempting.

Day thirty-eight: Friday

It's been the most extraordinary shock. Not just discovering what's really been going on, but to hear Reeves' voice as I've never heard it before. Nothing affable or warm about it; he must have made immense efforts to control his tone for our benefit. Or perhaps it's something he's done to everyone, for years, not just the lab members. I can't believe Wayne thought for a moment that he was helping with something so – underhand. So unethical. The man sounds crazed.

And I feel foolish, too. Gullible. Wanting to believe he wanted to help me and all the time he was using me. How could I have been so stupid?

The things he said about me – the suggestion that there's something fundamentally wrong with me – have shocked me. The eavesdropper can't expect to hear anything good about himself, but to hear such a catalogue of bad – to see myself through his eyes – has left me *wounded*.

Maybe he's right. Maybe all of my life has been spent at some slightly sub-normal level of which I've been – not blissfully, there's been so little bliss – but certainly completely unaware. It would explain so much.

And it would close the door to my ever finding Delphine again, to my ever being that happy again. I can't countenance it. She knew me better than anyone and that included knowing my quirks, my habits, the things which made me uncomfortable. She didn't find me strange.

I toyed with the notion of destroying the whole thing. Smashing the Dictaphone under my heel and getting rid of every last insane, vituperative comment. Instead, I telephoned everyone from Dream Lab. They were all shocked, though Julie and Sally both took it very calmly. Jag sounded so calm I realised he must be devastated. Simon was disbelieving at first; perhaps he thought I was playing some elaborate joke.

'No, really, Simon, it's true. All that time – before I even joined the lab – he was looking for people to experiment with. The lab began as a genuine project and even the Transmissions project had some scientific basis, but it all ended up as a cover for what he was really up to which was entirely to do with himself. With his own lack of dreams.'

'The bastard! I mean, I knew he was up to something, but this – this is appalling. Look, James, are you sure?'

In answer I set the gadget next to the telephone and pressed play. When the voice had stopped crackling I picked up the receiver. Simon was silent.

'So you see?' I prompted him. 'You see?'

'James?'

'What is it?'

'I'm sorry I thought you weren't all there.'

'No hard feelings. I probably wasn't. I'm more there now, I mean here now – I mean you were probably right.'

'What are we going to do about this? We have to report him. And you know, I think this suggests he's culpable in some way for Alfred's death.'

'Oh, I don't know if we can go that far . . .'

'Why not? He knew what an effort it was for the poor bloke to get there, how hard it was for him to talk. That would have all caused Alf more strain, you know, on his heart. I'm not kidding; I think Reeves helped finish him off.'

'I don't think we could prove that . . .'

'We don't have to prove anything. If we have some formal complaints to make then the uni will investigate them. And maybe the police.'

I hadn't thought of going through official channels in that way. I was still reeling from the discovery and its impact on everything else. The prospect of going through some long-drawn-out legal procedure seemed so uninviting. I never wanted this fight. But I'm at the centre of it all now, and I have to take up the gauntlet.

A few hours at my computer, a little judicious sifting – Huw Reeves had made frequent recordings but a lot of it was irrelevant and it seemed unethical to include his ramblings about other patients – and everyone from Dream Lab had received Reeves' revelatory voice files by email.

Polly used to copy us all into silly email cartoons and jokes; it's a shame that my first reciprocation is so unpleasant. But it's good to share.

I took the jacket and its replaced contents to the main reception at the university and left them for Reeves. I didn't leave a note.

Delphine is still in Ho Chi Minh. She sent me an envelope containing a sheet of white paper typed on both sides and a postcard. The card features a detail from a window in that little chapel in Tudley, commissioned by the family of a young woman who died in a boating accident. It's the figure of a girl in water. Surrounded by water. Delphine wept in front of that window.

James, there is something I never told you about me, about my life. I was waiting to trust you with it but never found the moment. And when I found out about Finn it was too late. I can't explain now but am pleased to report that I had a dream last night! I remembered it fully in the morning and wrote it down in great detail. You collected the others, didn't you? Have this one too.

The woman stares at the man behind the desk. Her infant son babbles against her shoulder. Her daughter stands by her side, squeezing her hand. The man taps a long, clean, white finger on the leather inlay and looks up. 'You understand what I'm saying?' She says nothing. 'This is your punishment. You have five minutes to make your decision. You can be assured that it will be carried out mercifully and swiftly if you make it within that time. However, if you fail to make the decision in the allotted time, the process will be prolonged by exactly the same additional time that you take. You see? Six minutes to make your decision and my men will take one whole minute to do the job. Ten minutes and they'll take five. And believe me; if you try to leave it an hour, a day, two days, they will rise to the challenge.'

She is about to plead but he stops her. 'No bargains. No you instead of them. You have come to the end of the road.' His voice softens slightly. 'Think of it this way. It could be so much worse. It's the decision that's the torture. Because there is no right decision and no wrong decision. Because it's all wrong. You see? Make it quickly. Close your eyes and point, or toss a coin. You will have one of them and the one you lose will go in an instant. It could be so much worse.'

He sets a clock in front of her and pushes the buttons until the display reads 'Timer'. He programs in five minutes. He looks at her. 'Ready?' She sways as though she is about to faint, but instead she stands up straight and nods. He presses. The numbers begin their count. 'Now.'

The boy is making the little noises he makes when he's hungry. Her breasts sting as the milk he's calling for begins to seep out. His body curves into her body as comfortably and easily as it did when he was curled in her belly only eight months before. His once navy blue irises have already turned to the amber brown of his father's eyes. His face nestles softly into her neck and he starts to make the long vowel sounds he's been practising for months. Her silence and stillness confuse him. He looks into her eyes and smiles; a broad, joyful four-toothed smile. There is nothing to him but beauty and love, unblemished.

There are four minutes left on the clock.

The girl at her side looks up. Her eyes are tired and her expression sullen. This morning they argued. Last night they argued. Every twist and turn of their time together is fraught with disagreement, anger and resentment. The woman can barely remember the time when her daughter was like this baby, as sweet and cheerful and eager for kisses as her brother always is. When she tries to hold the girl she sometimes stiffens, sometimes goes limp, sometimes struggles. Sometimes, so rarely, the child goes to her mother and hugs her fiercely or takes her face between her small plump hands and gives her a hard, hard kiss on the mouth. She is seven years old.

There are three minutes left on the clock.

The woman kneels on the floor. She hugs both of

her children to her tightly, until the boy begins to kick, and then she hands him to the girl. The girl doesn't understand, but her brother smiles at her, as he always does, and she hugs him. The mother takes him back and buries her face in the milky skin of his neck. He moves his head towards her breast, making the urgent noises of hunger.

There is one minute left on the clock.

There is no time. She stands. She looks into her baby's eyes, kisses him and holds him gently, her gaze alternating between his face and the clock.

The little girl is crying.

The final countdown begins and the woman's dry mouth shapes the numbers. 'Five . . . four . . . three . . . two . . .'

The man looks up expectantly. The woman holds the baby out to him and takes her daughter's hand as he is carried away. She hears him cry as he leaves the room without her but the crying stops very soon.

'You're hurting my hand!' complains the girl.

'Sorry,' her mother whispers.

'You may go now,' says the man.

The woman and her daughter turn and walk out, their hands no longer touching.

Babies again, always babies. I used to assume that Delphine was the mother in her dreams, but here she's the girl. The mother is always her mother, making that choice. I was constantly looking for fear and never considered guilt.

I began to keep my own dream diary. There are still only two entries, and the second one, from last night, made no sense at all – it was all about my old French teacher who seemed to be drowning and I kept trying to throw him things to cling on to but I couldn't reach him. God knows what that was about, but writing it down seems like a good thing to do. It's such a shame that I've nowhere to take them, no lab to bring them to and share with my fellow-dreamers.

I don't feel different. I don't walk around thinking – I can dream! The dreams have given me nothing but themselves, and that seems to me a fine thing. They prove only that I dreamt. Nobody can tell me they are right or wrong, nobody in the world will ever experience them as I experienced them, nobody can take them from me. We talk about our childhood dreams as though they are the same as *ambitions* – to be an engine driver, to own my own horses, to make Mother proud as I starred in the school play or captained the house eleven or won the prize for Latin. My whole childhood was spent dreaming of a happy future but now that more than half of my life lies in the past I've a great deal more material to draw upon. I can go back as well as forward. I can dream about the present. I can dream about things I've never imagined, people I've never met – or even about nothing of any consequence at all. And I have no control over any of it. Asleep, I'm at the mercy of myself.

When I was writing them up I tried to keep Delphine's dreams in mind and follow the same rules of being utterly factual and allowing no interpretation to sully the flow, but that reduced my selkie-bride dream to one sentence so I abandoned the theory and kept it very much as it appears in this journal. Perhaps soon I will have dreams that go over the page! I know who I'm writing them for too; I know that they are for Delphine to read.

I received a reply to the letter of condolence that I wrote

to Jacky once I realised I wouldn't make Alfred's funeral. Thankfully, I'd made no reference to marriage or anything else which might suggest my ignorance. This reply is very touching. Alfred obviously spoke to his partner about everyone at the lab and Jacky has mentioned that he said I was 'a real gentleman'. That's probably all he could say about me, but I take some small comfort from it. There's a reminder, too, about the memorial service tomorrow, to be held at the church where the funeral was held. Apparently Alfred was an organist and played at three services every Sunday! It never occurred to me to discuss Duruflé with him but it's more than likely he'd have been *au fait* with French sacred music. Another missed chance of connection which I'll have to try not to turn into regret. It's hard. Now that I've become aware of the things I've missed – not just understanding Delphine or making strong friendships, I mean the little things like having a chat to people before, or even without, judging them. And small, human acts I've always steered clear of, like trusting to luck, having a go, jumping right in. Everyone thought I'd just walked up to Delphine and taken her as though it was my right but that's so far from the truth. By never looking from side to side and acknowledging the presence of anyone else in any real, respectful way, I must have looked very much like a man striding ahead without a qualm to claim what he wanted. Gratitude, relief, humility – those aren't words that any of them would associate with me. And yet that's what I felt, amongst many grander and happier sensations, when I realised that my feelings for Delphine were reciprocated. If only I'd been able to express them better. She must have been very exasperated with me at times.

Day thirty-nine: Saturday

Today, I got the St Agnes breasts-on-a-plate postcard. Nice to have a change from Chagall. I don't know if it's one Delphine had with her or one she bought specially. All it said was,

So, James. Are you enjoying the locusts and wild honey?

Day forty: Sunday

Alfred's memorial service was utterly delightful. Rather more eventful than I'd expected, and typing is pretty painful as a result, but I feel more at ease now, this evening, than I have since Delphine left.

When I arrived in the little medieval church yesterday – the kind of hidden treasure you can still come across unexpectedly in parts of London – I found that Julie had saved me a space next to her and Simon, and Jag and Polly were sitting with them. Sally arrived at the end of the pew, a tiny bit late. I could see that they were all longing to talk about Reeves, as I was, but I still found myself able to concentrate on the service.

There was music and some poetry and Jacky said a few eloquent words. He's a fair bit younger than Alfred was and terribly handsome – dark curls just beginning to turn silver at the temples, a very fine profile, light brown skin and dark eyes. Some North African or Turkish blood, possibly. He spoke with the same accent as Alfred – they were brought up in neighbouring towns – and I remembered how amusing I used to find the way he spoke, how comical it seemed to me, but yesterday it sounded warm and gentle, and I thought of Delphine and her mother, their lips forming those wide, flat vowels; it was like singing. There was that, too – some beautiful choral pieces performed by the choir which Alfred had accompanied every Sunday for the past few years. The vicar spoke about his spirituality and his humanity. Everyone else present probably noticed both when he was alive but for me there was a revelatory mood about the whole service. And not just about Alfred.

During a lovely Purcell piece – 'Hear My Prayer, O Lord' the programme said – Julie turned to me and whispered, 'Almost makes you wish you believed in something, doesn't it?' and I nodded, moved. By the music and the light touch of her hand on my arm, the warmth of her breath on my neck.

At the end of the final hymn, Jacky and five others made their way to the back of the church and disappeared behind a curtain and I was surprised to hear, a few minutes later, the muffled sound of bells. I'd noticed the bell-tower but it hadn't occurred to me that they would actually be working, or that we would hear them that day. Bell-ringing makes me think of Oxford and the English countryside – rather obviously, I suppose – but the connotations aren't pleasant. A call to prayer seems very like a call to arms and both make me uncomfortable.

As our little group walked out into the tiny churchyard Simon whispered, 'You know, I could have sworn I saw Huw at the back of the church but whoever it was got caught up in the crowd. No sign of him now.'

'He wouldn't have the courage to come,' I said and Simon laughed.

'Yeah, he'd have to be pretty brave. Or very stupid.'

'Although of course, he doesn't know that we know.'

'He must suspect it – I mean, as soon as he realised he'd lost those recordings he must have been shitting himself.'

We were outside now and I put my hands over my ears. I was astounded at the volume achieved by bells which only seconds before had been chiming lightly and subtly inside the church. I looked up and saw six long, slatted arrow-slits in the stone of the tower. The sky was a cloudless blue. I felt hot and tired.

The vicar approached us, laughing at my wincing.

'Yes, it's much louder out here!' she shouted, 'They're doing a quarter peal with six bells so it's quite a powerful sound. They'll be done in another five minutes; why don't we go to the church hall now, there's some food and drink there?' She began to lead the way.

'I'll follow on in a moment!' I said.

Julie turned and gave me the thumbs up. I hoped I might catch Jacky after the peal.

I wandered around the graveyard and read any of the stones whose inscriptions had not eroded – nobody had been buried there for decades; the place was full. That was always the part of family holidays which alarmed me. We'd visit a church, as you always have to do in some dreary part of Britain when you're off school but it's not the summer and therefore you're not in France for a glorious month — and Mother would always have to pick her way solemnly through the churchyard and come back with the most poignant details to lay before us uninvited: a child's first name and two dates within mere days of one another, or 'beloved only child of' or a thirty-year-old woman 'mourned by her husband and their five children'. God, how I hated those morbid phrases, and how I hated Mother, her eyes welling up as she *wallowed* in the grief of other people, people she never even knew. Poor Mother. Her only way of expressing her softness was by being moved by the deaths of strangers, and I was truly unable to accept her being moved. We were both frozen into our heartlessness towards one another by then and neither of us could do a damned thing about it. I keep trying to remember her telling me stories, remember her singing to me.

The bells stopped ringing. As Jacky and his fellow ringers left the church I went to shake his hand and introduce myself. With little to say to him after expressing my condolences, I congratulated him on the bell-ringing, and so unlocked a floodgate of pleased enthusiasm.

'You liked it? It wasn't such a great one, but we did OK. Two of the ringers are quite new to the band but they're picking up quickly.'

'The band?'

'Yeah, it's a bit rock and roll isn't it, but that's what we say.'

The bell-ringers were walking towards the church hall, with Jacky and I lagging behind the group as we talked, when he stopped with an impatient groan. 'Damn, I left my bag in the tower this morning when we were cleaning up there. Listen, I'll catch you at the reception in five minutes.'

'Do you mind if I come with you?' I still didn't feel like joining the throng and, in a strange way, spending this little time with Jacky felt like a way of assuaging some of my guilt about how little notice I'd taken of Alfred.

He looked surprised but only for a moment. 'Course, if you don't mind hurrying.'

We trotted up the stairs and I got a speedy lecture on the weight and provenance of each of the bells in the tower. I mentioned how loud they had sounded from outside the church.

'It's amazing to think that those arrow-slits can make such a difference,' I said.

'Aye, the dream-holes do their job, that's for sure,' he agreed.

That threw me. 'You know about dream-holes? Don't tell me you're a rifleman? Or an archer?'

Jacky snorted. 'Not likely. What do riflemen know about dream-holes?'

'It's what they call these narrow windows. Snipers call a perfect place to shoot from a "dream-hole" because it's got all the benefits of an arrow-slit on a fort – high up, wide view, invisible, protected . . .'

Jacky looked puzzled. 'But it's nowt to do with war,' he said confidently, 'I mean, I know lots of medieval buildings have got arrow-slits and that, but this was never a fortified church, no battles were fought from this tower. The name definitely comes from church architecture, because they're holes to let out the "dream".'

It was my turn to look unsure. 'The *dream*?'

'Aye. It's from Old English. Alfred told me about this. *Dreman*. To make a musical or joyful noise.'

'Dream-holes are to let out the *music*?' I must have been smiling like an idiot because he was looking at me uncertainly and smiling back in spite of not having the faintest clue why I should be looking so pleased.

'That's right. To let the people outside hear the bells. To let them hear the music.'

'To let them hear the music!' I was laughing now; this idea delighted me for some reason I couldn't fathom, and I put my lips to the nearest dream-hole and whooped as loudly as I could. Jacky carried on smiling but he must have been wondering what the hell I was doing. I couldn't have explained it myself, but for the first moment since Delphine left I had felt something like joy. Even without her there. That scares me now, the idea of feeling joy without her being here, but it's liberating too.

In the silence which followed there was an awful moment when I realised that to Jacky my antics must have seemed akin to dancing on Alfred's grave, but he waved away my incoherent apologies. 'He'd have wanted folk singing, not long faces. Don't worry about it.'

Jacky and I walked down the stairs and I was about to go to the hall when I recognised the man who was swiftly crossing the churchyard towards the gate. He must have hidden at the back of the church until the coast was clear. I was about to let him go but then I recalled that in the tower, I'd had a *vision* of Delphine, rushing up the stairs and leaping into my arms. I'd had to blink hard and breathe in slowly to recover from that split-second, that flash of her presence. I couldn't do nothing.

'Reeves!' I shouted.

He turned, and for a moment it looked as though he might

run but his social sense prevailed and he walked towards me trying to look composed.

'Did you get your jacket back then?' I asked him. 'And your Dictaphone?'

As the implications of my having discovered his secret blatherings hit home his face paled. He didn't speak, didn't look capable of speaking.

Just then Julie came looking for me, but on seeing Reeves she turned on her heel and went back into the hall. She re-emerged with everyone from Dream Lab. Reeves and I hadn't moved. Jacky retreated, saying, 'Well, I'll see you guys in the reception then.'

'Huw, how kind of you to come!' said Sally, in a false, bright voice.

'I — I wanted to pay my respects, of course . . .' Reeves mumbled, but we wouldn't let him get away with that.

Simon was direct. 'You do realise, don't you, that we think you're partly responsible for Alfred's death?'

'That is preposterous! The man was ill; anyone could see that the man was ill!'

'But you didn't encourage him to get better!' shouted Julie. 'You just let him come to Dream Lab in case you could make use of him.'

'That's not true! Not in any sense that justifies your accusation—' He turned on Simon. 'And I'd advise you to be careful, Simon, you can't just bandy about that sort of talk without expecting me to take it further. I've a professional reputation to maintain—'

Polly laughed harshly and sing-songed, in a pretty good approximation of Reeves' accent, '*This might actually start making sense of the Thursday group. They'll have even more opportunities to drone on about their latest nocturnal exploits for even longer than usual.'*

He turned to me now, his pallor replaced with an angry blush. 'You – you took my private property – confidential material – and you – distributed it – out of context – to these people, how dare you think that . . .'

Sweat dripped into my eyes. The sun hit me like a slap. Reeves pointed his finger and jabbed it towards me, his ruddy angry face screwed up and his pink mouth and tongue making staccato movements, but no sound that I could hear.

So I hit him.

I hit him full on the jaw with my right hand. I didn't even know I'd made a fist. It was a perfect blow; he staggered back with the power of it and only just got a hand to the ground in time to prevent his falling flat on his backside. He stood up, wiping blood from his mouth, and my friends from Dream Lab stood closer to me. That finger began to wag at me again but I held up my palm and stopped him. The sun no longer bothered me.

'Enough. Your professional reputation is ill-deserved. You have abused all of us. We have yet to decide what we are going to do with the information we have. Go now.'

He was angrier than ever now, and redder than ever, but my blow had hit its target. I had the upper hand. And we had his future in ours. We had even taken his voice.

Reeves walked away quickly, in silence.

As soon as he was out of earshot, Simon came at me with his left hand raised.

'Whoo hoo!' he shouted, 'Put it there, Beauman!'

I did, and it hurt, so Jag shook my uninjured left hand vigorously, saying, 'Well done, man. Jesus. I mean, well done.'

Polly put her head on my shoulder and said, with a stage-struck sigh, 'My hero!'

'Those knuckles need looking at.' Julie bustled me into the toilets beside the church hall and applied wet hand-towels to my grazed hands and then she looked at me. 'James, are you OK?'

I nodded, because I was OK, but I was also shaking all over. It was difficult to speak, but finally I managed to get it out.

'I need a drink.'

We joined the reception and drank wine and talked until we were hoarse — a lot about Alfred to begin with, and then about ourselves, our lives since the end of the lab. Not about Reeves. There was a moment when we were all listening to Sally talking about her recent holiday and I looked around the group. Looked at them properly, each in turn. Simon had his arm around Julie's shoulder and she leaned into him and I saw that she was looking less tired than usual. The dark circles under her eyes were hardly there at all; she wasn't bloodshot and puffy skinned. Simon looked younger, somehow, and *cleaner*. Polly and Jag were laughing, their eyes shining. Nobody looked as though they needed a good night's sleep. I almost felt my spirits droop in the face of such energy, such improvements. But then I rallied, and I felt a small surge of warmth in my heart. It felt like it was in my heart, at any rate. I was able to feel glad for their recovery and their health and hopeful for my own.

I admitted quietly to Sally about my faint hope that Delphine would appear after all; that her reference to locusts and wild honey was a hint that my forty days and nights in the wilderness were about to end. A little later, when I had come to terms with my disappointment and was enjoying talking to the others, I comforted myself with the thought that she had been near me, in the bell-tower. Even though I had conjured her, it felt as though I really had seen her for that moment. Not like me to get so mystical about what is basically self-delusion, but then again what harm does it do? And it's a better delusion than many I've harboured.

The reception lasted until early evening and some of the others were going to eat afterwards but I declined their invitation to join them. I'm going to pop in to see Jag at the university next week though, see how he's doing in Polly's absence. He'll make sure it's when Reeves isn't around. And Julie and Simon are coming to lunch next weekend. But I wanted to come back here and I've been up until oh Christ all hours, reading this journal.

I never really expected her to turn up out of the blue. That's not how things happen. In any case, it was forty days but not forty nights. It would have been cheating.

Day forty-one: Monday

I slept for a mostly undisturbed five hours during which I dreamt that Delphine's mother was singing to me. She sounded like Edith Piaf and looked like herself but also a little like Delphine. I was wearing striped pyjamas, the kind I wore at boarding school, but was otherwise unchanged.

My first act on waking, after making a note of my dream and abluting, was to write an acceptance letter for the redundancy offer which I assumed, rightly as it turned out, still stood. I couldn't resist making Nica Jenson sweat for a little first, so I asked to speak to her privately just before lunch time, and when we were alone I said, 'I've decided I'd like to go overseas again,' and her face was a picture as she weighed the opportunity to send me to an unappealing posting abroad against her long-term plan to get rid of me entirely. She still hadn't responded when I continued, 'I'll be travelling independently . . . so, I'd like to take up your offer of redundancy. Here's my letter of acceptance of your terms.' As I handed it over she still hadn't composed her face into any definite expression. It's good to know I can discomfit her, but my hands were trembling as I left.

They'll give me gardening leave so I needn't come in again. I let my team know at once and a few people in my section began to murmur, as if they believed I would need persuading – oh, you must have a farewell drinks party, have a good send-off, chance to say goodbye properly – and I accepted the offer graciously.

'That's very kind of you, thank you. I'd like that,' I said.

They looked surprised too. Caroline stopped me before I left my room for the main office, having emptied my desk and taken the few items I wanted to keep.

'James,' she said tentatively.

'What is it, Caroline?'

'I just want to say . . . I just want to say that I hope everything works out for you. You know. Everything.'

It was eloquent enough, and she meant it, so I thanked her and said I would miss her, which is not completely untrue.

336

First stop Vietnam. I will look for Delphine but not slavishly. If she wants to be found I will find her and . . . well. I leave in a fortnight, and am going to send Mme Fournier an email to let her know my plans, with a request that she forward all of this – the whole damn lot, including those voice files – to her daughter. I think she will do that for me.

If she won't be found just yet, I'm not sure, but perhaps I'll travel. Offer my services as an interpreter on some of those schemes the office has been funding, go back to Africa to do voluntary service with some NGA or other. *Do* something.

I'm planning my escape from the tower I've constructed around myself and I want the world outside to be full of Delphine and other people. Perhaps she will take my hand and lead me down the staircase and through the graveyard, the two of us stepping amongst flowers and walking through the kissing-gate on to a path I haven't found before, leading us to the centre of that new life.

Perhaps I'll have to break out alone.

Dream Laboratory has helped my coming to consciousness. My trust has been broken, I have been deceived and betrayed, I have laughed, cried, despaired and hoped, but my heart remains whole. I've learnt a great deal about love and a little about how to honour it. I've found good people to be my friends. By seeking out my father and my son I have begun to feel like a father and a son. Each of these is worth more than the most spectacular dream I will ever have, but I have started dreaming too and that's no small achievement. Best of all, better late than never, I've discovered that dream-holes are for releasing not arrows, but music.

So, Delphine. My love. Hello. My best hope is that your mother has emailed this to you and that you have printed it out and are sitting in some colonial hotel bar left over from Saigon days with cane furniture and ceiling fans, sipping a French 75 while you read. You'll need speakers though, so maybe you're slotting *dong* into a pay-as-you-go internet café at the railway station, or more likely handing dollar bills to the proprietor, and scrolling down the days. If you've got to here, you'll know everything. There was a temptation to edit and prune, to remove some things and to soften others, but no, I must let it stand. This is what I have written since you left.

It began as my diary of Life After You – forgive the drama; I don't think you can imagine how bereft I felt, and still feel, without you near to me. But it has become more than a journal; it has turned into a story I told myself about all the strange things that have happened in the past two years. Some wonderful, some painful, some so confusing that I feared I would never understand them, but all most definitely strange.

The attached sound files have cleared up some of my confusions and presented me with a few new ones. I wasn't sure if I should send them but they are such a recent and important discovery; I think you should have the opportunity to make up your own mind. Naturally, his is the very last voice I want you to hear, but any mediation would blur the truth of it, and the truth is too diffuse already. And I must confess to getting a wholly dishonourable *frisson* about it: so recently he was whispering sweet nothings into your ear but here's the truth about Huw Reeves's mellifluous tone; it was a sham. He rasps, he barks, he growls. I trembled when I heard the change in him.

My trust has been abused, and yours, and all the members of Dream Lab have suffered one way or another; perhaps one of us paid the ultimate price. My fear at hearing that voice spilling its secrets soon became anger and then shame, at having been duped so thoroughly for so long. Anxiety, too, that he might have had some foundation for his cruel analysis of me. But those emotions have not once overshadowed the strength of my feelings for you. Nor have they blinded me to the pleasures of the new friendships the lab has brought me, and for which I have you to thank.

There are discoveries which I found floating in your wake – those crafty trails you laid for me – and others which perhaps even you never guessed I would find. I am not destroyed. I don't think you ever intended to destroy me but even so I have to tell you that I am – intact. Do you understand what I mean? At first this felt like I'd been left in an arid wilderness; nothing to cool or nourish me. Then as time has gone by I've found small puddles of rainwater and tiny tastes of something delicious. Not just in my memories of you, although they have been the source of much sweetness, but in the world. Even the world without you near me.

You know now that I know about your brother. It makes me additionally sorry to have behaved so stupidly about Finn. My life hasn't really prepared me for the notion that my son might make a good brother for my girlfriend, but I'm very happy to countenance it now. If you will let me, perhaps we could pick up all of the information your parents gathered to help you find your lost brother, together. I guess that's what you're doing already but it must be a lonely path, and one which might lead to more sadness. At least you will have followed it to the end; you will have done everything which love and blood require. I understand how important that is. I would like to help you. I understand if you don't want me to help you.

I want you to come back. But freely. Not out of pity or shame or indecision. I love your strength and vigour and would hate to compromise you. Perhaps that's what I've been doing.

Delphine, I want you to trust me and I know I can trust you. And I want you to help me carry on with some of the projects you've set me off on – being a better son, a better father. And for you, a better – what? I was going to say lover but I believe that as lovers we were, are, unimprovable. Boyfriend (hmm). Partner (yuk). Husband, maybe, if you'd like . . .? How I've avoided those nouns! But listen, I've been thinking – father again, perhaps. A rather decrepit father, granted, and a very scared one, but everything seems possible with you.

I know I've been very short of perfect in my behaviour towards you. I know that I can be quite strange myself; more than I realised. I know I can do better on both counts, given the chance. These are important lessons and they've taken me five decades to learn: a narrative about the past two years somehow manages to contain the story of my life. And you are here, everywhere; it, like its writer, has made itself yours.

Listen to me. Believe me. Let me sleep beside you, wake beside you, dream beside you. Let me find you.

Acknowledgements

Thanks to the management and staff of The London Sleep Centre, www.londonsleepcentre.com, particularly Dr Irshaad Ebrahim MBChB MRCPsych, Consultant Neuropsychiatrist, for information about sleep disorders and treatments, and Wayne Peacock RPSGT, REEGT, Sleep Services Manager, for technical advice. Also thanks to Dr Samantha Fisher, University of Swansea, for access to her research into dreams and nightmares, Bill Longhurst for help with FCO matters, and Roddy Lumsden, for stories of somnambulism. And to Daniel Buckroyd, as ever, for all the reading.

A NOTE ON THE AUTHOR

Clare Brown was born in Liverpool and brought up mostly in Sheffield. She worked in theatre for seven years before becoming Director of the Poetry Book Society, 1996–2003. She is the author of *The Creation Myths* and co-editor (with Don Paterson) of *Don't Ask Me What I Mean: Poets in Their Own Words*.

She lives in Nottingham.

A NOTE ON THE TYPE

The text of this book is set in Bembo. This type was first used in 1495 by the Venetian printer Aldus Manutius for Cardinal Bembo's *De Aetna*, and was cut for Manutius by Francesco Griffo. It was one of the types used by Claude Garamond (1480–1561) as a model for his Romain de L'Université, and so it was the forerunner of what became standard European type for the following two centuries. Its modern form follows the original types and was designed for Monotype in 1929.